RIMON TRACKED THE RAIDERS TO THEIR CAMP

They had stolen several Gens, one a red-haired girl, possibly Kadi. Now, hidden behind a large rock, Rimon watched in horror as the Sime Raiders whirled two Gen captives around in a wild tarantella. The shiltpron music grew faster, and the Raiders zipped crazily through the figures, gone mad with rapture.

Abruptly they pulled the last of the Gens from a tent and into the firelight. Flames gleamed on shining red hair. The girl looked like Kadi, and her arms were bound.

The leader of the Simes reached out and ripped away her bodice, exposing her breasts. He pounced on her, hands on her breasts, not fondling but grasping her tightly. When his tentacles grazed her skin, she realized what was happening and drew breath for a scream.

It was never voiced. Before the first sound, the Sime closed her mouth with his and stripped her of her life.

"The best-crafted book to date in this series. Readers of the first two books will want this one."—LIBRARY JOURNAL

FIRST CHANNEL

JEAN LORRAH &
JACQUELINE
LICHTENBERG

PLAYBOY
PAPERBACKS

FIRST CHANNEL

Copyright © 1980 by Jean Lorrah and Jacqueline Lichtenberg

Cover illustration copyright © 1980 by PEI Books, Inc.

Published simultaneously in the United States and Canada by Playboy Paperbacks, New York, New York. Printed in the United States of America. Library of Congress Catalog Card Number: 80-82658. Reprinted by arrangement with Doubleday & Company, Inc.

Books are available at quantity discounts for promotional and industrial use. For further information, write to Premium Sales, Playboy Paperbacks, 747 Third Avenue, New York, New York 10017.

ISBN: 0-872-16772-0

First published by Playboy Paperbacks January 1981.

To my parents, especially Daddy, who always knew I'd write a book some day,

To Mike Amsden, who sent me a copy of *House of Zeor*, and got me into all this,

And, of course, to Jacqueline Lichtenberg, who created a universe and shared a dream.

JEAN LORRAH

My work on this book must be dedicated to Jean Lorrah, and through her to the imaginative faculty that somehow allows people to share their dreams.

JACQUELINE LICHTENBERG

ACKNOWLEDGMENTS

Since publication of the second Sime/Gen novel, *Unto Zeor, Forever,* (Doubleday & Company, Inc., 1978, Playboy Books, 1980), the number of people involved in the work has risen steadily until now we have three fanzines dedicated to the Sime/Gen universe—*Ambrov Zeor, A Companion in Zeor,* and *Zeor Forum: Transfer for Ancients*—all three of which can be reached care of Ambrov Zeor, Box 290, Monsey, New York 10952. Please include a self-addressed stamped envelope.

We must acknowledge here the aid and assistance of the fanzine contributors and staffs in answering mail and providing information to the fans as this book progressed. We must also thank those who read and commented on portions of the manuscript as it was written.

In particular, we owe thanks to Anne Golar, editor of

5

Ambrov Zeor, Karen Litman, editor of *Companion in Zeor,* and Katie Filipowicz, editor of *Zeor Forum,* who is also working on a Sime universe concordance and so helped us with continuity, and to Judy Segal for the care and attention she has lavished on the story of Rimon Farris.

A separate acknowledgment goes to Mary Jo DiBella, the special production assistant on the *AZ* staff, who has spent untold hours helping us with this manuscript.

We would also like to thank Victor Schmidt of the Library of Congress, National Library Service for the Blind and Physically Handicapped for his personal help in providing access to the Sime/Gen novels as well as many other SF and *Star Trek* books to the handicapped readers. As we were finishing the rough draft of this book, we were on our way to the 1978 August Party. We stayed over at Mary and Vic's house, and Mary let us use her typewriter to finish the book. It takes a lot to maintain one's cool with two frantic writers as houseguests—but then Mary Schmidt is a writer, too, so she understood.

And as always, we must thank Doubleday for their quick and courteous forwarding of mail so that we have been able to meet and interact with so many readers. If ever the post office box number doesn't reach us, you can reach us through any of our publishers for more information on the sequel to *First Channel,* the sequel to *Unto Zeor, Forever* or its early drafts (being published in *Ambrov Zeor*) or other works that we are doing.

Jean Lorrah   Jacqueline Lichtenberg
Murray, Kentucky   Monsey, New York
July 1979   July 1979

CONTENTS

7

PART III

CHRONOLOGY OF THE SIME/GEN UNIVERSE

HERE AND NOW	PIVOTAL EVENT	PUBLISHED/PLANNED STORY	HISTORICAL BACKGROUND
?			
at least 1,000 years			First Simes appear; civilization collapses; Ancients die out. Nomadic existence. Some Ancient knowledge blamed for the mutation preserved secretly by isolated communities (e.g. School of Rathor: esoterica). Gens develop gunpowder; partition of world into settled Sime and Gen Territories, leaving nomad groups such as gypsies and Freeband Raiders.
several centuries			Organized Territory governments; Gens raised in pens in Sime Territory. Raiding across the borders. Ways of the Starred Cross help Gens escape from Sime Territory. Gen Church of the Purity calls Simes demons to be destroyed.
3 years	Self-identification of the first channel, Rimon Farris.	FIRST CHANNEL* (pub. 1980)	First known community of Simes and Gens living together, in Sime Territory. Channel transfer dominates there; some renSime (ordinary Sime)/Gen transfer.
9 years			
1 year	Zeth Farris, Rimon's son, takes over leadership, discovers anti-kill conditioning.	CHANNEL'S DESTINY* (1982?)	First recorded incident of unofficial Sime/Gen cooperation across the border.
few years			

few years	First Householdings formed, including Zeth's House of Rimon. They collapse; Zeth's son Del Rimon Farris founds Zeor.	UNTITLED*	Householdings spread to other Sime Territories, spurring technological redevelopment. First Tecton, barely legal organization of House-Holdings. Houses emerge as vital economic force.
2–300 yrs.	Risa Tigue becomes Sectuib in House of Keon.		
1–2 years		AMBROV KEON** (in development)	
few years	Klyd Farris, Sectuib in Zeor, meets Hugh Valleroy, leading to Hugh's founding House of Rior.	HOUSE OF ZEOR (1974)	
one month			
few years			
YEAR ONE	Third Order channels identified. Klyd founds "modern" Tecton. Hugh founds Distect. Keon opts for Tecton.	SHEN THE TECTON*** (in development)	Tecton takes over Territory government, initiates negotiations with nearby Gen government; they cooperate to eliminate last great group of Freeband Raiders. First Contract signed: Tecton undertakes to see that Simes never feel need. RenSimes denied direct Gen transfer. New calendar established. Simes allowed in Gen Territory, but with retainers confining their tentacles.
(10–15 years)			Schools for channels, Donors, and renSimes founded. Tecton spreads around the world. Householdings become non-localized corpora-

The Distect, supporters of direct Sime/Gen transfer for all, rebel, are defeated at Battle of Leander Field, and go into hiding.

Year (duration)	Event	Title	Event
yr. 131 (18 mos.)	Last chance to destroy Tecton in favor of Distect. Digen Farris, Sectuib in Zeor, supports Tecton.	UNTO ZEOR, FOREVER (1978)	Severe Donor shortage, alleviated at last minute by new training methods. Rior's version of Distect destroyed.
yr. 152 (1 year)	Ercy Farris, Digen's daughter and first fully endowed channel able to do psychokinesis and other "power functionals," leaves Tecton for School of Rathor.	MAHOGANY TRINROSE (1981)	Anti-witchcraft riots; Sime/Gen mutation blamed on Ancients' use of magic. Era of Channel's Secret, that some few Simes can do "magic."
yr. 224 (few wks.)	Mairis Farris, Ercy's grandson, invents comfortable replacement for retainers.	"Operation High Time" (1969)	Massive public relations campaigns in Gen Territory gain sympathy for Simes.
yr. 232 (15–20 years)	RenSime Laneff Farris campaigns for Mairis for World Controller; he wins and funds her project to prove her method of distinguishing Sime from Gen before birth. Results of Laneff's experiments 85% prove her risky method reliable.	RENSIME! (in development)	Secret neo-Distect rises; reactionary Gen groups.
		SIME FROM GEN DIVIDED (in dev.)	Gradual dissolution of the Territory borders.

perhaps 1,000 yrs.		Interstellar travel. Various groups, including Simephobes and House of Keon, emigrate to other planets. Endowed channels can use abilities publicly.
(1 day)	On a faraway planet, Yone Farris, not of Zeor, leads band of crash survivors in founding new way of life for Sime and Gen.	"The Channel's Exemption" (1977) — Distect is a force and still illegal; a few members survive with Yone.
some centuries		Klairon Farris, Sectuib in Zeor, discovers Yone's World, brings it into the Tecton Worlds.

COMPILED BY KATIE FILIPOWICZ.
Copyright © 1980 Jacqueline Lichtenberg.

* by Jean Lorrah and Jacqueline Lichtenberg
** by Jean Lorrah
*** by Jacqueline Lichtenberg and Jean Lorrah
All others by Jacqueline Lichtenberg

A SIME LEGEND

In the Days of the Ancients, Simes and Gens lived together without strife, the Gens freely giving selyn to the Simes, the Simes protecting and caring for the Gens. But then the Gens grew selfish. They wanted to keep all the selyn for themselves. The Simes grew weaker and weaker, and finally they went to the Ancients to ask for help, that they should make the Gens give up the selyn they could not use.

The Ancients called the Gens before them and asked why they kept for themselves the energy of life that they could not use. "It is a great treasure," they said. "See ow the Simes desire it. It must be very valuable, and erefore we will store it up."

At that the Ancients became angry. "You have not e wits to know that this substance has value only when you share it! For your foolishness, we make you subject to the Simes, to be their cattle. And to the Simes we give the power to take selyn from you, whether you will or not."

And so it has been ever since.

PART I

Chapter I

WHAT GENS ARE FOR

Rimon Farris woke with a start, his body instantly at full battle alertness, his mind crystal-clear. Before his eyes focused, he felt the bed bounce again as little Serri jumped on his feet, saying, "Rimon, come on! Mama says you gotta get up now!"

With a groan, he fell back on the pillow, quelling the shock reaction. The room went out of focus in a sickening whirl, and in a panic he fought for self-control.

The bed was still rippling up and down with Serri's jumping. Rimon said irritably, "Serri, don't you know better than to do that when I'm in need?"

"You can't be in need; not for another week!"

But she stopped bouncing.

The room steadied. A burning ache began to spread from the base of Rimon's skull down his back and into his arms. *Don't panic,* Rimon told himself. *Breathe evenly.*

Serri eased herself off the bed, her concern at his lack of response barely perceptible to Rimon. She was only a child. Her nager had no more power than Kadi's. "Rimon —you're all right, aren't you?"

To reassure her, Rimon hauled himself to a sitting position. "I will be if you'll go away and let me get up." He met her deep blue eyes for a moment, then buried his head in his hands, wishing he hadn't moved.

She backed toward the door, watching him dubiously. "Everybody else's finished breakfast. You better not fall asleep again, or Mama will scold me." She turned and skipped out, copper curls bouncing.

Stumbling to the shower, Rimon let the water wash over him, then turned it to cold and held his forearms under the stream to dull the feverish ache in his swollen

ronaplin glands. It was impossible. He couldn't hold out
for another five days. His father would understand, even
if Marna didn't.

"Hmpf!" Marna snorted as he entered the dining room,
"you've been augmenting again, Rimon, haven't you?"

"No, I haven't, Marna," he said. "I really haven't!"

"Then how did you get into this state so quickly? Rimon, you can have a new Gen every two or three weeks—
but what if your father couldn't supply them? What if
you had to wait your turn at the government Pens? You
kids! Playing games, I'll bet. But it's four years since
your changeover, Rimon. It's time you accepted your responsibilities as a man and stopped wasting selyn."

"Yes, Marna," he murmured, only half-listening to
the familiar lecture. Her accusations were unfair, but
there was no use protesting. The truth was that he had
not augmented once this month, and in spite of all the
self-discipline he could muster, he was in need after only
three weeks and two days. What was going to happen to
him? He hadn't been able to concentrate for the past
week—and it was getting worse, month by month.

Recognizing that a large part of his depression was
due to need, he tried to shake it off as he drank the trin
tea Marna had placed in front of him. He couldn't bring
himself to touch the bowl of cereal, though. The smell
of food turned his stomach. His guts were cramping, and
there was a heavy, tight feeling in the middle of his
chest. He wondered if he'd make it through the day.

As the tea settled his stomach, he began to feel better.
Yes, he could manage for a few more hours, put in a
good day's work to impress his father before he had to
ask . . . again.

He sat staring into his empty cup, gathering strength,
until his reverie was broken by a cheery "Good morning, Rimon!"

Kadi came in from the kitchen with a tray of clean tea
glasses and began quietly stacking them on the sideboard.
Immediately Rimon felt better. Kadi's presence always had
that effect on him.

He came up behind her, pushed her shining red hair
aside, and kissed the back of her neck. The dormant,

child's nager soaked through Rimon, unresponsive to his need, unthreatening. It was just a touch between friends. Kadi knew that; Rimon sometimes thought she knew every feeling that passed through his heart. She turned and kissed him swiftly—on the nose.

He grinned. "Good morning, slowpoke." He made a show of examining her forearms, although it was obvious from touching her that she was still cool, showing no sign of changeover. "When are you going to grow up so we can get married?"

"When I'm good and ready. I don't know why you're in such a hurry, Rimon. Always first at everything. You'll just have to wait for me . . . or marry somebody else!"

He looked deep into her blue eyes, but saw only laughter. No, Kadi wasn't worried, either about the dangers of late changeover, or about losing him. He'd never seen her afraid of anything; that was one of the reasons he loved her so much.

Rimon watched her putting the dining room in order. She was tall and slender, but at last the curves of womanhood were slightly softening her figure. It wouldn't be long now before she was his, completely. Determinedly, he thrust from his mind the thought that she might, instead, be lost to him forever. Oh no—not his Kadi. She was taller than average, true, but she was slender. Sime slender, he insisted to himself.

"Kadi!" Marna called from the kitchen. "If Rimon's through, bring his dishes in here and finish up the kitchen."

"Yes, Mama."

"I'd better get out to the Pens," said Rimon.

Kadi looked at him sympathetically. "You're having a bad time again, Rimon."

"Yes. I'm not going to make it to my assignment day this time, either."

"Try," she said. "I'll bring you some more tea later."

"Thanks, Kadi. I don't know what I'd do without you."

He walked out into the bright sunlight, steeling himself against the nager of the Gens. He was to supervise the cultivating of the hillside acreage today, but first . . .

In the Wild Gen compound he found Ran Morcot, Kadi's father, sorting out a new shipment. The Gens were crying and jabbering as Ran's helpers grouped them by sex and age, to determine which strong, healthy, spirited ones would be marked as prime Farris stock, which culled to sell to a local dealer.

The impinging fields grated on Rimon's nerves, as did the actions of the Gens. The wild ones acted too much like people.

They're not people! They're Gens!

As the men began moving a group of five good-looking Gens from one cage to another, one of them, a strong male, made a break for the gate. Instantly, on a burst of augmentation, Ran and two other Simes surrounded him and brought him back to the cage without injury.

"Don't bother to mark that one," Rimon said. "Clean him up and have him ready for me tonight."

Ran noticed him for the first time. "Your father won't approve of your taking prime stock for an extra kill. Take one of the culls."

"I'll talk to Father," Rimon said with a boldness born of desperation. "Taking a cull guarantees I won't be able to go four weeks. With this one, at least there's a chance."

"All right, I'll put him aside, but you don't get him until I have your father's say-so."

Relieved at not having to argue longer amid the emotional fields charged with Gen fear, Rimon set about his morning's duties.

The Farris Genfarm was the largest supplier of choice Gens in the Territory. They purchased the best Wild Gens captured, and also raised their own from the finest breeding stock. The Farris mark—a diagonal notch filed in the left front tooth—was a guarantee of health and spirit. As Syrus Farris said, "It doesn't cost any more to raise a spunky Gen than to raise a broken Gen." And spunky Gens brought more profit. Farris Gens were a luxury product that went to the choice auctions, the exclusive bazaars, and occasionally to wealthy individuals who would come to the Genfarm and pick out a year's supply at once.

One day, Rimon knew, all this would belong to him. And then what? Home-grown Gens made him nervous. He had never had one for a kill, and he knew that his father had him overseeing the cultivating to force him into proximity with them. *How can I oversee others when I can't oversee myself? What will I do when it's all my responsibility?*

The selyn nager of the working Gens was clear to him before he came over the crest of the hill and saw them toiling, sweating in the sun. They were all strong, healthy, equal to the task, the older children working beside them at the lighter jobs. Although everyone on the Farris Genfarm earned his keep, children of Gens were never mistreated. The children of these Gens could still lead normal lives if they should go through changeover. Some of the best overseers were Simes who had come out of their own Pens. But the supervisor of this particular group was Gen.

Seeing who it was, Rimon wanted to turn and run. Nerob. Once Nerob had been Yahn Keslic, son of one of the Sime supervisors. Years ago, the four kids, Yahn and Rimon, Kadi, and Rimon's cousin, Zeth, had been inseparable. Now Yahn was Nerob, one of the Farris breeding Gens. And Zeth . . . Zeth was dead.

Rimon shuddered, but forced himself to ride to the end of the row that Nerob was striding, to meet him when he finished that lap of his inspection. Nerob was conscientious, keeping his crew working steadily and well. No wonder. If Syrus Farris were displeased with him, he could be sold tomorrow.

"Tuib Rimon," Nerob said as he bowed, then looked up at Rimon still astride his horse, "Tuib Farris said you'd be checking this section today."

"I hardly have to check your crew, do I?" asked Rimon, sliding off his horse to make a perfunctory examination of the work. As they walked the length of the row, Nerob eyed Rimon, warily gauging his state of need.

Rimon dropped a few paces back from the Gen, sensitive to the fear-tension in the man's nager. About halfway down the furrow, Nerob stopped, waiting for Rimon to catch up. "I expect we'll make it to the irrigation ditch road by evening."

Rimon had to close the distance to hear and speak normally, consciously controlling himself. "Don't drive them too hard, Nerob. There's always tomorrow."

"Is there?" The Gen's eyes met Rimon's. Then, under

his breath, he added, looking away, "For you, maybe there is, not for us."

Rimon seized the Gen's arm and whirled him around. But then, despite Nerob's leap of fear, Rimon thrust the cringing Gen away, thinking, *You're alive, Nerob. You're Gen, and you're still alive. Zeth was Sime, and he's dead!* But Nerob wasn't to blame for Zeth's death. Rimon had nobody to blame for that but himself.

"You can't take me, Tuib Rimon," said Nerob. "I'm under your father's personal protection. You won't disgrace the Farris honor."

Rimon stood back, letting himself become conscious of the complex fields surrounding the Gen, reading the hidden meanings behind the man's emotions. *He wants to hurt me. He wants to use my need against me. He resents me more than I resent him. Why, when Father's saved his life?*

When Rimon came back to normal consciousness, the Gen was flinching away from the raw need in Rimon, his fear almost too much to bear. Shaking, Rimon said, "Calm down. I wouldn't take you—unless you goad me to it. We were—after all—friends."

Rimon whirled and stalked back to his horse. But then, instead of following impulse and galloping away, he sat and watched until Nerob had rejoined the distant group of fieldhands. Here in the field, those Gens felt temporarily safe. Anyone coming to buy today would be shown first the Wild Gens in the compound, and then the Domestic Gens down around the big house. Good workers could count on being safe until after harvest. Most of them settled into unthinking routine, their selyn fields high but unresponsive.

Gradually, Rimon's breathing returned to normal. He wheeled his horse and trotted toward the next group of workers.

Relief washed through him. He usually avoided Nerob and the few other Gens he had known before they established—began producing selyn. It was hard to remember that someone was not a person if you'd grown up with him. Gens looked like people, after all, seemed just like everybody else until the time of changeover when, instead of becoming Sime, they began producing selyn, the biologic energy that Simes had to have to live. Clearly, nature intended Gens to produce selyn for Simes, for Simes were faster, stronger, and equipped with special organs to draw the selyn from a Gen's system.

Those organs, the delicate lateral tentacles that lay along either side of Rimon's forearms, protruded slightly from their sheaths under the combined influence of his need and the impinging Gen fields. Deliberately, he retracted them, but that put pressure on his ronaplin glands, swollen with the selyn-conducting fluid that moistened the laterals for transfer.

Extending his handling tentacles relieved some of the pressure, so he extended all four on each arm, curling the ventrals around the reins and letting the dorsals lie across the backs of his hands, along his fingers. The primary purpose of those tentacles was to immobilize the arms of a Gen so the smaller laterals would not be dislodged during the selyn draw. However, they served that purpose only once a month, on the average. The rest of the time the strong, resilient handling tentacles were extra fingers—even extra hands. Gen arms seemed pitifully naked and awkward without them.

As he rode to the next group of workers, the fresh air revived Rimon's spirits. There the supervisor was Sime, as were all the others that he checked that morning. The flat fields of the Gens and the undisturbing fields of the Simes were little problem compared to what Nerob had put him through. All was calm and normal. By the time he had circled the furthest field and started working his way back, Kadi met him under the trees by the reservoir, bringing a double-walled container of trin tea, fresh and hot. They sat down under a tree, where the shade was still cool in the late spring morning.

"You're feeling better," Kadi said after Rimon had had a long drink of tea.

"Yes, I'm fine for the moment but I'm having trouble controlling around the Gens." Her nager remained unlinked to his, her body consuming selyn only at the almost imperceptible rate of a child.

She took his hand and laid it in her lap. Two fingers

stroked along the ventral sheaths, causing the tentacles to emerge from the wrist orifices. They twined about her fingers, and she squeezed them gently, then began to play with them, trying to tie a bow. Rimon wriggled them just enough to frustrate her, laughing at her attempts. She could always make him laugh, even when he was feeling his worst.

Finally, she stopped teasing his tentacles, and twined her fingers with his. "What are you going to do, Rimon?"

"Ask for another Gen. Tonight."

"What will your father say?"

"What can he say? He can see I'm in need. It happens to him sometimes, too—lots of times he can't make it a full four weeks."

"But not every month," she pointed out. "I know how hard you're trying, Rimon. I wish I could do something to help."

"You can. Will you meet me tonight, after . . . ?" The image of Nerob, twisted in the rictus of fear, floated to the top of his mind again, and the world shimmered into pulsing selyn fields for an instant. *No. It will be that big out-Territory buck. Not someone I know.*

Kadi said, "I'll be there, like always, Rimon." She squeezed his hand reassuringly. "I just wish there was more I could do than sit it out with you."

He wrapped his handling tentacles about their two hands, joining them. "Soon, Kadi. Soon you'll grow up, and we'll have each other forever." Soon—one day soon, he would be there to help her after her first time.

What would I do without her? he wondered as she left him to go back to her duties at the house. She was almost sixteen natal years old—few who changed over after fifteen survived, and those who did were left weak, unable to withstand the first illness, the first bodily strain that came along. And he wanted Kadi to marry him, to bear his children.

Again he thrust morbid thoughts from his mind. Going about his work, though, he found need forcing itself into his consciousness again. The soothing effects of the trin tea and Kadi's company wore off as he repaired a broken fence, instructed one of the Sime supervisors to take his Gens in early because he had driven them to exhaustion —his father would hear about that—and inspected several more groups that were working efficiently. That was the norm and the expectation on the Farris Genfarm; it was surprising that Rimon had found even one instance of poor work practices.

Toward late afternoon, though, Rimon was seeing everything as shifting field gradients, his Sime senses at their keenest peak. Fighting for self-control, he rode slowly up to the last work detail, supervised by an old friend, Del Erick.

As Rimon dismounted, Erick turned from watching two Gens open an irrigation gate. "Ah . . . Rimon!" Erick hesitated. "Shuven, Rimon, I know I said I'd repay you by yesterday, but I just couldn't get the money together . . . and . . . look, I'll have it by payday or you can take it out of my salary."

Rimon made a sweeping gesture, tentacles flying. Erick, poised on the balls of his feet, flicked back a step or two, startling his horse. As his friend brought the animal back under control, Rimon swore silently. *Even my best friend is still afraid of me!*

Rimon put a hand, tentacles carefully sheathed, to the bridle of Del's horse, and across the silken nose of the animal, said, "I know how hard it is sometimes, to raise cash. I can give you more time. I have all the money I can use."

Zlinning Rimon more closely, Del said, "You're—in need again—early."

"Dad has always been very generous with me. Don't worry about it. Pay me when you can. What are friends for, anyway?"

"I won't forget this."

"No obligation," said Rimon, holding up his closed fist, ventral tentacles extended. Del returned the gesture, twining his own ventrals around Rimon's for just an instant— aware how his high field struck through Rimon's aching body.

Rimon smiled, flicked a cursory glance at the working

Gens, and swung himself into his saddle. With an airy wave, he rode back to the big house and went straight to his father's office, determined to press his case. When even his closest friends were leery of him, it was time for something drastic.

Syrus Farris was an imposing man. He had the normal wiry Sime build, but stood unusually tall—a good three inches taller than his son. There was no doubt of their relationship, though. Both had the same black eyes and straight black hair; the same mobile, expressive lips, and characteristic chin.

Farris was busy with accounts when his son approached him, so Rimon had to sit down and wait, as he had done so often in this familiar room. It was a room for working, with solid, businesslike furniture, and undisguised files and other paraphernalia. The only nonutilitarian object was the portrait of Rimon's mother over the fireplace. It was hard to imagine his father loving that ethereal woman with her halo of soft blond hair, blue eyes looking calmly out at   world. Rimon had never known his mother, for sh   d died giving birth to him. Occasionally, since he h   grown up, he wondered if his father had ever completely forgiven him for that.

But no, his father had always seen to it that Rimon had everything he wanted. Marna often said his father spoiled him. If that were true, though, why was he so hesitant now to ask his father for something that he obviously had to have?

Farris looked up from his accounts at last. "Again, Rimon?"

"I am in need, Father."

"I can tell that. The question is, *why* are you in need? Marna says you've been augmenting unnecessarily."

"I understand why Marna thinks so, but it's not true. I have not augmented once this month." Rimon made no effort to control his selyn fields, letting his father read the truth directly from them. His father was exceptionally sensitive about such things. Nobody ever got a lie by him.

Farris studied his son. "Yes," he said, "you are telling the truth. Now . . . what can be done about it?"

"I don't know, Father. I seem to require more selyn than most people just to live. I will . . . simply have to work harder to afford the cost."

"It's not the cost that concerns me. Rimon, you're a grown man. Have you ever had a fully satisfactory kill? Have you ever—wanted to take a woman afterward?"

"Kadi and I have an understanding."

"No evasions, Son! Are you controlling the impulse, or is it that you've never felt it?" He paused at a new thought. "Or—no. Kadi's just a child. You couldn't. . . ."

"I wouldn't!" Rimon found himself on his feet, tensed. He made himself sit down again.

"I'm sorry," said Farris, and Rimon felt his furious embarrassment. "But I had to ask. I had to know. You've always had so much trouble. I'd hoped—well, it's been four years."

"It will be all right, Father, when Kadi's grown. I wouldn't—want—anyone else. Only—it seems I'm always in need, and I ache for the freedom of augmentation."

Rimon's misery communicated to his father. Farris picked up a ledger. "Ran told me you put your mark on one of the new catch of Wild Gens this morning."

"Yes, Father, a big male with a strong field. I want him. Now."

"You chose a Wild Gen with a strong field last time, and it didn't help. I think it's time you had a domestic Gen."

"No!" *Nerob!* The image choked him. "I'm sorry, Father, but you know why I don't want someone who knows me, who can talk to me—"

"Someone? Haven't you learned yet that Gens are not people, Rimon?"

"Please, Father. Your domestic Gens are valuable. I'll take one of the culls from this morning's shipment—"

"It's all arranged, Rimon. Gens who have lived among Simes understand more of what is happening. The emotions are more satisfying than the blind terror of the Wild Gens. Expense is nothing where my son's health is concerned. Not to mention . . . grandchildren."

Rimon was shaking his head bleakly. "Father, please, I can't. Not a Gen I know."

His father's expressive lips formed a hard line of annoyance. "Nobody ever takes a Gen he knows on this Genfarm. You know that, Rimon."

"Yes, Father. Forgive me." *How could I have thought . . . ?* Farris was a compassionate man. He kept as many established children of his friends as he could afford to, as breeding stock, giving them the chance to live as comfortably and securely as any Gen could hope to. When he could not afford to keep one—and of course there was no way he could afford to keep many males—he saw to it that such Gens were shipped far away, so their parents never had the slightest chance of hearing what finally became of them.

"This male came in today's shipment," Farris was explaining. "The raiders caught him at the border. It's not one you know, Rimòn, but he's from in-Territory—and spirited. He's been waiting for you all afternoon. This should do it for you, Son."

"Thank you, Father," said Rimon quietly. As he left, he steeled himself inwardly. It wouldn't be Nerob. It was just another Gen, and he would do what he had to do before he disgraced himself by taking an unauthorized Gen—or worse.

He put it all aside. The boy who awaited him was perhaps fourteen years old, stocky, with bronze-colored hair and expressive hazel eyes. He wore only the yawal, the clean white smock of the killroom, and a collar and chain. The chain was fastened high on the wall, so that although his arms and legs were free he could not move very far from the couch on which he sat—crouched, rather, like a frightened animal.

His fear burned into Rimon's strained nerves. Ravenous need sang through every cell of Rimon's body as he approached. The boy cowered for a moment. Then determination sprang to his eyes as he sat up straight and watched Rimon come nearer, glancing from Rimon's face to his wrists, where the laterals were now beyond any control, extended, drinking in the Gen's blazing field, dripping ronaplin.

When Rimon put out a hand to release the chain from

the boy's collar, the boy flinched, then held still, his nager flaring hope along with his deep fear as fingers and tentacles hit the eight points on each side of the collar to release the lock. When the chain fell free, the huge hazel eyes looked up at Rimon. "Are you letting me go?"

Simelan. He realized he had been hoping the boy would remain silent, making it possible to regard him as an animal, like the Wild Gens. Coherent speech was an unfair tactic. He jerked the boy to his feet. "You shut up!"

"Please, let me go. I'll do anything!"

As the boy continued to plead, his words disappeared into the swirling selyn fields. Rimon's Sime senses took over. No longer did his strong hands hold a physical body, but a bright field of pulsing energy. His emptiness screamed to be filled.

He seized the boy's forearms with hands and handling tentacles, seating the hungry laterals. As he contacted Gen skin, Rimon felt the long-ignored ache in his chest loosen, and instinct drove him to seek the fifth contact point with his lips. The Gen was a writhing mass of energy, charged with the fear that made it impossible for Rimon to resist. Energy poured from the Gen to him, satisfying his need, pulsing new life into every nerve, driven by the ecstatic force of the Gen's fear, completing, fulfilling, to burst into a brilliant rapture and a blissful moment's loss of physical awareness.

Rimon was brought back to reality by the tug of a dead weight on his arms. The Gen's eyes were still open, staring up at him accusingly. Like Zeth's. With a strangled cry, he dropped the corpse—no different in death than a Sime. It crumpled to the floor, still staring at him. Those dead eyes glaring from fear-contorted features held him, hypnotized.

With a groan, Rimon knelt and closed them, then lifted the body onto the couch. It was still warm, as if pretending to life—but there was no life there now. Every spark had been transferred to Rimon, so that he could go on with his existence.

Why?

Why do I deserve to live?

Why did he have to die?

There was no trace of the post-kill syndrome his father had predicted. He didn't want a woman, he wanted to vomit. With shaking hands, he pulled a coverlet over the body and yanked at the signal cord for the attendant.

This is what Gens are for. *This* is what Gens are for. It is what Gens are for!

He turned and fled from the killroom.

After his kill, sick and shaking, Rimon sought the only haven he had ever found since his changeover—Kadi's presence. Unaware of anything else, he headed out to where she had promised to wait for him, in the swing under the big tree in the back yard.

He dropped into the swing, staring at his arms. The tentacles were retracted tightly, painfully—but there was pleasure in the pain for a moment, until Kadi put one arm around his shoulders and the other hand over his clenched hands in his lap. In her soothing presence, he began to relax a little . . . almost to be a child again, one of the four Krazy Kids.

All within a three-year span in age, the four of them shared adventures, projects, and pranks. Zeth had the oldest, the leader until Rimon began to challenge m. Then the two had developed a spirited rivalry for Kadi's approval—and Yahn, the youngest, had entered in, even though he could never keep up with the older boys.

But the two Farrises could not help admiring the way both Yahn and Kadi refused to give up—hence the vow the four of them made never to separate. "And Kadi can be wife to all of us!" Zeth had joked—the only one of them at that moment old enough to comprehend the joke. Rimon, sensing that there was more to it than friendship, had had to conceal his jealousy under camaraderie—but soon there was to be no more rivalry for her affections. Time intervened to tear the Krazy Kids apart.

Zeth had changed over three or four months before Rimon did, and soon drifted away from the group, outdistancing them as he took on a man's duties, learning to use his new abilities as a Sime. Nonetheless, Zeth had tried to keep up their lifelong ties, including their childish vow of loyalty. So, when Yahn Keslic established selyn production, Zeth told him and encouraged him to run for the border. Rimon had been away with his father that day, and when Zeth told him on his return, he was furious. "You call that friendship? Why didn't you *take* him to the border, Zeth? You're Sime—you could guide him. Come on—let's find him and help him across."

When Syrus Farris' son was willing to brave his wrath, his nephew became more willing to lend his aid. All night Rimon and Zeth searched for Yahn, but couldn't find him. Toward morning they decided it was useless, and started back toward home—only to have Rimon begin changeover. Zeth made a fire, tended Rimon until he'd stopped vomiting, and then decided the best thing to do, as Rimon was drifting in and out of consciousness, was to go home and bring back a Gen for Rimon's first kill.

An augmenting Sime should have had no trouble, but Zeth had not taken into account the fact that the first stages of Rimon's changeover had been exceptionally rapid, and so was the last. Within half an hour, Rimon's tentacles broke free, and he was a full-fledged Sime in first need—the hardest and most terrifying need most Simes ever know. He set out blindly after Zeth. With the speed of desperation, he overtook his cousin when they were still more than an hour's journey from home—from the nearest Gen. To Rimon, Zeth's field seemed the source of all salvation.

Reaching to cling to that field without thought, Rimon found his tentacles twining about Zeth's arms in sheer reflex. He seized Zeth's laterals with his own; even so, Zeth did not fear. Only when Rimon, driven, made lip contact, completing the circuit, drawing selyn voraciously from Zeth's body—only then did Zeth panic, driving Rimon into the vicious stripping draw of a full-blown kill-mode attack.

Rimon did not remember much of what happened after that. In torment, he had wandered for hours, until suddenly there were people around him, and he was taken over by someone who let him collapse into a wagon, drove him somewhere—and then his father was bending over him, his concern flowing to Rimon through the new, confusing senses, saying, "Rimon? What idiot moved my son while he's in changeover?"

"He's through it," insisted the driver. "He came into the Northwest unit on his own power, then collapsed. I don't know what's wrong, but he was conscious when I put him in the wagon."

Farris smiled reassuringly at Rimon, reaching toward him, extending his laterals to read his field. "It's all right. You just didn't get a very good first kill. In a little while, after you rest, we'll—"

"No!" Rimon cried in horror, his own tentacles retracting painfully at the sight of his father's—organs of murder.

He felt annoyance beneath the genuine concern in his father's field. "Rimon, it's over. As soon as you get a decent kill, you'll feel fine."

"I killed him!"

Both concern and annoyance deepened, accompanied now by fear—and Rimon knew his father feared for his sanity. Well, so did he. But Farris said reassuringly, "Of course you killed. It's perfectly natural. That's what Gens are for."

Rimon rolled away from his father's touch, gathering in on himself, hating what he had become, what he had done. "No," he groaned. "Not a Gen. Zeth! He was trying to help me, Father, and I—killed—Zeth!"

It was terrifying now to be able to see the discrepancy between what Syrus Farris felt—fear, revulsion—and the control he exercised before he spoke. Other feelings came flowing in—sorrow, disbelief, even love for his son. But Rimon had seen—no, for the first time in his life, he *zlinned*—that first unshielded burst of emotion, and he could not totally believe the reassuring tone in his father's voice as he said, "If you did, you couldn't help it. Just tell me where, and I'll send someone. Then we'll get you to bed. You have to rest, Son. It's all right."

But it was not all right. Marna and Kadi put Rimon

to bed, but nothing they could do would stop his shaking. The sight of Marna's tentacles sickened him, and he hid his own under the covers, wanting to go back to yesterday, to be a child again.

He heard Marna and Kadi whispering. Zeth couldn't be dead, Marna said. A Sime could not kill another Sime that way. Rimon grasped at the thread of hope—what did he know of it? His senses had been so confused. He had drawn—but not enough, his father said. Then maybe Zeth was unconscious. They'd find him and bring him home. He'd be all right. They'd all be together again, the Krazy Kids, Zeth and Rimon and Kadi and—

No. Never again. Yahn was Gen. But if they hadn't found him, that had to mean he had escaped across the border. So Yahn would be all right, and Zeth . . .

He slept fitfully on and off through the afternoon and into the evening. It was after dark when a commotion outside drew his attention. They must have found Zeth! He raced to the window, and saw . . . Yahn, his father, and Syrus Farris. Farris was saying, his mouth thin with annoyance, "Keslic, you know I can't keep every male. . . ."

"Syrus, he came home of his own free will!"

Rimon couldn't believe it! Why had Yahn come home? Here he had no chance at a life as a person—only across the border was there any hope at all for a Gen. Was that what being Gen meant—losing all courage?

After an eternity, Farris said to Yahn's father, "All right, I'll keep him for a year. If he earns his keep, then he can stay on permanently, but he'll have to be a worker as well as a breeder." He didn't speak directly to Yahn, but to his father, as if Yahn could not understand.

"Thank you, Syrus," Keslic said. "I know Yahn will work well for you."

"No, not Yahn," said Farris. "There is no Yahn Keslic anymore. You understand that."

"Yes, N'vet."

"Take him to the Gen compound, and put him to work in the morning." Yahn would have a year to earn his life . . . and if he did, he would then be given a name. Meanwhile, he was a nameless Gen like all the rest.

Chills went through Rimon despite the warm night. *What if I'd been Gen instead of Sime? Would my father do that to me?* He shook off the thought, but it persisted. *It can happen to anybody. Father had only one heir— until Uncle Ryin died and Zeth came to live with us. When Zeth changed over, Father knew there would be one Farris to carry on. But I'm Sime, too, and I'm his son. . . .*

And surely Zeth is alive!

But the next day Zeth's drained body was brought in, and everyone knew: Rimon was different.

When the hope was gone, Rimon could not face the Gen they tried to tempt him with. He would no sooner touch Gen skin than he would collapse, his selyn currents in chaos. His father and Marna tried until he went into convulsions before they finally gave up and took the Gen away. He lay there, waiting to die . . . hoping to die. How could he ever kill again, after killing Zeth? No one wanted to look at him . . . until Kadi appeared with trin tea laced with apricot nectar. Her childish nager held no reproach—and no pity. There was true sympathy in it, and love. She had no tentacles—and yet she was not Gen. Somehow that was enough for Rimon, and as he drank the tea he managed for the first time to tell someone the complete story—a healing outpouring of the pain bottled up in him ever since Zeth had dropped lifeless from his grasp.

"Kadi, I wasn't going to kill him. I know I wasn't going to kill him! I didn't want to hurt—only when he tried to get away—something happened inside me. I—I—it was awful."

She crawled into bed with him, then, holding him for warmth as they had often shared a bedroll on camping trips. She had a child's body and a child's nager. But she believed him. She understood—and that was everything Rimon had to have at that moment.

Even with Kadi's help, Rimon almost died of attrition before finally, on the fourth try, he completed the kill of a Gen presented to him. That kill, and every subsequent one, became a reliving of Zeth's death under his tentacles.

Guilt, everyone said. But everyone knew, too, the awful fact that tormented him every month: Rimon is different.

Now, four years later, Kadi was helping him through it again. He didn't know what it was about her field, weak as it was, that soothed him even when he was most tormented. Slowly, he came out of the past, drew a deep, shuddering breath, and brushed his lips lightly, gratefully, over her forehead. Kadi pulled away to study his face, then took his hands and slid her fingers up around his arms, turning her face up to him for a full lip-lip contact. "Come on, Rimon. It will help."

He took her in full attack position, joining his lips to hers in a brief, glancing contact, and then withdrew, sheathing his tentacles. He sighed, deeply. "You always know what to do for me. I'm always afraid to do it."

Kadi kicked the swing into motion, working the tensions out of herself with the rhythmic jerking of her thigh muscles. "If you're in the mood to take orders, I'll tell you what to do for yourself next."

"What?" asked Rimon, stopping the swing with his long legs.

"Tell me about it, exactly what happened tonight. I saw your father. I know it was something pretty bad, because he was worried—but also hopeful."

"Dad, worried? Sure. He gave me one of his best Gens —and he's afraid it won't work."

"Well, did it?"

For a long moment, Rimon stared off into the distance, remembering. "I don't know, Kadi. In a way it was . . . good. But—I can't do it again. I don't know if I'll ever be able to face a kill again. I felt so sick—afterwards. I still do."

"What did he give you—one that knew you?"

"Of course not. But, Kadi—the kid—spoke to me. He begged me not to kill him. Begged. And the more he begged, the better it was. His fear—it was horrible and it was wonderful, and I hate myself. It was like Zeth—only better, do you understand? What am I, Kadi?"

She stroked his tentacles. "You're Sime. That's a very proud and beautiful thing to be, and I love you for it."

He turned and took her by the shoulders. "Could you love me if you were Gen and I was in need?" As he spoke, he let his tentacles touch her neck. "Could you love me then, Kadi? Or would you fear?"

"Don't be silly. Gens aren't human. They don't know the meaning of love."

"But if they did? What would happen if a Gen didn't fear?"

She shook her head. "You always talk this way when it gets to you. Rimon, look at Nerob—when he was a kid he was normal enough, but now look at him. Fear is a Gen's nature. The fear is there because the Sime is attracted by it—attracted to his selyn, like—like a flower's smell attracts bees. It's all part of nature."

"Is it? Well, when you've changed over, maybe I'll be able to show you what I mean."

"I only wish that would happen soon!"

"It could be any time. Maybe tomorrow. . . ."

"No. When I took his dinner in, your father checked. There's still no sign of changeover." He felt her anxiety, understood very well why she should be anxious—despite all her courage, she would face a very rough changeover at her age . . . if she survived it.

But then her mood shifted. "I'm just impatient," she said. "I want to be your wife, Rimon, and . . . you know what? Your father approves."

"He said so?" Rimon was surprised—not that he expected his father to make any objection to Kadi as the daughter of indentured servants—after all, the Morcots had worked that off years ago—but that he should express positive approval was unusual indeed.

"Yes. He actually said, 'I hope it works out.' That's an awful lot from your father, you know."

"I know!" But then, what other woman would have Rimon? His father would want grandchildren . . . oh, that was almost funny. He held Kadi close, trying to convince himself that once she changed over, she would be able to attract him as no other woman could. Despite four years with never a hint of sexual desire, he somehow believed that Kadi could do it. Well, she had saved his sanity—

maybe his life—many times in the first months after his changeover. If she could handle him that way when she was only a child, what would she be as a grown woman?

His thoughts were interrupted by a disturbance in the ambient nager. He stood up, startled, searching the west road against the setting sun. Kadi stood beside him.
"What is it?"

"Wagon coming. Gens—"

"What's wrong, Rimon?"

"Don't know—Nerob there, I think—alone in the wagon. He's left his crew out there unsupervised? No, he's not alone!"

Rimon began to run for the big house, shouting for his father. Kadi followed him through the hallway, past Farris' office where the older man joined them, and out onto the front porch, down, and across the yard.

The wagon pulled to a stop, horses blowing. Nerob got down from the seat, breathless, incoherent. "Tuib Farris—I tried to stop them. Soon as I saw—I got him away—best I could—Tuib Farris, don't—"

"Quiet!" ordered Farris as he and Rimon bent over the bruised and bloody form on the flatbed.

Rimon said, "Shen and shid! Don't you know better than to move a Sime in changeover?"

Farris vaulted into the wagon, probing the injured Sime. "It's not as bad as it looks. He's close to breakout. Here, you men, get Findel into the infirmary. Then go down to the holding Pen and cut out that male with the deformed foot."

In moments, men were scurrying everywhere, preparing to welcome a new Sime into the world. As the confusion cleared, Farris turned to Nerob, who had caught his breath.

"Let's hear it!"

"We were loading the last wagon, getting ready to come in for the night. Findel was missing. I had the men spread out and search—he couldn't have gone far. We heard a commotion—some of the men had found Findel in the irrigation ditch, helpless like that. Couple of my crew are out-Territory. They started it, and the rest went along—

trying to beat him to death. I lit into one of the ring-leaders—Klauf, knocked him down, grabbed Findel and ran for it."

"So you moved a Sime in changeover." Farris' tone was menacing, but his nager betrayed only curiosity. Rimon looked to the Gen, who was sweating.

"I'm sorry, Tuib Farris, but I couldn't hold off a mob. I figured it was either psychospatial disorientation or being beaten to death. This way he may hate me, but at least he'll live."

Farris considered that. "Hmmm. Quick thinking—shrewd thinking, for a Gen. I don't have many Gens capable of making that kind of decision." He paused, glancing at Rimon. "Nerob, name your reward."

Taken completely aback, Nerob dropped his gaze. "Why —I—wouldn't know. . . ."

"Is there, perhaps, some particular female you fancy?"

Nerob's head came up. His eyes turned to Kadi. Rimon heard through rising fury, "Tuib Farris, if you would, I have always wanted Kadi."

Rimon stepped forward, wanting to strike the Gen. "You brazen—!"

Farris stopped him with one warning tentacle. "Nerob, that was entirely inappropriate. Kadi is still a child."

"Then—if—it is ever appropriate," said the Gen, eyes downcast, visibly trembling at his own audacity, "if ever it can be, I want her as my only reward." Again he met her eyes for one quick flashing glance.

Kadi's skin crawled, and though her nager had little power, both Rimon and his father turned at her reaction.

Farris said, "I will keep this request of yours in mind, Nerob. You may go now and collect your crew. See to their injuries and bed them securely. Any more—trouble of any sort, and you may lose claim to any reward."

Rimon watched in disbelief as the Gen wheeled the wagon about and drove into the red sunset. Farris hadn't said no. He hadn't said yes, but he hadn't denied Nerob either. Rimon, sick, felt the cold dread gathering in Kadi. At that moment, he could have wrung his father's neck. If Kadi were Sime, fine, she would do well enough for Farris' peculiar son. But if she were Gen, Farris would casually hand her over to Nerob, use her for breeding—

It was only Kadi's discomfort that kept Rimon from going after his father in fury. Putting his arm around her, he said, "Don't worry, Kadi—you're going to be Sime, and you're going to be my wife. That's a promise!"

Chapter 2

BUT IF I'M DIFFERENT—WHAT AM I?

Two weeks later, Rimon was feeling elated because it was his turnover day. Normally, when a Sime reached the point at which half the selyn from his last transfer was used up and he began the slow descent toward need, he felt depressed. But when Rimon had wakened this morning with that hollow feeling, recognized it, and counted the days, he was delighted. A full two weeks. *This time I'm going to make it!*

Moreover, he was returning home with a sense of accomplishment, having taken a shipment of Farris Gens to a dealer in Scobla, and wound up with more money than his father had said was a fair price. He and Del Erick had spent a riotous night in Scobla, and were just slightly hung over today. They didn't talk much during the early morning, as they negotiated the empty wagon through the mountain passes. Around noon, Del, much more a participant in last night's activities than Rimon, adjourned to the bed of the wagon for a nap.

They were now on the Ancient Highway, the eyeway, which would take them straight home. Rimon hardly had to pay attention to his driving, as the broad roadbed scorched deep into the landscape by the mysterious Ancients ran straight as far as the eye could see—yes, eyeways was the right name for them.

The wagon jolted and creaked as the smooth roadway gave way to a wooden bridge across a gully. Del sat up with a groan. "Hey!" he complained. "Warn me when you're gonna run off the road!"

40

"We're on it," replied Rimon, looking back. "Quit sitting on my package!"

"It's soft," said Del, patting the parcel he was leaning against. "What is it?"

"Cloth," said Rimon. "Beautiful soft material the color of Kadi's eyes. Don't you tell her, though. It's a surprise, for her wedding dress."

Del patted the package. "All that for one girl's dress? There must be enough here to dress every woman on the Farm."

"Well, how should I know how much it takes for a lady's dress? Better too much than too little."

"Shendi, Rimon! You don't have to get so touchy about a little teasing!" Del's nager flashed slight pain and strong annoyance at him.

"Huh? I'm not touchy. What's the matter with you?"

"You're doing it again! Shen and shid—that hurts!"

Aware now of Del's actual pain, Rimon noticed that he had been ignoring a vibration of his own fields that was intensely irritating to the other Sime. As he strained to stop the vibrations, they only grew stronger. Fighting off panic, his body refusing to obey him, he let go of the physical world, sensing only through his Sime perceptions, and at last found control of his oscillating fields— or was it that the attack was waning on its own?

Swinging back to ordinary consciousness, he said, "Sorry, Del. I—"

Del shrugged. "You always fluctuate more than normal on your turnover day, but never like that!"

"I know. Kadi can stop it, though. I'll be okay as soon as I get home to her. Shen! Do you suppose my turnover symptoms would always build up to that if Kadi didn't stop them?"

"I don't know, but let's get you home to her!" Del climbed onto the seat and took the slack reins from Rimon, slapping them across the plodding horses' backs. "What I don't understand is how a kid like that can have any effect on a grown Sime. She's going to be one shendi-flamin' woman!"

"Yeah," said Rimon. "And she's mine."

Late that afternoon, Rimon and Del pulled the wagon

up before the big house on the Farris Genfarm. Rimon's eager anticipation faded beneath a strange foreboding. The first thing to meet his eye was Kadi's dog, Wolf, tied to the porch railing. At the sight of Rimon, the animal set up a pitiful whimpering, punctuated with howls as Rimon, led by the muffled sound of angry voices inside the house, hurried past without stopping.

The door to his father's office stood open. Inside were his father and three members of the Morcot family: Ran, Marna, and Serri. In a frozen moment, he took in the black anger on his father's face, along with the confusion of anger, compassion, and guilt in his nager; the grief in the Morcots, along with an almost equal anger in the two adults; the fact that the family was dressed for travel; and that while the two adult faces were stained with dried tears, Serri was crying openly.

Then he became aware of the argument going on.

"I don't understand, Morcot," Farris was saying. "After sixteen years of working together, why did you do this? Why didn't you trust me?"

"It was Kadi's choice," replied Morcot. "I knew you couldn't understand that."

"Kadi had no choice!" Farris said furiously. "She was Gen!"

Gen? Kadi? WAS!! The world around Rimon swirled dizzily into selyn fields. *Kadi—dead? Someone's kill? WHO??!*

He had to come back to ordinary consciousness to find out. No one had yet noticed him, and the argument was continuing.

"—would have kept her as a breeder," his father was saying. "You know I can always use healthy females. She would have been perfectly safe."

Marna spoke up. "You promised her to Nerob. You would have made her the property of another Gen! When she told me that, do you think I could hand my daughter over to you? I raised your son, Syrus Farris—I loved him as my own. If he had established, I would not have let him go to you—no, not your own flesh would you take pity on!"

Pain sang in Farris' nager, overshadowed by the greater

pain emanating from Kadi's parents. "A Gen is a Gen," he said harshly. "And the law is the law. She left my property. Ran, Marna—don't you know I loved your daughter, too? That I wanted her to be *my* daughter—my son's wife? Every family must face the possibility of a child's establishing—and being their child no longer. We must accept it just as we would have to accept it if she had died."

"Then she's not dead!" gasped Rimon. The others turned to him in surprise as he demanded, "Where is she?"

"There's nothing you can do for her, Rimon," said Farris.

"Where *is* she?" he repeated.

"The traders took her this morning," replied Morcot. "I think they're taking her to the Reloc Bazaar."

The Reloc Bazaar! The place that catered to all extremes of exotic—and perverted—Sime taste. If Kadi were sold there, she might be tortured first. She might be— Rimon didn't even know the possibilities, having heard the Reloc Bazaar spoken of all his life only in hushed whispers.

"Why?" he demanded. "Father, if you knew who had her, why didn't you go after her and buy her back?"

"Rimon, you know the law. She has family living here on my Farm; therefore, it would have been illegal for the traders who captured her to sell her to me. I tried, but they knew who she was."

"She has no family here any longer!" said Ran Morcot. "We are leaving. When Kadi told us about your promise to Nerob—"

Fury rose in Rimon. "You would have! Right in front of me, you would have handed her over to Nerob!"

Farris visibly struggled to keep from lashing out as angrily as his son. "Yes," he admitted. "Rimon, she is Gen. It is far better that she has been taken away. When you've calmed down, you'll see that things have worked out for the best."

"The best! I know what's best: I'm going to Reloc and buy her!"

"Rimon, you can't," said Farris. "What would you do with her?"

"Take her to the border! I'll buy her, all nice and legal

with my own money—and then I'll escort her to the border myself, and see that she has a chance at life!"

Rimon swept from the room and down the hall to his own room. Behind him, the raised voices faded to silence. Then, out the window, he saw the Morcot family leave, their meager belongings piled into a small wagon. Serri brought Wolf, dragging his feet and whimpering. She was trying to fasten him to the wagon when the rope came loose about his neck. He immediately took off at a dead run—in the direction the traders would take toward Reloc.

"Wolf!" Serri shouted after the dog. "Wolf, come back!"

"It's no use," her father told her. "He won't come back. He's Kadi's dog, honey. If he ever does come back to us— we'll know that Kadi's dead." He choked over the last words. Sobbing, Serri flung herself into her mother's arms. Ran climbed into the wagon seat, and the only family Rimon had ever known besides his father moved slowly but definitely out of his life.

It took him only a moment to pack a few things, including the leather bag containing all his ready cash, wishing he had the money Del owed him, too. He saddled two horses and mounted up, taking the road in the opposite direction from the way the Morcots had turned—took the road to Reloc.

It was a long journey to Reloc, Rimon reminded himself —a three-day ride. He wanted to gallop madly after the traders, but that would only tire his horses. Besides, leading the second horse made it difficult to gallop easily.

As he rode, the haze of anger and despair cleared from his mind and he began to plan. At first he had thought only of the bazaar, and had packed up all his savings. Now he realized that a single rider could easily catch up to the traders with their wagonload of Gens.

But the traders who visited the Farris Genfarm regularly all knew him. If they had refused to sell Kadi to his father, they would refuse to sell her to him. If he waited until she was on sale at the bazaar, he could buy her legally. No one there would know him. When she was tagged as his property, they could travel together—as long as no one caught him releasing her at the border, there would be no problems.

Except saying good-bye.

He drove that thought from his mind. It was replaced by bleak emptiness. There was no future now. *Kadi—oh, Kadi—*

If any Gen was able to be a person, a human being, it was Kadi. Gens had a culture out there—towns, it was said, roads, schools. She could live. He would see to it that she lived!

Meanwhile, he rode at a steady pace. The traders had eight or nine hours' start on him; he'd probably catch up with them tomorrow. He knew the way to Reloc, even though he'd never been there. About two hours out of town, he turned onto the less-traveled trail that connected the ancient highway with a modern main road a day's journey distant.

The sun was just setting when he emerged from a narrow pass between rocky ledges into a scene of destruction.

Two bodies lay in the widened roadway, flies already buzzing around them. By the side of the road a trader's wagon was turned on its side, an axle broken. One of the bodies was Gen. A lump in his throat, Rimon peered closely at the face. It wasn't Kadi. The Sime was a trader Rimon had seen before; the dead man's throat was slit. Was this the trader who had taken Kadi?

As he left the scene of destruction behind, Rimon realized that this far from the border, it could only have been Freeband Raiders who'd attacked the wagon. They were notorious bands of outlaw Simes who roamed the countryside, taking Gens or whatever else they wanted by force.

All senses keen, Rimon followed the road, watching for evidence that somewhere a group of people had left it. Another Gen body tossed casually aside told him he was going in the right direction, just as he was beginning to fear he had missed their turnoff.

He hadn't. Fresh hoofprints diverged from the road. They weren't even trying to cover their trail. Why should they? Out here, other travelers would just go on their way, thankful they were not the ones ambushed.

As Rimon followed the Raiders' trail, occasionally he began to sense selyn nager. As the sun set and twilight deepened, he relied more and more on his Sime senses.

Finally he found them. He could zlin the powerful combination of Sime and Gen nager, the Gens peaking a titillating fear, just a short distance ahead. They had stopped.

He left the trail, tethered his horses, and proceeded on foot. By the time he had crept up to where he could see them, they had made camp. He counted nine Simes and five Gens. Was one of the Gens Kadi?

On a wave of desperation, he realized that he would not recognize her. She had a Gen's nager now, not the child's nager he had known. He would have to get close enough to see the Gens to discover if Kadi were among them.

One of the Simes was circling the camp, well away from the cluster of lives in the center, zlinning the countryside to see if they'd been followed. Rimon ducked behind a large rock that would shield him to some extent, and deliberately damped his fields—the old scouting trick his father had taught him. The Raider passed by without a sign that he'd sensed Rimon.

Keeping a safe distance between them, Rimon followed him. When the Raider reached the camp, he called, "All clear. We'll be safe till morning, at least."

Rimon crept closer, knowing that his field would not be noticed amid the nageric clutter. He could see the Simes around the fire they had built, but they had pitched a tent and put the Gens inside it. It would be hot and stuffy in there. Apparently, they wanted to make their captives as uncomfortable as possible.

The Raiders were the sickliest people Rimon had ever seen; scrawny, skeletal, their skin loose over their bones, their faces wrinkled into masks of old age, although he had heard they seldom lived more than five years after changeover. They lived under constant augmentation, existing entirely on the kill, burning themselves out in one continuous flare of energy. And as fast as they died, new recruits seemed to filter across the border from Gen Territory—poor unfortunates turned true predator.

Beside one of the Raiders, Rimon would look like a Gen. His father insisted that all the Simes who worked for him eat two meals a day, with the result that they looked and felt better than average, and lived longer with fewer health problems. Most Simes ate at least a few meals each week, to provide the raw material for body growth and repair. The Raiders were the extreme, and looked it.

There were both men and women in the group, but one had to look closely to distinguish sexes. All were dressed in rags, with a few newer, recently stolen garments. No curves distinguished the women. And even from where he watched, Rimon could smell the foul stench of unwashed bodies.

They flitted about the camp, augmenting merely to move from place to place, wasting selyn profligately. Clearly they were addicted to augmentation and hyperconsciousness, not seeing beyond Sime senses, not caring what they did to themselves—or others.

Two of the Raiders pulled one of the Gens out of the tent—a young boy with unruly black hair and frightened blue eyes. His nager, and that of the other Gens, peaked from steady anxiety to desperate fear, and the Raiders cackled with scarecrow laughter.

A small man dressed slightly better than the others stood a few paces away, shouting, "Come here, boy!" as if accustomed to being obeyed.

The wide eyes stared at him, but the boy didn't move, paralyzed by fear. One of the women kicked him and he stumbled forward, only to be tripped by one of the other Raiders and land on his face at the leader's feet.

Yards away, Rimon was desperately fighting down the intil aroused by the boy's terror, but the Raiders around him roared with laughter. Jaded! None of them were in need—the kills along the trail attested to that—but the proximity of such fear would cause a normal Sime to react with a sharp sense of need—intil—unless he were satiated from a very recent kill.

One of the women picked up a stick and drew a circle in the dirt, within the edge of the circle of firelight. The boy watched her, his head turning, stupefied.

"Boy, you want to live?" the leader asked.

The boy looked up at him, climbing to his knees. The Sime's words kindled no hope in him.

"We'll let you go," the Raider said in a wheedling tone. "If we let you go, maybe you can escape across the border."

"You're not going to let me go," the boy said hopelessly, standing to face his tormentor.

"Yes, we will. I promise. All you have to do is get out of the circle."

Again the boy's eyes traced the circle, so small that he could run out of it in a second. But not faster than a Sime could augment. He knew that—but it was his only hope of life. He ran—and came up against one of the Raiders blocking his way, holding his arms up with tentacles extended but making no attempt to touch the boy. He, ducked in another direction. Like magic, a Sime appeared between him and freedom each time he approached the edge of the circle. He threw himself one way, then another, unable to stop until he wore himself out and collapsed in exhaustion, sobbing hysterically.

When one of the Simes bent to pick the boy up, Rimon hid his face in his hands and forced himself down beneath his Sime senses, down to hypoconsciousness, so he could not zlin the kill.

When he dared to lift his head, though, the boy was not dead. He was sitting up, drinking in great gulps from a cup someone had given him, his emotions so worn out that his field had gone flat. He sat, paying no attention to what went on around him as the Raiders brought another Gen out of the tent.

This time it was a girl, tall, awkward, heavy-set. She was twice the size of any Sime there, but her fear did not peak as the boy's had; she radiated only hopeless resignation.

"Hey!" said one of the Raider women, "we have to feed our Gens or they won't keep. Here, girl—make some soup!"

She picked up a heavy iron kettle and heaved it at the girl, who barely caught it against her stomach, falling backward with the impact. Blankly, she climbed to her feet and carried the kettle to the fire, then turned and said, "Where are the ingredients?"

The Raiders howled with laughter. "You think we carry fodder for Gens? Only for our horses. Horses we keep!"

Even that only caused a slight ripple through the girl's nager. She had clearly resigned herself to her fate long ago.

"Oh, you're no fun!" spat the woman who had thrown the kettle. "Let's have some music!"

One of the Raiders sat down with a shiltpron and began to play on the aural level. Rimon was glad of that. He'd been slightly drunk on shiltpron in Scobla—was it only last night?—and didn't want a hangover to impede his rescue attempts.

The Sime instrument required both fingers and tentacles and could produce music at both sound and nageric-field levels. The nageric level could become so intense in skilled hands that it produced actual intoxication.

"Dance!" cried the Raiders, dragging the Gen boy to his feet and throwing him into the arms of the Gen girl. Clumsily, they stumbled about, then were grabbed by two Simes who whirled them helplessly into a wild tarantella.

The shiltpron player began striking an occasional nageric chord. Rimon drew himself down to hypoconsciousness again, listening on the physical level only, so that the music would affect him less. Yet it kept intruding on the edges of his consciousness as he wished the Raiders would bring the other three Gens out of the tent so he could see if Kadi was there.

The music grew faster, and the Raiders zipped crazily through the figures, gone mad with the rapture of the shiltpron. Rimon realized he had a chance. If the Raiders were drunk, he might be able to dash in and snatch Kadi away from them. His fear that she was in that tent turned slowly to hope.

Despite his attempts to block it, the music was seeping through to him, affecting his field in a most curious fashion. Was his hope real, or was he hitting an emotional high because of the music? Why couldn't he block it?

Abruptly, he realized it was because of the Gens. His father would not allow a shiltpron on the Genfarm because its playing caused a resonance in Gen fields that gave an overpowering feedback to a Sime. That's what the Raiders were doing—deliberately. So jaded by Gen fear that it was not enough for them, they were multiplying the effects of Gen emotions with the shiltpron.

He had to get away. But Kadi was in that tent. He

could run right in and grab her—right under their noses. He knew he could.

As the music sang through him, he gave himself up to it, soaring on a cloud of ecstasy. The fear of the Gens was a balm to his soul—ahhh, he felt as a Sime was *supposed* to feel, at last. . . .

Somewhere, some tiny part of Rimon was horrified. It succeeded in keeping him where he was instead of running out to join the Raiders—but only because he was in a kind of lassitude. Why make any effort? Pure bliss was coming straight to him without his having so much as to think about it.

In the camp, the Simes finally opened the tent and pulled the other three Gens out into the firelight. Flames gleamed on shining red hair. Kadi!

No. Not Kadi. Another girl, short, freckled, snub-nosed. Not Kadi. Kadi wasn't there.

The tiny, isolated, reasoning part of Rimon felt intense relief—and then tried to goad him to leave. She wasn't there. He had wasted over an hour—two hours since he'd left the road. He had to get back to the horses, and head toward Reloc.

But the music held him, dominating the selyn currents in his body, leaving him deliciously activated yet utterly relaxed. The dancers in the camp were whirling flares of selyn, the Gens brilliant beacons of fear. He was bathed in the glow, the beauty of it all.

Then one of the Simes grabbed the boy they had first brought from the tent and tied his hands behind his back. Rimon could feel the boy's bewilderment—he wouldn't be killed for selyn with his arms in that position.

The other Gens were similarly bound. Then the leader of the Raiders chose the tall, awkward Gen girl. He pulled her to the center of the circle of dancers, and the music stopped. The dancers stopped to watch.

Rimon, like the other Simes, remained high, in ecstatic surrender, unjudging. The Sime reached out and ripped away the girl's bodice, exposing her breasts. She cringed away from him as he caressed her, but he hooked a leg behind her knees and sent her crashing to the ground.

The girl's horror of the Raider's touch soared out to every Sime there. He pounced on her, his hands on her breasts, not fondling, but grasping her tightly. When his laterals grazed her skin, she realized what was happening and drew breath for a scream.

It was never voiced. Before the first sound, the Sime had closed her mouth with his and stripped her of life.

Even at a distance, Rimon shared the killbliss of the Simes and the delicious fear of the other Gens when they realized what had happened.

The Gen boy bolted. Hysteria was rekindled in him as he came up against augmenting Simes each way he turned. Finally, he stopped, panting, backing away from the Sime before him—straight into the arms of one who had come up from behind.

He struggled helplessly when the steely arms came around his shoulders, hands on his collarbones—tentacles snaking out to his neck. The moist laterals sought the soft skin of his throat, near the jugular. His attacker took the fifth contact point at the nape of he boy's neck. It was the first time Rimon had ever seen a Gen killed in such a way that he could scream. The sound of his death agony resonated with the fear and killbliss and went on and on and—

Rimon came crashing down from his shiltpron-induced high into a spasm of nausea. The agony those Gens were suffering was prolonged—much worse than an ordinary kill. When the proper transfer points were not used, they felt more pain, took longer to die—and he had been reveling in it, letting it control him utterly. He, Rimon Farris, who dreaded his monthly kill. Was this what he would be without Kadi?

They were pulling the red-haired girl to the center of the circle now. It could have been Kadi there. He couldn't watch, couldn't feel her die.

He ran, unnoticed by the drunken Raiders, back to the horses, where he leaped astride and galloped away, back toward the road, toward Kadi, toward himself. He had to leave behind the image of himself watching—participating in—those perverted kills, enjoying it just as any Sime would have.

But the image rose again, and waves of nausea swept him. He had to stop to vomit, retching uncontrollably as chills swept through him with the old question become new reverberating in his head. *Rimon is different. Rimon is different.*

But if I'm different, what am I? What am I?

Chapter 3

KILL ABORT

Rimon caught up with the traders who had Kadi one day out of Reloc—and while he was scouting about to see if there was any chance of making himself known to her unobserved, Wolf caught up to him. The dog leaped on him, licking his face, barking joyously as if he knew Rimon was there to rescue Kadi. He managed to quiet the animal, and backed off, tying Wolf to a tree while he continued his search. Kadi was there, all right—how could he have thought he would not recognize her nager? She was still Kadi, only more so.

Amid the Gen fields ranging from terror to despair, he found one calm to numbness, yet glowing beyond the others with a sweetness he had never experienced before. She was in discomfort, but not pain—sunburned, dirty, sweat- and dust-begrimed, bruised from jolting over the rough roads, Kadi was in the state of any Gen being shipped to market after several days on the road. But this time it was Kadi. It was all Rimon could do to keep himself from rushing up to demand her release.

And the dealer was Brant, a pompous stickler for the legalities who would never sit still for a quiet little road-side transaction with a bribe to sweeten it.

So Rimon, Wolf in tow, followed them to Reloc, keeping to a safe distance as he watched Kadi delivered to one of the largest establishments. She was the last one in the wagon, huddled down at the bottom against the wall, half-asleep in her exhaustion. One of the Simes unloading the wagon flicked his whip at her bare feet, and Rimon gasped as if he were the one stung. Kadi struggled to her

53

feet, warily watching the Sime threatening to drag her out of the cage with his whip. "I'll walk, thank you," she said with dignity. Dirt, bruises, whip marks, dark circles under her eyes—and still she managed to hold her head high as she entered the compound and the door closed behind her.

Rimon knew it would take over an hour to prepare her, if they wanted to display her today. He also knew the procedures and closed his mind to them. She would be stripped, showered, and subjected to various indignities intended to frighten her. The guards would be allowed a kill—any Gen who made trouble, as an example to the others. Would Kadi be that example? He shivered in the bright sunlight and set about his preparations to buy her and get her away from there.

A short distance from town, he made camp. Kadi would be bone-weary, and probably hungry once she knew she was safe. As he had not brought enough food for a Gen, he did a little shopping and found a barber shop to help him put on his "prosperous jaded gentleman" look. With his boots shined, a fresh change of clothing, and barbered to neatness, he knew he gave the appearance of a man looking for an exotic kill. His increasing need only added to the effect.

He tied Wolf to a tree and went down the central street toward where he had last seen Kadi. There was a crowd in front of the display. Kadi had been dressed in a bit of filmy green material, and placed on a velvet couch between a blonde in blue and a brunette in red. Quite a picture they made; clearly that merchant knew prime merchandise when he found it.

Kadi was sitting very straight, keeping her legs together —the only way she could keep either dignity or modesty the way they had dressed her. She could hardly move anyway; the jeweled collar about her neck was attached by a fine chain to a stake driven into the dirt. All around her men and women were so displayed, three to a couch, each in a jewel-like setting. Guards in crisp livery made sure none of the customers examining the merchandise got carried away and took a kill before paying.

By concentrating, Rimon could sort Kadi's field out from

the others'. She had gone numb again—her spirits undoubtedly drooping even lower. He couldn't let her see
him now. He had to wait until something else stirred her
emotions, or the salesman might suspect something.

A couple approached her, the woman saying, "The sign
says she's from in-Territory. I wouldn't want to develop
such expensive tastes."

"You're right, of course, Bea," said her husband, "but
she intrigues me. See how steady she is? We could keep
her for a long time. I wouldn't take her accidentally, like
the last one."

"And look at her hands," said the woman. "She's used to
hard work. We can get a lot out of her while we work
her up."

A salesman came over. "You'll certainly get your money's worth with this one. Just zlin that field—solid and
packed and still rising. And she's well broken—a bit slow
to respond right now because she's been rushed through
production. Fresh in today. It makes them a little numb at
first, but there's the added advantage of not getting used
merchandise—almost like home-grown."

The woman became intrigued. "And just how much
would you want for such a one?"

The salesman named an outrageous figure. Kadi looked
up for the first time and said with a slight sneer, "The likes
of you could never afford me."

Startled, Rimon watched the three Simes zlin her. Then
the salesman said, "As I said, folks, when they snap out
of it, they come on very strong. Just zlin that nager!"

But the woman linked arms with her husband, pulling
him on. "The likes of you, my dear, could never handle the
likes of her—let alone afford her."

The salesman turned to Kadi and gritted in an under-
tone, "No supper for you tonight, and if you scare away
any more customers, I'll take stronger measures."

Kadi looked up at him, then away. He didn't scare
her. She leaned against the back of the couch, still carefully preserving her dignity. *She cares,* thought Rimon.
*Something in Kadi refuses to give up her humanity, even
when she thinks she doesn't care anymore.*

As Kadi was staring at her hands in her lap, Rimon

dared move closer. She looked much better now, clean, her hair shining again—but the scratches and bruises showed plainly on her fair skin. Another customer stopped, this time a tall blond man. The salesman said, "Have you ever felt a more seductive nager? She's ripe now, but I guarantee she'll get better in a month or two."

"How much?" the man asked, putting one foot up on the platform. A nearby guard unlimbered his whip, coming to full alert. The Sime said, eyes riveted on Kadi, "May I take a closer look?"

Rimon watched Kadi take in the bulging ronaplin glands along the man's arms, the trembling of leashed need. For the first time, he detected a faint glimmer of fear in her—and saw what it did to the Sime before her. His laterals licked out of their sheaths, and he leaned forward as the salesman named a figure. He was in no mood to haggle. "I'll take her."

Rimon felt a rush of pure pain and deadly fear that the man would take Kadi then and there. He made one step forward, but the salesman said, "You may examine the merchandise, but remember please that the price will be the same, and a private kill will be much more satisfying than taking her here with all these other fields interfering."

Kadi's contempt reflected Rimon's own—contempt for the man's public display of his need. He expected the man to back off at the derision pouring in from all sides—even from the Gen before him. Yet the Sime came even closer to Kadi, reaching out a tentacle to caress her bare thigh, savoring her nager. Rimon stepped up behind the man, expecting Kadi to look up then, but she didn't. She was staring at the Sime before her, her momentary fear gone—and because she did not fear, she was holding him mesmerized with her nager. Rimon had never seen such a thing. Slowly, Kadi's contempt faded, as did the soothing aura of her field. She was . . . deliberately stimulating the man's need!

"Are you going to let him do that?" Rimon snapped at the guard, who was just as fascinated as the customer. He came to just in time—the Sime's self-control snapped, and he seized Kadi's arms for a kill.

The guard's whip cracked, and the attacking Sime was doubled over, weak with the shock of shen. Rimon seized the moment.

"What's going on here?"

To his own shock, his voice rang in his ears exactly like his father's authoritative tones.

The salesman turned to look at the intruder, and his belligerence melted as he took in Rimon's carefully planned guise. With an obsequious bow, he said, "Yes, N'vet, may I help you?"

Taking his time, savoring the way people parted at his approach, Rimon circled the salesmen and guards and looked Kadi up and down as if he had never seen her before. But out of eyeshot of the Simes, he gave her a quick tentacle signal—*let me handle this.*

Kadi kept still, her nager ringing with surprise—but that was all right. Everyone on the platform was surprised, no one more than Rimon himself. But now he had to play out the role. "Yes, this one will do. There's nothing better here, and I'm in a hurry today. How much?"

The salesman named a figure twice what he'd asked of the attacker. Controlling his fields and swallowing a lump in his throat, Rimon nodded casually. "Fine."

By this time, the Sime who had attacked Kadi had pulled himself together. He confronted Rimon, still clutching his middle. "This Gen is already sold."

Rimon zlinned the man's fields. No, he was not still fixed on Kadi; the shen had broken that link. And, in fact, Rimon himself was in harder need. Indignantly, Rimon turned to the salesman. He didn't have to say a word. With a flick of two tentacles, the salesman ordered the offensive customer removed. The management could make amends to his kind later—he had to stay on the good side of a man who represented the very society from which Reloc made its living.

With another bow, the salesman said, "Shall I have her prepared for you here, N'vet? The Sultana Suite is vacant for the day."

Rimon looked down at the man. "Certainly not. I have my own methods. Have her prepared for the trail. I'll pick her up in ten minutes—no more than that." The only way he might possibly get away with it was to rush them, so they had no time to think. Yet he had to play the role.

He deliberately looked Kadi up and down again, then reached under his cloak for the leather bag of money, which he tossed negligently to the salesman. "That should cover it, and a nice tip for you, too." As he turned away, he reminded, "Ten minutes."

It was the longest ten minutes Rimon had ever counted off—but he let every second of it pass before he appeared again to collect his purchase, carefully suppressing a sigh of relief.

An hour later, Kadi was riding beside him through the open woods outside Reloc, Wolf running happily beside them. They kept silence as the heavy town traffic thinned, and the farmers and dealers leaving the market at the end of the day turned off onto side trails.

As dusk gathered, they found themselves alone, and Rimon led the horses aside through dense thicket. The little glade surrounding a small brook, where he had pitched camp, felt like home. Swinging down, he gestured at the ring of stones set for a fire, the little lean-to that sheltered some blankets. "Home," he said. "Or such a home as I can offer you, Kadi."

She sat her horse, very still in her plain white riding culottes and stiff white tunic, the collar and chain binding her to the pommel of Rimon's horse, the tags jingling every time she moved.

"Kadi? You haven't said a word to me. You don't have to act anymore. It's over . . . Kadi?" He loosed her chain, holding up his hands to help her down as he had always done. "Come on, let's get that horrid thing off you."

She let her eyes fall to his face. As if her courage and strength wholly deserted her, her body moved into his arms, and her next breath became a sob. Then she was crying, not hysterically, but thoroughly and from the depths of her soul. Rimon felt how every sob cleansed her, and in the end when she couldn't stop, he carried her to the lean-to and covered her with a blanket. "Sleep if you can, baby. I'll get the fire going and make some tea."

He unstoppered a canteen and made as if to bathe her face, but she groped for it, and he held it while she drank between sobs. She drank and drank until he pulled it away, saying, "Hey, whoa, how long has it been since you drank any water? When did they feed you last?"

She shook her head, her breathing finally quieting a little. "I'm all right, now. Oh, Rimon, how can you stand the sight of me?"

"You're as beautiful as ever to me, Kadi—more so, if you want to know the truth. And I haven't come this far just to have you die of starvation before I can get you to the border."

The fire was laid ready. Rimon flicked the striker at it, and when it blazed up he set some grain to cooking in the pot slung over it. Meanwhile, he cut a piece of fruit bread, toasted it lightly, and dipped it in the honey crock. He felt the aroma finally waking Kadi's appetite, but when she took the first bite, another tear trickled down her cheek. "Mama's bread."

With one tentacle, he smoothed her hair back and tucked a stray strand behind her ear. "It's been awful, hasn't it? But it's over now, Kadi. You're safe."

"Safe? Maybe to the border, if no one catches us. But then what? What can I do in Gen Territory—how can I earn my way? I don't even know the language—and now I'm Gen, I'm too stupid to learn."

"Kadi!" How could she think such a thing? "Kadi—you're just the same. You were never stupid—"

"Neither was Nerob."

Rimon swallowed his fears. *No, not Kadi.* "Baby, I'm going to take care of you until you cross the border, and then you'll make a life for yourself. I know you can do it."

"You knew I'd be Sime, too—" And then she shook her head, pulling her ragged spirits together. "No, none of this is your fault. It's just that—there's no safety for me in this world, not anywhere."

Rimon sat cross-legged, watching her nibble on the bread. "Do things look so different to you now?" He reached out one handling tentacle to caress her chin where the honey had dripped. Licking it off his tentacle, he asked, "Can't you tell I still love you?"

She stared at him, her nager edged with disbelief and hope. Then she stared deliberately at his lateral orifices, tightened against his increasing need. Out of long habit, she let a finger stray along a lateral sheath, seeking to gauge his condition as the familiar sympathy welled up from deep within her, assuaging his need with an incredible new strength.

For a moment, Rimon's lateral orifices softened and his breath came in a quelled rasp. He wanted her . . . she wanted to help him. He could feel it—NO! He tore himself away, on his feet and pacing around the fire. His voice shook when he said, "You shouldn't do that now, Kadi."

He felt her startle reflex as she realized what had happened—and yet it was followed by trust. He had to be worthy of that trust . . . all the way to the border.

To break the spell, he busied himself with bringing her porridge, but he could see that she attempted to eat only to please him. There was a new tension between them. Finally she abandoned the plate and said, "The world seems different." Then, her deep blue eyes sick with memmory, she asked, "At home—do they—? Oh, Rimon, I—I started to make friends with two girls in the wagon with me. Lynn . . . and Serri. Serri, like my sister. And then—in those horrible Pens, they stripped us, and the guards—It's chilling the way they look at you—*zlin* you, rather, looking for ones they can goad, so they can take a kill. One of the guards—Serri talked back to her—and she—she—she killed her, right there. And . . . then I knew I was Gen, Rimon, because I didn't do anything! I—I'm a coward, just like Nerob!"

"Because you didn't go get yourself killed, too? Kadi, that's just common sense!"

"No. You don't know how I felt. Oh, Rimon, have I changed so much? Things taste and smell different. And I've never cried like that before. I don't really feel like a different person—but I'm so confused!"

Everything in him wanted to comfort her. He reached out to cradle her face in his hands and kissed her as he used to do. For one moment, it was as if nothing had changed—and then, with a start, she drew back. "Rimon! Doesn't that make you—"

Puzzled, he searched himself. "It's gone," he whispered. "The need tension. No, not gone—faded away . . . Kadi, whatever it is you do for me, you do it even better now that you're Gen."

Rimon put his arms around Kadi in the old, sheltering gesture. She melted against his chest, and they sat for a long time watching the fire and holding each other, suspended in a moment out of time. Rimon felt all the tiny threads of self-control, of denial of need, mysteriously loosening within him. With any other Gen, Rimon knew that his current state of need would have been whipped into kill frenzy. How easy the last week of each month would be with Kadi to lean on like this. But—one flicker of fear in her, and even Kadi might be his next victim.

Yet, now that he'd tasted this—how could he give it up?

Two mornings later, they rode into the pass, taking a shortcut Kadi had learned of in the Pens. But in a few hours, they encountered such rough terrain they had to dismount and lead the horses. "Kadi, are you sure this is the way?"

"No," she answered irritably. "I'm not sure. I thought this was right, but after all, I'm only a Gen. I can get lost."

"Hey—I'm not complaining," said Rimon. "All I can tell is that we're near the border. This pass does go through, but it's awfully rough going—" He almost added "for a Gen," but thought better of it. Instead, he said, "Why don't you rest here for a few minutes while I climb that pinnacle over there? Maybe I can zlin the way through. It may not be as bad as it looks."

Away from Kadi, he felt need sharpen. Soon, though, he forced it to the back of his mind, as he had had to do so often before around the stock.

As he topped the craggy pinnacle, he saw the pass they had missed—an easy road cleared through the tumbled boulders clogging the slice in the hillside. He was about to scramble down when he felt selyn nager ahead. There was a group of Gens down there, not far from the border. A Gen border patrol? What luck! Kadi could go right to them, and have a safe escort into Gen Territory.

He turned to call to her, and paused for a moment. She was sitting on a rock, Wolf beside her, her hand on the dog's head. She had never been more radiantly beautiful. Her nager was like a golden halo all about her; he could feel it even from here. He knew all at once that despite days of steeling himself for this moment, he wasn't ready to send her away—not now, not ever.

It took all his strength to force himself to climb down, calling, "Kadi! This way—bring the horses!"

He led her to a vantage point where they could look down at the Gens. "I don't understand it," he said as they climbed carefully. "They haven't moved in the last half hour, and they're on the Sime side of the border, no place to make camp—"

At that point, Rimon sensed another, weaker, nager among the Gens, and slid hyperconscious to check his perception. "Kadi, there's a Sime with them—weak field— great pain—a changeover victim?" He scrambled heedlessly to the top of the rise and looked down at a lush valley dotted with trees.

Kadi joined him, and together they took in the scene below them. The group of Gens, all male, wore no uniform or identifying blazon, so they couldn't be an official Gen border patrol. Perhaps they were a band of vigilantes mounting a reprisal raid against nearby Larchmont Crossing—where Rimon planned to go for a Pen Gen to kill.

On the ground among the Gens lay their captive, a Sime woman wearing the green armband of the Sime border patrol. She was unconscious, but must have suffered for a long time before reaching that state, for Rimon could not believe the cruelty of what they had done to her. Beside him, Kadi choked and turned to bury her face against his shoulder, chills of horror running through her.

The Gens had a contraption Rimon had seen before, and hated: an animal trap. They often set them along the border to capture bears or wolves, or other fur-bearing animals. Rimon had occasionally released animals from Gen traps or, more often, killed them quickly to end their suffering.

The Gens had clamped both their prisoner's arms in the trap, the cruel teeth closed about halfway up her forearms. It was obvious that she had sustained a fatal lateral injury, slowly voiding selyn until she would die of attrition —*not long now*.

As they pitched camp, the Gens kicked her every time they passed by, to see if she was conscious. Rimon felt every blow deep in his own body. *They aren't civilized—they're just animals.* His need rose and his tentacles ached for the kill. That was really all Gens were good for.

"Rimon, I can't breathe!"

He realized he was holding Kadi to him so tightly his own shoulders ached. "I'm sorry. Here, that better?"

She wiped tears away and forced her breathing to steady as she looked once more at the group below them. "I can't go down there. I won't have anything to do with such sadists. Take me home; I'd rather belong to Nerob."

Rimon held her away from him, suddenly remembering that she was Gen. He told her what he'd just been thinking. "But that doesn't apply to you, Kadi."

"Maybe it will—one day—if I go down there."

"Somewhere out there, you'll find somebody good who'll want to take care of you as I want to—and can't. Kadi, go on down there. They won't be cruel to you—any more than the Reloc Pen guards would be cruel to a kid in changeover."

Kadi looked thoughtfully down at the Gens. "Maybe I can distract them, make them stop torturing her. Maybe —when they're not looking—maybe I could give her a quick death. I wonder if I could make myself do it."

"You're a full-grown woman, and you can do anything you set your mind to. Kadi, if you can distract them, get them away from camp a bit, I could probably get in there and help her die peacefully. If I have to, I could take one of them and be gone before they knew I was there. It would make your escape claim seem more valid."

Kadi's lips tightened. "You're going to have to kill— and soon—I know that. But—"

"It's different when it's real people involved? Yes—I know. But, Kadi—"

"Oh!" cried Kadi as one of the largest Gens kicked the prisoner again. "Rimon—you kill that one—the one with the barbed spurs on his boots. Do it for me."

This was the Kadi of free spirit and pure courage he had always known. "All right, if I have to take one of them, it will be that one. Now"—Rimon almost choked on the words—"now, go on down there and do what you must."

He could feel the emptiness in Kadi's heart as she stared at him for a long moment, as if she were engraving his features in her memory as he was hers. Then she turned and scrambled down the twisted trail toward the Gens. With one hand she loosed her hair, and with the other she smeared dirt over her skin so she looked much more trail-worn than she was.

She paused to kick a rock loose to signal her approach. Then, when she was sure they'd seen her, she veered off across the rock face, stumbling and scrambling, tossing fearful glances over her shoulder as if expecting close pursuit.

Several of the Gens broke away and came after her. Kadi redoubled her pace. Rimon could see her plan at once—to lead them a merry chase so he could get into their camp. But suddenly Kadi slipped, her ankle twisting under her, and went skidding sideways down the slope toward the Gens. He heard her yelp of pure surprise. She went into her panic act, screaming and kicking against the Gens as if they were Simes out to kill her and she were merely a runaway from the Pens. There was no panic in her nager, but the act was pure genius.

He held his breath, waiting to make sure her pain was nothing more than scratches and bruises. Then, seeing that her initial plan had failed, he decided he'd better find a more secure vantage point. He went back the way they had come, then up and over the side of the pass.

Hugging the edge of the valley, Rimon worked his way to where he could zlin what went on. By this time, they had Kadi by their fire, one of them tearing the Sime woman's shirt into strips to brace Kadi's ankle. The Sime woman was still unconscious, and from this close, Rimon could perceive the selyn leaking from her torn laterals. He fixed his attention on the big Gen with the spurs, for the first time in his life approaching a kill without the slightest hesitation or doubt—or regret.

Kadi let one of the men help her to her feet. It seemed that they had accepted her. Then the man who had helped her bent and scooped her into his arms, kissing her roughly on the mouth. Kadi began to kick and squirm, but the huge

Gen was more than she could manage. Then the Gen with the spurs pushed Kadi's captor, and in an instant the two big men were squared off for a fight, Kadi on the ground between them, just as Rimon had seen Gen males fighting over females in the Pens.

Animals—nothing but animals.

But these were Wild Gens. What were they doing? Did they make slaves of Gens from Sime Territory? Was that what he'd sent Kadi to? His first impulse was to charge in and break it up. But these Gens were not trained to obey a Sime, and one Sime in need against seven wild Gen males —no, no chance.

Before the two males began to fight, a short blond Gen shoved between them. With one hand, he plucked Kadi off the ground and shoved her at the Gen with the spurs. The leader rewarding his man.

At that moment, Wolf, whom Rimon had forgotten, dashed from the underbrush and began to nip at the Gen's spurred ankles, barking and snarling. As the big Gen danced away from the dog, the other Gens howled with laughter. One of the others took a lariat from his saddle and flipped it over Wolf's head, securing the snarling, prancing dog to a tree. *That won't last long,* thought Rimon.

During the distraction, Kadi had made a run for it, back the way they'd come. But they caught her before she'd fairly started. *I've got to get help,* thought Rimon. His eye fell on the green blazon now wrapped around Kadi's ankle. The border patrol never traveled alone. The Sime woman must have been part of a detachment, and some of them must still be in the area.

Rimon worked his way back along the edge of the valley to where he could overlook the whole green flatland to the border. In the distance, there was a haze of dust, and just in front of it, now that he was concentrating, he could barely discern the collective nager of a band of Simes—the border patrol. It had to be the border patrol—but any Simes would be delighted to attack that band of Gens.

Augmenting slightly, confident he would soon have a kill, Rimon went to meet them. They had already spotted the Gen nager ahead, and Rimon told them, "They have one of your scouts." In two-syllable words, he described what had been done to her. Then he said, "And they've got my—"

"Your Gen? You can prove legal ownership, I presume."

"Yes, of course." *Thanks to those tags!*

The patrol leader held out a hand, tentacles extended. "Then come!" Rimon vaulted aboard, suggesting a sheltered route back to the Gen camp. Soon they drew up behind a stand of trees, dismounted, and crept up with Rimon to survey the scene.

The Gens had a fire going, several rabbits and a grouse spitted over it. *Surely,* thought Rimon, *they think they're in Gen Territory.* Off to one side, Kadi's new owner was sawing away at her collar. The Sime leader took all this in, muttering something about a reprisal raid on Larchmont Crossing, and then turned to Rimon. "You wait here— No—" Changing his mind, he said, "I guess you couldn't. But, ware this—the girl with the tags is legally yours. The rest are ours. Understand?"

Rimon swallowed hard. He'd been counting on the one with the spurs. But patrollers didn't work for nothing. Once again he set himself to deny himself a kill. "Agreed."

The patrol deployed and charged into the Gen camp, whips cracking. Several Gens were caught and tied at once, but the Gen with Kadi had time to draw his rifle and get off a shot before dragging Kadi toward the horses.

In an instant, three patrollers were after them. Kadi was caught around the waist by a patrol whip and flung into Rimon's arms while the rest gave chase to the escaping Gens.

With the Gens scattering in every direction, patrollers after them but wary of their rifles, the camp was quickly emptied of all except trussed-up Gens, two dead Gens Rimon hadn't even seen taken, a dead Sime, and the Gens' captive, still barely alive.

Kadi was clinging to him, gasping for breath. "Rimon!" Her nager was no help to Rimon for the first time he could remember. He wanted a kill. He had to have selyn—now.

The pain of the injured captive assaulted him from one side as Kadi's strong field irritated him from the other. He thrust her aside—*must stop that pain!*

Bending over the trap, he released the catch. As the vicious teeth drew free of her flesh, the Sime woman's selyn loss rate redoubled. She screamed at the pain.

As Rimon lifted her, trying for a grip to snap her neck, she twisted and instinctively grasped at his arms as rapid attrition drained her life. It felt as if his own life were draining away.

He was slammed into hyperconsciousness, the whole world glowing selyn, the patroller's life pluming away in a burst of brilliance that made him ache with intil, need, attrition— And then she was dead, and he was in hardest need, desperate for the kill he knew he could not have.

Sick, dizzy, Rimon folded in on himself, gasping for air. It seemed a long, long time that he crouched there. Then, slowly, there was a warm, golden glow seeping through him, melting his locked muscles, soothing ravaged nerves. Pulse after pulse, brighter and brighter, the brightest Gen nager he'd ever felt, pure, solid, ruddy-gold glory. He went for the core of it without conscious thought as every cell in his body cried out—salvation!

A cracking shock of black fear sent freezing shards through every nerve of Rimon's body. The tempting field moved away from him and then fled. *Must have it.* Thrusting aside the lifeless Sime body, he scrambled to his feet.

The field he sought was ahead of him, fleeing madly. In seconds he was closing, dodging trees and rocks, vaulting fallen trunks with the ease of the Sime predator on the hunt. Skidding down a slope, ankle deep in pine needles, the musty smell coming to him in flashes of duoconsciousness, Rimon found a curious portion of his mind standing aside, untouched and remembering.

Once before he'd hunted—once before he'd killed—and once, only once before had he reached true satisfaction.

He was upon the fleeing field. Now, again, at last! Sweet familiar field of love and friendship and hope and life, now under his tentacles. Zeth!

But this time, Zeth—this time you won't be afraid. It was so good before you were afraid. It didn't hurt before you were afraid. Stop—Zeth! Stop. . . .

No. Zeth was dead. Long—long ago. . . .

The texture of the nager—the sweet delirious fear—was Gen. Gen—not Sime! Gen!

KADI!

With the most terrible effort of his life, Rimon shut off that selyn killdraw, choked it down and fought his way duo-conscious even as the imperative of the kill drove him, and saw that he held Kadi, and this time, his aching, dripping laterals lay along her arms as firmly as his lips contacted hers. A trickling of selyn activated the nerve-rich laterals. Despite her wild struggles, Kadi couldn't break that contact. No Gen could have.

In a time-stretched instant, Rimon stared into a face so distorted by terror that it wasn't Kadi, but just another Gen. Yet it was Kadi. That nager—unmistakable. All the years he had lived to rest within her nager.

She recognized that he was conscious, and a degree of her panic faded. Warily, she ceased to struggle, her terror turning to frozen resignation. Only then was Rimon able to break lip contact, cutting off that tempting trickle of selyn through his laterals.

Searing pain ripped through him, centered in his chest but lancing out in every direction, causing him to tighten his grip on Kadi's arms bruisingly. Through gritted teeth, he said, "No! I—will—not—kill—you!"

With the last dregs of his will, he broke lateral contact, aborting his kill in fiendish shen. Pain flashed. From some great distance, he observed his body convulse in agony.

Then there was nothing.

Chapter 4

THE FIRST DREAM

He was in pain. Immense, undeniable forces tore at his body. Raw, abused nerves screamed for release. Relentless spasms locked muscle against muscle, forcing him to awareness of every cell of his body, all burning in self-destruction, wasting his life-force out into empty nothingness.

Slowly, the nightmare turned to peaceful dreaming. On some sweet nageric plane, Rimon floated, gently buoyed up by a soothing golden field. Kadi, he recognized, but could not speak to her—his physical body seemed to disappear in her presence, beyond his control or caring. He knew he was dying, his life wasting away, but Kadi had eased the pain —it would be so pleasant just to drift away now to death . . . no more pain . . . no more responsibilities. *I didn't kill her.* It was all that mattered; in that one act of denial, he had accomplished everything life could possibly ask of him. At last he could rest.

He wanted to speak, just to say good-bye to her, but he had lost contact with his body. Somehow, that didn't disturb him—what had his body ever been to him but a source of frustration, need, and pain? Kadi was sad, he saw. *Don't be sad, Kadi. We're both better off this way.* But Kadi had her own ideas.

Bemused, Rimon remained passive, uncaring, observing what Kadi was doing without understanding it. She was touching him, her hands provoking flickers of pure delight along his lateral sheaths. He should have told her not to touch him there, but it felt too good, and he couldn't move anyway. . . .

Something surged from Kadi to Rimon—an emotion strangely akin to need, reawakening Rimon's need—but painlessly. For one instant he fought to remain in his numbed state, but then he felt his laterals lick out of their own volition, meeting Kadi's high and willing field. Rimon could not stop them, nor could he move his hands or handling tentacles. Somewhere in the back of his mind, the thought flickered that Kadi was in danger, but he couldn't focus on it.

As if she were the attacking Sime, Kadi moved her hands up on Rimon's forearms, and he perceived her sensation as his laterals licked at her skin. She grasped him firmly, and that strange feeling in her increased, piercing through his lassitude. Suddenly his body came to life. His handling tentacles lashed about her arms.

I've got to stop this, Rimon thought with no conviction whatsoever. He forced his eyes open, but saw nothing—of his physical senses, only touch seemed to be operating. But Kadi started, a moment's fear—for him, not of him—and then she pressed her lips to his.

Helplessly, he accepted the life flowing to him. He was not drawing—she was giving to him, filling him. As the flow became faster and faster, immeasurably sweet, he sensed her incredulous surprise at the pleasure—pleasure? —she experienced. Then a surge of power as she drove life into him obliterated all individuality between them so that they became one flowing force suspended in time.

When it was over, Kadi remained for a moment, lying on Rimon, her lips pressed to his. The physical world reclaimed him with a jolt—her weight was real, her lips warm, her hands firm on his arms. When she lifted her head, blue eyes stared into his, flaming hair a nimbus about her awestruck face. In a bare, shivering whisper, Rimon breathed, "Kadi?"

Afraid to believe it, he lifted a hand, barely dared to brush her cheeks with dorsal tentacles. Again he spoke her name, and she smiled—and he felt his own smile emerging from the recesses of his soul, swelling his heart to bursting. In buoyant elation, he touched her with hands and tentacles, all perceptions new. He wanted to zlin her, to make certain she was real and unharmed—but when he tried, it was as if he were a child again, or a Gen, not the briefest flicker of Sime senses at his command. "Kadi—I can't— zlin. Not at all. Is this attrition?"

But he knew before she answered, "You took selyn from me—I know you did. And it didn't hurt. I wanted to give —everything, even my life."

"But *why*, Kadi?" What she had done was inconceivable, even though he had experienced it.

She answered his question, but not the real question deep in his heart,. "You were dying! Rimon, you shenned yourself—for me. Everything for me. I know you must have defied your father to come after me. You were willing to break the law by releasing me at the border. But I was afraid—a coward Gen, running from you, terrified. When you caught me—you stopped yourself. You shenned yourself, and then the convulsions started. I was afraid this time you'd die—it was worse than I'd ever seen it, and—and I wanted you to live more than anything. I wanted to give. . . ."

Her words blurred in his mind. He wanted to ask her how she'd done it—not, why. That was important—*how?* But his grasp on the thought loosened and he drifted away, assured that they were both alive.

A warm, wet tongue licking his face brought Rimon awake. He opened his eyes to find Wolf greeting him enthusiastically, a bit of broken rope dangling from his neck. He pushed the dog away. "I'm glad to see you, too, boy. But if you don't mind, I prefer Kadi's kisses to yours."

"Are you all right?" Kadi asked, and Rimon's laughter faded as memory—and disbelief—returned.

But he couldn't help smiling at the sight of her concern. He felt marvelous—reborn. "Am I ever all right!" he chuckled. "We really did it, didn't we?"

"We did . . . something," she agreed.

He climbed to his feet, testing his limbs, his balance, and looked around. The horses were tethered to one side of the small clearing, and a fire burned merrily against a rock. While he'd been out, Kadi must have gone for the horses and made camp. *I'll never underestimate her again.* But she was still watching him suspiciously.

"Kadi, I feel great. Really. No aches, no pains, no dizziness—and no need. I feel like a kid again."

"You still can't zlin?"

He tried, then said, "No—but what does it matter? I don't think it's permanent . . . but if it is, I can get along as well as you can without it."

"Rimon, you're taking it too lightly," Kadi began.

"Baby, I have spent the past four years in varying degrees of misery. If I wasn't in need, I was feeling rotten after a kill. Can't you see it's worth anything to escape from that?"

He got up, stretched, and looked down at himself. "You changed my clothes."

"You had convulsions. I cleaned you up as best I could." But she hadn't been able to do a really good job of it.

Hearing the attractive sound of a waterfall off to one side, he said, "Ah . . . water. Come on, Kadi!" The fall was hardly more than a trickle cascading into a tiny pool. Rimon stripped and showered, shivering at the cold of the water, but enjoying it. When Kadi came near, he jumped out, dripping, and grabbed her playfully. She ducked away from him and ran back toward camp. Wolf joined the chase, barking merrily. Rimon caught Kadi and picked her up. "See? Now you're gonna get dunked!"

She struggled and kicked, and he let her escape long enough to strip off her clothes before Rimon caught her again and tossed her into the pool.

Wolf decided to join them, splashing around while Rimon tried to keep his footing on the slippery bottom of the pool as Kadi struggled playfully to escape. He slipped and went down backwards, and she squirmed free, soaked through, turning to laugh at the sight of Rimon sitting in the pool, grinning, while Wolf climbed out and shook, spraying both of them.

They stared at one another, laughing too hard to breathe. Then Kadi offered Rimon a hand, bracing herself lest he pull her back into the pool. He came out and leaned on her, still laughing. "Oh, Kadi, Kadi, we haven't laughed like that since we were kids," he gasped. "Remember—remember when we all used to sneak off to swim in the river on hot days?"

"The Krazy Kids," Kadi agreed.

"What happened to us?"

"Rimon," she said painfully, "you know what happened."

The laughter drained from him. He sat down heavily on the soft grass beside the pool, pulling Kadi down with him.

"Yes," he said, "I know what happened . . . but why did it have to happen? Why did Yahn have to turn into . . . Nerob? And Zeth. Why—" He choked over a sob. "Oh, Kadi, why? Why did I have to kill Zeth? Why couldn't it have been—have been—"

Kadi held him, supporting him as she always had when Zeth haunted him. And when his racking sobs subsided, she said, "It wasn't your fault, Rimon. You couldn't help it." How often she had said those words over the years. . . .

For the first time, Rimon suddenly understood. "I know that, Kadi." The slow marvel spread through him. "It wasn't my fault. . . ."

She hugged him tightly.

He struggled free and looked at her closely. "It's not guilt this time. It's grief. I can mourn Zeth at last because I know I was the cause of his death, but no more responsible than an avalanche or a forest fire is responsible for killing. I can think about it clearly now. Remember, I told you that—that time with Zeth, it was good during that first moment?"

"Don't think about it, Rimon. It's over."

"Yes, it's over, Kadi. So I can think about it now because . . . I felt that same good feeling with you today. But not just for a moment—the whole time was good. And that goodness did something to me—I don't know. It's as if—as if, because of Zeth, I didn't have to kill you. Oh, I can't explain it. I just feel it. Zeth didn't die in vain."

"I think I know what you mean," Kadi whispered, and something awakened a flicker of that delicious satisfaction he had been seeking so frantically all his adult life, only to find it right under his nose.

"Yes, I think maybe you do understand. Kadi, Zeth was Sime. He couldn't give up his selyn to me. But you could —because you're Gen. And that's what Gens are really for —not like Nerob, not like the Wild Gens. Like you."

"Rimon—do you really understand what happened to us?"

"You weren't afraid—that's all. You wanted to give me your selyn. Those two facts I'm dead sure of, because I felt them. Beyond that—the physical aspects—I don't really remember exactly what happened. Here, let me see. . . ."

He took her in killmode position, although for the first time he had no reason to seek her touch except curiosity. As his laterals touched her skin, he felt her respond with pleasure that swept through him with a relaxing warmth. Concentrating, he pressed his lips to hers. The tiniest trickle of fresh selyn passed between them, awakening in Kadi a pale echo of the wild joy that had consumed her before. Experimenting, he found that with the slightest effort, he could stop that flow, control it.

But then he became peculiarly aware of Kadi's physical closeness, the clean smell of her wet hair, the coolness of her skin beneath his hands and tentacles. For the first time, he noticed his bare thigh pressed against hers . . . and how exciting that suddenly became as his lips softened upon hers.

His hands loosened of their own accord, slipping up to caress her shoulders, her back, his tentacles exploring her skin. "Ohhhh—you feel so good. Why haven't I ever noticed how good you feel?" His lips buried in her hair, he whispered fiercely, "Kadi? Kadi, what's happening to me? I've never felt like this before. It's like . . . like hunger, but—"

"I know," she whispered back. "Me, too—"

They knew what they wanted, but only vaguely how to go about it. Then they found each other, and Rimon was lost in feelings. Kadi met his rhythm as if their hearts beat together, surging in a wave of shared pleasure to a euphoric peak . . . to fall into sweet contentment in one another's arms.

For a long time they lay still, but the sun was setting, and the air began to cool. Kadi shivered. "Come on," said Rimon, "let's go back to the fire."

They left the soft bed of grass beside the pool, picked up their clothes, and returned to their campsite to curl up together under a blanket, as they had done so many times before. But it was not like any time before. Rimon's arms were locked about Kadi, and he knew that all his strength existed only to protect her.

He was too happy to fall asleep yet, and so was she.

After a time, he said, "You are so beautiful, Kadi. I can't understand it. You seem to have that same glow a Sime has after a kill!"

She pulled herself up on one elbow to look at him. "You mean you can zlin again?"

He paused, searching. "Yes! Yes, I can, but—it's like normal now. I can, but I just don't want to. I only want to look at you like a child—there's a purity in that, you know."

She regarded him critically. "You know, I think you have that same post-kill glow, too. I can't recall ever seeing you look like that before."

He nodded. "I feel . . . right, for the first time I can remember. Kadi, you've given me what I'd been looking for all my life! Only I didn't know what it was until today. But—it won't be just us. You weren't afraid—and you didn't die! Simes don't have to kill! Gens don't have to die! I didn't kill, and I feel better than I've ever felt in my life. It's a whole new way of life, Kadi!"

She laughed. "Rimon, it's our old way of life—our old plan. We're as good as married, just as we always wanted to be, in spite of my turning out all wrong." Then she sobered. "But what are we going to do now? Where can we go?"

Rimon sighed. "Well, home, I guess, where else? Dad's always been pretty reasonable about my aberrations. If we can make him understand. . . ." He hugged her close. "Oh, we will, Kadi! It's so obvious we've found the way things should be. You are my wife, now. Our children will grow up unafraid—think of it! No more killing. Once we teach everyone what we know, no one else will have to go through what you've been through, baby."

"Rimon?"

"Yes?"

"Don't call me 'baby.' I'm not a child anymore. I'm a woman now."

He was delighted. "You certainly are, Kadi. We're neither of us children anymore. Because of you, Kadi, my love . . . my wife . . . at last, I'm a man. We are complete."

He hugged her to him, knowing that with Kadi by his side he could make the dream of a new way of life come true. Through the night, two lovers on a mountaintop lay in one another's arms, sharing their love and planning to change the world.

Chapter 5

HOMECOMING

It took five days to get home on horseback from the point on the border that Rimon and Kadi had sought after leaving Reloc. They met few people on the road, but those they did meet stared at them in disapproval or swung widely out of their way.

There was nothing unusual about a Sime traveling with a Gen tagged in his name—but there was no chain attached to Kadi's collar, no fear or resentment emanating from her, and nothing at all normal about the way Rimon and Kadi spoke to one another. Those who zlinned them also stared curiously when they perceived Kadi's low field. That had caused Rimon some concern on the first day of their journey, for he had expected Kadi's selyn field to spiral upward again, like that of a newly established Gen. When it did not, he feared for a while that it might be that a Gen only produced enough selyn to serve a Sime once—that he had taken her lifetime supply, even if he had not killed her.

Soon, however, he had perceived her field was rising slowly, apparently in perfect unison with his own rate of depletion. When he was in need again, Kadi would be highfield once more.

The only problem Rimon foresaw was figuring out exactly what they had done.

They had to stretch the small supply of food Rimon had brought. He had not expected to have Kadi's company on the way home. She didn't complain at having nothing but a handful of berries for breakfast the fourth morning, but by afternoon Rimon was berating himself for eating any of their supplies.

There were small communities along the way where they

could have purchased food if they had had any money.
"I'm sorry you had to spend all you had for me," said
Kadi. "The dealer asked a terrible price. It was lucky you
had enough to cover it."

"I didn't." He laughed, remembering with pleasure how
he had fooled that obsequious dealer. "There was just about
half what he asked in that purse."

But Kadi's alarm pierced him even when he was nowhere near need. "Then you didn't legally buy me! It's not
valid! They'll come and claim me!"

"Hey—calm down, Kadi! The papers are all legal. I
made sure of that, and I stamped your tags myself. If the
dealer was too stupid to count his money before signing
the papers, that's his problem, not mine. Besides, he got
more than a fair price."

Kadi was still upset. "Don't worry," he assured her. "I'll
pay him when Del pays me what he owes me. But in the
meantime, we've got to get some food for you. Maybe we
can stop somewhere that I can do some chores for a meal."

"That would look peculiar," Kadi said.

"We *are* peculiar!" he replied. "We're going to have to
get used to that."

When Rimon and Kadi rode up to the big house on the
Farris Genfarm, Wolf set up a loud barking to herald their
arrival. Rimon found himself expecting Marna Morcot to
come out onto the porch, to see what the fuss was and
scold Wolf . . . but of course Marna was not there, nor
Ran, nor Serri. *We'll find them and bring them home,* he
thought.

They dismounted and entered the house. In the kitchen
they found Su Thorbee, wife of one of the overseers, direct-
ing several children in preparing a meal. The results did
not seem very successful.

Su stared at them, zlinning them, and gasped, "Shendi!
Raf—run and get the N'vet!"

Rimon said, "It's all right, Raf. We'll find my father ourselves. Is he out at the Pens?"

"No," said Su, "he's checking that broken irrigation line
—but he should be back soon."

They went on out the back door, very much aware of

eyes following them. Kadi pulled herself tall, walking proudly beside Rimon, but he could feel the apprehension at the pit of her stomach. They stood in the back yard, not far from their playground swings. Soon they heard the sound of a lone horse.

Syrus Farris was riding alone, hastily, along the road to the house. Someone must have ridden to tell him the moment Rimon and Kadi had arrived. He galloped into the yard, an imposing figure on his huge black horse. When he pulled to a halt, the horse reared, forcing the two young people to retreat before the flying hooves. Then Farris controlled the animal and sat staring down at them, Rimon and Kadi at a clear disadvantage.

He took his time to zlin them before he spoke, his voice under careful control. "Rimon, why have you brought this Gen back with you?"

Aware of the gathering crowd, Rimon put his arm around Kadi's shoulders. She stood proudly, looking squarely at Farris. "Father," said Rimon, "this is no nameless Gen. This is Kadi Farris. My wife."

Rimon felt his father recoil and then surge with the fury that had always so unnerved him before. But he was no longer a child. He faced Syrus Farris as an equal.

Farris slid down off his horse. "Let's go inside where we can speak privately."

As they crossed the yard, Rimon could feel that the hard shell of his father's anger shielded a core of . . . fear? Despair? Disappointment in his son?

Farris indicated a bench in the hall. "You wait for us here," he said to Kadi.

"No," she said politely but firmly. "I will go where Rimon goes."

Farris gestured them inside and closed the door. As if stalling for time to think out what he wanted to say, he settled himself behind the desk, steepling his hands and running his tentacles between his fingers.

Rimon and Kadi sat down unbidden before the desk. Finally Farris asked, "Rimon, why have you done this?"

"Father . . . do you realize exactly what we have done?"

Farris was staring at his fingertips rather than at Rimon and Kadi. Almost imperceptibly, he nodded. "I find it difficult to reconcile my perceptions. What appears to be the case . . ."

"Is true!" Rimon said eagerly. "You know I was past turnover when I left here, Father. Kadi's field was climbing, but it's low now. Kadi gave me her selyn, and she didn't die! You have no idea how much better it is than killing!"

Farris' sensitive mouth curled as disgust rippled the enforced calm of his nager. "Rimon, I have had great patience with you because of the tragedy of your first kill. But now you have gone too far. You should have released this Gen at the border—people look the other way when someone can't allow one who was a friend to be killed. But to bring her home? Rimon, my son—take her to the Pens, and then we'll discuss your deed."

"Father, Kadi is my wife. Can't you see what she's done for me?"

The anger threatening to break through Farris' control met a barrier . . . no, a warmth that melted it away like icicles in sunlight. What was happening? Rimon, too, felt unbelievably calm and rational in the face of his father's implacability.

Kadi, Rimon realized, wanted desperately for Rimon and his father to discuss calmly what had happened. Without conscious intent, she was influencing their fields with her own, drawing them into harmony.

Suddenly Farris stared at Kadi. "You!" he gasped, and went hyperconscious for a moment. White with rage, he said, "Get out! Get *out* of this office and let my son have his own mind back!"

Bewildered, Kadi looked toward Rimon. "It's all right, Kadi," he said. "Wait for me outside."

When she had gone, Farris asked, "Can you think clearly now, Son?"

Startled to find compassion in his father's voice and nager, Rimon said, "Of course I can. I've been thinking more clearly than ever before since Kadi and I—"

"Rimon—don't you know what she was doing to you? And to me, for a minute? It's a trick—black magic."

"What?!"

"I've heard of it, among the gypsies. Gens who can control Simes . . . but I never believed it." Waves of horror shimmered through his nager. "She had you in her power!"

"Father, you don't understand. I love Kadi. She loves me —so much that she tried to give her life for mine, but she didn't die because she wasn't afraid."

"She's certainly not afraid now," agreed Farris, "but where did she learn that? I've never before felt anything like what she did to me just then."

"I guess now that Kadi's established, her field is strong enough to reach out further. She used to control my field, remember? She always had to touch me to do it—but she kept me sane. You never minded her controlling my field when I went to pieces after every kill."

"I—I minded, Rimon, but what could I do? She was the only one who could bring you out of those attacks. I know she saved your life many times over . . . but that was four years ago. You've outgrown your dependence on her. You must let her go, Son."

"No. What Kadi and I have," Rimon said softly, "we can share with you. We can teach you—and everyone on the Farm. Imagine everyone sharing—Father, think what it would be like if it didn't matter whether your son or daughter established or changed over!"

Again revulsion rippled through Farris' field, although this time he allowed no physical expression. "Rimon, you know that is impossible. You weren't gone long enough to have reached need. Were you augmenting?"

"I had to—to save Kadi! After that I was in hard need, Father."

"But it was early for you. Perhaps that is why you didn't kill her. I've seen Raiders so high on shiltpron that they'll kill while still pre-turnover . . . and once I saw a Gen too far into shock to feel fear survive such an attack. So . . . if you were not truly in need, and she was not afraid, yes, what you tell me is possible. But you're too sensitive, Rimon, like your mother. What will happen at the end of the month, when you try it again? This time you'll kill her . . . and then what will you do? Wouldn't you rather let her go now?"

"Father, Kadi is my wife."

"She is Gen. She can't be anyone's wife."

"We have pledged to one another. By law, our marriage becomes binding when she bears me a child. And she will."

Farris' eyes lifted to the portrait of Rimon's mother, over the fireplace. His field was unreadable at that moment, but his sensitive lips compresssed against some great sorrow. Rimon realized for the first time that it was not entirely from his mother that he inherited the sensitivity that plagued him. Finally, his father said, "You'll have to give her up, Rimon."

"No, I won't have to. Legally, Kadi is my property." He said it with distaste. He didn't own her—she was his wife.

Shaking his head, Farris pulled open a desk drawer. "Actually, she is *my* property, for you obtained her illegally."

As his father spread a sheaf of documents across the desk, Rimon's heart sank. Gone entirely was the momentary unity. Rimon was a child again, caught out in a prank more serious than he'd realized.

"I . . . I had to get Kadi away somehow," he tried to explain, "and I didn't have enough to cover the price they were asking."

"I knew that. I trust that my son would not deliberately cheat any man . . . for a lark. If I had not thought so, I'd not have paid your debt."

"But . . . how did they know me? I've never been to Reloc before."

"I have," Farris said. "Rimon . . . you didn't expect to get away entirely without paying, did you? Had you not been recognized?"

"I'll pay you back," Rimon said contritely.

"That is the least of your problems. You may have the Gen." He shoved the papers across at Rimon, scribbling his signature in the title-passed-to box. "It would be too disruptive to keep her here. Now, what are you going to do with her?"

"I've told you: Kadi is my wife. We're going to live together, raise a family, just like we'd always planned—only now we can love all our children equally, whether they're Sime or Gen."

"You're still determined to attempt this, in the face of all common sense?"

"Yes."

Farris got up, went to the mantel over the huge fireplace, and picked up an artifact of the Ancients, a pure metal globe of the world with the continents embossed in high relief, though worn now with Marna's constant polishing. As a child, Rimon had loved to make up stories about how that relic had been handed down in his family as an award for service and loyalty to an Ancient Queen. Pure fantasy. His grandfather had found it in the ruins. And Rimon had outgrown fantasy.

"Yes, Father, we're going to live together for the rest of our lives."

Farris put the globe down and turned to Rimon. His nager was grim and cold around Rimon as he said, "You can't stay here, then."

"But . . . this is where we can do the most good!"

"This is where you can do the most harm, Rimon! You've already disrupted the whole Farm. I shudder to think what rumors are flying—the Gen in such a state, your nager in this condition. And when Simes talk, Gens listen. We'll be lucky if we can keep our Gens from rioting if they hear that you came home claiming Simes don't have to kill."

"Is that all you care about? Keeping the Gens under control? Are you afraid I'm right—and that you'll lose your profitable business?"

Farris said angrily,"Yes, I'm afraid! Not of losing money, of losing my son—and our way of life! Rimon, you've grown up among Gens. You know what dangerous animals they are when they're not handled correctly."

"Kadi's not an animal!"

"She's a Gen. You've seen Wild Gens try to kill Simes in changeover. You've seen Gens like Nerob, grown up expecting to be Sime, turn crafty and cunning after they establish. And now . . . this female you have allowed to gain power over you. I ought to destroy her, Rimon, before she destroys you."

"I won't listen to this!"

"Yes you will! The best thing would be for you to let her go now, of your own free will. Let her go to her own kind and make a life for herself if she can. Or will you have to learn the hard way, when you kill her?"

"I'm not going to kill her."

"Rimon . . . I know what torture it will be for you when you kill this particular Gen. However, the greatest tragedy of all would be if you were right . . . if you really could teach all Simes to do what you claim to have done."

"Tragedy?" Rimon was at a total loss.

"Suppose . . . every Gen were capable of controlling Simes as this female does. Think of it, Son. The world would be run by Gens. Is that what you want? When you're away from her influence, can't you think clearly enough to see how dangerous she is? Possibly she has good intentions toward you—but think of other Gens. Would you like to see Nerob with such power? The Wild Gens? If they didn't kill us all off, they'd make slaves of us."

Astonished, Rimon could only stare at his father. *He's as much afraid of Gens as they are of us!* "Father . . . it won't be like that!"

"So I hope," said Farris. "Take the female to the border, and return. Or—take her to live with you, and don't return. Alone, my son, you are always welcome here. But as long as you call that Gen your wife, you are not. Take whatever you require—horses, a wagon, supplies—and try your experiment. When it fails, come home, Son."

Rimon got up. "We're not going to fail," he said. "We'll go." He thought quickly. "We'll homestead on that land near the border that I used to tell you about. You'll always be welcome there, Father."

He found Kadi sitting on the bench in the hall. She stood up anxiously, scanning his face. "He wouldn't listen to you. What did I do, Rimon? I didn't say a word. . . ."

"No, Kadi, it wasn't anything you said. My father is afraid of you."

Her blue eyes were huge with astonishment. "Afraid of me?"

"Yes, afraid. Come on, now. We've got to pack."

"Where are we going?" she asked, accepting without question the fact that they couldn't stay on the Genfarm.

He told her of his idea as they went to his room. There was good farmland available for anyone willing to clear it, and to chance the attacks of raiding parties from out-Territory. "It's the right place for us, now," said Rimon, "practically between the two Territories. Later, when more people have learned what we have—things will be different."

Rimon's room was just as he'd left it—including the package he'd tossed on the bed. Handing it to Kadi, he said, "A belated wedding present."

She opened it and lifted a length of the blue material. "Oh . . . Rimon. You bought this for me?"

"In Scobla. It was for your wedding dress."

She smiled, although her eyes were brimming with tears. "There's enough here for a whole wardrobe—and that's what it will have to be, since I don't have anything else. It's beautiful, Rimon—but you'll get sick of seeing me in blue."

He took her in his arms, as much for the closeness of her presence as to comfort her. Kadi, he was just beginning to realize, was the last part of his old life left to him—and the symbol of everything new. How could his father not trust her? He kissed her forehead. "Come on, Kadidid— you're the practical one. Help me pick out what to take with us."

People disappeared at their approach. Rimon was glad that Kadi couldn't zlin the way Su and her children rushed out the other door when he and she came toward the kitchen. By the time they entered, the room was empty, the partly prepared meal left unattended. Kadi couldn't help knowing what had happened, he thought, but she said nothing and neither did he.

"Pick out some basic utensils," he told her quietly. "Dad said to take what we required."

Kadi nodded and began methodically gathering a small pile, repressed sorrow in her nager. He didn't have to ask what made her heart ache: her mother's touch was everywhere in the kitchen—and Marna was also the only mother Rimon had ever known. *We'll still find them,* he thought, but he didn't share the thought with Kadi now. It was going to take time—and they would have to prove they could live together themselves first.

In silence, each deep in his own thoughts, Rimon and Kadi loaded a small wagon. Rimon wondered how aware Kadi was that they were being watched. Curiosity and suspicion followed their every move.

No one approached them, though, until Rimon brought the horses up to harness them to the wagon. Then Del Erick came across the yard from the bachelor's quarters, defiance and sympathy in his nager. He was leading his stallion, Lightning, by a hackamore.

"Rimon . . ." He looked sidewise at Kadi, hesitant. Then, daringly, he acknowledged her with a nod. "You're leaving?"

Rimon nodded.

Studying Rimon's nager, Erick said, "Together?"

Rimon stepped a little away from Kadi, minimizing the nageric interaction. "Del, I'm onto something exciting. I can't let go of it just because my father—prefers more traditional ways."

Chewing his lip, Del nodded again, considering. Then he dug into his shirt front and came out with a leather bag. "Look, you'll have to have some money to get started. Here are the stud fees I've gotten from Lightning. It's not the whole amount I owe you, but . . ."

Rimon pushed the little bag away. "Del, I can't take your last . . ."

"If you won't take the money, then here—" He thrust the horse's reins into Rimon's hands. "Take Lightning. You own more of him than I do, anyway. And you'll have to have horses—he could service your mares and next year you'll have foals to sell—or you could hire him out and get the money to pay your taxes. . . ."

Stunned, Rimon let his friend push the reins into his hand, but he was shaking his head. "You had such plans, Del, to go into business yourself. I can't let you give all that up for me and Kadi."

"I'm not giving up," said Del. "I've proved I can do it now. I can get another backer, find another horse, start again. I've got a job. You're going off into the blue. . . . Rimon, where are you going? How will you survive?"

"Remember that strip of bottomland, just this side of the river, where we camped that time? Kadi and I are going to homestead there. It's good, rich cropland."

"It's also a Gen Raider's corridor. You'd have to have an army to hold that land!"

"No we won't. We'll make friends with the Gens, somehow. Kadi and I—we can do it now, Del. We're going to start something new—no killing. We're going to live in peace and friendship with everyone."

Del's eyes misted over as he looked at the faraway dream. "Yeah, I remember the little grove we picked out for the main house . . ." Then he came to himself. "Kids' dreams. It's going to take more than two tentacled arms to make a go of it."

"I have Kadi."

Del blinked, looking back at her as she sat quietly on the wagon seat, holding the reins of the horses still not secured to the wagon tongue.

Del moved a little closer, one hand on the horse's withers as he studied her nager again. "Kadi—Kadi?"

"It's just me, Del, the same as always, only a bit more grown up."

He looked at Rimon, who said, "She's my wife, now—and a lot more than that. She gave me—a satisfaction I could never get from the kill. And she survived. And she's going to survive it again, next time." He turned to Del to look at him squarely. "She doesn't control me—and I don't control her. We're—married."

Rimon wound one tentacle around Lightning's reins and took Del's hands in his, gripping his friend's handling tentacles with his own in tight friendship. "Just feel what she's done for me. You could have it, too. We could teach you."

Del was tempted, but hesitant.

Rimon thrust the horse's reins back in Del's hands. "I can't take Lightning—not with what he means to you. And you've worked too hard for that money; you're too close now to give it all up. But you could tie Lightning on behind the wagon and come with us—out into the blue to homestead. We could certainly use the help."

Del's eyes went to Rimon's hands and tentacles, twined with his own. Without looking up, he shook his head. "I'm in need."

"Only just past turnover, if I'm any judge. Kadi?"

She edged down off the seat of the wagon, neatly managing the reins without spooking the horses. As her nearly palpable fields enfolded Erick, Rimon could feel the need-tension drain from his friend. It was like the ringing of a strident bell shut off suddenly. There was a peace in which mental clarity was possible above and beyond the normal.

"See?" said Rimon. "She doesn't control—she sets us free to be ourselves. If you don't kill your next Gen, he could do that for you—all month long, Del. All the time!"

"You could teach me not to kill?"

"There's not much trick to it," said Rimon. "It's mostly the Gen who has to be convinced not to be afraid."

"But—I *like* the fear. . . ."

"It's good—sure—but this is better. Del, if I can do this —with all my problems—surely you could do it, too."

Del thought that over, then said, "I'd like to go with you —you can't make it by yourselves, no matter what you think. And the whole idea . . ." He looked at Kadi. "All right, Rimon. I'm in."

Rimon smiled broadly at Kadi, squeezing her shoulders so tightly she squealed and they all laughed. Rimon said, "Go on up to the house and tell Dad you're quitting. Do you have a Gen lined up?"

"No. It's never mattered to me the way it does—did—to you. I've always taken whatever's available."

"The only way this will work is if the Gen is not afraid, and we have only a few days to convince him not to be. So—it has to be a Gen we can talk with."

Del paled. "A Domestic? One who grew up in-Territory? Rimon, I've never—"

"You're not going to kill him, remember?"

Hope and fear conflicting within him, Del nodded. "I've never collected a choice kill here, so I guess your father owes me one after two years."

Farris allotted his employees their choice of available Gens once each six months. Most, like Del, never chose the Domestic Gens marked for the bazaars and choice auctions.

"Go choose someone you can talk to," said Rimon, "someone Kadi can talk to. She'll be more convincing than either of us!"

Del smiled bravely, although Rimon knew even Kadi

could see his apprehension. "I haven't got much to pack," he said. "I'll be ready to go in no time."

As they watched Del walk determinedly toward the Pens, Rimon took Kadi's hand. "Del's the first," he said. "There will be others. We'll make it work, Kadi. Somehow . . . we're going to make it work!"

PART II

Chapter 6

VISITORS

Whack!

Rimon drove the axe deep into the wood, pulled it out, drove it home again—angrily working out his frustrations and anxiety by cutting firewood. There was already enough piled to last a week; still he worked steadily, holding back from augmenting. That would have felt good and made the work go faster—but he didn't want to finish the mindless task and have to face reality . . . his growing need.

They'd come here three weeks ago with such high hopes —two Simes and two Gens ready to start a new way of life. Del had chosen carefully, a boy from town who knew Del, Rimon, and Kadi, who could understand the chance they offered him. At first it seemed they could conquer anything—even the panic that shattered the boy's nager when Del picked him out of the Pen.

"I'm not going to kill you!" Del was saying—angrily, because the boy's fear was such an irritation to him—when he led him up to the wagon where Rimon and Kadi waited.

Kadi slid off the wagon seat and placed herself between the boy and the two Simes. "Don't be frightened," she said. "Nobody's going to hurt you."

"They're gonna kill me!"

"No. Look at me . . . Billy, isn't it?"

The boy nodded.

Kadi held out her arms. "Look—I'm Gen, like you. I'm not frightened, Billy, because Rimon and I have found out that Simes don't have to kill to take selyn from Gens."

Wide-eyed, the boy shrank back, shaking his head with his gaze riveted on Kadi. "No—no, they kill—they'll kill you no matter what you say or do."

93

"Rimon took selyn from me," said Kadi, softly, convincingly. "I'm just fine, see?"

In one long, tense moment, the boy's fight against hope became almost unbearable, and all Rimon could think was, *Kadi, do something—do the right thing—now!*

Impulsively, Kadi put one sheltering arm around the child's shoulder. Her calm nager dissipated the stifling scream of the boy's nerves, and the two Simes drew a deep breath. Rimon said, "We mean you no harm, Billy. Listen to what Kadi is saying—try to understand."

The boy didn't have much choice. Del owned him now. But as Rimon drove the wagon, talking softly to Del, the two Gens in the back also talked. By the time they made camp that night, Billy was not shrinking from the Simes, and his nager flared only if one of them made a sudden move.

It wasn't until the following day that Billy spoke to either Rimon or Del voluntarily, and he continued to stick close to Kadi. Finally, though, he began to relax and forget his fears for longer and longer periods.

As Billy relaxed, so did Del. By the time they arrived at the land Rimon planned to claim, he had come to accept Billy at his side, as Kadi stayed at Rimon's. When they unhitched the wagon, however, Del tended to Lightning and then left Kadi and Billy to tend to the draft horses.

As he came up beside Rimon, and began to help unload, he said, "Shuven! I'd forgotten all about my need!" He ran his fingers up and down his forearms to ease the sudden cramping there, the sick flutter in the pit of his stomach communicating forcefully to Rimon.

"Easy," muttered Rimon, breathing deeply, mustering his will as if to combat his own need.

After a moment, Del began heaving sacks with Rimon, saying, "What you said—it's true, Rimon. When Billy's around, I feel—pre-turnover. The first couple of days, when he was jumping at everything, it went through me like a shock, but now . . ."

"I know. He's learning. We're all learning, Del. It's going to take lots of time—but we're really onto something."

"I can see that—now. I had my doubts, but—Rimon, now I'm getting attached to the kid. What if—?"

· "No 'what ifs,' " Rimon said firmly, trying to will confidence into his friend. "You've never had all my crazy problems. It should be a lot easier for you, as long as Billy's not afraid."

"Yeah . . ." Del said uncertainly. Then, "Hey! What are you doing?"

"Huh?"

"Did you learn that from Kadi? Your field, Rimon—it's as if you're trying to calm me down the way she does. You don't have her—what can you call it? texture? Shen, there aren't any words for these things."

Rimon became aware of what he was doing. Yes, it was a poor imitation of Kadi's technique. He laughed. "It's incredible, Del—what we can learn from Gens!"

"Wherever you learned it, it sure is better than those mad fluctuations you used to have."

"Yeah. Well, I haven't hit turnover yet, but I'll bet that won't happen anymore."

It didn't. In fact, Rimon was hardly aware of his turnover; he simply found himself on the decline into need a few days later, when Kadi took Billy off for one last briefing before he and Del made their attempt at transfer. *Should have noticed,* Rimon thought. *My sex drive disappeared.* But he and Kadi had had no privacy since Del and Billy had joined them, so he'd only been relieved of an unfulfillable desire and had scarcely missed it. *By next month,* Rimon promised himself, *we'll have a cabin built.*

They had spent their time so far clearing one field and getting their first crop in, working side by side, the Simes doing the heavy work, the Gens driving the horses, planting the seeds, and otherwise contributing their share.

Now came the moment of truth. For the past two days, the same question had come over and over from both Del and Billy. "Just what am I supposed to *do?*"

Del repeated it again to Rimon as they waited for the Gens. Although Del's nervousness was grating on his growing need, Rimon tried to retain his calm. "You do what feels right," he said. "Del, it's really more up to Billy than to you. As long as he's not scared, it'll work."

"I really like Billy," said Del. "Not just because he can make me feel good, but he's a good kid, you know? Smart

—shendi, Rimon, I never got to know a Gen as a person before. Billy and Kadi are—real to me. I don't want them hurt."

"They won't be."

"I don't know. I'm so scared, I don't know how Billy can help it."

"Fortunately, he can't feel your fear, so all you have to do is put on a good act."

"I'll be able to feel his."

"I know. I wish I could tell you more, Del—but it couldn't have been worse between Kadi and me, and it worked for us. You're conscious, and Billy knows that it can work. Kadi didn't have that knowledge. She expected to die."

"She also loves you. Billy hardly knows any of us. He's trying hard, and I've been trying hard but . . ."

"He'll trust you after today, Del. Here they come. Let's do it—and then we'll have something to celebrate!"

It would be as much a first as Rimon and Kadi's first transfer. As Del and Billy faced one another, Rimon and Kadi stood on either side of them. Rimon could feel Kadi trying to calm them, and he tried to reinforce her efforts with his own.

Del summoned a shaky smile as he held out his hands to Billy, tentacles tightly retracted. "Come on, Billy," he said, the confidence in his voice at sad variance with the trepidation in his nager. "I'm not going to hurt you. I'm asking for your help—only asking. . . ."

"I know," Billy said, a palpable lie, although a genuine hope. He lifted trembling hands, placing them on Del's forearms as the Sime held himself completely still. Rimon marveled at the boy's courage, praying that it would hold long enough to complete the transfer.

When Billy's hands were gripping him firmly, Del allowed his handling tentacles to extend . . . and finally his laterals, relief flooding him as he released the terrible tension it had taken to keep them retracted in the presence of Billy's field. That relief counteracted the momentary shock Billy felt as the hot, wet laterals licked his skin. Rimon clearly felt both of them grasp emotional control. *They're going to be able to do it!*

Time hung suspended. Then Del said, "Billy—"

The boy nodded firmly. "Do it!"

Del pulled him forward, their lips pressed firmly together, and Rimon rose into hyperconsciousness, living Del's experience as if it were his own. The flow began, Del's draw riding on a wave of Billy's anxiety—but there was no pain, none of the searing, raw burn of killdraw. But Billy's faint trepidation fed Del's natural desire for killbliss—Rimon perceived Del's demand increase the speed of his draw, seeking that unique satisfaction provided only by Gen fear.

Slow down! Rimon willed, but his field was nothing to Del now against Billy's increasing agitation. The boy began to resist—and felt pain. Fear blossomed through his nager, adding fuel to the fire of Del's killbliss. All control gone, Del drew against Billy's pain and fear, pure animal instinct driving him to the ecstatic peak of satisfaction as Rimon reached out to tear them apart—

Too late.

Only at the moment of total depletion—of death—was Rimon able to wrench Del's hands and tentacles from Billy's arms. There was only a brief shock of shen, for Del had reached repletion, and Rimon had interrupted only the natural termination.

Simultaneously, Kadi understood what had happened. Her revulsion pierced the two Simes, and Del turned on her. Even as he was reaching toward her, however, post-kill transients plunged him into hypoconsciousness, and her field ceased to affect him.

He stared at her, seeing her as Kadi. Then his eyes turned to Rimon, sharing haunted anguish. Together they focused on the slight, crumpled form on the ground. Del went to his knees next to Billy's body, making half-articulate sounds, remorse so thick around him Rimon could almost taste it.

And then Del was crying. Kadi's revulsion melted to compassion, releasing Rimon's tears as well. Del touched the pitiful body, so full of life a few moments before. "I couldn't stop!" he said. He closed his eyes, able now to shut out the sight as Rimon could not—but he couldn't shut his mind to it. "Rimon, I didn't *want* to stop. I couldn't even think about stopping!"

"I zlinned what happened," said Rimon, his voice a tight whisper. "You did it right at first, Del. That's what you've got to learn to maintain—"

Del turned on him in fury. "You think I'm going through that again? Make a friend and kill him? What do you think I am?"

"You don't want to kill," protested Rimon.

"I didn't want to kill Billy. But I want to kill, Rimon. I'm Sime—and so are you. You'd better take Kadi to the border, or you'll kill her, too. Why did I ever listen to you? You couldn't tell me what to do, because there's nothing to be done! Last month was a fluke—you were unconscious. What are you going to do—have Kadi knock you out every time? You're going to kill her, Rimon, and I'm not going to stay and watch!"

Rimon knew that guilt and sorrow prompted Del's harsh words. Nonetheless, they preyed on him as his need deepened day by day. Over and over, Del's words came back, *I want to kill. I'm Sime, and so are you.*

Was Del right? Could Rimon keep from killing Kadi, or would the killbliss take him helplessly once again? He picked up the split wood and piled it with the rest—and saw immense irony in that great stack of firewood. Who was going to use it?

The test had to come soon. In another day, Rimon's need would be beyond even the control his peculiar history had given him. Beyond Kadi's control? He was afraid to find out.

He had deliberately left Kadi at their campsite today, sewing a jumpsuit for herself out of the blue material. Her few clothes were in tatters after their adventures and hard work.

His father's concern, Rimon realized, had also affected him. Was Kadi controlling him? He'd come away from her to try to think straight . . . and discovered that he was just as confused—even more so. No, he was sure it was not a false perception. Kadi only let him be himself.

She was waiting for him, wearing her new outfit, her bright red hair tied back with a strip of the blue fabric.

He sensed she was preparing herself for him, fresh and clean and new.

Stalling for time, he laid the armload of wood he'd brought back beside the small fire Kadi had started, saying, "Why don't you make us some tea, Kadi, while I clean up?"

She agreed easily, her nager soothing him as he washed up and came to sit beside her, accepting the tea. After they had taken a few sips, though, she said, "We ought to do it now, Rimon."

"Do it?"

"Have . . . transfer. I know you can drive yourself another couple of days, but you don't have to do that anymore. You're not avoiding a kill now."

"Kadi—"

"I want it, Rimon. I can't—can't stand to see you in need like this. It—hurts. I can't explain it—it just does."

Rimon met her eyes over his trail cup, aware of the swirling interlocked fields that made up her nager. It was almost as if he could see into the very center of her being, and he was falling, falling into eternity.

"Rimon?"

"Hmmm," said Rimon, blinking his way forcibly duoconscious.

"I said I want to give you my selyn, and then—I want to make love to you. It will be . . . a consecration of our new home."

He shook his head, not in negation, but bewilderment. "I wonder if all Gens are as—strange to understand as you."

Kadi cocked her head to one side, also bewildered. "It seems quite plain to me. The place of life and love is the place of home . . . no?"

Rimon put his cup on a hearthstone and watched it steam. "Right now, love is just a word. I remember it was nice—worth dying for, even—but I can't feel it. I'm too busy—dying—myself to feel anything else. Except fear. Kadi, what if I—what if I can't? What if I hurt you?"

"You won't. I'm not going to let you."

With a forced quirk of a smile, Rimon said, "What are you going to do, take a stick of wood and knock me out?"

Kadi laughed. "No." But there was an undercurrent of anxiety beneath it, increasing Rimon's own anxiety. That faint fear in Kadi's nager, which she was trying so hard to control, reminded him only too much of Billy's nager when he'd begun transfer with Del. Rimon knew exactly what had happened there: the slight anxiety had triggered killdraw against resistance; Billy had felt pain, causing fear; and his fear had driven Del to the kill.

If only I could control my rate of draw, Rimon thought. He sighed, and got up, walking to the edge of the space they had cleared, where their house would be. *If we ever have reason to build a house.*

Looking up the rocky hillside, he could see the mound of earth over Billy's grave, still a scar on the face of their new home. In his mind's eye, he saw a second grave yawning open, and shuddered with the effort of thrusting the thought aside.

Kadi came up beside him, putting her hand on his shoulder. "Rimon—look—maybe Del failed because it only works between male and female? We don't know. We don't know what makes it work, but we do know that, for us, it does work. Isn't that where every new advance starts? First somebody finds out how to do it. Then somebody makes a fancy theory out of it. First thing you know, everybody takes it for granted. Well, we're just starting. We don't have a theory. We don't have to. We just do it."

Edging toward hyperconsciousness, Rimon zlinned her. Her control of her emotional nager was close to perfect again. Still, that small nagging fear was there beneath her desire.

Desire?

She was reflecting his need somehow, absorbing it, amplifying it, and playing it back to him in a new form of intense but painless desire. Her hands closed gently around his wrists, barely touching, sending waves of pleasure through his nerves. Slowly she slid her hands up his arms as he stood helplessly, knowing himself in her control and not caring. He didn't care about anything except what Kadi was doing to him.

Her anxiety lessened as she settled her hands over his transport nerves. She was in command. Confidence rose in him . . . Kadi's confidence. His tentacles lashed about her arms of their own accord, his laterals drinking in the

pure joy of her field. It was Kadi who made the lip contact, Kadi who began to pour selyn into Rimon. In pleasant
surprise, he accepted . . . but it was tantalizingly slow.
Against his will, need and pure instinct drove him to draw
that selyn faster and faster to feed his depleted nerves.

Kadi started in surprise, on the edge of fear as Rimon's
draw increased. Reflexively, she resisted and felt pain, just
as Billy had. *No!* Rimon reached into himself and shut
off the voracious demand, his whole body screaming against
his will. And suddenly, Kadi relaxed, all resistance gone
as once more she began to push selyn at him, a little faster
this time.

And then there was no more pain, only soaring bliss for
both of them, the same intense joy they had shared a
month ago . . . no—this time it was better! Conscious,
Rimon could feel every sweet thrum of pleasure, the stark
terrors of need melting away to be replaced by—desire.

Even before the last trickle of selyn ceased, Rimon found
his mouth softening upon Kadi's to a demanding kiss. Her
lips yielded, and as the flow terminated with their fields in
perfect harmony, a desire almost as strong as need sang
through both of them, resonating and overpowering.

Rimon reached for the ties that held Kadi's jumpsuit at
her shoulders. When those and her belt were untied, the
garment slithered to the ground. He didn't want to stop
touching her long enough to shrug out of his own clothes,
but Kadi was helping him, and then they were in each
other's arms.

They made love eagerly, hungrily, driven by a mutual
yearning, Rimon delirious from the sheer tactile sensations
that faded so during need, and Kadi awakened after long
abstinence. It was better than the first time—an improvement on perfection, Rimon thought, as he became enough
aware to think again. His head was pillowed on Kadi's
breast. Too languidly content to sit up, he slid into a position beside her from which he could look at her face. It
felt so good just to look.

She turned to him, smiling. "I told you we could do it
again."

Smiling crookedly, he said, "Are you always going to say,
'I told you so'?"

"Only when it suits the occasion. You're glowing again."

"I didn't know I could feel better than the first time. But I do."

"Me, too. Maybe it'll just keep getting better."

"If it does, next time it'll blow out my whole system"—or yours. "Kadi—I hurt you. I know I did."

"Only for a moment. You just startled me, and—I think I resisted you, and it hurt. It makes sense that that's a Gen reflex, doesn't it—to try to prevent a Sime from draining away all his selyn?"

"Yes," he said. "Now that I've been fully conscious through a transfer, I know that's it. You can overcome that reflex, Kadi—but how are we going to teach other Gens to do it?"

"It wasn't just me! Rimon, you did something, and it stopped hurting long enough so I remembered how desperate you felt, and then suddenly I could feel it myself—a—need to give. . . ."

That sounded like a child's bad grammar—need to give indeed! But he remembered, "I think I did slow my draw for just a moment. I couldn't hold it though."

She put a hand on the middle of his chest, and he felt a little tingling tremor there. Suddenly there were pale ghosts of nager around things, and he was duoconscious, tingling pleasantly all over as she said, "Maybe next time you'll be able to hold it a little longer. We'll have to teach the Simes to go slower and the Gens not to resist."

"But *how*—!"

"I think we should wait a while," said Kadi. "If we build our house and get all our land cleared, and just live together, people are going to notice. Then, maybe if we show them how we do it—"

"Oh, no!" he groaned, nuzzling her hair and luxuriating in the feel of it. "Somehow I can't see us doing this in public. I'm certainly in no mood to give a lecture!"

Kadi had become intensely desirable again. The sun glinted on her bright hair, her blue eyes danced an invitation, she smelled deliciously sweet, and as he began to caress her once more, the very feel of her sent sparks of joy charging down his spine, wiping away the invisible scars of a lifetime.

He was aware that he'd lost duoconsciousness again, but his other senses were enough to take him to the limits of ecstasy. The future would have to take care of itself. At this moment, he had Kadi, and that was enough for any man.

Gradually Rimon became aware that the thundering in his ears wasn't just his racing pulse. "Horses! Kadi, wake up!"

It was close to sundown. They scrambled to their feet, stepping hastily into their garments as they turned to face a group of five riders approaching from the east. Rimon was relieved to make out five Simes. It wasn't a Gen raiding party.

The three men and two women reined in too close to where Rimon and Kadi stood, and then, without even reading the fields, Rimon knew they were being hazed.

The shortest of the three men asked, "Mind saying what you're doing here?"

"Does this land belong to you?" asked Rimon, feeling naked in such an exchange for the first time in his life. *How can you tell what they mean if you can't zlin? No wonder Gens are so scared all the time.*

"Don't belong to nobody," said one of the women. "What we asked is what you're doing here."

"Building a house."

The five of them burst out laughing. It was an ugly sound, but Rimon hadn't judged laughter by sound in so long, he had no idea what they meant. He put a protective arm about Kadi's waist, willing her not to be frightened.

"They're building a house, Risko, did you hear that? Farming, now I can understand that if you've a passel of Gens to feed till you can get 'em to market. But—"

"Quiet, Flieg." One of the women edged out the man's horse and confronted Rimon. "You get a good crop to sell, you come into town and see me. I run the holding Pen in these parts, do a little breedin' on the side. You got any Gens, you sell 'em to me. You got any grain, you sell to me to slop my Gens. I give a fair price. But I don't want no competition. Understood?"

She gave Kadi a penetrating look. "What happened to that one?"

"Nothing," said Rimon, grabbing innocence around him like a cloak. He wasn't sure who or what he was dealing with, but he knew that they had no chance against these Simes. This far from any real civilization, there was no law but the whip, and each of these under-fed but strong Simes was well armed. He even saw a dagger at the waist of one of the women, and shuddered. No self-respecting Sime would carry one of those.

"Well," said the lead woman, "if she doesn't recover, come see me. If I'm in a good mood, I may extend you credit. If not—well, I can always use workers."

The Simes whirled their horses and rode on into the west. Kadi turned into Rimon's arms, shaking but not crying. Somehow that made Rimon wonder all the more urgently if they'd chosen their neighbors wisely.

"Rimon. Wake up, Rimon," Kadi said, poking him.

Rimon stirred and pulled her into his arms. She pushed away, saying, "Wake up! Someone's coming. Can't you hear it?"

"Yeah," he said, immediately alert as he recognized the sound of hoofbeats, but even as he was reaching for his clothes, the rider came around the bend, and they saw that it was Del Erick. Rimon sank back under the blanket with Kadi.

Del pulled Lightning to a halt, jumped down, strode to the edge of their makeshift bed, and stared down at them. "You did it again," he said flatly.

"Yes—of course . . . but Del—" Rimon broke off in mid-sentence, propping himself up on one elbow to peer at his friend. Del had said he could never come back. Yet here he was.

Del followed the thought. "I—ah—I got to thinking about you and Kadi out here alone like this. What if— what if you'd—Kadi—I mean it wasn't like with Billy. You've loved Kadi all your life!"

Rimon put an arm around Kadi. "And I'll love her all the rest of my life, Del." There was an awkward silence until Rimon said, "Anyway, welcome back."

"Look, I—ah—I'm sorry I left like that. What happened wasn't your fault. I'd have come back sooner, only I found a town down the road, with a saloon . . . and I got drunk on porstan. I don't remember much about the last three days, until I woke up this morning."

"You really thought we couldn't do it again?" asked Rimon.

"I'm glad I was wrong!" Del said. "And now you can throw me off your land if you want to!"

Kadi said, "Of course we're not going to throw you out, Del. We're glad you came back. Look, want some breakfast? We're starved—I am, anyway."

"And," said Rimon, "when Kadi's hungry, everybody's hungry!"

"Oh, I couldn't eat—" Del started, then reconsidered, looking at Kadi. "On second thought—" They laughed together, and then Del said thoughtfully, "I haven't eaten since—since before—" He broke off, and nobody wanted to finish the sentence as his eye strayed toward Billy's grave.

Kadi said, "Rimon, where's my jumpsuit? You're letting all the cold under the blankets!"

As she dressed, Del frowned at Rimon, zlinning him closely. "What's wrong, Rimon?"

"Huh? Nothing's wrong. Things have never been righter!"

"Your fields—there's something—Rimon, you're still hypo!"

Rimon shrugged. "I can't zlin right now, but it comes back in a day or so."

"I never heard of such a thing!"

"Neither did I," said Rimon. "Del, we're the first, Kadi and I. And you—"

"No! Oh no, Rimon, I'm never going through that again!"

"But . . . you came back."

"To help you if you were in trouble. Since you're not, I can at least give you the rest of the money I owe you."

"Money? Where did you get—?"

"I don't remember it all too clearly, but sometime in the last couple of days there was a race. I rode Lightning, and I won. I must have—I ended up with more money this morning than I had before I arrived in town!"

"I didn't know anyone could get that drunk on porstan!"

"Oh, I remember someone playing shiltpron, too . . . I

think. Anyhow, I managed to blot out some time. There are parts I wish I could remember, though. At some point, I saw some wild horses in the hills, and that gave me an idea. I think I can capture some mares and start a herd."

"You're not going home?" asked Rimon.

"No—your dad knew I always planned on getting my own place."

"Won't you stay with us, Del?" asked Kadi. "At least for a while?"

His warm brown eyes looked into hers. "I can't, Kadi. I can't live like you and Rimon, so I can't live with you. But there's more land around here, good land for breeding horses. I'm going to claim some of it and in a few years I'll have the best herd in the Territory!"

"We can at least be neighbors, then," she said.

"Friends," asserted Del with a smile.

They shared breakfast and made plans.

A few days later, Rimon and Kadi went with Del to help capture some of the horses he'd found; then Del helped them plant Kadi's kitchen garden. The soil was rich, a pleasure to work with. Why had no Simes settled here, even if it was near the border? Certainly such fertile land was worth the effort of defending it.

Perhaps, though, it was simply that no Simes interested in settling down had come this far before. The riders who had stopped to laugh at Rimon and Kadi had scoffed at the idea of farming—and Del had described the nearby town as hardly more than a few huts thrown up as saloons and gambling places to milk the money from the Simes who hunted Gens across the border.

They saw the town for themselves a few days later, when they went with Del to pick out the land he wished to claim. Kadi shuddered as they passed the Pens on the outskirts, where dispirited Gens watched them pass, not even curiosity showing in their eyes. The town was a shabby place indeed, a block-long street of mud bordered with ramshackle buildings. There was a general store, stocked only with goods one might require on the trail, all grossly overpriced. Loud voices and music coming from some of the other buildings told where they might encounter trouble.

In the store, the two men flanked Kadi as she chose a

few supplies. Noticing the outrageous price of trin tea—
not even a good brand—Rimon hoped that the annual
variety Kadi had just planted would produce well enough
to see them through the coming winter.

The proprietor zlinned Kadi as she looked about. Finally
Kadi turned and looked the scrawny, unkempt Sime woman
up and down, then glanced at Rimon and Del on either
side of her, both strong and sleek, with glowing skin and
hair, the product of Farris' regimen. Rimon caught Kadi's
warm, protective pride—but so did the Sime woman. "Take
that Gen bitch outside," she said. "You got no right bringin'
it in here."

Rimon bristled. "I can take her anywhere. She's my—"

"She's his property," interrupted Del, "and he can do
what he wants with her. You know the law."

"Law!" She laughed. "No law out here but what we
make for ourselves. I know what you are—couple of fine,
high-minded lawbreakers yourselves, takin' little sister to
the border! Got no tags for her, do you, boys?"

"As a matter of fact," said Rimon, "I have." He pulled
Kadi's tags and papers from his pocket. "Not that it's any
of your business, but in case you were thinking of sending
the sheriff chasing after us, don't bother."

"Sheriff? Got no sheriff here, an' don't want none. You
goody-goodies better keep on goin', 'fore someone takes
that pampered Gen away from you."

Rimon wanted to lash out, but Kadi's discomfort faded
as she looked at him . . . and suddenly the whole scene was
vastly amusing. His anger evaporated. "No one would want
this Gen," he said. "She doesn't know how to be scared."

The Sime woman broke into helpless laughter. "Oh,
that's a good one!" she gasped. "A Gen that doesn't know
how to be scared!" Rimon felt Kadi's amusement go from
forced to real—and realized she was using her own emotions to affect the Simes. The atmosphere in the store remained one of high good humor as Rimon paid for their
purchases, the Sime woman wiping tears of laughter from
her cheeks as she took his money, still muttering, "Oh,
that's a good one!"

They left, got on their horses, and rode to the edge of
town before Rimon reached over and took Kadi's hand. He

was laughing now from his own genuine relief. "Kadidid, that was beautiful!"

"I can't believe it," said Del. "I saw it, and I can't believe it! Kadi, you're safe from Sime attack. You can make an attacker laugh himself to death!"

"It's more than that, Del," said Rimon. "Kadi protected *us!* We could have ended up in one shendi-fleckin' fight back there if she hadn't turned the whole thing into a joke. But Kadi," he continued, "be careful. That woman was pre-turnover. I'm not sure what would have happened if she'd been in need."

"Or if she'd reacted like your father," said Kadi. "Don't worry, Rimon. I'm not going to take any foolish risks."

As they left town, they splashed through a small creek, following a well-worn trail across the ford, and came to another small settlement. "What's this?" asked Kadi. "Del, you didn't say there were two towns."

"I wasn't over here," he said. "I remember now, though—somebody said some out-Territory Simes had settled here."

There were a number of homes clustered together behind a stockade. Although the gate was open, the place did not appear inviting to strangers. Rimon and Kadi peered in as they rode past, seeing neat houses with gardens, and children playing in the central green. Around the community lay carefully tended fields, a few Simes working in them.

Feeling a wistful envy in Kadi, Rimon said, "If they're from out-Territory, they grew up with Gens, expecting to be Gens. It makes sense that they'd want to learn not to kill Gens."

"You'd better wait until you know how you do it, Rimon," said Del.

"I think—Well, I guess we don't have the answer for sure, yet," Rimon admitted. "But I am going to find out exactly how Kadi and I do it!"

They did it again at the end of the month, easily this time, with the same deliciously inevitable transition from transfer to lovemaking. This time they did it indoors, in their own house, in their own bed—the one piece of furniture Rimon had gotten built so far. Resting contentedly, aglow with the joy of their double celebration of life, Rimon looked around at the home they'd built, with Del's help. It was a small cabin, just one room, but well made and weatherproof. A barrel Del had brought from town served as table and lamp-stand. Since there was as yet no storage space, most of their belongings were stored in the root cellar, as Kadi preferred to speak of the hole in the side of the hill. They had built their cabin flush against the hill, using the hill as one wall of the cabin.

Del and Rimon had dug the root cellar as a hiding place for Kadi. The packed dirt walls were insulation enough of her selyn field, and they had spent several days working with the doors, shooing her in and out, zlinning, adding insulation until she could hide there if necessary, safe from detection. Then they camouflaged the doors; once they were pulled shut from inside, they appeared to be a part of the natural hillside.

Some hours after their transfer, Kadi finally fell asleep, and Rimon soon joined her. When he couldn't zlin for a day or two after their transfers, he seemed to sleep undisturbed by the world of shifting selyn fields he was accustomed to, unaffected by the physical stimuli that were of secondary importance to a Sime.

"Rimon! Rimon, wake up! Someone's coming!"

He was awake instantly—nothing wrong with that Sime faculty—to find Kadi dressed. Pulling on his clothes, he found he could still not zlin, but he could hear Wolf's barking in the distance turning from curious to challenging to angry, charged with growls and snarls as he came back toward the cabin. His retreat was accompanied by the sound of a large number of horses, riding hard from the border.

Kadi edged up to the side of the window and peeked out the crack between the curtains. Ten or twelve Wild Gens galloped into view, Wolf trying unsuccessfully to drive them off. Kadi asked, "What do we do?"

"Stay low. They can't zlin us. Pretend there's no one home," Rimon whispered.

The Gens were all carrying guns. Rimon watched anxiously as they looked around, shouting to one another. The only word he could make out was "Sime."

Then, suddenly, all the guns were pointed at the cabin. Rimon thrust Kadi to the floor, falling on her as bullets raked through their house, making the curtains wave as if blown by a brisk wind. All went over their heads. Wolf's growling became a roar—punctuated by a sharp yelp, a howl of pain . . . and silence.

"Wolf!" cried Kadi. "They've shot him!"

"There's nothing we can do," Rimon said grimly, holding her down. "They'll shoot us if they figure out where we are!"

The rain of bullets continued for a few moments more, then stuttered to a halt. There was more shouting, followed by footsteps cautiously approaching the door. It was barred, and in the noise of the Gens shaking it, Rimon and Kadi scuttled into the root cellar and pulled the door shut behind them. They had insulated the door so well that they could barely hear what was going on outside—except the slam of their front door being battered down.

"The worst they can do is steal what's out there," Rimon murmured.

"Almost everything is in here," Kadi replied in the dark.

"Everything that matters," said Rimon, holding her close. His breathing became irregular as they waited. The palms of his hands were damp on Kadi's arms, and he found himself trembling. *I've forgotten what it's like to be in the dark and scared.*

Presently, when it grew quiet, she said, "I think they've gone."

"No, we'd have heard or felt the hoofbeats."

"What's that?" asked Kadi, alarmed at a muffled roar outside.

Rimon pushed the door open a crack, and then slammed it shut again as smoke and a blast of scorching heat poured through.

Kadi cried, "They're burning our house!" Smoke poured through their small ventilation slits. "Rimon, will the door burn through?"

"No—it's mostly mortared rock, remember?"

Kadi began to cough. Rimon pulled off his shirt and put it over their faces. "Get down on the floor," he said. "The smoke will rise."

But he, too, was seized by a fit of coughing and choking as they fell to the floor, clinging to one another, eyes smarting, each breath a fresh torture to their throats and lungs.

Kadi clung to Rimon, but he could do nothing but hold her. *Is this why I brought her here, learned not to kill her, just to have her die of suffocation?* He felt her go limp, unconscious. *So much for the grand scheme to make friends with the Wild Gens. So much for all my grandiose schemes to change the world—when I can't even protect the woman I love.*

Chapter 7

FORT FREEDOM

Rimon became aware of pain, every breath hurting his nasal passages, his throat, and his chest. A nauseating smell permeated the air. He opened his eyes to blackness, tried again to zlin, and couldn't.

He sat up, shoving away something that clung to his face—the cloth of his shirt. There was a trickle of fresh air. *Kadi!* She lay heavily over his legs.

Memory returned with a jolt. "Kadi!" he said, his voice hoarse. She was limp, unresponsive. He threw the doors of their hiding place open, not caring if the Wild Gens were waiting outside. Nothing was there but sunshine, and the sour smell of burned wood.

Kadi moaned, drew a deep choking breath, and began to cough helplessly. Kneeling amidst the ruins of their house, he supported her until her coughing stopped, and she opened her streaming eyes to look around.

The dirt floor was still warm from the fire and scattered with the charred remains of walls and roof. A fine powdering of ash rose to choke them. The heavy foundation timbers were still smoldering as Rimon lifted Kadi across them and set her on her feet again. They walked to the little brook that supplied their water, drank, and washed. Then, in silence, they surveyed the ruin of their home.

The shadow of the stone chimney pointed across the newly sprouted field at the wide trail the Gen riders had churned through the wheat. To one side of the yard lay a mound of brown fur—Wolf.

Still saying nothing, Kadi walked over and knelt beside the pitiful body. Wolf had been her constant companion for the last three years, since she had raised him from an abandoned puppy. Rimon stood helplessly, watching Kadi's tears fall brightly onto the dusty fur.

Blinking back his own tears, he turned his eyes away from Kadi, lifted them to escape the sight of the burnt-out cabin, and saw Billy's grave. *Billy trusted me. Del trusted me. And Kadi—And what did they all get for it?*

Just then Kadi rose and put her arms around him, clinging to him for support. "What are we going to do, Rimon? You could have zlinned those Gens before Wolf heard them. We could have gotten away, at least."

"I'm sorry," he choked out, helpless to comfort her.

But it wasn't comfort she sought. "You've got to learn how to do it, Rimon!" she said angrily. "We can't be blind and deaf for three days out of every month." She shook him, demanding hysterically, "You've got to learn to zlin right after transfer. You've *got* to!"

In dizzying force, Kadi's frustration penetrated him, overpowering despite her depleted field. "I'm trying! I'm trying!"

And—suddenly—he could.

"Kadi!" he gasped in pain at the heat of her emotion. Weakly, he tried to thrust her away, to shield himself. "Kadi, I can zlin. Oh, stop it, Kadi—you're hurting me!"

Surprised, she gasped, "I'm sorry!" And then, all at once her nager ached with shame. "It wasn't your fault—"

"Never mind—Kadidid, you did it. It worked. I can zlin." For a moment, he shut his eyes, zlinning the small grave on the hillside. "This was all my fault. They warned us about Wild Gens raiding through here! I should have . . ."

"No, Rimon, no," said Kadi, catching her breath. "They warned *us*, Rimon, not just you. Us. I could have insisted on moving. But I didn't. It's just as much my fault as it is yours."

Dizzily, Rimon realized he had again slipped into thinking of Kadi as a Gen, and therefore helpless, dependent. "I'm sorry. . . ."

She glanced around at the field, the ruins. "Sorry isn't going to help. We'll build somewhere else. Come on, let's see what we can salvage."

Following her toward the house, Rimon saw her cough raggedly, stopping to gasp for breath. Then she doubled over, coughing. He caught her and eased her to the ground, groping his way into duoconsciousness. He zlinned fluid collecting in her lungs, the bronchial tree swollen, the more irritated now for her exertions.

As she continued to gasp for breath, Rimon zlinned the accumulating fluids and began to fear for her life. *What would I do without Kadi?* Shoving panic aside, he spread his tentacles over her back, extending the laterals to zlin deep detail.

His concentration was barely interrupted by the dim shock of discovering that he was actually zlinning her body's cells. He could make out the sickened ones, selyn-dulled. But as his attention focused on them, the dulled cells began to throb weakly with selyn production again. It was as if his use of selyn caused her to produce selyn.

Perhaps, if he could fool her cells into thinking he was in need, he could induce the dulled cells to produce selyn again—to rejuvenate.

Suddenly, as she gasped again under his hands, he wished with all his heart for need, even attrition. With a shock, he found himself hyperconscious, unable to see or feel, though he felt no real need. The memory of hunting mode, that's all it was. But under his touch, her cells began to surge with life, healing themselves, clearing the swelling and congestion miraculously.

Before long, she was laughing with him as they bent to the chore of cleaning away the ruins.

They were burying Wolf up on the hillside, next to Billy, when Del rode up that afternoon. The Gen Raiders, he reported, had struck the out-Territory Simes working in the fields around their small community. Although there was not usually much amity between the two communities of Simes, the common enemy, Wild Gens, had drawn Simes from both sides of the creek to ward off the attack.

"I got in on the tail end of it," said Del. "The Raiders shot down three farmers and headed back across the border when other Simes started to the rescue. It was only when someone said they'd come from this direction that I realized you two might be in trouble."

"We were," said Rimon. "Fortunately, we had that hiding place."

Del looked down at the ashen ruin. "Well, you can't stay here anymore. This is the way the Gens always come through."

"That's why those Simes laughed at us for settling here," said Kadi.

"There's plenty of land over by my place," said Del. "I'll help you pack."

"The land around yours is no good for farming," said Rimon.

"Then why farm? Come in with me and raise horses."

It was tempting, but Rimon shook his head stubbornly. "Food prices in town are outrageous and—Del, we, of all people, have got to be self-sufficient. We've also got to be able to support other people who join us. You know how important it is for Gens to eat well. . . ."

"And Simes have to eat, too," said Kadi, "or have you forgotten? You look as if you haven't eaten since you left us."

Del's face twisted momentarily. "I haven't," he admitted. "My last kill was . . . . pretty horrible. I kept seeing Billy."

His nager rang with such pain that Rimon couldn't breathe, but Kadi said firmly, "I'm hoping you'll learn to live without killing, the way Rimon does, if only for your own peace of mind."

Del turned away from the grave on the hillside. "I don't think anyone else has a chance. Rimon found you first."

She felt it then, but all she said was, "Come, Del, and have tea with us."

Rimon and Kadi went back to camping until they could rebuild on a spot away from the Raiders' trail. Meanwhile, they cleared more ground, and salvaged what they could of the trampled field. In return for Del's help, they spent several days helping him build his cabin. He had already broken several of the wild horses and sold them in town; as he had money, he often bought things Rimon could not afford—presents for Kadi, he would insist.

One such present was a supply of jars for canning the products of Kadi's garden. "It's not a gift," he insisted. "I expect homemade jam to come back in some of those jars, and I intend to exact payment of a part of your tea harvest. The stuff they sell in town is wretched!"

One day Del arrived for an unexpected visit, bringing with him a young Sime woman and two small children, in a wagon that Rimon didn't recognize. The woman was Carlana Lodge, one of the out-Territory Simes from the neat little community that Kadi always admired. She spoke Simelan with a heavy Gen accent, and was the first Sime other than Rimon and Del to be willing to speak with Kadi.

Kadi at once took a liking to the Sime woman. She was a breathtaking natural beauty, with pale skin, huge blue eyes ringed with thick dark lashes, and straight dark hair worn center-parted and pulled back into a coil at the nape of her neck. She wore a dress with a high bodice and skirts to the ground, even in the heat of summer. The sleeves of her dress looked as if they'd been designed to come down to the wrist, but then cut off and hemmed at the elbow instead, to avoid pressure on her tentacle sheaths. Apparently Carlana had carried an extreme form of Gen modesty with her across the border.

When they showed her around the garden, Carlana said, "Your tea plants are doing much better than mine. I never heard of trin tea before I . . . came here, but it is such a necessity. I don't think anyone in Fort Freedom grows it as well as you do."

"Fort Freedom?" said Kadi, struggling with the odd accent.

Carlana translated, apparently unaware of the irony in the name—for the out-Territory Simes had walled themselves in against whatever freedom Sime Territory had to offer.

Rimon and Del stood back, watching the women talk, and for the first time Rimon realized Kadi must be missing the company of another woman. They were soon chatting amiably, and he ignored them until there was a small nageric shock from the end of the garden. He looked over to see that Kadi had put her arm around Carlana. He heard her say gently, "I don't think nature intended us to kill one another." She took her arm away.

"Del—Mr. Erick—told me something about you, but I didn't expect . . ." Carlana spread hands and tentacles. "I'm sorry."

"I'm getting used to the fact that I'll never have them," Kadi reassured her.

But Carlana rushed on, not hearing her. "They're so repulsive. You shouldn't have to look at them."

". . . what?"

"They seem to have a life of their own," the Sime woman apologized. "Of course, we all use them for working—we can get so much more done—but that makes it hard to remember to keep them decently sheathed in company."

"Carlana . . . are you saying you actually try to hide your tentacles? But they're beautiful!"

Carlana took Kadi's hands, holding her arms up. "No, Kadi, you are beautiful. Normal. Not a mutant monster like me."

Rimon glanced at Del. "Carlana comes from Gen Territory," Del said. "She has a lot of strange beliefs . . . but I guess I can sympathize with some of them now."

"Do you know," Kadi told Rimon after their visitors had gone, "Carlana was surprised that I call myself a Gen? She thought it was purely a derogatory term for the Pen-raised Gens that are hardly more than animals."

"What do the Wild Gens call themselves?"

"People."

Rimon stared at Kadi, then chuckled. "Of course!"

"And most of the Simes at Fort Freedom were members of something called the Church of the Purity in Gen Territory."

"What's that?" asked Rimon.

"It's an . . . organization to worship God. I think. I didn't really understand it all," Kadi admitted. "They seem to believe that if a child changes over, it's a punishment from God for the parents' wrongs. They think Simes are inhuman monsters visited on the Earth because of witches and sorcerers who once tried to control the forces of nature, instead of obeying God's Law. Really, Rimon— she told me this in all seriousness!" Rimon stared. She added, "Did Del tell you about Abel Veritt?"

"No—Del was too busy telling me how wonderful Carlana is. He likes her kids, too. I think we're going to see him settling down pretty soon."

"That fast?" asked Kadi. "Carlana only lost her husband

last winter—and the way of life she's found at Fort Freedom means a lot to her. I'm not sure they can adapt to one another's customs. And from the way Carlana talks about Abel Veritt—their spiritual leader—I don't think Del will be welcome in Fort Freedom if he questions anything that man teaches!"

Wistfully, Rimon said, "You want to be welcome there, too, don't you, Kadi?"

"Well—yes. And I'd like to have Carlana and her children for friends. She wants us to come talk to Mr. Veritt—that's what they call each other, Mister this-or-that, some kind of—Genlan?—honorific, I think."

"They call their language—English. I always intended to study it, but never got around to it. I was sick so often during my First Year after changeover when it would have been so easy to learn. . . ."

"I think you should tell Carlana all about Zeth if you get a chance. Rimon, she killed her mother in First Need."

"Her *mother!*"

"I think we should go talk to this Abel Veritt. These people could use our help as much as we could use theirs. They're all from out-Territory, and most of them have never had any contact with—civilization. Can you imagine what they go through—believing they've become demons? At least Veritt has given them some self-respect, but they've got a long way to go."

"Even the ones who don't think they've become demons have a hard time," Rimon said. "Remember Charlie Horvan? Even after my father hired him, he was still depressed all the time, couldn't learn Simelan very well, poisoned himself a couple of times, and finally hanged himself."

"I remember," Kadi said. "Mama and I had to take care of him when he made himself sick. Your dad came in one day and bawled him out for being such a fool . . . but I don't think he knew those things he ate were poison, Rimon. We couldn't feed Gens a lot of Sime foods. Surely there are things that Gens can eat that would poison us. You," she amended, with a chuckle. "I'll ask Carlana. There's no reason to restrict our larder to food suitable for both of us."

Kadi got her chance to ask a few days later, when she

and Rimon were invited into Fort Freedom to meet Abel Veritt. The leader of the community was an imposing man who reminded Rimon of his father—not in appearance, but in air of command.

Veritt was actually shorter than Rimon, but stockier than most Simes, with broad shoulders. There was no malnutrition evident among the Simes in Fort Freedom. Apparently they kept up the Gen habit of regular meals.

It was difficult to judge Veritt's age, although his hair was so silver that one couldn't guess the color it had once been. His face was suntanned and weather-beaten, his eyes squinting out from a mass of lines.

Rimon noticed that Veritt did not zlin them—not even Kadi, who usually drew curious attention. Instead, he invited them into his parlor, offered them tea, and introduced them to his wife and son. Mrs. Veritt said little. She served tea and then disappeared into the kitchen. Only after she'd gone did the conversation turn to the reason Rimon and Kadi were there.

Rimon did most of the talking at first, explaining what he and Kadi had discovered so far. As he answered Veritt's questions, Rimon noticed Jord Veritt, Abel's son, watching in sullen silence. He showed the same effects of good diet and hard outdoor work as his father, and the few times he spoke up—objecting, probing—it was in faintly accented but fluent Simelan—of course, thought Rimon, he'd been born on this side of the border.

Rimon had a sudden insight into Jord's status. Kadi had mentioned that one of Veritt's teachings was that if Simes lived "good lives," their children would be Gen. Jord must be regarded as a symbol of his father's failings. And, at the moment, Jord was in need. Small wonder he was so belligerent.

Veritt heard Rimon out. Then he sat back, elbows on the arms of his chair, fingers steepled before him. It was a familiar posture, except that Veritt kept his tentacles sheathed.

Recalling Carlana's apology for displaying her tentacles, Rimon carefully kept his own sheathed. Veritt noted that and nodded approval. Then he asked, "May I have permission to zlin you and your wife, Mr. Farris?"

"Yes, of course," said Rimon. "I was wondering why you hadn't done so already."

"We believe in privacy . . . and modesty. Although we bear the curse of the Sime nature, it is our goal to turn the Devil's gifts to God's purposes. It would be presumptuous of me to examine your soul without your permission."

"My . . . soul?" asked Rimon.

"It is the human soul that is reflected in one's nager," said Veritt reasonably. Then he addressed Kadi for the first time, "Mrs. Farris, you are not like the soulless creatures provided here for our need. So—it disturbs me that you choose to ally yourself with a Sime—and yet you have taught him not to kill. I cannot easily judge what you are."

"Zlin me," Kadi invited calmly.

Holding his hands toward Kadi, Veritt said, "Will you forgive me if . . . ?"

"Mr. Veritt," said Kadi, carefully using his form of address, "I am neither frightened nor offended by the sight—or touch—of tentacles."

"I'm not in need," he reassured her.

"I can see that," she replied evenly.

Considering the way Carlana had delivered the invitation for this specific day, Rimon had known Veritt had timed the interview so that his judgment would be completely unclouded. Kadi had caught that nuance, too. She said, "You killed two or three days ago. It's your son who is in need."

"A witch!" Jord gasped. "Father, these are evil spirits come to tempt us!"

"Silence!" demanded Veritt. "If you can't control yourself, leave us!"

The younger man sat back in his chair, sullen again.

Knowing how one Sime's need could affect another, Kadi rose and placed herself between Jord and his father. As the older Sime held his hands toward Kadi, cautiously extending his laterals, Rimon watched Jord tense. But Kadi only stood quietly, projecting tranquillity.

When Veritt's eyes refocused, he said, "I've never felt a nager like yours. I can't judge, for I have no basis for comparison."

"I'm no witch. Surely you can tell that."

"I sense no lie in that—but—" He looked from Kadi to Rimon, reserving judgment. "What do you ask of me?"

"Friendship," Rimon answered. "Kadi and I have started a homestead."

"Yes, Mrs. Lodge told me. She's very much impressed with you."

"I like Carlana," said Kadi. "But she seems afraid to be my friend without your permission."

"I am spiritual advisor to this community," explained Veritt. "I won't forbid anyone's friendship with you."

"Father—!" Jord protested.

Veritt fixed him with a cold stare. "I have not that right. However, for the time being, I must forbid my people to experiment with your attempts to avoid killing Gens. I have two reasons for this. The first is practical: you have not proven that you can teach your method to others. Your friend Mr. Erick is in great distress, Mrs. Lodge tells me, because he killed someone who had become his friend."

"True," answered Rimon. "So we're not trying to teach anyone else until we're sure we can do it. You have my word."

"My other reservation is more serious, because I can see no way of proving what you are. There are legends of Simes and Gens living together among the gypsies, practicing sorcery. I have never seen this. We drove the gypsies away from our town when I was a child, but there were no Simes among them. On this side of the border I've seen Sime gypsies, never Gens. Yet it's known they indulge in secret practices—and if they do, so may others.

"You don't seem like a sorcerer, Mr. Farris—but the Devil works most effectively through those who seem innocent. God revealed to me many years ago, when I recognized the soulless state of the Gens grown here, that Simes have souls. I amended my life from that day, and have, with God's help, brought hope to the people of Fort Freedom.

"Now you bring a new hope—that it may not be necessary for Simes to kill at all. Is this a new revelation from God? Or is it a false temptation to lead us into the practice of witchcraft? Because I don't know, I'll not forbid your welcome in Fort Freedom. Yet I can't ask you to join our community."

Rimon smiled. "I think you'll soon see we're not sorcerers."

"I shall pray and meditate that God may let me see this matter clearly. Meanwhile, go join your friends."

Del and Carlana were waiting for them at Carlana's home. The Sime woman was delighted with Veritt's decision. As it was very warm, they joined the children in the neatly fenced yard. At one end was a patch of strawberries, a few late berries still ripening. "Why do you let these grow?" asked Kadi. "They're poisonous."

"Not to the children," Carlana replied. "They love them. They're not poisonous to you, either, Kadi. Try some." At Kadi's hesitation, she laughed. "Really—when I was a child, strawberry season was a great time at home. Everybody in the family ate them. I'd no idea they were poisonous to Simes until the people here warned me not to eat them. It seems a lot of new Simes make that mistake—and some of them die from it."

"Yes," Kadi recalled. "One time that Charlie Horvan poisoned himself, it was with strawberries. I guess nobody thought to tell him what everybody knows!"

"And here you have no one to tell you what you can eat, have you, Kadi? There are, oh, certain mushrooms, for instance. Someday we'll go out gathering some, and I'll show you which ones my parents taught me to pick."

Just then Carlana's little boy, Owen, began to cry. His mother darted to his side and picked him up, discovering at once that he was merely frightened at having fallen. He was only two, and his sister Jana, a year younger, was crying in sympathy and tugging at her mother's skirts. Carlana spoke soothingly to the children, but Rimon didn't understand what she said.

When Owen quieted, and Carlana kissed both her children and sent them off to play again, Rimon asked, "You're teaching your children the Gen language?"

"Yes—both languages," Carlana replied. "It's a difficult fact: I want my children to be real people—Gens. But if they are, they will cross the border, and I'll never see them again. If they change over, though, they'll have to kill to survive. I don't want that for my children!"

"Carlana," said Kadi, "by that time, surely we'll have learned how all Simes and Gens can live as Rimon and I do. And then it won't matter. It simply won't matter anymore if a child changes over or establishes."

Carlana studied Rimon and Kadi, hope and despair fighting in her nager. "I shall pray, Kadi. Every day, when I pray for my children, I shall pray that you are right!"

Chapter 8

WILD GEN RAID

That first summer on the homestead was a happy, carefree time. Their crops thrived, and they developed friendships at Fort Freedom. Not everyone was willing to accept them—especially the younger Simes who had been born this side of the border and had changed over here. Chief leader of the group was Jord Veritt.

Kadi and Rimon seemed to grow closer, if that were possible. Each transfer was as ecstatic as if it were the first time, and the lovemaking that followed as joyful and fulfilling. Rimon no longer had difficulty zlinning immediately after transfer, so they could indulge themselves as they pleased, with no fear of interruption without warning.

The talk of Fort Freedom was the successful rout of a small group of Freeband Raiders. Rimon and Kadi had been visiting Carlana when the alarm had rung, and Rimon had joined the men who rode out to challenge them. None of the women with small children had joined them.

"They escaped across the border," Rimon reported when he returned. "I suppose they'll find plenty of prey over there . . . but what could we do?"

Abel Veritt, who had ridden up beside him, said, "Nothing. We can't ride into Gen Territory, even after Raiders. People would shoot us on sight as quickly as they would the Raiders. I just hope they don't do much damage."

"I hope they're shot down at the border!" Rimon said. "For the first time in my life, I actually wished today that I had a Gen gun and knew how to use it!"

"Rimon!" Kadi exclaimed, moving quickly to his side.

"Kadi, you haven't seen them in action," he said, remembering all too keenly the time he'd thought Kadi snared by such a band. "They don't just kill—they torture."

"He's right, Mrs. Farris," said Veritt. "The Freeband Raiders are an abomination upon the face of the Earth—and yet, we must not judge even them to be irredeemable. I speak from personal experience. I was once one of them."

Rimon and Kadi were the only ones shocked by this statement. Apparently, Veritt hid nothing about his past from his people.

"I lived that way for nearly six months," he told them, "if you can call it living. It was more a flight from life. We killed . . . people, self-aware Gens who understood what was happening. I didn't know there was any other way to live as a Sime. When our band fell upon hard times, we raided Pens, and I discovered that here there are soulless creatures in Gen bodies. They provide the selyn we must have to live, yet killing them is no more than slaughtering a steer for the meat."

Rimon felt Kadi's gorge rise at the thought. Then she controlled her disgust. Veritt continued as if he hadn't noticed.

With his "revelation," he had left the Freeband Raiders. Penniless and in poor health, he'd been fortunate to find a woman who owned a stable and gave him work, letting him sleep in one of the stalls. With her help, he regained his health, perfected his knowledge of Simelan, and discovered that most Simes were honest, hard-working people like those he'd grown up among.

As he learned to zlin subtleties, he perceived what to him seemed a second revelation: there was something in common in the nager of both Sime and Gen grown up as "people," the element that was missing in the nager of the Gens from the government Pens. Veritt perceived that element as the soul, and determined to return to the border and teach his new doctrine to other new Simes fleeing in despair into Sime Territory.

"He's saved most of us from suicide," Carlana said when Veritt had gone, "or maybe from joining the Raiders. Most of us killed a friend or relative in First Need, you know. But the marvelous thing is, we can all see for ourselves that what he teaches is the truth. There is such a difference between Kadi, or one of our own children who establishes, and one of the Gens raised for our need. They're just animals."

Rimon and Kadi said nothing. They were afraid to shake the faith of either Veritt or Carlana. It would be unnecessarily cruel to question beliefs that allowed these people to accept the necessities of their existence. So they quietly went home.

And then harvesting began around Fort Freedom, and every hand or tentacle was welcome. Rimon agreed to work in order to make the money to buy the things their homestead couldn't produce. *And the tax on Kadi,* he thought, anger clouding his mind every time he thought of it. Even out here where the government was no protection, the tax collector had come around—and the date on Kadi's tags told him how much Rimon owed, almost wiping out the little cash they had left.

He was working in the fields, happy at the sound of coins jingling in his pocket, when the alarm bell from Fort Freedom sounded. At first he didn't recognize it as an alarm, but by the second peal he was anxiously scanning the horizon for the source of the danger. The other Simes were frantically gathering the children, forming a phalanx. Then Rimon spotted a band of Simes riding from town toward the Fort and pointed.

As the field workers began to gather, running toward the Fort, Rimon sensed a massive Gen field closing in from another direction. He stopped, scanning the hills. Even as he was turning, it grew stronger, emerging from behind the insulating hills as a large band of Wild Gens galloped toward them.

"No, this way!" shouted Rimon, and simultaneously, the most sensitive Simes in the field were turning, yelling to their neighbors. The Simes closed ranks and, under full augmentation, charged at the Gen riders.

Shots rang out. The Wild Gens had rifles. The Simes ran zig-zag, weaving a complex pattern as they formed a crescent to engulf the Gens. To Rimon's left, one Sime fell, screaming in pain, but no one dared break formation to help him.

Sara Fenell and Herg Lol, who were approaching hard need, moved out in front, the Sime predator instinct roused to fever pitch by the high-field Gens. They selected their prey and grasped at the horses' reins. The Gen that Herg had chosen brought a shortened rifle around and fired. Herg Lol was caught full in the face, dead before he hit the ground. The Gen's horse reared, and two other Simes plucked the hapless Gen from the saddle, one wrestling the stump of a gun from his hands and bending the barrel so it would never shoot again.

The Gen screamed in utter panic, and Rimon, only six days fresh from a perfect transfer, felt his need awaken. On the other side of him, at the same time, Sara was pulling her frozen victim from his horse and killing with a savage glee. Then, all around them, Gens were unhorsed and killed.

Panic spread quickly among the Gens as every Sime past turnover was driven to a berserk lust for the kill. The Gen horsemen broke ranks. Then the Simes from town rode into the melee, laying about them with whips. Each Gen lashed by a Sime whip flared nagerically with a promise of exquisite delights.

Caught up against his will, Rimon helped to pull three Gens off their horses, only to have each snatched from his grasp and taken, as some feeble corner of his being fought to keep him from killing one himself. Augmentation was eating selyn, though he struggled to keep it to minimum, and the urge to kill grew stronger and stronger. *It's only intil!* he told himself. *Can't be need!* But it felt like need.

Later, he was never certain if self-restraint kept him from a kill, or if it was simply that all the Gens were dead before he managed to get one. With the death of the last Gen fighter, the provocative nager cooled, pain and panic faded beyond the power to disturb him, and, without having killed, he found himself coming down from augmentation to a still-life scene of carnage.

Dead Gens were scattered across the wheat stubble like broken dolls, drained of life, nagerically nonexistent but visible to the eye. Satisfied Simes, glowing with post-kill repletion, stood languorously among the dead.

Off to one side, a girl, one of the older children who had

been helping with the harvest, was kneeling beside the body of Herg Lol, sobbing. His daughter, Rimon realized. Abel Veritt went to her, putting his arms around her—himself still resonating with post-kill. He shared her tears, offering words of comfort.

Behind Rimon, there was a dull sobbing, edging into gasped words. "Oh, God. What have I done? What have I done. . . ." It was Carlana Lodge. Del knelt beside her, saying, "Protected the lives of your friends and your children —that's what."

"But I killed," she sobbed. "I wasn't in need—and I killed—I killed a real person—and—and I enjoyed it!"

Abel Veritt signaled to his wife, who came to take the sobbing girl from his arms. Then he turned to the Simes around him, those from Fort Freedom all beginning to realize that they had violated their beliefs.

"Listen to me!" he said firmly. "No one here sinned today. We killed, yes—I killed with you, in defense of our community. Gather now and let us pray together that we will never yield to the temptation of the kill for its own sake. Let us thank God that we were warned in time to prevent even more senseless slaughter. Let us not forget the people from town who came to aid us."

The Simes from town had stayed apart during all this. Now one of the men said, roughness covering his embarrassment, "We only come to get them Gens. . . ."

"Whatever your motives," Veritt replied, "we're grateful for your help in our time of trouble. I see you've lost three of your number. We shall pray for their souls."

"Much good that'll do 'em!" said the woman from the store. Then, under the impact of Veritt's sincerity, she added, "I guess your prayin' for 'em can't hurt 'em none."

"Let us pray, then, for all the souls perished here today, and for our own." Rimon, feeling as out of place as the Simes from town, stood silently, as did Del. But he saw Carlana's anguish dissolve as she prayed. Whatever Veritt had, it was clearly good for the Simes who followed him. But Rimon wondered at the idea of the pleasure of the kill being the wrong rather than the kill itself. With Kadi, he had the pleasure—without the kill. Would Veritt consider that a sin?

After the prayer, as they began to clear away the bodies, Veritt came up to him. "I see that you have prayed with us, though you yourself resisted the temptation of a vain kill. Yes, I saw you twice surrender a Gen to one in true need. It is on the battlefield that one comes to know a man."

Rimon shook his head, restraining an impulse to gesture with a tentacle. "I can't take credit for . . ."

"And that, itself, is to your credit, young man."

Suddenly they heard a gasp. "Risko! He's still alive!"

The woman who ran the Pens in town was kneeling beside the still form of a Sime Rimon recalled seeing before —oh yes, one of the riders who had laughed at him for his choice of homestead. Well, they'd been right.

He went to the woman's side, and found that the man's body was not merely pluming off residual selyn as a dead body did, but pulsing slightly with escaping life. There was a gaping wound in his chest.

He must have taken a kill just before he was shot or he wouldn't have survived this long. Rimon zlinned him.

Abel Veritt said, "Can you help him, Mr. Farris?"

"I don't know." He'd helped Kadi, a Gen, overcome some aches and pains—but what did he know about healing a Sime of a mortal wound?

"If we can't stop the blood and selyn loss," said the woman, "he's a goner. I don't know no way to do that!"

"He's not in attrition yet," Rimon said, kneeling beside the man. "Let me try." But he had spoken on impulse. He had no idea how to go about it. He strove to make nageric contact with the Sime's wavering fields as he always had with Kadi. But she was Gen; she fitted neatly into his patterns. He fumbled and then—suddenly—he had it. Not stopping to wonder how he did it, Rimon found the man's weak but pulsating field with its gross anomaly at the point where cells were dying. But it felt as if the selyn were being drained out of him, drained and drained, and he was dying. He came up out of it fighting for breath, his nerves screaming attrition.

He was lying on his side, curled into a tight ball, shaking. Abel Veritt and the Sime woman from town sat him up, coaxed him back to life, watching him expectantly. Rimon felt closed in, claustrophobic—surrounded by Simes, the world empty of life. Simes replete from the kill but using selyn, consuming it irretrievably, draining away all the life in the world, with no way to replenish it. . . .

"Kadi!" gasped Rimon, aching for her constantly rising field.

"Shall I send someone for your wife, Mr. Farris?" asked Veritt, deeply concerned.

"Yes! . . . No, wait. . . ." Something—at the edge of consciousness . . . "She's here."

Rimon couldn't even wonder how she got there, couldn't question the miracle. "Help me, Kadi . . . this man . . . I'm trying to stop the selyn loss."

Coming to him, Kadi gasped as she saw Risko's wound. She put one hand on Rimon's shoulder as he knelt over the wounded man again, and her attention focused onto him. Calm again, he forgot himself and zlinned the dying man. The entire selyn field had darkened around the edges; all selyn was drawn to the dreadfully bright area of the wound.

In Kadi's Gen field, the anomalies were dark areas in which the cells did not produce a steady pulse of selyn, and he had eased her pain by inducing an increase to normal levels of production. In the Sime field before him, the cells about the wound were drawing too much selyn from Risko's body, both consuming and wasting it at an accelerated rate, death coming in a black wave from the farthest points of his body.

It didn't frighten him now, with Kadi's field enveloping him. But he had to stop that selyn loss. He lowered his hands into the plume, his laterals extending. He had that funny, wobbly trembling in his chest that Del used to complain about, but then it stopped, leaving a strange, intense clarity that was painful deep in his chest. But Rimon ignored that, concentrating on the selyn plume, willing it to diminish.

And, gradually, it did. He could zlin the stillness about the wound now, the flesh cooling—the blood clotting.

At last the wound was closing. Every time Rimon's attention wavered, small rivulets of blood and selyn would break free again. He concentrated, holding and holding,

waiting until the healing was strong enough to hold by
itself.

At last he took his hands away, and the wound held.
There were soft gasps in the pure silence around him. He
leaned back against Kadi, breathing in long, panting gasps
as if he'd been running a race. He was more tired than he'd
been from the battle itself. The world began to wobble
again, but he blinked it away, drawing strength from somewhere.

The Sime woman was staring at him in astonishment.
Rimon smiled at her. "You can move him now, if you're
careful. He's not unconscious, just asleep. But he's going
to need a kill again tomorrow—maybe the next day. I
think it might do him good if you brought his kill to him
as soon as you can."

"I can supply him with the best," said the Pen woman.
"I owe him my life more times than I can count. But—"
She ran her hand, tentacles extended, over the wound.
"How did you do it? He was dyin'!"

"A miracle," murmured Abel Veritt.

"No," said Rimon. "I don't think so. He's so low-field—
even the selyn plume was weak. All I did was block it with
my field—a kind of nageric tourniquet."

"I seen a gypsy do that once," said the Sime woman.
"Over to Ardo Pass—man got mauled by a mountain cat.
No way to stop the bleedin'. This gypsy man done what
you done—or something like it."

Veritt now looked at Rimon in infinite sadness. "Is that
where you learned to heal? Is it a gypsy trick, sorcery?"

"No," said Rimon, "I figured it out—just now. I wasn't
even sure it would work—but what did he have to lose?"
Rimon's mind felt sluggish. He didn't want to argue, yet he
knew it was important for Veritt to understand.

"Mr. Veritt," said Kadi, "why are you so afraid of the
gypsies? They're just people who wander around, keeping
to themselves. I've never known them to hurt anyone."

"I was taught as a child that the gypsies still practice the
Ancient sorcery that destroyed the world."

"You were also taught as a child," she said boldly, "that
Simes don't have souls."

Veritt stared at her in shock for a moment—and then his

face crinkled into one of his rare, warm smiles. "Kadi—may I call you Kadi?—I think you may have the power to convince Simes that down is up! But you're right; we shouldn't condemn without knowledge."

The Sime woman spat. "A Gen philosophizin' and a Sime listenin' to 'er!"

"I couldn't have healed your friend without Kadi's help," Rimon said very quietly. "You saw what happened when I tried."

She paused, then said to Veritt, "'S right! And that there gypsy feller, he had no Gen. What Rimon here did—must be different." She turned to Rimon. "Risko's one of my best men—been with me for years. I owe you for this."

Rimon began to protest, but she cut him off. "No, listen here. End of the month, you come by my place and pick out the best I got—not the free ones, the choice stock."

To her bewilderment, Rimon, Kadi, and Veritt all broke into laughter. Rimon finally caught his breath and said, "Thank you. I appreciate your offer, but—I don't kill."

"I know you won't kill *that* one—but nobody don't kill."

"Do you remember last spring, when you and Risko and some others laughed at Kadi and me for homesteading where we were? I didn't have anyone but Kadi with me then, and I haven't been to your Pens in all these months, have I? What did you think I was doing?"

"Never thought about it."

"Kadi supplies me with all the selyn I need. Every month."

The woman stared from Rimon to Kadi and back again. "Well, I'll be shenned," she said. "That's why she ain't scared."

"Miss Slina," said Abel Veritt, "we should get Risko indoors where it's warm and dry so we can bandage that wound. Bring him to Fort Freedom for the night. You can take him back to town tomorrow."

Sara Fenell, who had been looking on for some time, said, "I have a Gen set aside that I won't be using. You can have him for Risko."

"Now that's more than friendly of you folks. . . ."

"You, and the others from town, did a great service to Fort Freedom today. If it hadn't been for your warning, we wouldn't have been massed for the attack, and many more lives would have been lost."

Slina laughed. "Don't thank me for that—thank that crazy redheaded Gen."

Rimon started. "Kadi?" For the first time, he realized that the Wild Gens must have crossed the border near their homestead.

The Sime woman was saying, "She come ridin' through town, yellin' there was Wild Gens comin'. Never seen nothin' like it in my life, the way she stood up to a bunch of Simes. You'd a swore she was a leader of a border patrol, not a Gen!"

One of the gathered Simes added, "I thought she was runnin' for the border. When I tried to claim her, she swore at me like some Freeband Raider!"

Radiating embarrassment, Kadi murmured, "I rode off in such a hurry, I left my tags at home. But the storekeeper recognized me."

The storekeeper shrugged. "I knew she was legal, even if she is plumb crazy."

"That was a very brave thing to do," Veritt said.

"I wasn't brave. I was scared for Rimon, and all of you. I had to do it."

Slina was studying them. "I don't understand. You was all alone out there by the border, and you didn't just go on across? Why do you stay with this guy who keeps you for selyn?"

Kadi smiled at her. "Why does any woman stay with her husband?"

"Husband!"

"Yes," said Rimon. He chose his words carefully, recalling the reaction of another Gendealer—his father. "Kadi and I have something special. So far, we haven't been able to teach it to anyone else, but that won't stop us from living together."

Slina shook her head again. "Weird. I got customers like to make it with Gens, sometimes. But I never heard of nobody wanting to marry one! That ain't legal, is it?"

"There's no law against it," Rimon pointed out.

"Clearly Rimon and Kadi are married in the eyes of God," said Abel Veritt.

Slina shrugged. "Your business. I guess if you have kids you'll be officially married, no matter what anybody says."

Kadi nodded serenely. "We'll have children. Rimon and I are settled into our home now, we're making friends—life is good."

The Sime woman said, "I don't envy you. Folks don't like nobody who's too different. I guess you're better off around here than most places . . . but I sure wouldn't want to be in your place!"

Chapter 9

FAREWELL CEREMONY

After the battle, Rimon and Kadi stayed in Carlana's house, watching her children while she and Del went for a ride after dinner . . . and didn't return until dawn. Carlana blushingly apologized while Del tried to hide his smug satisfaction. Rimon knew that his kill in battle that day had been without remorse for the first time since Billy's death.

A few days later, Del and Carlana came out to help Rimon and Kadi. The four of them worked together for a while, but Kadi couldn't keep up with the Simes. She could drive the wagon, though, bringing it in for the others to load, then helping to unload.

At one point, as they finished loading the wagon, Carlana climbed onto the seat beside Kadi. "I'll do it this time," she told Del and Rimon.

Rimon, who had been riding to the threshing floor with Kadi each time, found himself stepping forward, as if to challenge the Sime woman's right—and then pulled himself back, embarrassed. Carlana was pre-turnover. Probably the two women just wanted to talk woman-talk. Kadi had little enough time for that.

At Rimon's hesitation, Del said with studied casualness, "All right, Ana. We'll have another load ready when you get back."

Rimon caught a peculiar glance from Del as he deliberately turned his back to the departing women and started working. After a few minutes, apparently convinced that Rimon was normal enough, Del said, "Rimon, I've decided I want Ana to be my wife."

"Hey! That's great!" said Rimon. "Married life is . . ." But Del was uncertain. "What's wrong?"

"I—I just don't know, Rimon. For the first time since

135

Billy, I've found something to live for. But . . . she deserves better than I can give."

"Don't be silly," said Rimon. "Since you started that ranch, you've become the best catch this end of the Territory. You're young and strong and well on your way to getting rich—what more could a woman want?"

"For one thing, someone who shares her beliefs," said Del. "Her . . . relationship with God, the teachings of Fort Freedom—it's all so important to her, and most of it means nothing to me. I know that bothers her. And the one piece of knowledge we do share—that's what's tearing me up. Gens are people. She knows that as well as you and I do—except that to preserve her sanity, she accepts Abel Veritt's teaching that the ones grown in the Pens are just bodies without souls. If I could believe that—oh, God, if only I could believe it!"

Del stopped his savage hacking at the wheat and upended his scythe, staring at the wicked blade. "They almost convinced me."

"What?"

But Del, lost in reverie, didn't hear him. "This month, I had a good kill. I killed a man who was trying to kill Ana. Shen—that was the best kill I've ever had in my life! Real, alive, alert, undrugged—and no guilt, because he deserved to die. But the month before . . ."

Rimon didn't like the way Del began to finger the edge of the scythe blade. "I wasn't going to kill, Rimon. I'd had all I could take. Or maybe—maybe I really hoped Ana would stop me and convince me—I just don't know. I was crazy!"

Deeply concerned, Rimon tried to make his field soothing to Del, wishing desperately that Kadi were here, and on the other hand glad she didn't have to hear this.

Del glanced at him, and smiled grimly. "I'm all right now —for the time being. But that day I decided to kill myself."

Rimon leaned on his own scythe. "But you didn't."

"No. Ana found me. Maybe I hoped she would. She took me to Abel Veritt—shen it, Rimon, he stayed up all night talking with me, to be sure I wouldn't go off and try again the minute his back was turned. And then . . . he brought me one of those Gens they kill, passive, drugged, and he kept telling me to zlin it, to see the difference—and I was so deep into need by then, I had to believe him. And there *is* a difference. Nothing—nothing like Kadi . . . like Billy—" Tears were sliding down Del's cheeks, unnoticed. Rimon was able to take the scythe from him, make him sit down. "But, Rimon, after it was over, I—I couldn't accept it anymore. I want to. But I can't. Just can't."

Rimon put an arm around Del's shoulders, helpless. Finally Del said, "You and Kadi—that's the only thing that gives me hope, Rimon, hope enough to take Ana and the kids and stay alive until—until you—"

When Del couldn't finish the sentence, Rimon said, "Yeah. Until." *This is what I've done to my best friend. Now what?*

At last Del pulled himself together and went to the brook to wash his face. The women, bouncing the wagon across the empty field, ignored Rimon.

"Do you love Del?"

"Oh yes, Kadi," Carlana replied. "I loved my husband; he was an honest, hard-working man who cared well for me and our children. But—Del is a—gentler man. Haven't you seen the way he gentles the horses? He is a very easy man to love."

"I know," said Kadi, her nager humming with strong emotion. She turned to Carlana, securing the reins. "You said yourself that he loves your children as if he were their own father. Grab him, Carlana. Grab him while you can."

With a silent, welling bitterness, Rimon thought, *And I'm not an easy man to love. Not at all.*

Carlana climbed down from the wagon, careful to keep her long skirts in place. Kadi, wearing denims, jumped down beside her. "Here comes Del," she said. "Go ahead and ask him."

"I wish to. It would mean leaving Fort Freedom, but we would not be far away. The only thing I could wish is that we could be married in the chapel."

As "marriage" to Rimon and Kadi meant living together, Carlana's statement made little sense. "You mean a pledge ceremony?" asked Kadi. "Most couples do that with a big party. I'm sure Del would be delighted—why, it would almost make this country seem civilized!"

Del joined them to find his fate sealed—but Rimon sensed that he was relieved that the women had made his mind up for him and were already making plans concerning plum cakes and whether there was enough of Kadi's blue material left for a wedding dress. When they went off to the house to see, Rimon turned to Del and said, "Congratulations. You are doing the right thing, you know."

"I know," said Del. "The right thing for me, anyway. I just hope it turns out to be the right thing for Ana."

If Del was worried about taking care of a wife, Rimon was equally worried, with more reason. Kadi had carefully preserved a store of food for the winter, and they had their house—the problem was money. Rimon had never had to worry before about not having enough cash. He was down to what he'd earned in Fort Freedom's fields, worrying about paying Kadi's head tax, when, after the Wild Gen raid, they were awarded four of the horses taken that day —and the right to have them shod once by Fort Freedom's blacksmith. The Gen guns would be melted down for their precious metal. Rimon sold the saddles in town, adding to their meager supply of money.

Thank goodness, there would be no property taxes until their two years of homesteading were up, and Rimon could claim the deed to his land. By then surely they'd be doing better!

Kadi seemed content with their progress. They even had a goat now, a present from Slina, who claimed to have taken it in trade. "She'll drop kids in the spring," she told them, "and you'll have milk and cheese after that. You can use her; to me she's a nuisance."

Paradoxically, the local Gendealer was friendly toward them because of Rimon's healing of Risko, while a good number of the people of Fort Freedom were not. Rimon noticed it particularly the day Del and Carlana were married, a glorious day with the crisp cool of early autumn in the air.

It was a simple ceremony, with Abel Veritt presiding and just a few friends to witness. Mrs. Veritt was there. Jord Veritt was not. While he would not oppose his father openly, he spoke to others in the community, warning that the "outsiders" were trying to destroy their way of life.

Somehow, a number of people became convinced that Del's taking Carlana and her children away was part of a plot directed by Rimon and Kadi.

More and more, there was a distinct coldness from those who sided with Jord—the younger Simes born in-Territory, with whom Rimon should have had the most in common. Soon after Del and Carlana were married, they learned one of the reasons the Sime children of Fort Freedom might foster feelings of resentment.

Rimon and Kadi were invited to a "Farewell Ceremony" for Elin Lol, the girl whose father had been killed in the Wild Gen raid. She had just established as a Gen—cause for rejoicing in Fort Freedom.

The celebration began at dusk, in the chapel. Both factions were there, Abel and Jord Veritt officiating jointly. Those approaching need carefully placed themselves on the periphery, those most recently satisfied, in front and along the aisle. As Elin had established only yesterday, her low field would have put her in little danger; nonetheless, every precaution was taken for her safety.

Rimon and Kadi were placed in the front row, Abel Veritt saying, "When you two are together, no one can tell where you are in your cycle, Rimon."

He could feel all eyes on them, and the effort of those approaching need to avoid zlinning. Many were resentful of their presence, and even those friendly to them were affected by the hostility.

A large proportion of Fort Freedom's Simes had killed within the past three days, as the Wild Gen raid had been four weeks ago. Only a few members of the community were past turnover, so the atmosphere was not tense. A stilled hush fell as all were assembled, expectant and reverent.

Elin, in a white dress, a wreath of chrysanthemums on her hair, came down the aisle between Abel and Jord Veritt. At the front of the chapel a table was covered with a white cloth, and on it were laid out a pitcher and three cups, an unlit lamp, and a lighted candle.

Elin and Jord took the two chairs that stood to one side, and Abel Veritt faced the congregation. "We're here tonight," he said, "to rejoice in God's blessing upon Elin Lol, child of this community—child of Simes and yet herself not cursed with the Sime nature."

Elin Lol was attempting to smile, although her eyes were flooded with tears. This was the best Sime Territory had to offer a Gen. Elin didn't face a terrorized flight to the border, or the prospect of being killed by a friend, sold into the Pens, or captured by Gen hunters. She knew the Gen language and customs, and something of what to do when she got across the border. Nonetheless, she was leaving the only home she'd ever known, never to return.

Veritt was continuing, "We all question the will of God at times. Every Sime here has wondered why God would curse anyone with the Devil's form. To that question, no one can give a complete answer—yet we know that God is working for good because every so often we see His plan revealed to us.

"Here sits Elin Lol, blessed by God. He chose the Lol family, tried and tested them, and they did not waver. Two years ago, their son died in changeover, and they found strength in the thought that God took him before he could kill. Last year Riled Lol died, and her husband turned his energies to caring for his daughter, remaining always a good and pious man. And finally the test came upon Elin. Her father was brutally murdered. She questioned, and yet she placed her faith in God's justice and mercy. And now the Lol family has been blessed.

"Let us all pray that Elin Lol will continue to live in God's grace. May she find good friends across the border. May God bless her with a good husband and healthy children, none of whom bear the Devil's curse."

There was a prayer in unison at that point, in which Rimon and Kadi did not participate. Rimon was fascinated by the way Veritt had taken the harsh facts of a hard and sorrowful life and woven them into a story of faith and hope. Yet life wasn't that simple, and Rimon was certain Veritt himself knew that. He deliberately kept his teachings to black and white, good and evil to ensure that his people didn't have to think too deeply about their faith.

Hope and joy permeated the nager in the chapel and seemed to enter Kadi, too, lifting her to a euphoric contentment. Rimon basked in it until he felt Jord Veritt zlinning Kadi from all the way across the room, despite the heavy nager. Rimon took her hand protectively. She looked at him, then at Jord, and suddenly became transparent, visible to Sime senses only as a brightness. Startled, Rimon had to look to see that it was still Kadi sitting beside him.

The prayers ended. Elin Lol and Jord came to the table. Jord poured water into the three cups. Abel Veritt said a blessing over them, and handed cups to Elin and Jord, keeping one himself.

"We celebrate our sameness," he announced. "All life, from the smallest plants and animals to man himself, both Sime and Gen, must have water to exist. Thus we remind ourselves that we are all part of God's plan, even those who bear the curse of the Sime nature."

The three drank from the cups, and Jord set them off to one side, placing the lamp in the center of the table. Then he gave Elin the lighted candle. It caught the tears swimming in her eyes and picked out highlights in her hair. All in white, she looked like a shimmering apparition, a vision of hope.

Abel Veritt said, "Elin Lol, you leave us now for a better life here on this earth. Live it so that you may know an even more blessed existence after death, and that your children may never be cursed with the Devil's form. Go with God, Elin Lol, leaving behind you the flame of hope."

Tears streaming down her face, Elin turned to the congregation. "I—I love you all. I'll never forget to pray for you. May God bless and protect you."

Then she lit the lamp from her candle. Jord put the chimney on, and the flame flared brightly as around the chapel all the other lamps were extinguished, and then Elin blew out her candle. The only light in the chapel now was the lamp on the table. The Simes, though, could perceive Elin's nager, even low-field as she was, as a glowing, growing flame of hope.

Of course, there wasn't supposed to be another Gen in the chapel. Kadi's nager was much brighter than Elin's, but there was nothing to be done about it. Perhaps, though, the strange custom of Fort Freedom's Simes of not zlinning under formal circumstances extended to their religious practices. As the Veritts guided Elin down the aisle, Rimon put his arm around Kadi's waist and guided her out. He knew she didn't miss the way he deftly avoided Jord Veritt and kept his own body between Jord and her. As they were mounting up, she whispered, "What's the matter, Rimon?"

"Nothing," he said tersely. "Button your coat. It's going to be a chilly ride."

The stars were bright and clear, the moon just rising. There would be frost by morning. Rimon and Kadi joined the band of ten Simes escorting Elin to the border, for they would take her to the easy crossing-place on the edge of their homestead.

They took the hill trail, passed Rimon and Kadi's home, and went on to the border crossing. There Abel Veritt asked Rimon to go up to the top of a hill with the most sensitive Simes of Fort Freedom to zlin any danger spots ahead.

Elin knelt before Abel Veritt for a last blessing, and then made as if to kiss his wife good-bye, but the woman stepped back sharply, warding off the contact. Just past turnover, Rimon judged. They exchanged a formal little gesture he didn't quite follow.

"It's all clear as far as I can zlin," Rimon reported, and with stiff determination, Elin Lol mounted and rode away, leading a heavily laden packhorse, the discipline of Fort Freedom keeping her from looking back. Blinking back a tear, Kadi pulled Rimon's arm around her. The Simes stayed at the top of the hill, watching until no one could perceive Elin's nager any longer. Then they all turned and rode back along the trail.

Abel Veritt dropped back to ride with Rimon and Kadi. "I was sorely tempted tonight to say something about the hope you have brought to our community. When we put the lights out, I was sorry I hadn't, for Kadi—"

"I know," she said. "I shouldn't have been there to distract from Elin's moment."

"No, no. It was as if our ceremony were reflected and expanded. The little candle flame beside the flaring lamp, and Elin's low-field beside yours. Kadi, you are a symbol of hope."

"She's the Devil sent to tempt us, Father." Jord Veritt had come up beside them. Rimon bit back bitter words.

"You will not speak so!" ordered Veritt.

"It's time I spoke out. If this Gen has formed an unholy alliance with a Sime, what can she be but a demon in Gen form? What other form would you, our leader, trust more?"

"Jord, you will be silent," said Veritt. "Rimon and Kadi have learned to live together, Sime and Gen, without killing. One day, may God be willing, they'll teach us, and then our children will not have to leave us."

"Father, they're seducing our people from the faith. Mrs. Lodge left us to live with one of their Godless followers. Who will be next?"

"Mrs. *Erick* comes to all our services, and brings her children," Veritt replied. "She lives with her husband, as is only right and proper. Jord, I want you to apologize for this outburst. You have no excuse—not even need."

"Father, these people are blinding you to your own teachings."

"Jord," said Rimon stiffly, "Kadi and I had no intention of coming between you and your father, but how can one prove intentions—or spiritual merit?"

Jord studied Rimon. "You are willing to give proof?"

"Certainly, if you can think of a way."

Jord looked Kadi up and down while Rimon fought for self-control. "Since you already know how not to kill, take one of the Gens from Slima's Pens this month—and let Mrs. Farris teach me."

"Why you—!" Rimon leaped for Jord's throat, tentacles spread for a killing grip, knocking the other man from his horse, the two of them rolling, struggling on the ground.

Abel Veritt dismounted in a flash of augmented motion, coming between the fighters, his wife at his side in an instant, pulling their son back while Veritt grasped Rimon. "Stop this!" he thundered. "Will you prove that Simes are no better than beasts?"

Kadi came up beside Rimon, trying to project calm. "Rimon, please!" she begged. "Jord doesn't understand!" Veritt relinquished Rimon into her care, turning to his son.

"Oh, he understands!" he said, advancing to where Jord

stood. "You disgust me! Flesh of my flesh and child of my sin. You're the punishment God has meted out to me for being seduced into the Freeband Raiders when I first changed over. Your birth killed your mother, who had rescued me from a life of sin. Now you stand there, a disgrace to the woman who raised you as her own son."

"All I ask is for these people to do what they say they can do!"

Rimon felt the urge to leap at him again, but Kadi held him back as Veritt berated Jord. "Do you think we're all fools? Do you think we have not all experienced the lust of the flesh which follows repletion of selyn? You lust after another man's wife, Jord. Did you think to hide that shame beneath your garbled logic?" He took a breath, and said firmly, "You will go directly back to the chapel and spend the rest of this night on your knees, begging God's forgiveness. Perhaps tomorrow you'll be ready to beg forgiveness of Mr. and Mrs. Farris."

Veritt and Jord stared at one another fiercely. Then Jord dropped his gaze like a whipped animal. Kadi, standing with her arm around Rimon's shoulders, felt a surge of pity for Jord that brought Rimon to his senses. *Fighting like dogs in the street! A Farris!* He took a deep, shuddering breath and gathered himself to face Abel on his own, his control still tenuous. "I must apologize, Abel—Jord—Mrs. Veritt. I overreacted. I'm not in need and have no excuse."

"You were provoked," said Veritt. "You're young—and Sime. In all the time you've been here, I've never seen you lose your temper. I was much older than you before I achieved such control over my nature."

"Thank you," said Rimon, still wanting to protest.

"We'll go home now," said Veritt, "and leave you and Kadi to rest. I'll see that my son never again makes such an indecent suggestion."

Rimon and Kadi rode home in silence. As they prepared for bed, though, Rimon was thinking that they did indeed owe people some proof of what they promised. He said, "Jord was right."

"You—want to try his experiment?"

He turned on her, enraged at that idea. "Is that what *you* want? Is it, Kadi?"

"What do you mean, Rimon?"

"I noticed how you sympathized with him after he as much as called you a whore! If you were Sime, you'd know how enticing you are."

"Well, I'm not Sime! And I'm glad!" said Kadi.

Fists on his hips, Rimon looked her up and down. "What an uppity Gen! Choice kill, that's for sure. Small wonder Jord and his friends are after you. The very idea they could have you and not kill you, so that afterwards they could have *that,* too! It must surely be driving them crazy."

Her shock thrilled through him, her pain a pleasure to his overwrought nerves. She fought for control.

"Rimon, why don't you relax and let me make you feel better?"

"Oh yes—let you make me happy and carefree, so you can do as you please? You really have become a witch, haven't you? It's like Dad said—you can get a Sime in your power and control him completely! Well, you're not going to control me. I'm my own man, and you just keep your killusting field out of my nager!"

He reveled in the shock and pain that went through her at his vile gutter language. Then he turned and stalked out of the house, holding himself from zlinning lest she somehow reach out and affect him again.

He walked around the side of the hill, half-expecting Kadi to come running after him. But she didn't. *Shen the wench anyway!* He plunged on, fighting the desire to enter hunting mode, until he was beyond Kadi's influence. In the darkness, where the moonlight didn't penetrate, his left foot came up sharply against a small rock. Feeling like some stupid, stumbling Gen, he kicked spitefully at the rock.

Somehow, the pain cleared his head. He sat down, removing his boot and rubbing his foot as the pain subsided. No, he hadn't broken any bones—but why was he behaving like a Sime in hard need? What did he want from Kadi? When she tried to help him, he pushed her away—and when she held herself aloof, he resented that, too. He didn't understand her. How could a Sime understand a Gen? How could she help always doing the wrong thing? She was only a Gen.

Pulling on his boot, he limped back to the house. Kadi was asleep, her tear-stained face buried in Rimon's pillow, which she clutched against herself. He pitied her helplessness, zlinned her, and found that she was cold.

She woke as he drew the blanket over her, and reached for him. He drew back. "Not now, Kadi."

She sat up as he stripped off his clothing and pulled on pajamas. When he stretched out on the edge of the bed away from her, turning his back stiffly to her, she still sat there shivering a little. "Rimon. We've got to talk."

"I'm tired," he replied gruffly. "We'll talk tomorrow."

"No," said Kadi, firmly. "If you don't want me anymore, I'm leaving tomorrow."

He sat up, eyes wide. "What?"

"If I'm hurting you, controlling you, turning you into something unnatural, then I can't stay with you. I can speak the Gen language now; I know something of their customs. Carlana will give me some clothing that Gens think proper for a woman. If you can't give me a horse, Del will. I'll make out."

"Kadi—no!" His tentacles extended, gripping air in shock. "I can't let you go. . . . I didn't mean what I said—any of it. Not any of it, Kadi. Believe me, oh, please believe me." The tears were his own now, not an echo of hers.

"Then what's wrong with us to make you say those things?"

"It's not us, it's me. I don't know what's wrong with me. I just go crazy thinking of anyone laying a tentacle on you. And when I watch someone zlinning you, it's like a knife in my guts, twisting. . . ."

She put her arms around him, bewildered. "But Rimon, I've never wanted anyone but you. I can't even stand the thought. . . . Zlin me for the truth of it, Rimon—zlin me deeply," she said, pulling his hands into position and coaxing his laterals into contact with her arms. "I'd never give transfer to anyone else, certainly never let them have me afterwards. If I leave you, I go to live alone for the rest of my life. I know that—and I know my life wouldn't be very long. But I don't care, if it would make you well at last."

He disentangled the contact and drew her to his chest. "Kadi, you could survive without me—but I couldn't survive one month without you. I think that's what scares me so. I'm only beginning to realize how much stronger you are than I am. You can walk away from me—anytime you want."

"No, I can't," she said deliberately. "Unless you throw me out."

Oh, never! Holding her, he let her field penetrate into him. Then, puzzled, he held her away. "Lie down. I want to check something."

"What?" she asked as she lay flat and he extended his laterals again, spreading his hands over her chest, running them down to her abdomen, seeking the source of the faint anomaly he'd zlinned.

"Yes!" he said, brightening suddenly. "Yes, it is! It is, it is, Kadi, it *is!*"

"What!" she demanded, though he sensed she knew.

"Our baby! We're going to have a baby!" Then he sobered. "My baby. My heir. So soon. So soon."

Kadi beamed, completely missing the dread fear that threatened Rimon's happiness. He pushed it aside. They'd manage—hadn't they managed to survive everything so far? He let himself dissolve into Kadi's delight.

Chapter 10

TRAGEDY OF IGNORANCE

In the days that followed the discovery that Kadi was pregnant, Rimon made a deliberate attempt to control his emotions. The way he'd lashed out at Jord Veritt—and then at Kadi—disturbed him more than he wanted Kadi to know. One night he wakened in a cold sweat, his laterals fully extended, convinced that he was savagely draining the selyn out of Jord. He hadn't been able to sleep for three nights after that, and when he did finally fall into a doze, it deepened into an episode of near coma, and he woke to Kadi's frantic efforts to rouse him.

He'd had need nightmares all his adult life until Kadi established, but never before turnover. He didn't dare tell her about them. She was so happy now, humming and singing as she prepared for the winter and made plans for the baby. For her, the fight had cleared the air, making everything fresh and new again. But Rimon kept remembering how he'd stormed out on her, with the killrage singing in his veins, wanting to *hunt*. That feeling wasn't gone after the fight. Every few days, in a dream or while riding within zlinning distance of Slina's Pens, or in the presence of a post-kill Sime, it would come back sharp and clear. And his resolve never to kill again would be shaken, and that scared him more than anything. Never had he felt this way about the kill.

He couldn't discuss it with Kadi. How could a Sime discuss killust with a Gen? There was no Sime he could discuss it with either. Del had his own problems. Carlana and the people of Fort Freedom—no, they'd lose faith in him. He had to fight—and win—this battle alone. He couldn't lean on Kadi now.

Despite her age in natal years, she was still only six months a woman. However much he had yearned for their child, it was too soon. Her cycles had barely begun. His father never bred female Gens until they'd been established for a full year or their cycles stabilized completely. He wasn't even sure if she *had* stabilized. He had been so frantic to relieve himself, he hadn't even been aware of her fertility.

If anything goes wrong, it's my fault, my fault.

The next day, as they went about their work in the house, Kadi watched him warily, sticking close to his side. At midmorning, she straightened from spreading the straw they were using for warmth on the floor of their house. "Someone's coming."

As soon as she said it, he heard the hoofbeats—but he zlinned no one, either Sime or Gen. "Children?"

They went outside, as the horses started around the side of the hill. He did, indeed, zlin the faint nager of children.

"Mr. Farris? Mrs. Farris? Is anyone home?"

They walked down the hill to find two visitors from Fort Freedom dismounting: Drust Fenell and his girlfriend— Rimon fumbled for her name—Vee, that was it. Vee Lassiter. Both were on the brink of adolescence, and as inseparable as Rimon and Kadi had been at their age.

"Hi!" said Drust. "We've come to trespass on your land."

"No one from Fort Freedom trespasses here," said Kadi. "You're always welcome."

"Thank you," said the boy. "My ma sent you some wool." He untied a roll of heavy cloth and handed it to Kadi. "It was supposed to be a coat for me for the winter, but I'm not gonna be here to wear it."

"Why not?" asked Rimon.

Drust laughed. "Look at me! Even Mr. Veritt says it's not presumptuous to say I can't possibly become Sime, now."

It was true. The boy was not only already taller than Rimon, but filled out to a muscular Gen build. His hands were large and square, callused with hard work, yet he was gentle as he put an arm around the waist of the girl with him. "We're going up top of the pass to look over to Gen Territory and decide where we're going to meet."

"To meet?" asked Kadi.

"Drust will establish any day now," said Vee. "Later, if—"

"*When*," said Drust. "When Vee establishes, she'll come to me. I know where Elin Lol went, and others from Fort Freedom. It won't be so hard to go, knowing Vee will join me."

Rimon nodded silently. Drust rushed on, "Mr. Farris, my ma says you're awful sensitive. She can't zlin anything yet, but maybe you could . . ."

"Of course," said Rimon, awed to be consulted by this boy who so wanted to be Gen. He wondered—a boy like this, raised by Simes—could he learn to be unafraid, like Kadi?

He thrust the thought from his mind as he remembered Billy. No experiments with the children of friends!

"Come on," he said. "We'll have to get away from Kadi's field."

Need slid into his consciousness as they moved apart from Kadi and Vee, but it was not strong yet—just enough to sharpen his perception of Drust's field. He'd done this often enough with the whelps of his father's Gens, looking for the accidental Sime among them.

"Uh, Drust, I'll have to make lateral contact to be sure."

"It's all right, Mr. Farris. Jord Veritt's been screening me for weeks now. I'll be still."

As Rimon circled to put himself between Kadi and the boy, he said, "Can I ask a—personal question?"

"Sure."

"Did—uh—do your parents ever touch you with their tentacles?"

"Oh, yeah, of course." He reached for Rimon's hands confidently.

"All right, be still then for a moment." He concentrated, zlinning Drust right down to the cellular level. Nothing.

As he dismantled the contact, Drust started, but his nager had so little power that Rimon didn't even react. "What's the matter?"

"It's all over? You did it?" He looked at his arms. "You didn't even bruise me."

Rimon realized he had held the boy very loosely. "I trusted you not to move. You wouldn't have wanted to hurt me." Which was rather strange, he realized. He'd never trusted a child like that before. Was Kadi destroying all his reflexes?

"Oh," said Drust, with a trace of reverence Rimon wasn't sure he liked. Then, "What did you find?"

Rimon smiled, shaking his head. "Not yet. There's not the slightest sign of establishment—or changeover, either."

Drust shrugged. "I'm glad. I'm not ready to leave, but Ma thought maybe . . ." Drust was Sara Fenell's son. Rimon wondered if she feared that her kill—and enjoyment of it—on the day of the Wild Gen raid would condemn her son to life as a Sime.

"I'm glad, too," said Vee. "Maybe we'll both establish together."

Rimon zlinned her with senses sharpened by the exercise with Drust. *Oh, no*—

"Vee," he said gently, "I think we'd better take you home. Both of you."

"Oh, but Drust and I are going to picnic up top of the pass! We have permission—honest."

"You're not going to feel like picnicking in an hour or two," Rimon said. "Come on. You'll be most comfortable at home."

"Should we take her in the wagon?" asked Kadi.

"No! There's nothing wrong with Vee!"

"It's not wrong," Kadi said. "It's just changeover."

Vee screamed. It was the agonized, despairing cry of a trapped animal.

When Vee caught her breath, she cried, "No! You're lying! I'm not a Sime—my parents are *good!*" The raw self-loathing took Rimon completely by surprise, though it shouldn't have.

Drust took her into his arms. "It's not true," he said. "Mr. Farris must be wrong. You're fine—Vee, you're not even feverish." He held a hand to her forehead, glaring at Rimon.

"Drust, you know I'm right."

"No one can tell before the fever starts!" He cradled Vee against him, as if Rimon were trying to curse her.

"Drust, you're not helping Vee by denying the truth," Kadi said. "She'll be more comfortable at home, with her family, and you can stay with her until it's over."

Vee turned tear-drenched eyes up to Kadi. "I don't want to be Sime! I'm not a monster!"

Kadi recoiled. "How could you possibly think you were? Your parents, Mr. Veritt, all the Simes at Fort Freedom are good people—and now you won't have to leave them."

"Drust will have to leave—and now I can't go with him!"

"If you're Sime, I'll pray to become Sime, too," said Drust.

"Drust—you mustn't! You can't pray to be cursed!" said Vee.

"Won't that guarantee it? Vee, I'm not going to leave you."

Rimon met Kadi's eyes. Hadn't she said almost the same thing to him the day they brought him home on the flatbed wagon, the blood of breakout crusted on his hands, Zeth's selyn sustaining his life? He could see she was thinking the same thought. He gave her a let-it-be signal with one tentacle, and went to hitch up the wagon.

By the time they reached Fort Freedom—stopping only to ask Slina to send a Gen to the Lassiter home—Vee's fever had begun, and she was responding to Kadi's field. Her parents accepted their daughter and Rimon's diagnosis without complaint and took her to her room. But under the veneer of calm, Rimon sensed the father's shock, and his brief savage fight with denial, before he went out to get Abel Veritt.

"Please, Mrs. Lassiter," said Drust quietly, "I want to stay with her."

The woman nodded. "You can come in when I've put her to bed."

"I'll help you," said Kadi.

"Thank you," she replied. A tear slid down her face. "It's not her fault. Her father and I—we've tried, but—"

"It's no one's fault, Mrs. Lassiter," said Rimon. "Changeover is a perfectly natural process." He was furious at Abel Veritt's teachings. They might give hope to the newly escaped Simes from Gen Territory, but look what they did to the two thirds of their children who would change over!

Just then Veritt arrived with Vee's father. As Mr. Lassiter went into his daughter's room, Veritt said, "Rimon— you discovered this sad event?"

"It's not a sad event! It's nothing but a perfectly normal changeover. If you'd stop making the poor girl think she's turning into a monster, she might even survive it!"

Veritt paused, shocked at Rimon's vehemence. Drust was staring at both of them, wide-eyed.

Then Veritt said mildly, "Her survival is in God's hands now. We'll try to keep her comfortable, and we'll pray." He looked at Drust. "Come, Drust. Your prayers will help."

Veritt and the family stayed in the room, conducting their prayers, while Rimon waited outside in the main room. He wondered how long they'd inflict themselves on the poor girl. He could tell it wasn't going smoothly. He could feel Kadi's field swamped by the emotional vortex in the next room. Peevishly, he thought Kadi should be out here, shielding him.

He sat there for hours, ignored, alternately fighting down jealousy over Kadi, and magnanimously allowing her to help Vee. After all, the child was going through the worst experience of her life. If Kadi could help her, he had no right to take her away. He was only one day past turnover, perfectly capable of controlling himself. He was only being selfish.

Finally, it dawned on him that while he sulked the changeover had turned into a deathbed vigil. Suddenly shamed out of self-pity, he went into the bedroom.

No one had much to say. Vee had fallen into an exhausted sleep, pale and drawn. The Simes, who had shared Vee's pain and would suffer worse before it was over, all had the look of strain. Only Kadi seemed calm.

Vee moaned, her pain filling the room once more. Rimon felt the ache along his own arms as her new tentacles, still sealed in fluid-filled sheaths, went into spasm again. Kadi held her hands, pleading wearily, "Not yet, Vee. Don't clench your fists—"

"Has she been doing that all along?" asked Rimon.

"Yes, and I can't make her stop. She's worn herself out."

He picked up the feebly twitching arm. The field was depleted, and the membranes were still hard and thick over the wrist orifices. The tentacles themselves were immature. Another random spasm hit, and Rimon watched selyn drain uselessly away as the girl tensed against the pain. But he did detect a slight trickle of selyn tracing out the major nerves to the laterals.

"Wait! There's still a chance she might live!"

Drust lunged into the middle of the room. "She's dying?"

Veritt came to his feet. "What's the matter?"

Rimon turned on them, stunned. "You've been sitting here for hours, not knowing she's dying? I could zlin that outside!"

Veritt's eyes went to the bed. "Can you help her, Rimon?"

"I don't know. I don't really know that much about attending changeover. Who usually does it around here?" He looked around the room, wondering why they were leaving it to Kadi, a virtual stranger and a Gen.

"What do you mean?" asked Mr. Lassiter.

"Who specializes in assisting changeover, training the children for it?"

Veritt shrugged. "What can be done to assist changeover other than to submit to God's will?"

"You don't train your children? You don't lift a tentacle to help them! What are you, some kind of—of—lorsh?"

Veritt recoiled in horror. Rimon had always kept a civil tongue around the Fort Freedom people. He'd often thought the gutter language used in town went over their heads.

Veritt said, "I've never allowed one of our own to be abandoned in changeover. You have no reason to call me—*that*."

Vee moaned again, Kadi struggling to keep her from going rigid against the pain.

"I see it now," said Veritt, zlinning. "She's going to die without killing. Let us pray for God's mercy."

Rimon stood astounded as Veritt led them all in prayer, devoutly thanking their merciful God that this girl was dying. His eyes met Drust's, and the boy's pain became Rimon's own. What if Kadi had gone through changeover before him, and had been allowed to die? As the prayer ended, Drust said to Rimon, "But I want her to live—I don't care how, just to live."

Veritt came to Drust. "Nobody wants her to die, but we must accept God's will. She'll have lived a good life and died without killing. Who could ask more?"

"I can," said Drust defiantly. "I won't—"

Vee screamed, her whole body going rigid.

Rimon grabbed Vee's father and shoved him toward Drust and Veritt. "Get them out of here, and bring that Gen in. Mrs. Lassiter, get some water boiling—hurry." For a long moment she just stared at Rimon. He said, "If you really love your daughter—*move!*"

In seconds the room was cleared, and he was alone with Kadi and Vee. *Now what?* "Kadi? Do you remember what your mother used to soften the membranes?"

"They don't have anything—I asked. Rimon, I didn't realize she hadn't been trained at all. I didn't think—"

He sat down on the sweat-soaked bedding, wondering if Vee wouldn't have been better off out-Territory, hounded and beaten to death rather than loved to death. "Sometimes," he said to Kadi, "when we'd run out of creams in the winter, Marna used her own ronaplin to soften the membranes."

"That's right! I saw her do it once. But the child died."

"Well," said Rimon grimly, "ronaplin we have in abundance." He extended his laterals, flushed with the selyn-conducting secretion in sympathy with Vee's growing need. Vee stirred again, striving to extend her own tentacles. The membranes bulged, but didn't break. The contractions were premature and weak.

At that point, Mr. Lassiter arrived with the Gen Slina had sent over hours before. Despite the frontier operation she ran, Slina's Gens were always healthy and clean, though heavily drugged, as the Fort Freedom people preferred.

As Mrs. Lassiter came in with the hot water, Rimon said, "Hold the Gen over there until she's ready. Mrs. Lassiter, will you take my wife outside? Vee's going into breakout."

He turned back to Vee, dipping a towel into the hot water and applying the hot compresses to her arms, hoping to induce the swelling necessary to break the membranes naturally. As he let his field relax to normal, so that the Gen in the corner would seem more attractive to Vee, he kept the compresses hot and applied ronaplin to the membranes themselves.

Tossing and moaning, Vee became more frantic as moments went by. Rimon sensed the gathering contraction and put the wet towels aside, rolling the edge of the blanket up and thrusting it into her palms. As soon as the rough material touched her sensitized palms, the contraction hit, hard.

"That's it, now, Vee! Harder . . . harder this time. . . . Come on, you can do it!" Rimon coiled one tentacle around each of her elbows and ran it down her arm to her wrist as the contraction peaked, hoping to force the fluids she had against the membranes and break them open.

Her frustrated need grabbed at him. For a moment, he was shaken by an attack of killust. On the brink of attrition, Vee uttered a choked cry, convulsed by the worst breakout contractions Rimon had ever seen. And then in one bright, searing agony, the membranes tore open, releasing the new tentacles in a flood of warm fluids.

Panting, gasping out little stunned chuckles of pure amazement, Rimon and Vee clutched at each other. In those seconds, stolen from the flow of time, Rimon knew again the dizzy euphoria of Sime rebirth coupled with an odd yearning ache. In one moment of spinning reorientation it was gone, and Vee's long-deferred need exploded outward, commanding them both to killust.

Vee, blind now to ordinary senses, zeroed in on Rimon's field, laterals extended. Augmenting, fighting off the killust, Rimon avoided her grip and bounded across the room to grab the drugged Gen from Lassister's grip.

There was no understanding in the Gen's eyes, no fear in his nager, even when Rimon thrust him toward Vee. Her father came two steps after Rimon, and stopped, alternately piercing Rimon with his gaze and frowning at Vee's feeble groping for transfer grip. She could not raise herself from the bed.

Rimon slapped the Gen's face to try to rouse him from his drugged stupor. There was a flicker in the boy's eyes.

The nageric backlash from the slap hit Rimon like a shower of icy nails, and all at once the savage killust was back. The boy saw it in Rimon—and understood.

Rimon shoved the dull, throbbing selyn source toward Vee, forcibly retracting his own tentacles. He was augmenting, so it all seemed to happen in slow motion as he waited in anticipation of the kill. The Gen's fear peaked to terror as Vee's killbliss flooded Rimon, wakening his yearning to participate fully—*No! No!*

Abel Veritt loomed before Rimon's gaze, the last sight he saw as he blacked out. He came to seconds later, sagging in Veritt's arms as the older Sime was in the act of lowering him to the floor. A moment of sick, dizzy chaos hit him before the world steadied. It was over; the ambient nager had quieted. Rimon struggled to his feet, but couldn't seem to co-ordinate.

Veritt pushed Drust past them into the room, and then Lassiter followed them out onto the front porch. It was dark, the night crisp and cold with bright stars shining. Rimon gulped the air into his lungs, fighting strange, threatening sensations that swept through his body.

"That's it, Rimon, take it easy now," Veritt coached softly, as he walked Rimon around in circles.

"Did you zlin what he did?" Vee's father asked, amazed. "He used his own killust to rouse Vee from the brink of the grave, then to stir the Gen so she could fix on him— then he simply relinquished the Gen to her. Abel, anyone else would have killed that Gen himself, but Rimon just— just gave her away. And now there's no trace of killust in him!"

The two men looked at Rimon with something approaching awe.

"Well, what could I have done, let her die? In attrition? Is that what you do?" As the two men looked at him blankly, he gasped. "You worship a merciful God and that's the kind of mercy you practice? Letting kids die in First Need—for no reason at all?"

Veritt's eyes closed, his hands clasped in what Rimon had come to recognize not as a masochistic practice, but an attitude of prayer.

"The wisdom of the young often surpasses that of their

elders," said Veritt. "This is a lesson we must ever be learning. I will not offer the excuse of ignorance. I am guilty. I have sinned."

Taken aback, Rimon said, "I—I don't understand, N'vet?"

Veritt drew himself up straight. "I had two sons. I have a daughter, somewhere on the other side of the border. But my younger son was Sime . . . and died in changeover, as Vee might have died today, had you not saved her. We have rejoiced that it was God's will that our children die without having to kill. But it was not God's will, but our own! Rimon, you must teach us—you must help us."

There was such intensity in Veritt that Rimon had to take a step backward. "Abel, I swear we didn't know you didn't know."

"Will you teach us?"

"Of course I'll do what I can, but—there was nothing really wrong with Vee, except that she believed she had been cursed, and it almost killed her. All I could do for you, Abel, would be to teach your children that it isn't a curse to be Sime—or Gen either—any more than it's a blessing or a curse to be male or female."

Veritt sat down on the top step, heavy with age. Rimon joined him. Lassiter slipped quietly inside, leaving them alone. Veritt sighed. "Ah, but it is a curse to be Sime."

"Maybe it's merely that we're not strong enough to withstand God's blessings?"

Veritt looked aside at Rimon, startled. "The more I know of you, the more I am sure God sent you here for a purpose. But still I believe and must teach that it is a curse to become Sime, and be unable to resist the kill. Perhaps, when we see your children grow up in a house where a Sime lives without killing, perhaps then I can see it as a blessing too strong for a mortal to withstand. It's a new thought, Rimon. You shake the foundations of my faith."

"I'm sorry," said Rimon hastily.

"No, don't apologize. I feel renewed. It's almost as it was when I was young, riding with the Raiders—and suddenly, a whole new world was opened for me when I discovered we don't have to kill people. Tonight, I feel young again. I don't know yet where it will lead, but tonight I saw you in killust and now it's gone, yet you didn't kill. Perhaps, indeed, you'll teach us all not to kill."

It was a terrible responsibility. "What—what if I fail? What if—Abel, you saw. Kadi's pregnant. She'll be able to give me transfer again this month, but next month—the month after, at latest—she won't have enough selyn for me. Then I might hurt her—I suppose I might even kill her. I don't know."

"Are you certain, Rimon? Where did you learn all this?"

"I—I've grown up in-Territory. I've zlinned pregnant Gens. That's always the way it is; the field just bleeds away."

Rimon would never be able to follow Veritt's strange mode of thinking. He was surprised when the man suddenly turned to him, taking his hands, shaking with suppressed enthusiasm.

"Rimon, it's clear to me now! You'll take a Gen from the Pens, and you'll not kill, but use him again and again to supplement what Kadi can provide for you. You'll prove to all that Simes don't have to kill to live. When you can take selyn from any Gen—not just Kadi—and refrain from killing, then you'll be able to teach others."

"I hope so," said Rimon, "because there's nothing else that I can do—now."

"Son, I think I see now why God made me Sime," said Veritt. "Fort Freedom is here, not just to help the Simes fleeing across the border in despair, but to offer a welcome to you. You will teach us all not to kill. I *know* it, Rimon! Because of you, Rimon Farris, I will not die a killer!"

Chapter 11

WILLA

When the news of Kadi's pregnancy spread, the little sod house was inundated with gifts—mostly from the people of Fort Freedom, but a few from people in town. When Rimon protested, he was informed that everyone would be insulted if he refused the offerings. Milk and cheese arrived daily, along with warm blankets and winter clothing. One day Abel Veritt, Del Erick, and others helped Rimon build a cistern atop the hill, to catch rain and melting snow. They wouldn't have to carry water up the hill anymore.

Drust Fenell, expert at woodworking despite his youth, made Kadi a rocking chair. He had still not established— and now he was determined he was going to change over. Rimon was conducting classes in changeover training at Fort Freedom which, when they became known in town, softened the contempt toward the Fort people. It had been out of ignorance, not callousness, that they had let their children die in changeover.

But Rimon knew that if it hadn't been for Drust's infectious enthusiasm he wouldn't have had much success. The attitude of Fort Freedom's children was, "I won't require that training; I'm going to be Gen. My parents are *good* people."

But Drust was there at every meeting, as was Vee Lassiter, who wanted to learn how to teach others. She had emerged from her ritual seclusion wholly resigned to her fate. At first Rimon was puzzled at her swift reversal of attitude, but he soon found that her new calm was only on the surface. With the twisted theology of Fort Freedom, she just might suffer terrible guilt if by some fluke Drust should change over, feeling that he had cursed himself for love of her. On the other hand, should Drust establish, she'd lose him—and Rimon was sure she would be even more devastated by that. Either way, what kind of a teacher could she be?

When Rimon hesitantly discussed the problem with Abel Veritt, the older man replied, "It's in God's hands—but He may be working through you, Rimon. I can't imagine what is holding up Drust's establishment otherwise—the boy has looked Gen for almost a year."

"Drust isn't the problem, Vee is," said Rimon. "No matter what happens to Drust, she'll be destroyed by it. What can we do?"

"You are closer to God than I. You should know."

"I don't share your theology. I haven't yet caught onto the trick of reasoning inside it. But I do think you've misjudged my place in the world."

Veritt sighed, as if shouldering a tremendous burden. "Drust and Vee are in love. I'm sure you can understand that. You and Kadi shared the same kind of young love. Their situation is no different than yours was—only they have you to guide them. Or they will have, after this month, when you've tried out your method on another Gen and know how you do what you do. Then you can teach us—through Vee and Drust."

"Abel! You haven't put that idea into the boy's head—have you?"

"No! But I think you'll find he has already thought of it for himself. One scarcely has to be a prophet to see it."

Rimon let out a long breath, surprised that he was shaking.

"It's a terrible responsibility God has placed on you, Rimon. I don't envy your place. But my job is not easy, either. I've had to speak to Drust and will again, to remind him that at the first sign of establishment, he will be escorted to the border with our love. And I will enforce our law, if I must. But while I was speaking, in my heart I was praying that even if he were to leave tomorrow, within the month we could call him back. Rimon, I dream of the day when we send our next established child into Gen Territory, not to exile, but to bring our other children home!"

Rimon had to seize the older man by the shoulders and zlin him deeply to offend him into sensibility. "What if I can't do it? What if I kill again? Abel—it's bad enough if I kill a Gen this month. Must I be set up so that I kill your dream, too?"

"My dream?" asked Veritt mildly. "Isn't it yours, too?"

If they shared a dream, Veritt also insisted that they share the attempts to achieve it. He would not hear of Kadi accompanying Rimon to Slina's the next day, but came along himself. "You won't kill," he insisted, "and if you will allow me to zlin your transfer, perhaps I can learn how you do it."

What they both learned, though, was that Rimon was fixed on Kadi. He could not work up an interest in the Gen Slina gave him, even though he was in hard need and the boy was undrugged. Riding with the Gen before him on the way out toward the homestead, Rimon felt nothing but pity for the boy, who snuggled against him for warmth in the cold of early winter.

When Veritt reined in at a camping place along the road, Rimon pulled up, vaguely, wondering why the older man was stopping. Veritt got off his horse, saying, "No one else will stop here this time of day. Come on, son."

Unquestioning, Rimon dismounted, then lifted the boy down and walked him over to the ring of stones laid out as a fireplace. Veritt sat down carefully on the other side of the ring, and zlinned them. "I thought surely you'd fix on the Gen by now. It's still Kadi you want, isn't it?" At Rimon's helpless nod, he said, "Then you shouldn't be anywhere near her, or your desire for her could interfere with this transfer."

"Say it—I'll kill her, too!" Rimon flared.

"Easy," whispered Veritt. "That fear is all the more reason to do it here and now. Face the fear and end it."

"Yes," Rimon agreed listlessly. He faced the Gen. His body needed the boy's selyn, but he felt no real compulsion to attack. Taking the boy's hands, he looked into the empty eyes. When Rimon extended his handling tentacles, the boy looked down at the movement, and watched without fear.

Rimon slid his hands up the Gen's arms, settling his handling tentacles in transfer position. He let his laterals find the Gen skin, and slid effortlessly into hyperconsciousness, smoothly seeking the fifth contact point, still with no driving urge to kill. What would happen now? Would he simply hold contact, no selyn flowing?

But no, Rimon was low-field even compared to the dull Gen. Selyn began to flow into him. He let it come, neither satisfying nor enticing, warming a part of him.

It wasn't enough. Some subtle shift awakened true need, intil soaring, and he began to draw selyn. No pain, no fear—and no satisfaction. Craving the ecstatic pleasure he found with Kadi, Rimon increased his speed. The boy's nerves screamed with raw pain and Rimon basked in it until— *No! No! I won't!*

And suddenly it was as if he were healing someone. The shrieking drive to killbliss left him. Need was still there, but he was distant from it. By an act of will, he slowed his draw to a trickle. The boy's pain diminished. Rimon cut off the flow in that moment, severing his contact with the Gen in ripping agony.

Stomach heaving, he found himself hypoconscious, the limp Gen body on the ground before him.

I killed. I killed again. Oh, Kadi! Oh, no!

Off to one side, Veritt moved, disturbing the hairtrigger balance of the nager, and suddenly a burning pain spread in waves from some central point in Rimon's chest.

That was the last he knew as pain overtook him. "Kadi!"

"I'm here. It's all right, Rimon. You're all right."

Kadi was bending over him, her hands on his arms. He opened his eyes, and she was still there—trees—stones— *it's real.*

She pressed her lips to his, giving him the presence of her steady field to guide him in fighting the turmoil of his selyn system. There was a quiver of need within him at her touch, quickly silenced in the thick warm blanket of her nager.

Kadi and Abel Veritt put blankets over and under him. "Rest awhile," said Kadi. "Then we'll take you home."

"Kadi . . . I killed." Wretchedly, he forced out the confession, unable to look at her face.

She knelt and made him look at her. "No, Rimon—no, you didn't. The boy is alive, right here. See? Zlin him."

A few feet away, also wrapped in blankets, was a still form. But there was a faint Gen nager, fluttering.

"Bring him over here," said Rimon, struggling up to his elbows. "If I can't help, he'll die!"

Silently, Veritt brought the boy closer. The Gen's body temperature was way, way down. Veritt must have gone for Kadi, leaving them both here.

Rimon hesitated to touch the Gen. But even Kadi's field didn't entice him now. He brought himself into what had become known as his healing mode, reaching for nageric contact with the boy's cells. As he fumbled, the spark grew ever fainter until, quietly and without pain, the Gen body ceased producing selyn and in Rimon's loose grasp, gently died.

Veritt carefully took the boy away, saying, "You didn't kill him, Rimon."

"If I hadn't taken his selyn, he wouldn't be dead."

"But you didn't *kill*."

"What difference does that make?"

"It makes a great deal of difference," insisted Veritt, bringing them tea he had brewed over the fire that now danced in the circle of stones. "I zlinned the whole thing. You fought down killbliss and then—there at the end, you came back into that same state you use to heal people. Your field joined with the Gen's. You almost had it. Rimon, what if you'd done the whole thing in—in your healing mode?"

"I don't know."

"Yes, you do," said Kadi. "Next time I'll be there to help you, and you'll use your healing mode."

"Kadi," said Veritt, "perhaps I should have let Rimon come home to you today. I'm sorry."

"Someone had to zlin what happened, Abel," she replied. "I couldn't. But next time we'll *both* be there for Rimon. And next time, the Gen won't die."

A few days later, the first heavy snow of the winter fell. It was only a few inches, but it drifted to block the trails. Rimon went out only to feed the horses and the goat; the rest of the time he worked at filling in the chinks around the windows, where the chill wind crept through, while Kadi sewed on the flannel shirts she was making for both of them.

They could not afford glass for the windows, and so Rimon had covered them for the winter with wooden shutters. That made it dark inside, even in the middle of the day. It didn't bother Rimon much, as he could zlin by Kadi's nager inside the house, and if necessary even through the shutters. But by the second day, Kadi had to get out, snow or no snow. Rimon joined her, and they became children again, pelting each other with snowballs and laughing as they floundered in the drifts.

The next day, they had visitors. Del Erick arrived with little Owen before him on his horse. "The two kids together, shut up in the house, were driving Ana crazy," he explained. "Besides, Owen wanted to come along."

"Pa's gonna teach me to ride inna spring," Owen informed them. "Then I can have my own horse."

"Not till you know how to handle one," Del chided gently.

Each time he saw Del with Carlana's children, Rimon was amazed at how easily their friend had taken to instant fatherhood. Of course, he and Carlana would have their own child soon—about a month before Kadi was due. Rimon knew that that child was the result of post-syndrome after Del and Carlana had killed in the Wild Gen raid, but it didn't matter—the marriage was so clearly good for both of them.

When Del was ready to leave, Rimon and Kadi walked out to his horse with him. The snow was melting into slush. "The road's already clear through town," Del said, "but I wouldn't try to take a wagon over the hill trail for a few days yet. It looks like a hard winter coming. You'd better stock up."

"We have plenty of everything," said Rimon.

Del looked to him, then to Kadi, and back to Rimon. "I mean—Gens. A Gen, anyway, as soon as you can get to town to claim one. You don't want to be stuck out here, with just Kadi when . . ."

"Yeah," said Rimon. "Don't worry, Del. I'd never put Kadi in danger."

Del mounted, and Rimon handed Owen up to him. Del settled the sleeping child into a comfortable position. Watching, Rimon said, "You care for that boy as if he were your own, don't you?"

"He *is* my own," said Del. "He may be the only son I'll ever have. He's certainly all the son any man could want."

As Del rode away, Rimon and Kadi stood staring at one another. So it was that bad. "Kadi, I've got to get it right this month."

A few days later, Kadi went with Rimon to Slina's Pens. Slina was horrified. "Kadi, you get yourself all upset, you're gonna lose that baby!"

"I'm not upset, Slina."

"You're askin' for trouble. Rimon, I know you got only a little bit of a house. You got no place to keep a Gen so Kadi won't be always runnin' into 'im. Listen, I been in this business nigh fifteen years, an' I know better'n ever to take for my own kill a Gen I've nursed through sickness or injury, or one of my breeders that's got too old. They take on a kind of personality, and it spoils the kill."

"I know that, Slina. But I'm not going to kill this Gen."

Slina heaved a sigh, flicking a tentacle over the papers on her counter. "I dunno. You two sure are turnin' life upside-down." She shrugged. "You pay your taxes, you take your pick. That prime Farris-bred I was expectin' hasn't come in yet, though." Rimon felt the start run through Kadi, and her immediate control when Slina zlinned her.

Rimon shook his head firmly. "The same as last month for me. One you've raised. That boy didn't get scared until . . . until I hurt him. I'm not going to hurt this one."

Slina showed them to a holding room, bare and bleak, firmly shuttered but quite chilly. Yet it was clean, and so were the five Gens who sat on a bench, leaning against the wall. They didn't even look up as the customers were shown in, didn't notice that Kadi was Gen, too. Drugged.

"What do you give them?" Rimon asked.

"Metadine. Finest grade I can get my hands on. Keeps

'em easy to handle, but too numb to make trouble. Won't try to breed or nothin'—don't even fight."

"Yes, of course, or you couldn't put the males and females together like this."

"Yeah. The Fort Freedom people want 'em kept drugged right up to delivery. Most folks, though, want 'em alert. Metadine wears off overnight and don't make 'em sick. You want one of these, or—" She gestured toward the Pens.

Kadi had been looking over the five Gens, two males and three females. They all wore the same gray smocks, but they were clean and healthy. "We'll take this girl," she said.

Rimon controlled his astonishment, saying, "All right, Kadidid. I'll trust your judgment."

Slina started to say something, then merely sighed and plucked the girl from the bench. The Gen was Kadi's height, but built more solidly. She had dark blond hair and wide blue-green eyes in an otherwise plain face. She seemed sturdy, the kind of person you'd find on a pioneer homestead.

They took the girl home, fed her, and gave her a bedroll by the fire. The next morning, as promised, the drug had worn off. She looked around the house, but remained docile, obedient to the simplest commands, "Come," "Sit," like any trained dog.

She was Kadi's responsibility, as Rimon was in his last week's descent into need, and tried not to come near her without Kadi between them.

The second day, the girl began to follow Kadi around the house, out into the yard, down into the tunnels they had dug into the hill under their home. When Kadi handed her some jars of vegetables, she carried them up into the cabin and watched with interest as Kadi made a rich soup. She ate with relish, and Kadi told Rimon, who was pretending more than eating, "It's nice not to be the only one with an appetite in this house!"

"I hope we've stored enough to see both of you through the winter."

That set the tone for the next few days. Neither Rimon nor Kadi admitted aloud that anything could go wrong.

They spoke of the girl as a permanent addition to their household, and even gave her a name, Willa.

Abel Veritt arrived bright and early on the appointed day while Kadi and Willa were still breakfasting. Rimon was seated between them, at Kadi's insistence, nervously sipping tea.

Abel looked at the group, and said, "I'm just here to observe."

But something in his tone made Kadi ask, "Do you observe something already, Abel?"

"Yes! There's . . . there's some kind of connection between all three of you."

Rimon nodded. "I have the weirdest sensation that if the two of them were to walk away from me in opposite directions, I'd just melt away into a puddle on the floor."

Kadi said quietly, "Nobody's going to walk away from you, Rimon."

Willa was chasing the last of her cereal around the bowl, unable to capture it with her spoon. Finally, she dropped the spoon, lifted the bowl, and shoved the last bit into her mouth with her fingers.

"Willa, your table manners leave much to be desired," said Kadi, taking the bowl from her.

"Don't scold her," cautioned Rimon.

"No, not now," agreed Kadi. "Your lessons begin with lunch, young lady." She explained to Abel. "We've been careful not to do anything that might frighten her."

"I hope—I hope you'll be able to train her to be some help to you."

"She is already," said Rimon. "She follows Kadi around like a puppy and tries to imitate everything she does."

"She's like a child, Abel," said Kadi.

"Perhaps," replied Abel, but he was clearly more comfortable with Rimon's comparison.

They talked idly for a few minutes more, and then Kadi said, "Rimon, are you ready?"

"Not really—but I guess that's good. I should have some control."

"Come on, then."

They sat on the edge of the bed, ignoring Abel Veritt.

Kadi put Rimon between her and the girl, saying, "Willa, watch."

With Willa's attention on her, Kadi held out her hands to Rimon as she had done many times during the last few days, letting Rimon grasp her forearms with his handling tentacles. Kadi controlled her yearning to give him transfer herself, and just held steady. Rimon was trembling already. She smiled at him, projecting reassurance, and he steadied.

"There," said Kadi. "Can you go into your healing mode now?"

Barely breathing, Rimon nodded. He sought that strange state—and felt peace descend as he got it. Kadi let her confidence flow to him, and gently disengaged one hand, reaching for Willa's.

The girl's hand came eagerly into Kadi's, and did not resist being placed on Rimon's arm. When she had both Willa's arms gently circled by Rimon's handling tentacles, Kadi moved to kneel behind him, her hands on his shoulders. He leaned back against her for a moment, gathering strength, then began to speak soothingly to Willa.

His laterals licked over the girl's forearms. She looked down at the sensation, then up at Kadi, who nodded reassurance as Rimon murmured, "Good girl, that's the way, keep steady. No one's going to hurt you. . . ."

Confidence seemed to soak through him, and he drew Willa into lip contact. He took selyn easily, steadily, without pain. There was none of the intense satisfaction he felt with Kadi, but neither was there the agony of the kill. There was nothing but a solid, steady flow. When he had drawn as much as he could, he disengaged. Willa stared at him uncomprehendingly.

She's alive!

The thought was echoed in Kadi's nager. "You did it!" she cried, hugging Rimon, and then hugging Willa.

Abel came to take the girl from her arms, saying, "Our prayers have truly been answered, and nothing will ever be the same again!" He moved the girl near the fire and began to pray.

But Rimon remained on the edge of the bed, feeling as he had never felt in his life. When Kadi moved away from him, he gasped in anguish. "Kadi! Something's wrong! I'm still in need."

Kadi rushed back to his side. "Didn't you do it?" She reached out to him, letting him take her in transfer position. For one moment there was a delicious sensation of flow, but then he recalled that he dared not take her selyn. Besides, he had Willa's, if he could just reach it. . . . As he thought that, the strange imbalance within him seemed to shift. Life poured back into his depleted nerves.

"What happened?" asked Kadi when he released her.

"I don't know! I was . . . full of selyn, and yet—I couldn't use it! Then you somehow released it into my system. That doesn't make sense! Abel, you were zlinning me. What happened?"

"You drew from Kadi at first, I think, but then—everything shimmered—I can't explain it, and I couldn't even try to do it."

Kadi moved to serve tea and get Rimon something to eat while the two men discussed what had happened. As they all sat down around the table again, Veritt said, "I—ah, guess I'd better be leaving now."

"Not yet, Abel," said Rimon, and the older man took a place opposite them, accepting a slice of fruit bread. He turned to Kadi and said, "I couldn't even begin to describe what you did, either. How in all God's creation did you learn that?"

"I've been doing that for Rimon since I was a child. Before I established, Rimon used to have a terrible time after every kill, and I just sort of learned how to help him."

Abel tilted his head to one side, studying Rimon. "You know—I tend to forget that you ever killed. Now that you've proved that you'll never have to again—are you willing to talk about why you've been so desperate to learn not to?"

"Uh—some other time?" Rimon said. "Abel, I'll tell you the whole story—but it's pretty sordid."

"It couldn't be worse than my life with the Raiders, son. And my people at Fort Freedom—many killed someone they loved. Is that it? You got caught in need, with a friend or relative who had established?"

"My cousin," admitted Rimon.

Zeth's ghost had been laid to rest long ago beside a waterfall, but Rimon still remembered how Simes used to fear him during need. What would Abel think?

"He didn't know he was Gen?" guessed Veritt.

"You don't understand," said Rimon slowly and deliberately. "Abel—my cousin was Sime. Zeth was Sime, Abel—not Gen. Sime. And I killed him in transfer. It was the best kill I ever had—until Kadi. You explain it. I can't." He waited for the older man's rejection until Abel digested that.

"Rimon, can't you see now that the shock you suffered was the same shock suffered by every new Sime who comes fleeing to us from Gen Territory? You killed one of your own kind—and so it seems to every Sime grown up among Gens. But you have used that terrible tragedy to teach yourself not to kill. Today is your great triumph. Look at this girl. Zlin her. She reads like a newly established child, yet she lives!"

"You're right, Abel," said Rimon, smiling at last. "Because of Zeth, Kadi is alive"—he reached over and squeezed her hand—"and now Willa is alive. I won't ever have to kill again."

"And others will follow. But," said Veritt, "I realize that first you must teach me how to go into healing mode."

"Yes," Rimon said. *He plans to be next.* "It really isn't as difficult as it looks once you get the trick of it."

"Rimon," said Kadi, "you ought to rest a little before you take off on a new project."

Veritt rose to go immediately. "I don't know why I'm intruding like this. I really should have left an hour ago." Then he laughed and said, "It's time we shared the good news. Why don't I take Willa on home with me, and you two come over this afternoon? We'll have a celebration in the chapel this evening—a new kind of welcoming ceremony instead of a Farewell—to thank God for allowing this next step on the road to freedom from the kill."

"Why don't we all go?" asked Rimon.

"Rimon!" Kadi said with annoyance. She projected sexual frustration, and Rimon started, turning astonished eyes on her.

When Abel had gone, taking an unwilling Willa, Rimon

said, "Kadi, you didn't have to broadcast *that* right in his face!"

"How else was I supposed to get through to you? Abel knew—that's why he kept trying to leave. Rimon, it's almost six weeks since you made love to me. Soon I'll be getting too fat and clumsy to have much interest . . . and it's not good for you to go too long without sex. Remember what your father always said?"

"Oh, terrific!" he snapped. "Now you want to make love to me as some sort of—therapy!"

"No. I want to celebrate! We've always celebrated life that way."

She moved close, her desire flowing into him. His anger evaporated.

Still, there was no urgency in Rimon. He let himself be carried on Kadi's desire, feeling love, gratitude, but no excitement. He made love to her with tender affection, making sure that she was satisfied; but he was not, nor did he want to be. He found it pleasant to give to her without seeking his own gratification—yet he knew he would never have thought of it had Kadi not provoked him.

When they lay together afterward, Kadi took his hand, running her fingers along his ventral sheaths, making the tentacles emerge. He felt her contentment in knowing she could do with him what she would. He snatched the tentacles back into their sheaths and sat up, his arms around his knees, closing her out.

He felt her momentary anger—and then the way she damped it, trying to get him back into her power.

"Stop that!" he snapped.

"What? What am I doing?"

"You're controlling me again! I can't live without you—but how can I live with you when I never know what you're really thinking?"

"Rimon—I have never lied to you."

"Your nager lies to me all the time! I know you're angry now— but you don't *feel* angry."

"Yes," she said, letting it show. "I am angry! You couldn't have asked more of today. It was absolutely perfect! Yet you're determined to be depressed. What's wrong with you? Why aren't you deliriously happy?"

"Because I couldn't do it alone. I had to have you there to straighten out my fields. I'm becoming more and more dependent on you. You've got the power now, haven't you, Kadi? I'm trapped. I acknowledge it. And it's poetic justice, after all."

"Rimon—what are you talking about?"

"Ever since—ever since there's been a Sime Territory, we've raised Gens, used them, controlled them. And now, the only way we can stop using them . . . is to let them use us."

"No, Rimon!"

"No? You've just used me, Kadi—used me as your sexual plaything. I felt no desire until you turned me on."

Uncertainty in her nager, she said, "I love you, Rimon. I thought you loved me."

"I do. Oh yes. It's just that I wonder if I ever had any choice in the matter?"

Chapter 12
♦
GROPING IN THE DARK

As their first winter on the homestead closed in around them, Kadi made an obvious effort to keep from controlling Rimon. Sleeting rain kept them housebound much of the time. Willa was becoming more and more of a help, her clumsiness slowly disappearing. She was a cheerful child, still eager to please as a puppy, ready to cry at a harsh word, but delighted with any praise or comfort.

They went to Fort Freedom often, traveling as much as the roads allowed, and now Willa giggled with delight when the wagon was harnessed, eager to go anywhere Rimon and Kadi went.

Abel could not achieve healing mode before he came into need again, and so resigned himself to another kill. "The last, may it be God's will."

The next day, when Rimon and Kadi came over as planned, they found him looking worn out instead of fulfilled.

"Abel, you tried to keep from killing," said Kadi as they warmed themselves before the fire.

"I had to try," he replied.

"But it spoiled the kill for you. Here, let me help you—" Automatically, she held out her hands to him.

But before she could touch the older man, Rimon leaped between them, a surge of fury driving him to shove her savagely back. She would have fallen into the fire had Willa not caught her, whimpering in terror. For one blazing moment, Rimon perceived a ravening Raider about to snatch his Gen. Under attack, Abel flicked into battle mode, and that goaded Rimon on.

Then the older man's nager froze, throbbing with bewil-

174

derment. "Rimon, I'm not going to take her! I'm not in need. Zlin me!"

The tension suddenly drained from Rimon. "Shidoni, Abel, I'm sorry! I don't know what made me do that!"

"It's all right," Abel said gently. "Nobody's going to take Kadi from you."

"Kadi!" He turned, stared. "Kadi, did I hurt you?"

"No, Rimon—you just startled me, that's all. If you don't want me to help Abel, then I won't. I'm sorry I upset you."

But he could feel the apology like gall in her throat. Then he couldn't zlin her emotion, but only the tight control she held on it. *Control. That means she's lying again.*

He turned. "Abel, I don't know what came over me. Of all the people in the world I can trust you to . . ." Unable to find words, he sat down dejectedly on the couch. "I—wonder if I'm going mad?"

"Of course not!" said Kadi, sitting beside him and putting her arm around his shoulders. But he could feel her uncertainty.

She looked to Abel for help, and he drew up a stool and sat cautiously before Rimon. "Son—look at me." Reluctantly, Rimon raised his eyes. "I know you didn't mean to attack me. I know you're upset because your actions seem irrational. But haven't you seen other Simes act irrationally when they haven't had satisfactory kills?"

"I've had—"

"No. Not for two months now. Willa—poor soulless creature. She can give you selyn, but not the caring Kadi gives you, that must take the place of killbliss. Two months without that—I don't know how you even survive it!"

"It started before I gave up Kadi's transfers," said Rimon. "You—you were there the first time I did something crazy. The night I attacked your son."

"Jord provoked you unforgivably."

"Rimon," said Kadi, "that's the night you discovered my pregnancy! Maybe as my body adjusts, it's affecting you!"

"That may be," Abel nodded. "We have much to learn."

"Yes," said Rimon, "and we'd better get started." Abel wasn't suffering the kind of wobbling imbalances Rimon usually suffered, but his nager was dulled. "You can't work in this condition, Abel. Let Kadi—"

"No," Abel said firmly.

"Why don't you try it with Willa?" Kadi suggested.

At the sound of her name, the girl got up from where she had been crouching before the fire and came to Kadi. She was calm now, as they had calmed down.

"Kadi's right," Rimon said eagerly. "Any Gen who's not scared can do it—even a child."

"I know," said Abel sadly. "I caught Drust Fenell doing it for Vee after her last kill and I didn't forbid it because of what you'd told me. But if she comes to depend on him, what will happen to Vee if Drust establishes and has to leave?"

"We're so close, Abel," said Kadi. "Surely Vee can live in hope until Drust can come home again."

He nodded. "I pray you are right—and we'll never learn if we don't try. Willa?"

He got up and turned to the girl, who smiled up at him. "Willa, I'm going to touch you—" He stopped in amazement as she placed her hands confidently on his out-stretched forearms.

"I've been working with her," Rimon explained. "We don't want her ever to be frightened if—if anyone should try to take her."

Abel said, "Good girl." Willa smiled again as he extended his tentacles. As soon as they were firmly in place, Willa leaned forward expectantly, and with almost awed reverence, Abel bent his head to press his lips to hers. When he released her, his tension seemed to have gone, and he put his arm around her shoulders and guided her to sit beside Kadi, repeating, "Good girl, Willa," as if to a trained housepet.

He sat down then in his armchair and was silent for a moment. "She doesn't feel like Kadi—and yet there is a difference from the Gens we take. It must be the drugs," he concluded and Rimon and Kadi didn't suggest otherwise.

"Where's Del?" asked Rimon. "He ought to be here by now."

"I'm sorry," said Abel. "I forgot to tell you. He had a chance to sell some horses over at Ardo Pass. Carlana wanted to come and observe for us, but she is pregnant, too, and I don't think she should be involved in these emotional matters."

Rimon agreed. "Who's going to do it, then?"

Since Rimon couldn't observe his own field from outside, he couldn't tell if Abel were imitating his healing mode, so Del had been joining them, trying to zlin the differences between their fields. The results were frustrating; both Del and Abel insisted that Rimon's field became obscured by a bright nageric haze when he went into healing mode.

Now Abel sat, fingers steepled. "Rimon, I know that you and my son have had your differences. Yet Jord has more sensitivity than anyone but you. Perhaps he can zlin through that haze."

Rimon asked tensely, "You've spoken to Jord about this?"

"He asked me—some time ago. And the point of conflict between my son and me is that he thinks I'm deluding myself in saying the Pen-grown Gens have no souls. Can you not see that his desire to learn not to kill is all the more sincere for his belief?"

Rimon nodded. "Then by all means, Abel, let's have Jord work with us."

For the first time, Jord Veritt did not look sullen. He was determinedly polite at first, and then as they began to work he became eager; no longer acting, but caught up in what they were doing.

"No, Father, it's still not right," he said as Abel tried once more to imitate Rimon. "You've got to—*to project* like a Gen. Can't you just—*project*—"

"Project! You keep saying that!" Abel moved away in frustration. "What do you mean, project!"

"I've always thought of *project*," offered Kadi, "as the opposite of *quell*."

"No," Rimon said, "it's more the opposite of *draw* in the special sense of selyn movement."

"I always thought it meant more like *discharge*," Jord said.

"No, that can't be!" said Rimon and Kadi together.

They laughed, and Rimon said, "We're trying to find words for something that can't be put into words—no existing words, anyway." And neither Abel nor Jord was a native speaker of Simelan.

"Well, *I* know what I mean! Just imitate Kadi's field." Jord was frustrated, too. He moved to stand beside his father, facing Kadi.

Abel frowned thoughtfully. "May I zlin you, Kadi?" But he was looking at Rimon. Tensing, Rimon nodded.

Veritt zlinned Kadi, and his field shifted. After a while, Jord said, "No, that's not it." Veritt paced away, working off tension again. He seemed ten years older.

"Father," said Jord hesitantly, "let me try it."

Abel started, and then said, "Why not? Rimon?"

"Sure. There's no sense in not letting anyone who wants to try it."

Determined, but not defiant, Jord came to sit where Abel had been, facing Rimon. Obviously, he had killed within the past three days. Remembering that when they'd first met, Jord had been approaching need, his cycle several days behind his father's, Rimon realized that if he was now ahead of Abel—had they aligned the day of the Wild Gen raid?—he must have a short cycle, like Rimon's. Syrus Farris also had a short cycle and extreme sensitivity—maybe the two went together.

Abel sat down across from them. "Anytime you're ready."

Rimon returned to healing mode, and waited. He felt Jord zlin him, and then make a determined effort that caused their fields to clash painfully. Gritting his teeth, he held steady as Jord's field distorted, flowed—and then meshed with his.

Abel rose, coming closer, tears welling up. "Jord!"

Jord snapped back to hypoconsciousness and faced his father in astonishment. Abel snatched him out of the chair and hugged him, crying, "You did it! Jord, my son. Oh, thank God, we can learn it." He was crying too hard to say more, and Jord was crying too, father and son in a painful reunion.

Then Abel said, "You're young, both of you—more flexible than I am. We must have Del try it, too."

Just then Jord sagged heavily against his father. Solicitously, Veritt guided him to a chair. Jord was shaking, sweat standing out on his skin. Kadi said, "Rimon used to react like that—remember the first time?"

"It gets easier with practice," said Rimon, "but I always feel exhausted right afterwards, especially when I'm really healing someone. It passes in a few seconds, though."

Several minutes passed, and Jord still sprawled in the chair, limp with overwhelming fatigue. "Don't you feel better, yet?" asked Abel anxiously.

"I'm all right now," said Jord. "I just don't want to move." But he sat up, looking toward Willa, who was playing with the fire tools.

"What is it?" asked Veritt.

"I just realized—if I can go into healing mode when I'm next in need, and hold it long enough—"

"You won't kill," said Abel. "Jord, forgive me. My son, I thought of you all these years as the symbol of my shame—but you're the greatest blessing God has yet granted to Fort Freedom. Can you forgive me for being so blind?"

Jord stared at his father for several seconds. Then he said, "When I was just through changeover, I used to dream of revenge for the way you treated me. Now I've had my revenge—I've done what you wanted most in all the world to learn. Only—Father, I wish you'd done it first."

Veritt looked away. "I think we both must pray."

The emotional intensity must have made Mrs. Veritt more curious than she could resist, for she came out of the kitchen, wiping her hands and inspecting them. Veritt told her the news, and then swept them all outside to ring the bell and announce to everyone that his son had learned one of Rimon's key techniques.

Drust Fenell and Vee Lassiter found one another in the crowd. As Veritt made his announcement, Vee's face lit, and she whispered something to Drust.

As the crowd adjourned to the chapel for prayers of thanksgiving and petitions that everyone might learn the healing mode as easily as Jord, Rimon worried about those two young people, so much as he and Kadi had been just a year ago.

Chapter 13

YEAR'S TURNING

Although plans were made for Rimon to work with the most sensitive of Fort Freedom's younger Simes, he was unable to get back again for the meeting because another blizzard struck, trapping them in their house for two days.

Their front door was blocked by a drift of snow up to the roof; the only way in and out was through the tunnel entrance at the bottom of the hill, where the wind through the wide pass kept the snow from piling deep. "It's a good thing the Wild Gens can't travel in this weather," said Rimon. "That trail in the snow tells the whole world exactly where we are."

The trail didn't remain for long, however; storm after storm came out of the mountains, piling new snow on the old. Days became weeks, and it was as if Rimon, Kadi, and Willa were the only people in the world.

Rimon's second transfer with Willa went easily, though again Kadi had to help him balance his fields afterwards. "Next month, I'll see if I can use Willa to complete the job," he said.

"I don't mind helping you, Rimon," Kadi said. "I miss being able to give you transfer."

"Kadi—there was a flow again—and you can't afford to lose any selyn later—in the last months of pregnancy. So by then, I must learn to do it without your help—for the baby."

After that, it seemed Kadi made less effort to control him, and Rimon felt much better. When the snow let up, he congratulated himself—in the whole time he'd been confined with Kadi and Willa, he'd managed not to lash out irrationally at either one of them.

The clearing roads made him wonder what was happening at Fort Freedom—would he find that Jord, too, had managed transfer without killing? In hopes of finding progress had been made without him, Rimon decided to ride over there. Kadi wanted to go, but he didn't want her riding horseback as her pregnancy advanced, and Willa hadn't yet learned to ride.

He was glad he'd gone alone when he found both Abel and Jord haggard and upset. Jord had tried a healing-mode transfer and failed; Abel was still failing to achieve healing mode at all. Rimon didn't stay long; although the Veritts were polite, he sensed they were holding back from him, trying to cover something—probably the same resentment he felt from everyone else in Fort Freedom.

As he rode home, he wondered if he should ever go back. All he'd done was cause misery. Depressed, he yearned for Kadi's sweet, comforting field.

As he approached their house, however, he sensed something wrong in a strange tangle of fields within the house. Without conscious intent, he slipped into hunting mode, every sense alert. He tethered his horse and approached on foot.

There were three fields in the house. Willa's he recognized, alone, neither frightened nor concerned. The fearsome anomaly was Kadi's field, inextricably twined with that of another Sime, a bottomless black need—

He's going to take her!

In full killmode rage, he flung open the door. Hyperconscious, he felt as if the other Sime was pulling selyn from Rimon through his touch on Kadi. He had to stop it —do anything to stop it.

Rimon attacked, the world slowing around him as he leaped across the table at the other Sime. But the other eluded his grasp. Gen fear soared all around him, goading him to hunting frenzy.

He drove the Sime back against the wall—and suddenly found himself staring into the brown eyes of Del Erick. And Del, also abruptly duoconscious, was staring back, poised on the edge of the irrevocable act.

Their fields joined intimately, Rimon felt the other's activated killust focused deep in his own body. One flicker would unleash Sime violence upon them both.

Rimon knew he had to do something, but all he could think to do was go into healing mode. It was hard—harder than it had ever been, but when his systems were re-aligned, Del shuddered, and said, barely breathing, "Don't move, Rimon, or I'll—"

He's fixed on me as if I were a Gen!

In a moment's insane inspiration, he thought, *Then I'll be Gen for him!* Summoning all his memories of Kadi's soothing need-to-give, he imagined that he was Kadi. He felt his own fields expand, pulsing outward in gradually increasing intensity like a Gen's, masking his own personal selyn consumption.

Del's eyes closed, tension lines smoothed out of his face, and then he slumped against Rimon. Rimon caught him and scooped him into a chair, collapsing wearily beside him, his fields returning to normal. He felt as exhausted as he had the first time he'd tried healing mode.

Gradually, it came to him that he'd done it again—only this time he'd nearly killed a close friend—poor Del, who had lived with this nightmare since Rimon's changeover. Dropping his head into his hands, Rimon said, "What's wrong with me! Can't I trust anyone?"

Del, still gasping and shuddering, said, "Rimon, maybe nothing's wrong with you. I might have tried to take her— I wanted to."

"I wouldn't have let you," protested Kadi.

"Maybe," said Del, "but *I* couldn't feel that. Rimon, don't you see, you've been behaving just as if you were fixed on Kadi for a kill, permanently fixed on her, not just when you're in hard need. You've never had to face down another Sime trying to cut you out of a kill, or you'd recognize the feeling. But we should have understood. I'm sorry . . ."

Rimon examined Kadi's nager. "Abel says I'm just acting as if I'm in need all the time. But I think you've got it."

"If everyone understands that," said Del, "especially Kadi, you won't have any more trouble."

The short winter day was drawing into night, and Del took his leave—still in need, Rimon noted, and facing his next kill with the same agony Rimon had lived with for four years until Kadi had delivered him from it.

Alone with his two Gens, Rimon felt himself relaxing almost against his will. His Gens made him feel safe somehow—safe from all the horrors only a Sime could know. *But I'm paying for it,* he thought. *I'm more and more in her power every day. But I'll get used to it. I've got to.*

Over dinner, he told Kadi about Abel and Jord's problems. "What have we started, Kadi? We're making all our friends sick, and nobody's any better off for it."

"Is that all Abel told you?" she asked, obviously not wanting to pursue that dead-end argument again.

"That's about all, except that Fort Freedom is preparing for some kind of annual celebration. I didn't quite understand it all, but I gather it's some out-Territory custom. Simes would never think of celebrating by eating—feasting, they call it. Eating with religious connotations. We're invited."

"Hmmm," said Kadi. "Following his own customs, Abel has kept his people on a regimen very like your father's. And look at him—despite having been a Raider, he's strong and healthy for his age."

That week there was no snow, just cold, crisp days and clear starlit nights. Rimon, Kadi, and Willa bundled up warmly and drove over to Fort Freedom the day before the festivities began. They stayed in Carlana's house, which had remained empty since she'd married Del.

Rimon had protested at first that Del and Carlana would want to use the house, but they insisted they lived close enough to ride in each day. It was a major project for Rimon and Kadi to move—Rimon drove their spare horses over to join Del's herd, while the goat was installed in the back yard, happily cropping the remains of the garden.

Kadi laughed. "You think it's bad now? In a few years— if we want to go away for a few days, we'll have to pack up not only horses and a goat, and Willa, but three or four kids, some cows, a dog and some cats—and maybe Willa's husband and children!"

They were sitting on a bench by the fire. Willa was lying on the hearth rug, staring into the flames. "I don't think Willa will ever grow up enough to have a husband and children," said Rimon. "Pen-grown Simes rarely achieve normal lives—even those that were never drugged as heavily as Willa was."

"Give her time, Rimon," said Kadi. "She can't grow up overnight. Look at the progress she's made in the short time we've had her."

At least the girl was a help to Kadi, taking over all of the cleaning and much of the cooking. She had learned proper table manners, too—she wouldn't embarrass anyone at the feast.

If she never developed beyond where she was now, she'd probably never be unhappy with her lot. But if Willa came to understand herself as a woman and wanted a husband—where was she to find him?

"Perhaps we should get a male companion for Willa."

"Rimon, what are you thinking of? A male you brought from the Pens could only react as an animal—and a year from now there'd be a baby. They'd be stuck with one another even if they didn't like each other once they both grew up. Honestly, Rimon, sometimes you still think of Gens the way your father does."

He stared at her, his Kadi, so beautiful in the flickering firelight. Her blue eyes sparkled with animation. Duoconscious, he admired the way her pregnancy filled out her childish figure into womanly curves, while on the nageric level her field still outshone Willa's.

"Hey," he took her hand, "I'm still learning. Forgive me if I slip up sometimes?"

"Of course. I forget—it's only two months since you proved you could take transfer from any Gen without killing. It's only now you can drop your own defense against seeing Pen-grown Gens as people."

"You're saying I've been doing the same thing Abel does, only without the theological explanations?"

"Haven't you?"

He nodded. "There are Simes, and there are Gens . . . and there is Kadi. Abel and the others see their established children as I see you. But they must have their defenses until they learn—if they can learn—"

Kadi's nager became a soothing blank, her eyes suddenly sad.

"Kadi, what's wrong?"

"There's something I must tell you, Rimon—or you'll find out about it without preparation."

"What are you talking about?" Her nager gripped him.

"The day Del came to visit, when you were away. Del was so depressed. You see, during the snow, when no one could travel, Drust Fenell established."

He couldn't wait for her to say it. "Vee killed him."

Kadi nodded. "And herself."

Rimon was numb, suffocating. "Why did they let them try?"

"Nobody let them. They managed to get off alone—and—"

"Oh, Kadi, what have we done?" Rimon forced the words out in a harsh whisper. He felt as if he were struggling against an oppressive weight. "Kadi! Let me grieve!"

She gasped, and he felt her control slip away. Grief flooded through him then, but he was able to cry it out. She held him, crying too. Willa came over to them, worried, touching them, beginning to cry herself without understanding.

The feast was a difficult experience. Fort Freedom was divided into those who still saw Rimon and Kadi as hope for the future, and those who had become fearful of the pain they had brought.

Abel Veritt was showing his age more and more, and Jord was haggard. Mrs. Veritt hovered worriedly over them. Both the Lassiters and Sara Fenell avoided the Farrises, and Rimon felt too guilty to go up to them and offer condolences. Kadi, however, insisted, and so they made the attempt. The responses were cold, but Rimon felt better for trying.

Rimon helped to bring the trestle tables out of storage. There would be a prayer ceremony tonight, and then the chapel would be cleared of benches and the tables set up for the feast tomorrow. As he worked, Rimon felt resentment from some people, while others refused to come near him. Clearly, he and Kadi were no longer welcome.

But Abel said, "Tonight, in the chapel, I will make my vision clear to everyone. Be there, Rimon, with Kadi. Then, if you still feel you do not belong here, leave before the feast tomorrow."

In the chapel that evening, sitting with Del and Carlana, Rimon felt the tension all around them. First there were prayers of thanks that the small community had survived another year, that the crops had been good, and that five babies had been born and had survived.

When he lifted his head at the end of the prayer, Rimon felt the ambient nager shift toward indignation. After a moment, he realized they had expected thanks for all who had established.

Veritt stepped out from behind the lectern, and called, "Carlana Erick." Carlana left them, and at the front, Jord seated her on one of four chairs. "Miral Coyne." Another woman, heavily pregnant, moved forward and was seated beside Carlana. A third woman, also obviously pregnant, was called forth, and so Rimon was not at all surprised when Veritt called, "Kadi Farris."

Kadi stopped before him. "Abel, I will be pleased to have your blessing and your prayers for the health and safety of my child. But, if you're going to pray he'll be Gen, I can't participate."

Smug satisfaction filled the air around Rimon, then was shattered into disbelief and anger as Veritt replied, "No, Kadi, I shall not pray that any of these children be either Sime or Gen—only that they be born healthy."

A gasp went up, and then people began rising to leave, muttering indignantly. "Wait!" called Veritt, his powerful voice silencing the murmurs. "Hear me out before you condemn!"

Reluctantly, the people reseated themselves. "I promise," said Veritt, "if you cannot accept the new revelation God has granted me, I'll step down as your spiritual leader."

He returned to the lectern, placed his hands on the sides, and extended his handling tentacles.

This time the gasps of horror took the form of words: "Sacrilege!" "In God's Own House!" "How dare he?"

"I dare," Veritt answered them, "because I am a Sime. God made me a Sime." He lifted his right hand, tentacles spread. "God made my tentacles, as surely as He made the rest of me. I learned long ago not to question the will of

God. If it is wrong to question His will, is it not equally wrong to deny His gifts?"

"Gifts!" The exclamation stuttered from several points.

Veritt was silent for a moment, allowing the heat of emotion to die, retracting his tentacles and becoming once more the calm and pious leader they were used to. "Every one of you has had to change the beliefs he grew up with, in order to survive. In Gen Territory, you were taught that Simes have no souls."

Rimon felt the first melting around the edges of cold indignation.

"I have taught for twenty years that the Sime nature is a curse. But in this past year, God has seen fit to demonstrate to us that it's not our nature that is a curse, but what we do with it. He has sent among us a man—a Sime—who lives entirely without killing. Look at the girl seated to his left, a Gen from Slina's Pens—a Gen we would have taken for the kill had Rimon not chosen her—and here she sits, safe in the midst of Simes, not because she can protect herself, but because Rimon Farris protects her. Look at Rimon's wife, a Gen, who will bear his child this year. Kadi Farris is a miracle in herself, for she was able to keep Rimon from the kill until he could learn to take selyn from any Gen without killing. Rimon Farris is our hope for the future—and you would have me banish him from Fort Freedom?"

There was instant response from all sides. "He killed Drust and Vee!" "He's a devil sent to mislead us!" Others, though, cried out, "Rimon wasn't even here when Drust and Vee died!" "He's a healer!"

Veritt held up his hands—hands only—for silence. "Yes," he said, "there are those who recognize what Rimon has done already. Since he began changeover training, two of our children have come through, if not easily, certainly with far less pain than most of us knew." He added solemnly, "But it is true that two other young people died. We all loved Drust Fenell and Vee Lassiter. Yes, it was in my heart, as it was in all of yours, that they might have been the first among us to live as Rimon and Kadi Farris do. Had they waited, they might have succeeded. Do you think

Rimon learned what he does at his changeover? No—it took him *four years!*"

Another murmur—and the first hint of sympathy. Veritt seized upon it. "I have seen you looking at me, at my son, at Mr. Erick. I have heard you say that Rimon brings only death, pain, and illness to those who try to learn what he does. But it cannot be learned overnight—and is it not worth any amount of suffering to learn to live without killing?"

Before anyone could shout him down, Verrit raced on. "I've called these four women before you for our traditional prayers for those with child. They know they face the pain of childbirth—yet each one rejoices that she will bring a new life into the world. There will be pain in our learning not to kill, pain as inevitable as the pangs of childbirth—but will the results not be as well worth the suffering?

"Traditionally, we have prayed this night each year that the children in our midst establish, that the babies to be born grow up Gen. I submit we have blasphemed by asking for God to do our will, not His Own! Think. Count. God's will has been to make two out of every three of our children Sime—and often we have allowed them to die! Rimon has taught us to save them. Will you go back to letting your children die horribly—or will you pray with me and with Rimon and Kadi Farris, that when these children grow up, it will not matter if they are Gen or Sime?"

He turned back to the congregation. "If there's anyone here who in good conscience cannot pray with me, I ask you to leave. If you all leave, then I shall leave Fort Freedom. For I have sworn a vow that no matter how I may suffer, and no matter if it takes me the rest of my life, as God is my witness, I will not die a killer!"

There was a silence in the chapel. Then, at the back, a rustling as Sara Fenell stood. "Drust believed in this new vision of yours," she said, "and because he believed, he's dead. I can't accept that his death was God's will—it was a punishment to him and to me, for turning against God's Law. Now you'd have us believe it's not a curse to be Sime? If Vee were here, she'd tell you what a curse it is!"

With tears threatening to choke her voice, she said loudly, "I believe in the old ways, the true ways. Until you return to them and cast these demons out of our midst, I can no longer follow you."

Alone, head high, she walked toward the door. Dan Whelan, the blacksmith, rose, and with him a pale woman and a boy of about ten. As they followed Sara out, others got up and left—perhaps twenty people in all. The chapel door closed behind them, the heavy sound echoing in the silence.

Rimon looked back to Abel Veritt. He was staring at the door in stricken disbelief. Then Jord came up beside him, putting an arm about his father's shoulders. "All cannot accept the truth immediately," he said. Then, to the congregation, he said, "There will always be those who doubt. We must not condemn them. Once they see us fulfill our vows, they'll return."

Veritt straightened. "That is true. My son is right. We must pray even more for those who have left us tonight, for they have rejected the chance to be among the first to learn to live together, Sime and Gen. Come, then, let us pray for God's blessing upon us all."

Am I going to be responsible for destroying Fort Freedom, too? Rimon wondered. *Where will it end?*

Chapter 14

FIRST WORDS

After the scene in the chapel, the atmosphere in Fort Freedom was strained. The feast was held, as planned, but the absence of six families in so small a community was strongly felt. Even Willa, who enjoyed anything resembling a party, was subdued. Those who had walked out remained behind closed doors all day, with curtains drawn.

After the feast, Rimon and Kadi began preparations to return home. The temperature was dropping sharply, and even the well-built house they were staying in had only a small circle of warmth near the fire.

Del and Carlana spent the evening with them, and as frost formed on the windows, Del said, "That does it. You're coming home with us until the cold spell is over."

"Yes," agreed Carlana. "The cold this time of year is vicious."

"We've got a good house—" Rimon said.

"Sure," said Del, "but with the fire out, your walls will be *cold*. Besides, we can use three extra warm bodies at our place for a couple of days."

"People will gather in the tightest-built houses here in Fort Freedom," Carlana added. "Really—body heat makes a difference in this kind of weather."

Rimon knew his friends were avoiding mentioning the fact that their home was better built than his—especially that they had a wooden floor raised off the ground. Kadi and Willa would feel the cold more than the Simes—and, mostly for Kadi's sake, he agreed.

In the few months they'd been here, Del had expanded the simple cabin Rimon and Kadi had helped build into a three-room home with a loft where the children slept. The blue curtains Kadi had made still hung at the windows of the main room, but Carlana had added a couch with a yellow cover with two pillows of the same blue, and a braided rug on the floor of neutral browns and beiges with just a touch of blue and yellow.

There were double panes of glass in the windows—a real extravagance, but they kept out the cold. Another luxury was the stove. Not only did it heat the main room efficiently, but Carlana could cook on it more easily than over the open fire as Kadi had to do.

Rimon thought of his small store of cash, and the fact that the tax collector would turn up any day now—and this quarter he owed on both Kadi and Willa. No, he couldn't see how he could afford to buy even a stove, although, with two Gens to feed, and a baby on the way—it was a necessity.

The sense of challenge he'd felt last summer was gone. Then, roughing it in the warm weather, making it on his own where no one knew he was his father's son, had seemed exhilarating. The lack of ready money had seemed a minor inconvenience. But now, he looked at Kadi marveling at Carlana's stove, and the knowledge went through him. If he didn't have the money to provide for her, she could die from the cold.

The irony of it. The one thing Rimon knew was Gendealing. In nine months, he had claimed only two Gens. He could claim six more—but he could no longer sell a Gen like an animal, and if he kept them, he'd have to pay tax on them.

He reached turnover the second day at Del's, and both Del and Carlana began to treat him as if he were in hard need, never ever getting between him and Kadi.

Willa left her play with the children and attached herself to Rimon's side, his shadow, as Kadi spent most of her time with Carlana, or preparing meals.

The cold snap continued for four days. Only Rimon and Del went out at all, and then only to see that the animals were all right, hurrying back inside as soon as they could. The fourth evening, Del told Rimon, "Ana's using a lot of selyn—too much, too fast. And there's no telling what the weather will do next. Rimon—I've got to go to Slina's tomorrow—"

"Of course," said Rimon. "I'll help you, Del. If we each take a Gen on a horse, we'll be a lot warmer and faster than with a wagon."

Del studied him. "Thanks, Rimon. I hope the weather breaks before we need them, but—"

"But you can't take chances with your life, or Carlana's. I understand. Kadi understands. Willa is the only one who doesn't understand the kill, Del. If you or Carlana must kill before we leave, let's try to keep her from knowing about it."

Del nodded. "The children have never seen it, either. They'll grow up soon enough and have to learn, but for now—Rimon—how long can you shelter Willa?"

"Until she's had many transfers—so that if she does see a kill, she won't associate it with what she does for me."

Slina's Gens were the usual nonentities. Although Rimon held himself deliberately in check, he found they didn't even tempt him. Partly, he knew, it was the drug, but partly it was that they didn't seem to have what he wanted.

They took the Gens in through the back door to the small storeroom that shared a wall with the well-heated main room. When they emerged into the main room, though, Willa was at the side door, trying to see what they had brought.

"No, Willa," Rimon said firmly, closing the door.

Willa made a questioning noise, and pointed to the door. Owen and Jana left their toys to find out what was going on.

"No, Willa," Rimon repeated.

This time the sound she made had a demanding tone, and her nager said she was determined to satisfy her curiosity. He would have to distract her.

"Come on," he said, "let's play with the children. You're going to miss them when we go home, aren't you? But Kadi and I will soon have a baby for you to play with. You'll like that, won't you?"

He wondered how much Willa understood as she studied him, listening intently. When Rimon turned Willa and guided her back toward where the children had been playing, Jana scampered to her toys, picked up a doll, and said, "Willa, play baby!"

Rimon went to look at Carlana, who was asleep on the couch. Her field was still dropping too rapidly. Tomorrow she'd have to kill. "Kadi, I think we'd better leave tomorrow morning."

"Yes," she agreed. "I'd rather not be here when Carlana has to kill, but until then I can ease her somewhat. She's having a wretched time, but Mama always said that kind of misery would stop when the baby started to show. Carlana ought to be fine after tomorrow."

"I hope so," said Rimon, not telling her of the unhealthily bright anomaly in the Sime woman's field, where the baby was wasting selyn. He knew Del had noticed it, too, but had decided it was not a danger sign. Rimon was not so sure.

That night, Rimon lay beside Kadi, keeping her warm as the wind rose outside. He and Del were taking turns restoking the stove, but even though it was going full blast, Rimon felt cold. He realized after a while that the ambient nager carried the chill from the Gens out in the storeroom, even though they'd been given all the extra blankets.

Rimon got up and went to see if perhaps he could get a little more heat out of the stove. He'd have to help Del split some more logs before he left in the morning. Inserting one more log, Rimon knew Del hadn't even noticed the chilling of the ambient. *What makes me different?*

Restless, he went to the window, certain that he detected a change in the weather. When he saw the clouds boiling up from the horizon, he knew he'd known it all day—snow. Would they be able to get home before it hit?

He went back to lie beside Kadi, consoling himself that at least snow meant the temperature would rise. Soon he drifted into an uneasy sleep, drawn down and down by the collective Gen nager.

They woke to a white-blanketed world, knee-deep, the heavy sky warning of more on the way. Rimon helped Del shovel out to check the stock and bring in more wood, glad to get away from the tensions in the house. There was no question of their going home until the roads were clear again, and they all knew what that meant. *Maybe both Kadi and Willa can shield me from Carlana's actual killbliss.*

Kadi was making breakfast when they returned. Del frowned. "Carlana isn't up?"

Rimon detected Del's worry, but Kadi said, "Let her sleep. Sleep is the best medicine."

"Not at this time of month," Del replied.

"We've got four Gens in this house," said Rimon. "They had me sound asleep last night. Carlana's exhausted—small wonder if this nager keeps her asleep. It's good for her, Del."

Dubious, Del took two bowls of the cereal Kadi had made, stirred powder into them, then went into the back room. The food would drug the Gens again—thus the one Carlana must take today would be unresponsive.

Willa, who was sitting at the table between the children, stared after Del suspiciously. Then, as Kadi was dishing out cereal, she got up, slid Jana down the bench to sit beside her brother, and took Rimon's arm, guiding him to sit beside Jana. Curious, he allowed her to seat him. Then she poured him some tea, and finally sat down next to him and began to eat her cereal. Kadi watched the performance, and said, "Good girl, Willa. You're learning how to keep Rimon from feeling bad." Then she said to Rimon, "If Willa keeps on at this rate, soon she'll be as safe anywhere as I am."

Rimon stroked the back of Kadi's hand with one tentacle, letting their fields mesh. Vaguely, outside his concentration, he felt a painful disturbance, but he blocked it away.

Then the side door banged open. Del ran from the storeroom under a screaming burst of augmentation, darting into the bedroom. Rimon jumped to his feet, instantly realizing that the vague stirring of pain was in fact a blinding-hot lance.

The moment he left the shelter of Kadi and Willa's fields, he was fully immersed in the pain. He managed one staggering step and then doubled over with an aching cramp in his gut. Then Kadi was at his side, gasping, "What's wrong?"

He could breathe again. "Not me—Carlana!"

Feeling the fear rise in the childish nager of Owen and

Jana, Rimon added, "Willa—come with me. Kadi, take care of the children." He went toward the bedroom.

Kadi also started for the bedroom. "But Rimon—I've got to help her."

He caught her back. "No! I won't—I can't risk you, Kadi. Carlana's going to have to kill. Willa can't explain to the children—but she can help me."

Del appeared at the bedroom door. Rimon took two more steps, pulling Willa after him. Del said to the children, "It's a lot warmer outside today. Why don't you go out and play in the snow? Kadi will help you bundle up, but come right in if it starts to snow again."

Owen came over to Del. "Mama's sick. Pa, is she gonna die?"

"No!" said Del, too hastily. "No, Owen. Rimon is going to help her."

"Our dad died," said Owen. "Mr. Veritt couldn't help him. God couldn't help him. He died anyway."

Rimon could feel the conflict in Del as he sought a way to reassure the boy. "Owen, if God has a plan for us, it's so big that one person can never understand it all. I don't know why your father died, except that that left you and Jana and your mother for me to love. You know I love you, don't you? That, no matter what happens, I'll take care of you?"

Shocked, Rimon turned to protest Del's suggesting to the child that Carlana might die, but what he saw was Owen hugging Del, reassured that there was someone strong in his life. "Good," Del murmured. "Now you go play with Jana. She's too young to understand, so don't let her get scared. We're going to see that your mother gets well."

When the boy had gone, Del closed the door and turned to Rimon. "God's plan," he said bitterly. "Only God knows God's plan, and what comfort is that to a poor, scared kid?"

"Del," Carlana said wearily, "please don't."

"Ana," he came to her side, "just lie still. Rimon's going to help you."

Tears slid down her cheeks. "The baby is dying. *Our* baby. Oh, Del, I wanted it so much, even though—"

"Hush!" he said, his voice edged with emotion.

"Del, you've got to understand. I killed. And I enjoyed it! And then we—"

"We loved!" said Del. "We still love."

Through clenched teeth, she insisted, "I sinned!" And the pain grew again, sweat standing out on her forehead as her swollen belly rose visibly under the thin blanket. Del looked up at Rimon.

"Carlana," said Rimon, groping desperately for the right thing to say. "Think about what Abel Veritt said at the year-turning ceremony. God's will is to make two out of three children born at Fort Freedom Sime. Not a punishment, Carlana—just a fact of life that God leaves us to deal with . . . just as He leaves us to deal with something like this."

She smiled weakly and let her eyes close, gritting her teeth as the pain mounted and mounted.

Rimon sat on the edge of the bed, Willa behind him. He placed her hands on his shoulders and said, "Stay there, Willa." Her hands gripped him once and relaxed, as if to tell him she understood. Her field was steady, reassuring.

Duoconscious, he saw immediately the flaring consumption of selyn as the child within Carlana's womb fought against death. But the selyn consumption was sporadic. The tiny life Rimon now studied drew selyn from its mother's system in demanding gulps, but grew weaker even as Rimon watched.

Rimon looked up at Del. Lips tight, Del nodded. In a faint whisper, he said, "Save her, Rimon. If you can't save them both, save her."

I'm supposed to work miracles! But it was already hopeless for the baby. Carlana would be all right if she didn't bleed to death or die of attrition in the contractions. He let go of physical perceptions and dropped to the cellular level. He tried to surround that tiny life with his own field, as if he were Gen, but even that did not slow the mad consumption. Yet it did stop the drain on Carlana, so he held there, shuddering in the death agony of that small life as it flared, flickered, and finally went out.

When Rimon emerged to duoconsciousness, still in touch with Carlana but grasping for a partial respite from pain, she was crying softly, and holding tightly to Del's hands.

Willa's field was also filled with sadness, but she remained where she was. Rimon put his hands over hers for a moment, murmuring, "Good girl. You're doing just fine. Stay there, Willa. There's more to come."

It came almost immediately, as Carlana's body heaved with the last efforts to expel the dead fetus. The pains were not so sharp now, but they came more frequently. Again Carlana heaved, giving an open-throated, inarticulate moan. "Good, Carlana, once more should do it."

She nodded, drawing a deep breath, and, working with the next contraction, forced the dead tissue from her body. Rimon returned to the cellular level to control the wild loss of blood and selyn. As he had done with Risko, he used his own field as a tourniquet. It was easier now; his system no longer threatened to go into spasms as it had then.

Del let out one trembling breath, and Rimon knew he understood how close Carlana had come to death. Their eyes met, and Del, still in deep rapport with his wife, let go of one of her hands to reach over and grip Rimon's shoulder near Willa's fingers. Silently, he mouthed, "Thank you, Rimon." Rimon smiled weakly.

"Del, I'll bring one of the Gens. You finish this up."

As Rimon started to move, Del reached for the towels he'd brought and turned back the blanket. At the sudden sight of blood, Willa screamed.

Fear knifed through the girl's nager, throwing all three Simes into killmode.

Carlana, verging on attrition, made a reflexive lunge in Willa's direction, only her weakened condition preventing her from connecting. Willa fled in terror, and Rimon, his fields a throbbing tangle of agony, would have attacked her, but he was compelled by instinct to stand and fight off the other two Simes seeking the same prey.

The tiny instant it took for him to turn back and face off against Del and Carlana was enough to prompt déjà vu. This had happened before; but he had stopped it before, too. Yes—become Gen for them . . .

Carlana collapsed back onto the pillows. Del gasped, then stared in astonishment. "Shen, Rimon, you did it again!"

But he couldn't hold it. The wobble in his fields was

back, becoming a mad fluctuation. He was thrown into Carlana's desperate need, then back into that weird state of feeling like a Gen. Carlana moaned, and Del cringed. "Stop it!" he gasped. "Rimon, stop it! Kadi! Kadi!"

As Kadi tore the door open, Willa ran into her arms. Kadi thrust the girl behind her and came right up to Rimon. Her presence seemed to flicker from the physical to the nageric as the fluctuations inside him grew wilder—but he sensed no Gen fear now, only concern, covered with—

No! No, there was fear. Deep under the surface calm. Rimon could sense the core of fear, bright and hard and beckoning. He had no will to resist. It would slake the pain, the constant torment that had been nagging at him for months.

He stalked the retreating source of selyn, hyperconscious, wild with need and ready to kill. It backed away from him, toward the other source of selyn—but that first one had become dull beside the one he sought.

He could feel the swirling emotions in the Gen. He was zlinning deeper than ever before, through the calm to the barely controlled panic underneath. He recognized the protectiveness now—not of him, but of the second life within the primary field.

Something made him want to stop and think at that. Second life? But just then another Sime in need moved toward him. He turned his head, feeling a growl rise in his throat, warning off the threat to his prey. Then he reached toward the source of selyn, tentacles extending—to find the calm back in the field.

Conflicting tensions tore him—he wanted to take that throbbing field, pulsing in rhythm with his own, so clearly marked as *his*—and at the same time he wanted to let his need be quelled by the promise of sweet fulfillment. As he hesitated, he felt hope flare in that welcoming field—hope, relief—

He dropped to duoconsciousness and saw Kadi before him, calm on the surface, murmuring, "Come on, Rimon—you can do it!" She was controlling him again!

"Hypocrite!" he spat, zlinning through that shell of calm to the panic beneath, deliciously roused by his word. He took another menacing step toward her, deliberately toying with her as prey to be terrified before the kill.

The inviting field before him froze, shifted, and rang with denial. She would refuse him. The threat of shen lanced through his hypertense nerves, and with a snarl of pure Sime anger he lunged for her, driven to strip away her selyn against the potent pain/pleasure of her resistance. The best kill ever!

Willa sprang between them, pushing at Rimon, shouting, "No, Rimon!" The words were slurred, but intelligible. "No—no!"

With a negligent flick of one hand he thrust her aside, focusing wholly on Kadi. But Willa bounced back between them, insisting, "No! No! No!"

His hands came to her forearms to thrust her away, but Willa's automatic response was to grasp his arms in return, her fingers right over his lateral transport nerves but grasping hard, trying to push him back. With that searing pain, Rimon gave one scream and fell into blackness.

He came to in that same state of paralysis he had been in the first time Kadi had given him transfer. He felt her hands moving gently over his tentacle sheaths, assessing the damage and at the same time easing his pain. As he tried to move, his awareness spread to Willa, kneeling beside Kadi in the same kind of concern, to Del, his concern obscured by his need and worry over Carlana, watching them, zlinning to be sure Rimon was alive, then edging purposefully past them.

Then Kadi's fingers pressed gently on Rimon's lateral extensor nerves. The delicate tentacles emerged on a wave of pain, releasing Rimon's paralysis as he sat bolt upright, crying out.

Relief flooded Kadi's field when he moved. Even though he had to clutch at his arms, his teeth grinding together to keep from moaning, it penetrated his misery that she had been afraid he was dead.

Kadi held out her hands to him, now nothing but sincerity in her field. "Take transfer, Rimon, if you must—"

"No!" he gasped. "No. The baby—" He doubled over again, shivering uncontrollably.

She recognized the problem. "Let me balance your fields."

"Yesss," he agreed, but couldn't pull his arms apart to reach for her.

As Kadi tried to take his hands, he realized why he dared not touch her. "No," he said raggedly. "Can't do it, Kadi. Want you too much."

"Let me give you transfer, then," she said. She had given up the protectiveness of the child within her in her fear for Rimon's life and sanity. She was making him need her, and he wanted to take her so badly.

He was drifting from duoconsciousness to hyperconsciousness and back. "No control," he gasped, staggering to his feet to escape Kadi. "Dying for you." He sank to his knees, feeling the fluctuations growing stronger, moving toward convulsions.

Kadi moved after him, not understanding. "Then take me, Rimon. I can't let you die."

"Kadi—no—the baby—"

Willa suddenly came to Rimon's rescue, pulling Kadi's hands away from Rimon's. "Willa," she announced, holding out her hands to him. And he felt in her field a reflection of Kadi's need to give.

But Kadi's field, her yearning, outshone Willa's, drawing him against all the control he could muster. He was fixed on her. "Kadi, stop—please. Please."

Don't do this to me, Kadi!

But it was his choice. Need compelled him, yet if he could just let Kadi balance his fields, he could control the need.

No—he woudn't be able to resist. He felt his tentacles reaching toward Kadi, even as he shook his head in denial. Kadi quelled her yearning to respond, and somehow, Rimon was able to drag his attention away from her, toward Willa. As he turned to the girl, he felt one momentary pang of jealousy from Kadi—and then she was so firm in her conviction that he could almost read her thought. *Not what we want. What is right.*

He dragged his gaze from Kadi's and grasped Willa. It was over in seconds. As Rimon withdrew his lips from Willa's, he began to cry in dry, heaving sobs. The girl put her arms around him, patting his back. "Good girl, Rimon," she said.

The relief in Kadi's laughter was amost hysterical as she said, "No, Willa—*you* are a good girl. Rimon is a man."

It had happened so fast that Del was just whisking the drugged Gen into Carlana's room. Willa turned curiously at the sound of the closing door, but Kadi held her. "Willa, come," she said, getting to her feet. "Make tea."

"Tea," said Willa, looking over her shoulder at the bedroom door.

Kadi turned to Rimon. "You did the right thing," she told him. "Oh, Rimon, everything's going to be fine now." She released the girl to hold Rimon. "And Willa—" She tensed. "Willa, no! Come here."

Rimon saw Willa edging toward the bedroom door. With a flicker of augmentation, he was at her side, pulling her back. The girl resisted stubbornly. Kadi met Rimon halfway, but even with two Gens supporting him, he felt the shock of Carlana's kill. When it was over, he wilted with exhaustion and stumbled to the couch. Willa pulled a blanket over Rimon, patting it into place, and said, "Willa make tea."

Rimon gathered himself and stared at her.

"Yes," said Kadi, "she's started talking, and we didn't even notice."

Rimon began to laugh—laughing because it had all become too painful to cry about. Willa was already heading for the kettle as the bedroom door opened. Kadi signaled Del to wait, and quickly bundled Willa up and shoved her feet into boots.

"Go out and bring the children in, Willa. Bring the children, then make tea." She gave the girl a hug. "Oh, Willa, this should be your celebration. We'll have a party for you tomorrow. Now go get Owen and Jana. They'll be cold, so you make tea for them. All right?"

Willa pulled the door open. "Then make tea," she repeated.

"Right," said Kadi. "Good girl, Willa." She shut the door and went back to Rimon. "Come on, Rimon," she said, trying to get him to sit up. "Let's go up to the loft where we'll be out of the way of the children."

But he knew what she wanted him out of the way of. Del came out of the bedroom, carrying a still form wrapped in a blanket. Rimon followed him with his eyes until the store-room door closed behind him. He continued to sit on the couch and stare listlessly at the closed door.

Willa came back with the children and Del came to help. The aroma of trin and toasted bread filled the room, and there were the sounds of the family at the table, Del's low murmur hushing the children so that Carlana and Rimon could rest.

And then Willa's blurred but recognizable words: "No, no, Jana!"

Del said, "Jana, don't take Willa's—" He broke off and added hoarsely, "—oh—my—God!"

Rimon sat up, staring in the direction of the table. Kadi knelt beside him. "Don't worry, Rimon—Del wouldn't— Willa's all right."

"Del—" He looked at Kadi then, and forced himself to look away from her, to the group around the table.

Del was staring at Willa as she traded little pieces of honeyed toast with Jana and Owen, getting the sticky honey all over the table and their clothing. Del's face was pale. As they watched, he turned to meet their eyes.

Rimon looked up at Del, and said, "I didn't know. I didn't know it would happen like that. Please believe me, Del, when I asked you to come along out here—I didn't know what I was doing."

"None of us did. How could we?"

"It's all my fault! Everyone I touch—you, and Billy, Carlana, Abel, Drust, Vee—but most of all you, Kadi. Oh, why do I have to love you so? It's going to kill you!"

Del didn't understand Rimon's outburst.

Rimon just shook his head, his eyes locked with Del's. "Willa can talk—just like Billy." Del came over to Rimon, nodding, and Rimon continued. "Every time, Del—every single time you zlin a Pen Gen you'll be zlinning Billy. How many more times can you do it, Del?"

Del just shook his head.

"So I've killed you, too. And Carlana—she doesn't know Willa can talk yet, but what will she—and Fort Freedom

—make of that? And you, Kadi—I've killed you—because I couldn't learn control and when you die, I can't live."

"Rimon, you've just proved you can take selyn from any Gen, use any Gen as you use me. So I'm going to live, and so is the baby."

He said bitterly, "You're still a child! I never gave you a chance to grow up—before we made love—oh, Kadi, that was so wrong. Dad always waited a year before breeding a female Gen—"

"I am not one of your father's breeding Gens!"

"No! Oh, no, you're not that—but physically, Kadi, you weren't ready. I forced myself on you—and then didn't even watch for your fertility. Every time we had transfer, I lost control completely—like an animal in rut!" His eyes flashed to Del. "That's not normal any more than complete impotence is! Is that the kind of life you want, Del?"

"Rimon!" Kadi interrupted. "Don't say such things! You'll feel differently as soon as we can have transfer."

"We won't," he said desperately. "I see it now—oh, I see it all now. Why didn't he tell me? Why? Because you're just a Gen?"

"Who?" asked Del.

"Dad," said Rimon. "Zlin her," he said with a commanding gesture of one tentacle. "Zlin how the baby is draining her." He turned to Kadi, infinitely relieved to say it aloud. "I've killed you as surely as if I'd drained away your selyn that day at the border. My child is draining you—oh, why didn't I *think?* Farris men kill their women. My mother died giving birth to me. Zeth's mother died at his birth—you remember, that's why he came to live with us after Uncle Ryin died. Grandpa died when I was seven—but where was Grandma? She must have died at Ryin's birth."

"You don't know that, Rimon."

"Why don't they remarry? Dad, Grandpa, Uncle Ryin—none of them ever took a second wife. Why? Farrises are rich—I've even been told we're attractive to women."

"You are," Kadi said. "You're also faithful."

"No. I see it now. Carrying a Farris baby drains a woman—the way you're being drained, Kadi. They couldn't watch that happen more than once—so they didn't remarry."

"Maybe," said Kadi, "Farris men are really meant to marry Gens who can manufacture enough selyn to bear their children. Didn't you say my selyn production is going up as the baby drains it away? How can you be sure I won't be able to match the baby's drain—after all, I've matched your demand, and you're no baby." She moved over to hug him close. "Don't you know by now, Rimon Farris, that we were made for each other?"

Chapter 15

HORNET'S NEST

It was three days before Rimon and Kadi could leave Del's home. By then Carlana was up and around, physically healed but still emotionally unsettled. Despite his approaching need, Rimon felt more stable now than he ever had before. Willa watched him, but didn't remain glued to his side.

To the children's delight, Willa's vocabulary increased rapidly. Soon she had garnered enough words to ask Kadi, "Why Carlana hurt?"

"She doesn't hurt anymore, Willa. She's going to be fine."

"No, no. In there." She pointed to the bedroom. "Why?" She rubbed her abdomen. "Why hurt?"

"She lost her baby, Willa."

"Baby?" Willa looked over at Jana with a puzzled frown. Clearly, she could make no connection between what she had seen Carlana go through and the little girl who had been used to teach her the word "baby."

Kadi tried, with words and gestures, to explain that babies grew inside their mothers. When she had Willa thoroughly confused, Carlana came to her rescue with a few well-chosen words. Afterwards, though, Kadi had to hold Carlana for nearly half an hour while the older woman cried helplessly. It was after Kadi left Carlana napping that Rimon realized he had felt sympathy, not jealousy, at the touch of another Sime on Kadi.

A few days after they got home, Rimon took transfer from Willa again, using her to balance his fields afterwards. He knew it bothered Kadi, not to help him at all, so as soon as he had thanked Willa and sent her to make tea, he put his arms around Kadi and said, "You know Willa can't satisfy me the way you can, Kadi. Even though she's

205

improving, look how short my cycle is—and it will be shorter still, because I'm taking her before she reaches full capacity each month."

"You'll have to have another Gen. You'll be able to alternate them," she said bleakly.

"No, I'll have to get along with only Willa until the tax collector finds his way through the snow. Then—you're right. I'll have to claim another Gen, and hope to find a way to pay the tax on her by the end of the next quarter."

"On *him*," insisted Kadi desolately. "Now that Willa is thinking and talking," she went on, "I think she can handle herself. We can watch them—there's certainly no privacy here as long as it's too cold to be outdoors!"

"Spring will come—and I don't think Willa understands much about sex. We treat her like a child, but a male Gen from the Pens wouldn't."

"All the more reason to get one now. Rimon—don't you realize that Willa is in love with you already?"

"You're not serious!" *Is that what's bothering her?*

"Right now it's a brotherly sort of thing, but if she doesn't have someone else to be attracted to when she's ready for romantic love, she's going to be badly hurt when you can't respond."

"But she's still just a child. I think you're blinded by your own lovely °madness. Of course, I'm delighted that you're in love with me, but that shouldn't make you think that other women would be!"

Two weeks later, however, they found that Kadi was at least partly right. They went over to Fort Freedom, where Willa's progress was shaking the foundations of many people's faith. As she learned and understood more, Willa's nager was assuming the characteristics that Abel Veritt had for twenty years associated with the "soul." This revelation increased the determination at Fort Freedom to learn not to kill—but the result was only more and more gaunt and haggard people suffering guilt after every kill.

That afternoon, Rimon and Jord were to teach the changeover class in the chapel while Kadi and Willa visited with Abel Veritt and his wife. When Rimon and Jord got up to leave for their class, Abel said, quietly, "Something has happened to you, Rimon."

Kadi said, "You're right, Abel. Rimon—you know those angry outbursts have stopped altogether. I hope they're gone forever!"

"I do, too," Rimon replied. "I—I think they are."

"It looks to me," said Abel, "as if you've passed a crisis —a period of adjustment. Perhaps the Sime system has to adapt to not killing. As others learn, we'll be aware of such symptoms, and help each other through that period."

"Abel, after all the disappointments, you sound more confident than ever that you'll learn not to kill."

"I have sworn it," the older man replied serenely. "This I know. God guided me to build this community, even though I misinterpreted some of His intentions. I'm not going to fall into the trap of trying to interpret the rest of His plan, but one thing I do know is that He will not let me be forsworn."

As he and Jord worked with the children in the chapel, Rimon blotted everything else out of awareness. Since the chapel was stone, it provided fairly good insulation, so he did not pick up the blazon of anger from outside until the door opened and Abel entered with his wife, Kadi, and Willa. Rimon and Jord both leaped up as the ambient nager struck them, but Veritt was closing the door, instructing, "Margid, you take care of the children—and keep Kadi and Willa safe. I don't think anyone will desecrate the chapel."

It was the first time Rimon had heard Mrs. Veritt's first name. His attention, however, was on the commotion outside. Peering through one of the narrow windows, he saw the crowd of dissenters who had walked out of the Year's Turning ceremony, led by Dan Whelan and Sara Fenell.

As Veritt went out to face the dissenters, Rimon watched Kadi, Willa, and Mrs. Veritt gather the children and take them out the back way. Then he and Jord looked at one another, and without a word went out to stand on either side of Abel. Thus Rimon couldn't do anything when Kadi and Willa returned to the chapel.

"When I taught that the Pen-Grown Gens had no souls,"

Veritt was saying, "I was honestly mistaken. Behold the miracle God has sent to show us His true intentions!"

Whelan shouted, "Keep the Devil's spawn away from us! Cast out this sorcerer from our midst—they have defiled our chapel!"

Somebody back in the crowd yelled, "Purify it with fire!"

Whelan shouted, "If we must do that—we will! But Abel Veritt can cast this evil out by a turn of heart. We must purify our hearts before we can cleanse our grounds! Abel," he continued, turning toward the veranda where Rimon and Jord flanked Veritt. "Seek God's help in casting out Rimon Farris and the cursed succubi he has brought among us!"

Other people were coming from their homes and gathering in a semicircle around the band of protesters, listening curiously.

Veritt held up his hands, tentacles sheathed. "Rimon Farris is a Sime who does not kill, who brings that hope to all of us, and he has shown us that we must all learn not to kill, because all Gens have souls."

There were angry shouts, quieted by Dan Whelan. "Abel, do you know who this misbegotten son of the Devil really is?" He pulled from under his coat a scroll of paper, and dramatically unrolled it into a poster, holding it up for all to see.

AUCTION

PRIME FARRIS GENS

FINEST WILD GENS

MOST SATISFYING DOMESTIC STOCK

PRIME KILLS!

The name "Farris" had been circled in red.

Rimon blanched. Abel and Jord merely looked puzzled.

Whelan, after displaying the poster, took a step toward Rimon. "Will you deny it? Gendealer! Raider! Will you deny you hunt across the border?"

"Where did you get that?" asked Abel.

"From Slina. She had it on her desk yesterday—said she

couldn't afford to attend that auction—the prices would be right off the map. Said only once in a while can she pick up one or two Gens of Farris stock. *Farris* stock, mind you!"

"*Rimon* Farris?" Abel challenged.

"She didn't say," Whelan admitted.

"It's a common enough name," said Veritt. "Let me see that!" Picking the poster out of Whelan's hands, Abel scanned it briefly and pointed to the fine print at the bottom. "*Syrus* Farris! What makes you think there's any connection?"

Sara Fenell stepped forward, half-facing the crowd so her voice would carry. "This Syrus Farris—Slina says he's so famous because he consorts with gypsies. He must use magic to produce these"—she spat out the words—"'prime Farris Gens!'"

"And if that were so—what is that to us?" asked Abel. "Rimon is no Gendealer. He doesn't even kill."

"But look what he's done to those two Gens—he's given them souls, Abel, *souls.* Isn't that what people call 'prime kill'—Gens who are real people! If that's how this Syrus Farris does it, then that's where Rimon Farris learned it! And all he's done for us has been to gain our confidence." She added defiantly, "Ask him, Abel. Ask him right here in front of all of us and see if he can lie. Zlin him and ask!"

As many of the Simes allowed themselves to become duoconscious, their eyes flicked first toward the spot where Kadi and Willa stood listening. Rimon felt Willa's vague anxiety, and Kadi's steady support.

"There is no necessity for you to answer this man's insults," said Abel. "We all know you, Rimon."

Bracing himself, knowing this time Abel would surely be repelled, and that it would hurt as badly as his own father's rejection, he said, "Abel, the truth is going to come out sometime, and better now than later. I grew up on a Genfarm. Syrus Farris is my father."

A gasp rose from the assembled Simes, not just the protesters in the center, but all those who had supported Abel Veritt and Rimon. Even Jord took a step away from Rimon, too shocked for words. Only Abel kept his composure and calmly imposed silence on his people again. That calm acceptance allowed Rimon to continue.

"I didn't mention it because I didn't think it was important. There's no magic involved. Any Gen, well treated and not drugged, develops rudimentary abilities. And apparently—if you treat them like people, they respond like people because they *are* people."

Veritt prompted, "You have left the life of a Gendealer behind you?"

"Forever!" Rimon said fervently.

"And your father?"

"He—wouldn't listen to me when I discovered I could live without killing. He—he threw me out."

Abel turned to the crowd. "There you have it. Can a man help what family he's born to? What more can you ask of him than that he change his ways when God reveals the right path? You accept me, although you know I've been a Freeband Raider. If you can accept my past, you can accept Rimon's past. Judge him for what he is today."

"My son died because he believed Rimon Farris," said Sara Fenell. "I pray Drust is in heaven, but I know Vee, whom he loved, whom I loved almost as if she were my own daughter, is in hell! Rimon Farris destroyed her *soul!* Will you let him destroy yours as well?"

Abel replied, "I can't think that God would condemn her for the result of her attempt to live without killing. The will of God is only slowly being revealed to us. Only in the past few weeks has He seen fit to reveal that I was wrong in one of my early teachings. Willa, please come out here!"

When Willa appeared, silence fell. Abel led her forward. "You all saw this girl among us at the Year's Turning. Rimon took her from Slina's Pens—if necessary, to convince you, he can bring her papers. I was witness the first time he took selyn from her—and did not hurt her at all! I've seen what it's cost him to learn to do this, yet he has never hurt her. Willa, you tell them. Has Rimon ever hurt you?"

"No," she answered. "Rimon never hurt me. He never will."

The onlookers were staring, openmouthed. Then Dan

Whelan said, "She *is* possessed! He's conjured up a demon to possess the body of this soulless Gen!"

"Gypsy sorcery!" cried Sara Fenell.

"Nonsense!" snapped Abel. "Willa is an innocent child, learning to talk only now because she's been drugged all her life. Willa," he asked, "do you believe in God?"

"God made the world," she replied—the way Rimon had defined God for her when she had insisted on knowing the meaning of the word she heard so often at Fort Freedom.

"You see?" said Veritt. "Already she understands that much. Come, speak with her. See for yourselves she's no demon!"

"She's a puppet, made to speak by that sorcerer!" cried Sara Fenell, real fear in her nager. "I'll not come near her!"

Whelan added, "Look at what's happening. This man arrives among us, promising to teach us not to kill—but how many have learned? Not one! He has lulled us with promises, yet no one except Rimon Farris—supposedly—can keep from killing. How do we know he doesn't hunt across the border—perhaps among our children? And what has he really taught us with his changeover classes? Just how to keep more Simes alive to kill and kill, and kill again!"

Abel Veritt, in a voice of calmest sanity, said, "Are you through?"

"Yes," replied Whelan, "through with these lies and sorcerer's tricks. These people stand with me. Who'll join us to drive this Farris and his demons from our midst!"

There was a tense moment during which no one stirred. Then Mr. and Mrs. Lassiter, Vee's parents, moved from the back of the crowd. Rimon's heart sank and Dan Whelan grinned in triumph as it appeared they would join the group of protesters. But they kept walking, on up onto the veranda, to stand beside Abel and Willa. Others followed, until there wasn't room on the porch and they lined up before it, facing the accusers.

It was Jord Veritt who broke the silence. "We stand for the hope of life against capitulation to superstition and death. We admit our mistakes, and we're going on to a better way of life, as my father once did, as Rimon did, as I'm prepared to do. Will you go to your death one day, knowing that you never even tried not to kill?"

"I'll go to my death knowing I followed God's true way, Jord Veritt," replied Sara Fenell. "I, for one, can't live where God's Law is thrown aside at the word of a conniving Gendealer who begets children on his own stock. When you can tell me you've stopped killing, Jord—you come talk to me then about standing for life!"

Again, she turned and led the group of dissenters from their midst, but it was a smaller group than before. Rimon saw that one family, a man and woman with two adolescent boys, had dropped back to join the group by the porch. They were welcomed with open arms. Then Abel led a prayer, and the crowd dispersed.

As they went back inside, Rimon said, "I should have told you earlier who I am, Abel."

Kadi said, "He just didn't want to ride on his father's fame, Abel; please believe that." Rimon was too ashamed to stop Kadi from making excuses for him. "If we had known what people would think, we'd have told you who we are."

"I know who you are," the older man replied. "It makes no difference who your father was, Rimon—" He broke off, astonished at his own words. "God chose to show me today how very wrong my teaching was on that point! Clearly, you are not what you are because of anything your father did."

"Abel—you do know I don't hunt across the border?"

"Son, I've been with you. I've zlinned your field, and Kadi's and Willa's. You've never been high-field, for no reason. Everybody in Fort Freedom knew that accusation was nonsense."

"And—you know I don't practice sorcery?"

"Sorcery?" He laughed. "Forgive me, but if you had magic at your command, you'd never have built a house to be burned down, and you'd not be struggling to pay your taxes. You'd harness a demon to—"

"What's a demon," asked Willa, interrupting.

"An evil being," Abel told her. "You're not evil, Willa. You're good."

She nodded, smiling. "Yes. I'm a good girl. I'm learning to count. Do you want to hear me?"

Abel listened patiently while Willa counted to five on the fingers of one hand.

"Very good," he said, and began to turn away from her.

"Can I count more when I get tentacles?" she asked.

It was the first time she'd spoken of noticing the difference between Simes and Gens. Kadi said, "Willa, you're a Gen, like me. You won't get tentacles."

"Why can't I have tentacles? Carlana has tentacles."

Well, thought Rimon, *she finally has male and female straight.* "Good question," said Rimon. "But you're a Gen, so you have no use for tentacles."

"I could do more."

"You do enough," Abel said. "You don't understand how much you do for us that you couldn't do if you had tentacles."

"I help," she agreed, and did not pursue the matter. Rimon was relieved that Willa accepted "because you're Gen" for the moment, but knew that he and Kadi would soon have to explain the difference between Sime and Gen to her—and transfer, too.

As Rimon considered the difficulty of explaining to Willa, he remembered his own introduction to the knowledge of the kill. Krazy Kids already at four years old, Rimon and Kadi had been caught by Syrus Farris in the loft of the holding barn, trying to see what went on in there when Wild Gens were brought in. Turning Kadi over to her own father, Farris had taken Rimon off with him for a lengthy but somewhat vague lecture. Rimon and Kadi, comparing notes afterward, found they'd been told the same story. "Well, Gens are just animals!" said Rimon.

"We don't kill animals," said Kadi. "Would you kill Kitty? Or one of the horses? I'm not going to do it."

"Kadi, we'll have to do it. Dad says you can't help it— it's the only way you grow up."

"Well," said Kadi, "maybe I won't grow up!"

Although their parents had spoken as if Rimon and Kadi were assured of growing up Sime, it had slowly come through to them that some children don't. Rimon was nine when that fact emerged from his subconscious in agonized nightmares—pale previews of those that tortured him after changeover.

But our son won't have nightmares! He hugged Kadi, sensing their growing child. She returned a flood of warm happiness, and again he wondered how closely she could follow his thoughts.

When they got home that evening, and Willa took off her coat, Kadi noticed blood on the back of the girl's skirt. Rimon busied himself on the other side of the room, glad to leave that problem to Kadi.

"Willa, you're growing up so fast," she began, trying to pass the event off as a good sign of normal maturity. "Let me show you what to do about—"

But when Willa saw the blood and realized where she was bleeding, she started to scream. Rimon dashed to help, but pulled himself to a halt as Kadi flung herself between him and the terrified girl.

"Willa, it's all right!" Kadi said. "It's normal. You're just growing up."

"Baby," sobbed Willa.

"No, no, Willa—it's because you're *not* having a baby." She looked up at Rimon, who was recovering from the discovery that Willa's terror had provoked nothing but sympathy in him. "What she saw, with Carlana," she explained.

"Of course," said Rimon. "Yes, Willa, you saw Carlana lose a baby. But it hurt her, remember? You don't hurt, do you?"

"No."

Kadi gave him a thankful smile, and cast about frantically for the right thing to say. Rimon admired her calmness—he would have expected her to be dying of embarrassment.

"Willa," she said finally, "what's happening to you is normal. It happens to every woman every month. It shows that you are not having a baby, Willa—but it shows that you can have one when you're ready."

"I can have a baby?"

"Yes, Willa, once you're grown up yourself."

"I want to have a baby, like you, Kadi."

Kadi came up with an answer Rimon had heard her

mother use. "You will have your own children, Willa, but first you have to practice and learn how to be a mother by helping me take care of my baby. You'll help me, won't you?"

For a moment, Rimon thought Willa was going to cry, having been denied what she wanted. Then, very solemnly, she nodded. "Willa helps." Then she had another thought. "How did you get your baby?"

Kadi said, "Rimon gave it to me."

Willa turned to Rimon, her eyes lit. "Will you give me a baby?"

"I can't, Willa."

"Why?"

"Because I'm Kadi's husband. Like Del is Carlana's husband. One day you will have a husband, and he will give you babies."

Kadi gave him a warm smile of gratitude. He winked at her, and went off to finish caring for the horses.

Later that night, however, after Willa was asleep, Rimon said to Kadi, "You realize that if I were on a normal schedule, today would be my turnover?"

"Your turnover was three days ago."

"Yes, but it should have been today."

"So?"

"Willa's cycle had adapted to mine. If she were married to a Sime whose need did not exceed her selyn production, her fertility would come at their transfers, as yours does at ours."

"You think she'll marry a Sime?"

"To any Sime who could face the prospect of marrying a Gen, she'd be practically irresistible."

"And Fort Freedom is full of Simes who could easily face the prospect," Kadi added. "Oh, Rimon—what hornet's nest will we stir up next?"

Chapter 16

WILLA'S DECISION

As it turned out, the next Gen to come to live with Rimon and Kadi didn't come from Slina's Pens. He was Jon Forester, whose parents brought him from Fort Freedom at his insistence. They were horrified when Rimon immediately took him to Slina's to have him tagged as a runaway he had "caught," but he left Kadi to explain the law to them. Once they understood that Rimon would have to pay to keep their son, they gave her the tax money for Jon for the quarter.

Alternating Jon and Willa, Rimon was able to get back to an almost normal cycle, although he still took all his transfers in healing mode, and afterward had to balance his fields. Kadi could help him less and less, for she tired easily, and that made her irritable and often snappish.

Rimon bore it all stoically, even when her lack of emotional stability set his teeth on edge. But he couldn't blame her for what her body chemistry did to her. He wondered, though, if her depression was the source of his own. He felt as if he were in chronic need from insufficient kills: restless, fretful, depressed and without much appetite. Yet he was getting enough selyn now.

In the late winter, too early for plowing or planting, there was no way Rimon could earn extra money. One time Del asked him to take a consignment of horses over to Birmington, and he did it even though they all knew Del could just as easily have taken them himself. What Del paid him made it possible to pay the first-quarter tax on Kadi.

With the spring, they learned another reason they had been laughed at for homesteading just here. Hoping to get work in the fields around Fort Freedom, Rimon plowed his own fields early, as soon as the ground could be worked. Thus he would be ready to plant as soon as the threat of frost was over—and if he were too busy, Jon and Willa could even do the planting.

Out-of-doors, working off his tensions, his temper, improved, and that made Kadi happier. But in the end, all his hard work went for naught: when the mountain snows melted, their little brook swelled to a raging torrent, overflowed its banks, and turned their fields into a lake. The place where they had built their first house was completely under water, the charred timbers scattered over the lake. At one point, the lower tunnel entrance was under water, and they had to move everything from the lowest storeroom where they'd huddled as the cabin burned.

During those days, Rimon spent a lot of his time on the top of their hill, surveying his fields, wondering if nature were trying to tell him something.

But when Abel Veritt arrived to survey the situation, he said, "It's mud now, but it's enriched soil that should give you the best crops in this whole area. Next year you'll know better than to plow too soon."

Veritt went down on one knee and ran his fingers through the soil, smelling it, patting it smooth again. "If I were you, I'd grow trin in this soil. The tea you've been serving me is better than anything we raise, and ours is better than any the townspeople can import. They already buy every bit we can spare—and there's more market than Fort Freedom can supply."

"I didn't grow the trin crop. That came from Kadi's kitchen garden— all her own handiwork!"

Abel laughed. "Will you never stop surprising me with your talents, Kadi? I've never known such an accomplished woman!"

Kadi could do very little of the physical work of extending her garden patch of trin into a whole field, but Rimon carefully followed her instructions, and by early summer the field was lushly green. But Rimon also put in grain and corn, beans, and peas against another hard winter.

By that time, Kadi was no longer able to travel back and forth to Fort Freedom. Rimon went seldom now, too, refusing to leave Kadi for more than an hour or two at a time.

They had many visitors from Fort Freedom; either Abel or Jord almost every day, Jon's parents at least once a week. Jon moved among Simes now as easily as Kadi or Willa, and when he was low-field he would often go home to his family for a day.

Dan Whelan, Sara Fenell, and the others who had broken with Veritt's teachings, moved out of Fort Freedom. Just across the creek from the seedy little border town they built a row of neat white-painted houses, their own small chapel at the end of the row. They began to work the land which stretched along the creek.

That much Abel told them. Rimon found out for himself that during the spring three more families had become disillusioned and joined the dissenters. Privately, Veritt was worried about what would happen when next a new Sime came to them from across the border. Would the dissenters fight to gain a newcomer—and, if so, how would they fight?

"The whole schism is my fault," Jord told them. "It all came to a head when I spent all night trying to bring Karl Risaki through changeover. He'd had your training, but it didn't do any good. He died."

"That happens sometimes," said Rimon. "Kadi's mother was the best changeover attendant I've ever seen. But sometimes she lost even a kid who'd been taught everything."

"Well, after that, I was exhausted," said Jord. "Rimon, I can't keep it up the way you do, and after all night with Karl, I was in no condition to help Suzi Hamilton. She was the one who developed pneumonia. Her family—and some others—blamed me for trying to help an accursed Sime—while Suzi deteriorated so that by the time I got there, there was nothing I could do. Or maybe I could have, if I'd been fresh!"

"You didn't have a Gen to help you," Kadi pointed out.

Jord shook his head. "Rimon and I brought Evva Blant through without Gen help, remember?"

"True, but we didn't start out exhausted," said Rimon.

"When I have Kadi or Willa with me, I work much better."

"Jord, why can't I help you?" Willa asked suddenly. She had just joined them, with tea for everyone. Now she settled next to Jord, who relaxed perceptibly as Willa's field began to work on him.

He stared at her. "You—might get hurt, Willa."

"No. I help Rimon heal people. They hurt. I don't."

Jon Forester suddenly spoke up. "Jord, she doesn't really understand the danger, but I do. Why don't you teach me what to do?"

Willa pouted. "I did it before you came here!" Jord winced, and Willa was immediately contrite. "I won't hurt you," she said, putting her hand over his.

"I know you won't," he replied, "but I can't protect you —or you either, Jon—the way Rimon does. Pain raises intil. I could turn on either one of you."

"For transfer?" asked Willa. "Why not?"

Jord looked from Rimon to Kadi and back. "When are you going to tell her?"

Willa stared at him—and the question finally came. "Why don't you have your own Gens? Or Mr. Veritt or the others? Rimon has Kadi and Jon and me. Why don't you have Gens to live with you and make you feel good?"

Jord stared at her helplessly.

"Tell her, Jord," Kadi said.

He looked at her protestingly, and then at Rimon. He nodded and pulled his chair up before Jord and Willa, in range to interfere should Willa become frightened. "Willa is a grown-up girl now. She has to learn to live in the grown-up world."

Willa straightened proudly, aware of something important about to happen to her. Jord acknowledged Rimon's precaution with an embarrassed smile. Then Willa said, "Tell me, Jord, why don't you have Gens living with you? Why did Jon leave Fort Freedom instead of living with you?"

Jord licked his lips. "Because, Willa, we kill Gens. No other Sime in all the world—can take transfer the way Rimon does, without killing."

Willa frowned. "Killing? You say that all the time. What does it mean?"

"The Gens—die," said Jord.

Death Willa knew. She understood that Carlana's baby had died, as had a baby bird she had found fallen out of the nest. "But—why? Die from transfer? I don't understand."

"Neither do I, child," Jord said sadly. "It should be possible for any Sime to do what Rimon does—and yet we can't, no matter how we try. The Gen becomes frightened —and—"

Willa turned to Rimon. "When Carlana lost her baby, I got scared. And you—"

"Lost control," he said tightly.

"But—you went to Kadi, not me. I remember—I didn't understand except that Kadi was scared."

"And you saved her life, Willa, and probably mine."

"I hurt you."

"Willa, you couldn't hurt a Sime," said Jord.

"No, I hurt Rimon," she said. "I'll show you—but I won't hurt you." She quickly slid her hands into transfer position on Jord's arms. Rimon started to protest, but was caught in the sympathetic backwash as Jord gave a yelp of pure pain. Willa let go, putting her hands on Jord's shoulders, soothing him. Kadi reached out to Rimon as well.

"I'm sorry," said Willa, "I didn't know you'd pull away. Rimon says never—ever—do that to him. I didn't mean to hurt!"

But Jord's eyes were filled with tears—of pain, and something else. "Child—what have you discovered in all your innocence? God be praised, Rimon, why didn't you tell us this?"

"Because—it doesn't seem much of an improvement to trade the death of a Sime for the death of a Gen. Suppose Drust Fenell had known this—or found it by accident as Willa did? He must have panicked when Vee tried to take transfer—and if he'd known how to injure her lateral nerves, she'd have been lucky to die immediately of the shock. Otherwise she'd die a slow, agonizing death because she couldn't take another kill. I saw an injury like that once. I hope I never have to see it again!"

"But Rimon, if a Gen knew he was safe, that he could stop the Sime if he felt pain—then he wouldn't feel fear!"

"That fear is not rational. Jon, you remember your first transfer?"

"I was scared silly," Jon admitted. "And I knew Rimon doesn't kill. But that didn't help. Rimon didn't hurt me—but Jord, if I'd tried it with Mom or Dad, and they did hurt me? If I—If I—" He couldn't even say it, staring down at his hands. "Oh, God, now that I know what I can do, I couldn't touch another Sime—especially not somebody I love."

"I will do it," said Willa.

"Do what?" asked Kadi.

"I will teach Jord."

"Willa, you don't understand," said Jord.

"I do, I do!" she insisted. "After Kadi has her baby, Rimon won't need me anymore. Then I will give you transfer, Jord. I've never been scared of transfer."

"Child, you don't understand what we've been talking about. Rimon, tell her you won't allow it!"

Kadi interposed. "Willa, you like Jord, don't you?"

"Yes," the girl replied.

"Do you understand that every time he has ever taken transfer, the Gen has died?"

Jord tensed, but Willa said, "Yes, because they were scared. But," she said, looking at Jord, "you don't want them to die."

Intense with desire, not denial, Jord said, "Rimon, tell her it's too dangerous!"

"I think Willa understands what she's offering, Jord. If she's willing, I have no right to stop her."

"I shall consult with my father," said Jord. "We'll pray together for guidance. Willa, child, you can't possibly know how much I want to accept your offer—but I'm afraid."

When Jord had gone, Kadi told Rimon, "Willa suddenly grew up today."

"She did indeed. I wish I knew the right thing to do. I was zlinning her, Kadi. I think she really does understand that she could die. I think it's truly a considered, adult decision, in which you and I have no right to interfere. But—"

"But if something goes wrong, we're going to feel responsible," Kadi said. "We'll think she was still the child Jord calls her, and that we should have forbid her to try it."

"Yet if we never let her try, we're thwarting one possible way for other Simes to learn not to kill."

As the heat of summer set in, Kadi was more and more tired. Finally it seemed that she did nothing but eat and sleep as the days passed, until she woke up one dawn in pain. Fear stabbed through her, bringing Rimon running to her side.

She didn't have to control her fear, though, for it disappeared when Rimon said, "It's only a contraction, Kadi! It's time!"

She gave a weak laugh, relief sweeping through her. Rimon said, "I'll send Jon for the Veritts. Mrs. Veritt's helped with most of the births at Fort Freedom, Jord can help me support your field, and Abel—well, you know Abel would never forgive us if the baby were born without him here."

As Rimon moved, she said, "Don't let Jon go through town alone. There's time. That was only the first contraction strong enough to wake me up."

"Rest now," he said, kissing her forehead. "You'll require your strength later."

Chapter 17

MIRACLE

As Kadi slept, Rimon worried. Her field was as low now as it had ever been after transfer, and the worst drain was yet to come. He knew what could happen; he had seen it on the Genfarm. Occasionally a female Gen had symptoms like Kadi's, entered labor with a low-field, and was totally drained before she could expel the child. Usually they lost both mother and child.

Once in a while, after the mother was dead, they had cut a living child from her body. Syrus Farris had always taken special care of such infants, saying they were likely to be Sime, but Rimon could remember only one that lived more than a few days in the nursery—and she had been only two years old when Rimon and Kadi left. But his father's beliefs came not from a single instance, but from generations of experience passed from father to son.

To me, thought Rimon. *And what good is all the Farris wisdom now?* He sat beside Kadi, trying to encourage her body to produce more selyn, and wondering where her strength came from when her field responded—again.

It was more than half an hour before a second contraction brought Kadi awake again. She smiled at Rimon when it ended, and took his hands. "It won't be long now," she said, and he realized she didn't know how much time had passed.

He forced a reassuring smile. "We'll soon get to meet our son," he agreed. "Do you feel strong enough to let us get you ready?"

Jon soon returned with the Veritts. Mrs. Veritt inspected Rimon's preparations and said, "Good job. I've never met a man before who knew anything about midwifery."

In Rimon's world, no man would leave his wife alone in

labor—yet it was obvious Mrs. Veritt expected to take over now, shooing the men outside.

"I must stay beside Kadi to support her field," he explained. "Zlin her, Mrs. Veritt. She's very weak."

The older woman did so, just as another contraction hit Kadi. Mrs. Veritt gasped, almost doubling over, gripping the bedframe to support herself. When it was over, her eyes focused on Rimon. "I have—helped a Gen give birth before, Rimon. I was the oldest girl in our family, so I had to help the midwife when my brothers and sisters were born. But that was before—"

"Before you could sense fields," said Rimon. "You'll find Gen pain affects you much more than Sime pain, even low as Kadi's field is. Willa, you help me. Jon—" He looked around, and had to zlin past the fields around him to find the boy. "Why didn't he come in?" He went to the open door. "Jon, come in and help Mrs. Veritt."

"Help deliver a baby?" he asked in shock.

Jord said, "You know how to shield a Sime against pain. Mother can't do this alone."

Jon entered the house, but still hung back from the bed.

"Come on," said Willa. "You stand over here."

Jon remained where he was. The battle between Willa and Jon for pecking order had amused Rimon up to now; today it only annoyed him.

"Please, Jon," Kadi said softly, "help Mrs. Veritt. I can't."

Still the boy hesitated, a mass of conflicting emotions, his age and upbringing making him vulnerable to embarrassment.

Jord said, "You think Rimon and Kadi are going to feed and clothe you so you can refuse to help when they ask you? You weren't raised to be a freeloader, Jon."

At that, Jon squared his shoulders and pulled his emotions under control. He looked over at Abel. "You think it's right, Mr. Veritt?"

"Yes, Jon, it's right. You're the only one who can do it."

Jon went over to stand beside Mrs. Veritt. "I'll do my best."

The day dragged on. Kadi drifted in and out of consciousness, only coming really awake when the contractions hit. By midafternoon they were still fifteen minutes apart, and Kadi's field was faltering. Her selyn production had lagged behind the baby's consumption for months; now, for the first time, production itself was slowing from its mad rate.

Willa shielded Rimon well, at the same time gently wiping Kadi's face after each contraction, making her as comfortable as possible. But as Kadi's complexion turned ashen, concern grew in Willa, echoing Rimon's.

They had carefully prepared Willa, explaining that yes, it hurt to have a baby, but the pain was not beyond endurance and well worth the joy of having a child. Nonetheless, even Willa could see there was something wrong.

Trying to zlin Kadi's dilation, Rimon found himself constantly caught up in her pain—and now came the sharpest yet as she clutched the sheet, gritting her teeth, and then Rimon felt the momentary relief as her water broke.

"That's a good sign!" said Mrs. Veritt. "Won't be long now."

Gasping for breath, Kadi said wryly, "I'll be glad of that."

Willa cleaned up the mess, and Rimon was astonished to see Mrs. Veritt feel for the baby with her hands. Fearing infection, he started to tell her to check by zlinning when she said, "Good. He's in position. Now really work with the contractions, Kadi."

Kadi was wide awake as the contractions came more quickly, but each time she fell back afterward, gasping for breath. Rimon could see her field fading, and knew that their child would not be born in time. In healing mode, he conjured the specter of need in himself to encourage Kadi's cells to produce more, and ever more selyn.

But their son—*his* son—drew selyn inexorably through her nerves, outlining her vitality in a sparkling glow. The periphery faded; all was drawn to the center, the connections lost, as if parts of Kadi were dying, dying of attrition—

"No!" cried Rimon, not realizing he'd shouted aloud, but sensing Jord there, zlinning helplessly.

Rimon let go of all awareness beyond himself and Kadi and the small life struggling to glean enough selyn to live.

He'll kill her. No! No, my son will not begin his life by killing!

Frantic, Rimon seized Kadi's limp arms, falling directly into transfer position, searching for any spark of life in her. Peripherally, he felt Jord wrench himself out of intil as Willa's support suddenly shifted to Jord for a moment, then returned, steady, worried but unexcited. Jon was low-field, thank goodness, for his shivering anxiety was a growing irritant to the other Simes. But all of Rimon's attention was on a hard, bright core at the center of Kadi's otherwise black field.

Suddenly, Rimon was elsewhere—careering trees blurred by, the musty smell of old leaves somehow penetrating him as Zeth died under his tentacles, his system forced to give up selyn. For a moment, Rimon became Zeth, feeling selyn drawn from him.

He jolted to present reality, dizzy, whirling downward toward bottomless dark, pouring forth his life in willing catharsis. The flow was so good that Rimon began to force selyn outwards from his system, faster and faster as within him a chronic, nagging ache dissolved, and for the first time in months he felt free of need. The more selyn he forced away from himself, the better he felt. He kept going even when resistance rose against it—kept forcing and forcing selyn outwards—

PAIN!

He was dashed down to hypoconsciousness, hearing Mrs. Veritt saying, "Once more—push once more, Kadi!"

While at the same time, Jord yelled, "Stop it, Ri—"

As Kadi's pain relented, Rimon was aware of the searing ache along his arms where Kadi's fingers had bitten into his flesh just above the sensitive nodes. He was also aware of a distinct change in the ambient nager, but couldn't place it.

Kadi looked up at him with huge blue eyes, gasping, but conscious.

"You're alive!" he said.

Before she could speak, another contraction overtook her. "Push, Kadi!" said Mrs. Veritt. "Here comes the head."

Now, the child was not drawing—it was settling already

into a normal child's pattern, unaffected and unaffecting. The nageric link between mother and child had severed— the baby had to be born quickly now, allowed to breathe air before its blood supply failed.

But as the last contraction gathered, her pain flared through him until it was impossible to endure, and all faded to blackness.

Rimon became conscious of Kadi beside him, alive, pulsing again with selyn production. He wanted to take her in his arms, but she was sleeping, weak and in mild pain— but alive.

The child!

Trying to sit up, Rimon felt as if an axe descended to split his skull in two—but that was nothing to the searing, torn feeling in his chest. Jord was immediately there, pushing him back down on the bed. "Lie still. Everything's fine. I don't know how you did it, but you saved both of them."

As Rimon's eyes focused, he trembled inside with a peculiar, sick feeling. Everything hurt, but from somewhere came the memory of not being able to locate Jon. "Did— did anyone get hurt?"

"No," Jord reassured him. "You put us through hell, but it doesn't matter."

"It was worth it," said Mrs. Veritt, bringing a small bundle to show Rimon. She lifted the blanket away to reveal a red wrinkled face. "Your son—strong and healthy, thanks to you, Rimon."

He had seen newborn children before, but nonetheless that mite of humanity seemed small payment for all Kadi had gone through. *You almost killed her,* he thought resentfully. Then he remembered. *What did my father think when he first saw me?*

All the pent-up love for his son suddenly flowed out, released by the end to his worry. He reached for the child, even though the movement made his head whirl. Jord supported him, Willa put pillows behind him, and Mrs. Veritt gently placed his son in his arms.

The baby stirred, and opened his eyes for a moment— black eyes, like Rimon's, startlingly dark for a newborn. The dark fuzz on the tiny head made him already seem like a Farris. His tiny mouth worked, and he squirmed and began to cry fitfully.

"He's hungry," Mrs. Veritt said. "I think Kadi can feed him once she's rested—but don't worry, Rimon. I asked Mrs. Ennis not to wean her baby yet, in case you require a wet nurse."

And you were prepared in case she died, Rimon thought, but he only said, "Thank you. And thank you for being here today. All of you."

"You did everything that saved your wife and your son," said Abel. "I've never seen anything like it—a Sime giving selyn to a Gen? That's how it appeared to me. Both Kadi and your son were dying, Rimon. I was praying for a miracle—and you performed one!"

Rimon didn't feel much like a miracle worker. The headache was beginning to pound and spread from the back of his head down through his arms to his laterals, then back up into his already burning chest, where the waves of pain met and clashed under his breast-bone. The tenuous balance he'd been holding over his fields dissolved into vibrating chaos. He wanted to turn to Kadi, as always, but he dared not disturb her rest.

"Here, Rimon," said Mrs. Veritt, gathering the baby away from his arms. "You'll crush him. What's the matter?"

"Willa!" called Abel, urgently. "Help Rimon."

Instantly, Willa appeared and, sitting on the edge of the bed, pried Rimon's arms from clutching across his chest. She slid her hands down his arms into transfer position, her field steady, self-assured; he could rest against it, damp the oscillations until the whanging pain let up. This was worse than he'd ever had before. But eventually, the pain subsided to a sick ache. "Thank you, Willa," he murmured, falling back on the pillows.

"Tea now?" Willa asked.

"Tea won't help this," he said, and frowned. "Fosebine might. And it would certainly help Kadi."

"Fosebine?" asked Jord

Fort Freedom. At the oddest moments, the gulf yawned between these people and everything Rimon had ever known. "It's a medicine—a mild pain reliever most people don't use because it tastes so bad it's easier to endure the pain. They used to force it on me—after a kill—and when I didn't vomit it up, it helped sometimes when I felt like this."

"Where would we get this—medicine?"

"Oh—nowadays, lots of Pens use it. Slina probably keeps some around."

"I'll go ask Slina," said Jord, and left quickly.

Rimon thought—*I've hurt Kadi. What if she learns to fear the pain? Oh, God, what have I done?*

As Jord's nager faded, Rimon realized that something had been bothering him. Jon should have been with Jord. Rimon zlinned the house and grounds outside, finding no sign of Jon. "Abel, where's Jon? Why isn't he helping Jord?"

"He's probably across the border by now," said Abel.

"What happened!"

"I'm not blaming Jord," said Abel. "He had to leave himself vulnerable to assist you. But he was depending on Jon, and—"

"What happened," demanded Rimon.

Willa answered, "Jon got scared and that made Jord want him, and that scared Jon more and poor Jord—"

Abel said, "He attacked Jon, but Willa intervened and Jon ran. I don't know where he went—we were too busy to—"

Rimon sat up, swinging his feet to the floor, trying to balance his head carefully on his shoulders. "We've got to search for Jon. God alone knows what he's going through!" But the pain was so great, Rimon couldn't zlin his hand in front of his face, let alone run around searching for a Gen.

"Rimon, get back on that bed," said Mrs. Veritt. "You're—"

"I'm responsible for him!" said Rimon. "Suppose the border patrol catches him—he doesn't have his tags—"

"He knows the way across," said Abel.

Before Rimon could answer, Mrs. Veritt said, "Willa, help Rimon sleep now. He feels very bad, and Jord has gone to bring medicine. Help Rimon now, all right?"

Rimon let them put him to sleep, admitting that he simply couldn't move. It was Kadi's pain that woke him, a searing flame in every nerve. Desperately, he shut out her pain

—his own was bad enough. He had to stay hypoconscious to avoid hers, and that just made his worse—but he resolved to endure it in silence. Kadi had endured far more.

Mrs. Veritt lifted Kadi and held a cup to her lips. "This will make you feel better."

She took a breath and gulped the vile-tasting stuff down. It did ease her pain. Then Mrs. Veritt asked, "Rimon, can you drink this down now?"

Rimon thought of the taste and his unsteady stomach and wanted to say no, but he had to try something. Abel was standing just outside the front door with Jord, scanning the night. They hadn't sent anyone after Jon. "I'll try," said Rimon, taking the cup from her hands.

Taking a deep breath, he gulped it down, and the fosebine immediately spread a soothing warmth through his aching nerves. "I guess it's going to stay down," he said, handing the cup back.

Kadi turned to him. "Rimon. Our baby!"

Rimon said, "He's fine, and beautiful, too."

"He's sleeping," said Mrs. Veritt. "Let him rest until you're strong enough to feed him, Kadi."

"Yes," she whispered. "I remember, I saw him. But—Rimon—what did you do to me?"

"He saved your life," answered Abel quickly, coming in from the night.

Kadi was assembling the fragmented memories of the past day, and arrived at the pain. "Shidoni, Rimon—you hurt me!"

"I didn't know it would hurt, Kadi—I felt you dying, and I just took a desperate chance. I'm so sorry I hurt you—"

She met his eyes, and rubbing her arms absently, she said, "Well—we lived through it, and now we have our son, and everything is all right."

It was full dark outside, with no moon. Willa was clearing the table after a meal, but water was boiling for fresh tea. "Kadi," she said, "I have your soup. Rimon, will you eat some, too?"

He was surprised at how good the idea sounded, how Kadi's sudden appetite was getting to him. "Yes, Willa—thank you."

He looked at the cradle. He couldn't see his son, but he could zlin the completely normal childish nager. *It's real.*

"Where's Jon?" Kadi asked.

From where he was sitting in Kadi's rocking chair, staring into the fire, Abel told her what had happened. Jord stood by the window, staring out into the night, defeated.

"Rimon tried to go after him," said Mrs. Veritt. "But he simply could not. I'm sure God will take care of Jon. He's a good boy."

"No," said Willa unexpectedly. "It was all Jon's fault. Jon is a bad boy." She went over to Jord and put a hand on his wrist. "Jord is good. Jon is bad. Jon was afraid."

Mrs. Veritt took the abandoned soup bowls from the table and brought them to Kadi and Rimon. Rimon watched Willa, amazed. She had never asserted herself like this before.

Jord said, "Jon was afraid of exactly what happened—that the pain in this room would cause one of us to turn on him. It makes sense to be afraid of what's bound to hurt you."

"I don't know a lot yet," said Willa, "but I know it wasn't Kadi's pain that made you turn on Jon. Jon made you do it. It was his own fault."

Abel Veritt came up behind Jord and put his arm around his shoulders. "Son, if it were the pain and lack of control on your part, Willa couldn't have brought you out of it."

"What exactly did she do?" asked Rimon.

"What she's doing right now," said Jord. "I could let her do that forever. It's addictive, you know."

"I know," said Rimon, reaching over to squeeze Kadi's hand. As he did, he saw the burn marks his tentacles had left on her arms—and the pattern of her fingers etched in purplish bruises on his.

"Rimon, somebody has to go after Jon," said Kadi.

"Maybe Del will show up by morning, and I'll send him."

At that moment, Kadi noticed the marks on their arms. She put down her spoon and stared. Then she traced the marks on Rimon's arm with a delicate finger. "Did I do that?"

"And they say Gens aren't as strong as Simes," said Rimon, basking in the soothing delight of her touch.

"Oh, Rimon, I'm sorry!"

"Don't be," he said with a wry chuckle. "It was a cooperative effort." He looked back to Abel and Jord. "If Kadi and Willa can learn to control themselves around Simes, why couldn't Jon?"

"I'm going to learn."

The door to the hillside tunnels opened, and Jon Forester entered. His trousers were grimy, and his face was streaked with dried tears, but he pulled himself erect as he entered the room. "I'm sorry," he said to Jord. "If I'd made you kill me, it would have been my own fault."

"We thought you'd run for the border," said Abel.

After his initial relief that the boy was safe, Rimon said, "Jon, we'll gladly give you a proper Fort Freedom sendoff —anytime you want. But don't ever try to run for it alone!"

Jon shook his head. "I have no place to go over there. Everybody I care about is here. I want to stay if you'll let me. I promise I'll earn my keep."

"You always have," said Rimon, although he felt uneasy. Well, they'd make sure not to place the boy in such a situation again until he could handle himself.

"Jord," said Jon, "can you forgive me?"

"I forgive you," said Jord. "I've a lot to learn, too— especially how not to react to a Gen's fear. Like Rimon. He didn't react to your fear today."

Rimon chuckled despite the way it made his chest hurt. "To tell the truth, I never felt it. All I knew was Kadi. Now, let's put that behind us. Jon, you're starved. Go eat."

Mrs. Veritt made a place for Jon at the table and supplied him with soup and bread. The baby began to cry. Jon jumped up, wide-eyed. "He's alive!"

"Of course," Willa said, plucking the baby out of the cradle as if Jon would contaminate it. "We knew what to do."

"A lot you had to do with it!" Jon snapped. "You're just too dumb to be scared!"

"Jon!" said Abel. "That's enough! Willa saved your life today."

"Huh?"

"She stopped me," said Jord. "Your life—my soul. We owe a great deal to Willa."

Shamefaced, Jon sat back down at the table as the baby began to scream in earnest.

"Oh, please, give him to me," said Kadi.

With Mrs. Veritt's help, Kadi was soon nursing her child, looking down at him in delight. "We have to give him a name."

"It should be an appropriate name, Kadi," suggested Abel. "We witnessed a miracle here today, when Rimon gave of his own life-force to his wife and his son. God showed Rimon the way; the child should have a name that indicates God's inspiration."

Rimon thought back to the moment when he'd lost Kadi to death. The flashing picture in his mind of a green forest—his First Need. "The inspiration—came from my first kill," said Rimon. "Abel, you remember? I told you about my cousin. He was Sime—and I killed him when I drew selyn from him, forced his system to work backwards. Today, I remembered that—and I made my own system work backwards—and Kadi's, to accept selyn."

"That must be what caused that incredible pain," said Veritt. "But how did you do it?"

"I don't know. But I know our son's name—for the person whose death made me aware of what I could do today. Because he died—my wife and my son live."

"Zeth," said Kadi. "He didn't die in vain, Rimon. I've always told you that."

"Zeth Farris," said Abel. "A truly appropriate name. May God bless the child who bears it, and guide all of us privileged to see this miracle to do His will." He bowed his head. "God, You have given us a miracle this day. We pray for Your guidance to speed the day when we shall all be as this young couple you have sent to be an inspiration to us. May it be Thy will to bring that day soon, Lord—oh, please, let it be soon!"

PART III

Chapter 18

INFORMED CONSENT

One warm, late-summer day, Rimon and Del rode triumphantly home from Ardo Pass, where the largest horse auction of the year was held. They had sold every horse, at prices among the highest at the auction. Their wagon was loaded with the rope Del had wanted, kegs of nails—some on consignment for Fort Freedom—a saddle for Owen, and three huge bales of wire for Del's fences. The wire was an incredible extravagance, but his stock had to be protected.

After five days, Rimon was eager to be home. Del was just as eager to see his family—Carlana and the children were staying with Kadi at the homestead, and as they rounded the bend in the trail, Rimon could zlin the whole group on top of the hill above their home. Carlana must have pointed them out, for as they came in sight Owen and Jana were jumping up and down and waving, and came running pell-mell down the hill to leap into Del's arms as soon as he jumped off the wagon.

"We're having a picnic!" Jana announced.

"Come on up the hill!" Owen added excitedly.

Kadi, Carlana, Willa, and Jon were waiting atop the hill —Kadi holding seven-week-old Zeth. Rimon kissed her, and took the baby, who gurgled up at him happily.

Del was passing out presents to his family, Carlana exclaiming, "Del, you'll spoil the children—oh! but that's so expensive!" as he presented her with a sheer scarf in soft blue and yellow.

"You deserve the best, Ana," he told her. "And if I can keep on this way, you're going to have it!"

Rimon said, "Already some people knew Del's name from last winter. By next year's auction, everyone will be bidding on Erick stock!"

What Rimon had for Kadi was a small bag of coins. He had agreed to help Del for a percentage instead of a fee—and his confidence in his friend had paid off.

Kadi counted the money. "Oh, Rimon! Now we can pay our taxes, and still—"

"Buy a stove!" he said. "We're going into town tomorrow to order one, and glass for the windows! No more cold, dark rooms for you, Kadi."

But he had also bought a few trinkets—a rattle for Zeth, a set of tea-glasses for Kadi, a plaid ribbon for Willa, and for Jon something from out-Territory: a compass. "With that, you should find your way in the hills as easily as a Sime!"

"How does it work?" asked Jon.

"I'll show you," said Carlana.

"How are things at Fort Freedom?" asked Del.

"About the same—according to Abel," said Kadi.

"Yes, the same," Carlana said bitterly. "Dan Whelan and the others—those ingrates are destroying him, Del, after everything he's done for them—"

Rimon had never seen Carlana angry before—but her righteous indignation brought her laterals forth in uncontrollable response. Jon, with whom she was still bent over the compass, jerked back with a start of fear. Carlana turned on him but then held back, and his fear died away. "Forgive me, Jon," she murmured.

"It's Jon who should apologize," said Kadi.

Covering his fear with anger, Jon snapped, "She startled me!"

But the stab of fear had been clear to the three Simes—particularly Rimon, who was now approaching need.

Later, after Del and Carlana had gone with their children, Rimon sat before the fire holding Zeth on his lap. "He's grown just in the time I've been away."

"He changes every day," Kadi agreed, watching Zeth grasp his father's finger and pull it to his mouth. "He's getting stronger all the time."

"Tough little frontier kid—he'll do better than either of us. Kadi, was Jon that jumpy the whole time?"

"No, of course not. But it looks as if I'll have to do some more work with him."

"He seemed so much better since Zeth was born."

"Rimon, he calmed right down today. There's no way to control the startle reflex—it happens to me sometimes, too. Don't scold him. You know how hard he's trying."

But trying's not enough. "He's got to learn not to be scared every time something new happens—or we'll have to send him off across the border. Maybe we ought to . . ."

"He wants so badly to stay," Kadi said. "Give him time."

Rimon felt that Kadi wanted to get his mind off any problems while he was in need. But it was so comfortable to be back in her presence again that he didn't care what she did!

She stayed close to him for the next two days. Willa relinquished without protest the place she had become accustomed to. Nonetheless, Rimon became gradually more nervous than he had been in months. Early on the third day, before anyone else woke, he went out to work off tension by chopping wood. It helped, as always. And in the evening, he knew, they'd have their privacy, for the first thing Rimon had done after Zeth was born was to build another room onto their little house, so they now had their own bedroom.

Over morning tea, he looked into Kadi's eyes and said, "I'm glad we'll have only Gens and a child out here. It's convenient not to have to insulate for privacy, as you do in a Sime household."

"What happens when our kids change over?" she teased.

"By then," Rimon said brightly, "we'll have a bigger house!"

Willa and Jon were stirring now. Jon went outside—to milk the goat, Rimon assumed—and Willa began to prepare breakfast. Zeth started to cry. Kadi laid him on Willa's bed to change him. Rimon sat at the table, staring into his half-empty cup. A sudden shock brought him to his feet. "Yeee! Jon! What the bloodyshen do you think you're doing?"

Kadi, carrying Zeth, followed Rimon to the door. Jon turned to stare at them in astonishment, a small trickle of blood running down his chin.

He had set a small mirror on a stump, and was attempting to shave. Obviously, he had just cut himself. "I'm shaving."

"You have no more beard than Willa does!" said Rimon.

His dignity injured, Jon said, "I do so! And besides, how am I going to learn if I don't practice before it gets heavy?"

"Well, practice tomorrow! Don't *do* things like that when I'm at my most sensitive!"

Jon was immediately contrite. "I'm sorry, Rimon. Sure, I'll wait until tomorrow."

As they went back inside, Rimon said, "I guess that proves he's not afraid of me, even when I'm in need." He managed a wry chuckle. "What was I saying about the convenience of living in a house full of Gens?"

Early that evening, Kadi fed Zeth and left him in Willa's care. Then she and Rimon retired to their room. After all the months of denial, both of them were slightly shy—and yet he sensed Kadi's yearning to give him transfer. Rimon assured her she wasn't fertile now, so they could do as they pleased.

They undressed and got into bed. Rimon drew Kadi close, eyes closed, tension in his body. "After all those months—I thought I'd never survive it—and now you're here again—"

"You know I am," she said. "Every month from now on."

"Until I get you pregnant again," he said bitterly.

"We'll worry about that when the time comes." She pushed back his unruly black hair, kissed his forehead. "Relax, Rimon. You don't have to hold back anymore. Everything's perfect."

She let her own delighted anticipation flow to him. They lay thus as Rimon's tensions slowly drained away. Then he caressed her arms, his laterals teasing her with anticipation before they finally settled into place, and he drew her into lip contact.

A heavenly relief filled Rimon as selyn flowed from Kadi's nerves, tingling through every portion of his being, Kadi's satisfaction growing as Rimon's draw increased, peaked, and slowed. But Kadi wasn't ready—she clung to him, wanting more. He could feel her need to give more, but he could take no more, felt himself sinking into hypoconsciousness, leaving her hovering on the brink of completion.

"What happened?" she asked. "Oh, Rimon, have you grown so used to unsatisfactory transfers that you're holding back with me?"

"No," he whispered. "Kadi, I—That was—Oh, Kadi, that was the best ever, for me. But—you—" He paused to zlin her, with an effort. Then he said, "You're still almost high-field—well, not relative to me, now, but you have more selyn. Kadi, I'm sorry." She was forcing back tears, the first since Zeth was born. "You're feeling a little like I felt after Willa or Jon. Let me try to help—"

He took her into transfer position again. As he sought to ease her discomfort, he found the knack. Her grief faded. "Better?"

She looked up as he retracted his tentacles. "You did that?"

He nodded. "I just—I don't know what I did, but I found a way to take that extra selyn. Now you feel better, and so do I."

"But you controlled me! Rimon—oh, Rimon, I'm sorry for all those times I controlled you. I didn't know how it felt!"

But he was in the full grip of post syndrome while she remained essentially unmoved. Curbing impatience, he leaned back to talk to her. "Don't worry about it. We were just off phase from one another. Today puts us back in phase, and next month it will be right for both of us again."

"Yes," she murmured. "We have to get used to each other again."

"That's right." He kissed her gently, and as he began to caress her tenderly, in all the ways experience had taught him, she slowly began to respond. But there was no trace of the urgency they had always known after a transfer before. Rather there was the gentler sensation that usually characterized their lovemaking a few days after transfer. Had that urgency been abnormal—was this the way it ought to be?

Rimon couldn't spend much time pondering the fact that he hadn't satisfied Kadi in transfer. Everyone's immediate concern now was Willa. Only the girl herself was unconcerned, talking of her upcoming transfer with Jord with happy anticipation. Jord, on the other hand, was as nervous and edgy as Rimon had ever seen him.

When the day came, Rimon, Kadi, and Willa assembled at the Veritt home. Jon went to visit his parents, who were also caring for Zeth today, but Rimon knew that every mind in Fort Freedom was on that one neat house in the center of the community.

They took every precaution. Abel and Margid Veritt had adjusted their own schedules the past three months so they were pre-turnover when Jord was in need. Rimon was less than a week into his cycle, at his steadiest.

As Rimon took up his position behind Jord, Kadi at his side, he couldn't help remembering Del and Billy. *But Billy was afraid,* he reminded himself. *Willa isn't.*

The plan was simple enough: both Rimon and Abel would be zlinning the transfer. Should Willa feel the slightest pain, Rimon was to grab Jord and Abel Willa, and pull them apart. Rimon and Kadi would then do whatever they could for Jord, who had insisted Willa's safety must come first.

As the moment arrived, Jord's nager was troubled, haunted, Rimon knew, by echoes of a series of unsuccessful attempts at what he was trying again today. With an extreme effort, Jord went into healing mode, but need threatened to kick him over into killmode at any moment.

Rimon entered healing mode too, supporting Jord. There was a now-or-never desperation in Jord's field as he held out his hands to Willa. She grasped his arms and pressed her lips to his almost before his laterals had seated themselves against her flesh.

The flow began at once, pleasantly, but too slowly—the same frustration Rimon had endured for months on end during Kadi's pregnancy. *But it is endurable!* he willed to Jord.

Grimly, Jord held steady, slowly meeting physiological necessity while he fought the urge to increase his draw speed. Willa was steady, just as she had been every time for Rimon.

Nonetheless, frustration was weakening Jord's control, and long before he reached physical satisfaction, without warning, something flipped inside-out. The draw leaped instantly to the speed of the kill.

Even as Rimon was reaching for Jord in the agonized fear that he was already too late, he felt Willa's response: delighted surprise and intense pleasure.

The girl reacted as Kadi did, cooperating, pouring forth her life-force as fast as Jord could take it, pure joy springing through her as she gave and gave.

When it ended, Rimon was plunged with Jord into hypoconsciousness. Willa was staring up at Jord, looking utterly beautiful. His tentacles had withdrawn, and his fingers were lax on her arms. When Rimon moved from behind him, he saw that Jord's eyes were closed, as if he feared what he would see. He glowed with selyn.

"Jord," said Willa in awe. "You do that better than Rimon!"

"God be praised!" he whispered. Then, as the fact that she was truly alive and well sank in, he caught her into his arms, his tears falling into her hair.

Abel Veritt, too, was crying openly, as was Mrs. Veritt. They both embraced their son as Abel said, "At last! Oh, thank God, thank God!" Then even he was speechless.

Rimon was prickling with the reaction after the fact. He put an arm around Kadi. "We did it!" he said numbly. "We actually taught someone else!"

Abel Veritt turned to Rimon. "My faith has been rewarded, despite my errors. Jord," he turned back to his son, "God has blessed you."

"Father," said Jord, "I didn't do it! I lost control, and—it was just like every other time—except for Willa."

"It was the way I started," Rimon said. "I had no control at first. It was all in Kadi's hands. It still is, except that now I know I can control, if necessary."

"Willa," Abel said reverently.

"I said I would teach Jord." Her nager was as innocent as ever. "I kept my promise."

"You certainly did!" agreed Abel. "Jord, Rimon, we must talk about your experiences later, decide how to proceed from here—but now we must let everyone know that their prayers have been answered!"

When they were on the green, Abel rang the bell with

sweeping strokes that gave it an oddly festive sound. People poured from their homes. When they saw Jord and Willa together, both alive, tears and laughter mingled, and families embraced each other—particularly parents hugging their Sime children, reaffirming the knowledge that they were not cursed.

Then everyone went to the chapel to give thanks. Abel ended with a prayer for guidance in teaching everyone. Then he went to the lectern and stood looking out over the congregation.

"I have watched the hard, painful effort both Rimon Farris and my son have put into learning not to kill. I have witnessed the devastation wrought by their failures—failures with nameless Gens from the Pens, not close friends or family. Yes, I know, you don't wish to hear this—but for that very reason I must say it, and you must listen. *There will be no unsupervised experiments.* At the present time, only one person is qualified to supervise, and that is Rimon Farris. Jord?"

"I agree absolutely, Father. Today's success was much more Willa's doing than mine. I have a great deal to learn before I can teach others."

"Therefore," continued Abel, "no one will attempt transfer unless Rimon judges that both parties are ready. Especially the Gen. And that," he paused, looking over to where the Forester family sat, "means you, Jon Forester. *When* Rimon says and *with whom* Rimon says. You understand?"

"Yes, Mr. Veritt," Jon said clearly.

To himself, Rimon thought, *when Jon wants it as badly as Willa did, not before.* No wonder Jon felt like a fat rabbit surrounded by hungry foxes. No one in Fort Freedom would think of taking Jon against his will, or against Abel's proscription—but a Sime in need didn't think at all.

Abel was speaking to the whole congregation again. "In the months ahead, each time a child establishes as a Gen, he and his family must decide whether he will stay here or cross the border to safety. For we must all remember that there is danger here for such children—*and we are that danger.*

"Until each and every one of us learns not to kill, we

must avoid temptation. You know the way; we have practiced it at Farewells for years. A Gen in our midst is to be surrounded by those who are high-field. Anyone approaching need must keep away. Is that agreed?"

"Agreed." It was a reluctant murmur.

Surveying the congregation nagerically, Abel continued. "That had to be said, and I zlin that you all understand. But this is a day of celebration, when we all renew our vows to seek the road away from the kill. God has set my son's feet on that path, and I vow again to follow. Let us rejoice in this day's miracle, and in the hope it brings for all the days ahead!"

As they left the chapel, Rimon and Kadi found Del and Carlana at the back.

"Another miracle!" said Carlana, gazing at Willa and Jord.

"It's a fact we must adjust to," said Rimon to the Sime woman. "Killing can be a matter of choice."

Abel joined them, saying, "Everyone wants to congratulate Jord and Willa. It's their day. Why don't you all come over to our house? Rimon, we must make some plans."

As they walked, Del said, "I wouldn't let Carlana come here today when I heard what you planned to do with Willa. But when we heard the bell—"

"You came, the way you did that time to see if I'd killed Kadi. You are a true friend, Del."

"Yes," said Abel. "You'll learn quickly—you're sensitive—"

"No," said Del, "that's just it—I'm not sensitive. Rimon always could zlin further than I could. When I'm observing, I don't know what Rimon and Jord are talking about half the time, fields within fields. Maybe it takes that kind of supersensitivity to learn not to kill."

They settled around the Veritts' table, Mrs. Veritt soon producing tea and little biscuits. While Kadi ate, Abel toyed with his tea and shook his head. "No, God would not condemn some Simes to the kill and not others, so it can't be mere sensitivity. But perhaps sensitivity allowed Rimon and Jord to learn without a teacher."

Carlana gave a plate of biscuits to Owen and Jana and shooed them off to play. Abel was still thinking. "We must put our heads together, go over every piece of information we have—everything Rimon has ever done, or Kadi, or Willa. And the failures—yes, we must never make the same mistakes again."

"Abel," said Kadi, "it seems clear to me that we must teach Gens not to fear. That's Willa's secret, and mine."

"But how do we teach that?" asked Abel. "Why did Willa learn so easily, while Jon is still uncertain?"

"Jon knows too much," said Rimon. "Willa had been giving me transfer for months before she found out Simes kill Gens. Jon—in the past year, that boy has had to go through drastic adjustments in his thinking, and he doesn't have that tremendously increased learning capacity and adaptability of the first-year Sime."

Kadi made a rude noise, her whole nager shining with derision. When Rimon looked at her, suitably shocked, he found her blue eyes laughing at him. "The fact is that I adjusted, and Willa adjusted—but Willa had no previous beliefs to conflict with what we taught her, while my adjustments were all positive."

"I don't understand," said Abel.

"I grew up knowing Gens were cowardly animals. With Rimon's help, I learned I'm the same person I was before I established. But Jon grew up knowing Gens were the real people, better than Simes. And then just when he turns into a Gen, you go and change the rules on him. And Willa shows him Pen-grown Gens are people, too, and he's no better than she is. Is it any wonder the poor boy is confused and scared?"

Abel pondered that a moment. "You're right, of course. I shall counsel with Jon and his parents. We must all help him to adjust before—"

"Before someone convinces him he's being selfish," said Rimon. "Watch out for Jon's pride, Abel. He feels he should be able to do anything Willa can! I'm glad you made the point before the whole town that there are to be no private experiments."

"You felt how everyone gravitated toward Jon. I'll admit, it crossed my mind, too—but I've seen him break under pressure. No, next month Willa can teach someone else, and—"

"No, Abel," said Rimon, "you mustn't take her away from Jord."

"But—how are others to learn? Jord already knows the healing mode. Next month he—"

"He would lose control and kill again. Give Jord a chance to build up his health and his confidence."

"His health?"

"He hasn't had a satisfactory kill since Willa spoke her first word. No one in Fort Freedom has."

Abel stared at his steepled fingers. "It's longer than that," he said. "I don't think Jord has ever had a satisfactory kill. I've never seen Jord so—at peace with himself as he is now. You're right. We can't take that from him yet."

"What are you going to do about them?" Del gestured. "Out there? Everybody in town will think up some reason he should be the one to have Willa next month."

"I can give you a good reason to hold them off for two or three months," said Rimon. "It took me that long before I even learned healing mode."

"Jord knows that already. No one else can perceive it, let alone imitate it."

"Have you tried every Sime in Fort Freedom?"

"No—but now everyone, men and women, must attempt it. We must do something to show progress, and healing mode is important. Rimon, did you not take transfer from Willa in healing mode, every time?"

"That's right," he said.

"But Jord couldn't hold it today—he broke at the same point he has broken each time. At that point, the Gen feels pain and then fear—and is killed."

Del said, "Terror seems to be the natural state of the Gen. From a Sime point of view, that is," he added, glancing at Kadi. "I haven't been able to keep a Gen from becoming scared, no matter how drugged they are, no matter how careful I am. Even—Billy, who knew better, panicked—and I'm sure it's the sensation of selyn movement that causes the panic and—the kill."

Carlana looked from Kadi to Rimon. "Abel, they love each other. That's important—Willa likes Jord, and she likes to make Simes feel good, as she puts it."

"Good will," Abel said, "or even love, isn't enough. Vee

couldn't do it. Rimon could—he slowed his draw. And, come to think of it, I've zlinned him doing it, and I don't know how he does it."

"The Gen has to know enough not to be afraid," said Kadi. "But the Sime has to care enough to force himself to go as slowly as necessary. It takes two to make a transfer."

Abel frowned, and then asked, "Can we raise our children not to fear?" He looked from Rimon to Del and Carlana. "The Gen is the primary key—I'm convinced of it. Imagine a community in which Simes did not kill because Gens didn't expect to be killed! I wish Jon had been here today to see Willa's face. I wish all the children had seen it. Imagine growing up, seeing transfers like that all the time. Who would be frightened then? Who would resist? Rimon—surely that is the way God planned Simes and Gens to live together!"

"In the days of the Ancients," Kadi murmured.

"What?" asked Abel.

"The way so many fairy tales start, you know, the kind of stories people tell their—oh."

Rimon stepped into the breach. "I think the story Kadi means is the one that starts, 'In the last days of the Ancients, when Simes and Gens lived together—' It pretty well describes the kind of society you're talking about."

Kadi told them the story, with Del filling in some details of another version. Abel smiled tolerantly. "Obviously a Sime legend—blaming the Gens for the way the world is. Yet—isn't saying that the Gens wanted to keep all the selyn for themselves a way of saying they—resisted? There is always truth within a parable, if only we can see it. Who are the Ancients supposed to be?"

Rimon, Kadi, and Del stared at him in astonishment. "Why—the original people. Humans, before they mutated into Sime and Gen—the builders of the ruined cities—the eyeways—"

"But Gens *are* the original human race," said Abel. "Simes are the mutation."

"I don't think so," said Kadi. "If the Ancients had all been Gens, what would have been the point of their selyn production? With whom would a person have fulfilled his potential? No, I think both Simes and Gens are mutated, to fit with one another."

"Well, either way," said Abel, "we're clearly meant to live together. I wonder why it has taken all these centuries to figure that out?"

"Maybe some people have," said Rimon. "There are other legends, stories. Kadi, do you remember old Brova's tall tales?"

"Yes. He claimed to have traveled all the way around the world, and he'd spend hours telling us about strange places."

"Instead of working," added Rimon. "I don't know if Dad fired him for that—or for telling us kids about the island of—what did he call it?"

"I don't remember," said Kadi. "We were only seven or eight years old, but I remember that story, about an island where Simes and Gens lived together without killing. He claimed the Gens would go right up to any Sime in need and offer themselves, and that they didn't die, and afterwards—"

Rimon squirmed, and interposed, "They were just stories!"

"But were they true?"

"I doubt it," said Rimon. "Brova was an old man—the oldest man I've ever met. He claimed to be fifty years past changeover, but nobody lives *that* long. He was probably thirty or so, and senile."

"Still," said Kadi, "he had to get the ideas somewhere."

"The idea is always around," said Rimon. "Brova just embroidered on it." He noticed a Gen field approaching outside. "Jon—"

The sun was setting. As Mrs. Veritt rose to light the lamps, Jon entered, bringing Zeth to Kadi. "He's hungry," he said.

She smiled up at him, saying, "I know," as she took the baby and prepared to nurse him.

"We'll have to be going home soon," said Rimon. "Jon, do you know where Willa is?"

"I think she went off with Jord somewhere. Rimon, may I stay at home tonight, and come out to you tomorrow? Both Mom and Dad are pre-turnover."

"But you are high-field, Jon. No, we won't take any chances like that."

"That's not fair!" Jon flared.

"What's not fair? Protecting your life?"

"A lot you care! It's blackmail, that's what!"

Out of the corner of his eye, Rimon saw Abel flinch from the Gen's field, and Abel wasn't in need. He moved to put himself between Abel and the boy. With the tension relieved, Veritt said, "Jon, just what is disturbing you?"

"I'm sorry, Mr. Veritt," said Jon, but Rimon felt the boy's inner rebellion. "It's just that if I can't visit my parents—or anybody—just because I'm high-field, then I may as well go live out-Territory!" He turned to Rimon. "Since you've got Kadi back, you don't need me, so I'll never be low-field again unless I give transfer to someone else."

Rimon pondered that, disturbed by the truth of Jon's conclusion. But another idea occurred, a chance to test something that had been on his mind since Zeth's birth. "All right, Jon, come here."

He held out his hands, and almost by reflex Jon put his hands into transfer position. Rimon slipped into healing mode, made lip contact, and drew enough selyn from Jon to leave the boy low-field. It was over in an instant. "All right, Jon, you can go home now."

Jon stared at him suspiciously. "What did you do?"

"I lowered your field."

"You took transfer without even asking me?"

"No, I didn't take transfer. I did what you asked—made it safe for you to stay with your parents tonight. Now go on—but I expect you home by tomorrow sunset, no later, understand?"

"Yeah, uh, thanks, Rimon." Self-consciously, he exchanged polite words with the Veritts and Carlana and left, almost stumbling over his own feet in the manner of adolescents—and Gens.

Rimon noticed Del and Abel zlinning the boy. "He is low-field!" Del said. "I was afraid you were faking to give him confidence."

"What did you do?" demanded Kadi. "Rimon, you've thrown your whole cycle off!"

"No I haven't," said Rimon quickly, aware of a near panic in his wife. "And I don't have to balance my fields, either. Abel, Del, zlin me. Am I any higher-field?" He looked appealingly at Mrs. Veritt, but she wasn't zlinning. She was watching Zeth, and Rimon had the impression she had hardly heard a word since the baby came in.

Del was shaking his head, mystified, when Abel finally said, "No, you're not any higher-field. What did you do? Where did Jon's selyn go?"

"The same place all that selyn came from that I transfered to Kadi when Zeth was born. I've thought about that a lot. I was horribly sick afterward with those fluctuations in my fields, nerve burn—but I wasn't in need. That doesn't make sense, Abel! I transfered to Kadi—oh, at least twice what I get from a transfer with Jon or Willa—and yet I wasn't in need. I fell short again that month—but no more than the month before. So where did all that selyn come from?"

"I have never questioned that it was a miracle," said Abel. "God provided."

It was one of those moments when Abel's faith proved an immense barrier to understanding.

Finally Rimon said, "Well, maybe God did, but not the way you mean. Del—remember how I used to get that crazy wobble in my fields before—before a kill?"

Del nodded. "Most peculiar sensation—used to give me a sick headache to be near you."

"And it intensified my need to the point where I couldn't fight it off anymore—even with Kadi's help." To Abel, he added, "That was before she established." And to Del, he said, "Well, I had another attack of it after Zeth was born, and it got me to thinking and kind of feeling around inside myself."

Veritt was nodding. "Yes, Rimon's distress affected all of us. It's a high price you pay for your healing ability."

"Maybe not, if I can learn to control this selyn storage system. That's what was fluctuating—I was going almost into healing mode then coming right out of it again, and each time some selyn would leak into this storage system— like a reservoir for extra selyn. I've always had a short cycle—a month's selyn would never last a month, and nobody knew why. My dad was the same way."

"And Jord," murmured Abel.

"Yes! I think what happens is that each time, some of the selyn goes into that reservoir—and stays there, permanently, unless the person learns to get at it."

"Rimon," said Kadi, "considering what you and I went through when Zeth was born, I don't think you've found the way to get at it."

"Oh, but I have! When I take transfer in healing mode—all the selyn goes into that reservoir. That's why I'm still in need until I balance my fields. What I really do is draw the selyn into my system, ready for use—and that doesn't hurt at all!"

"You may be right, Rimon," said Abel, "but if you do have this 'reservoir,' what is it for?"

"Survival. A Sime who has it can store up two months' worth of selyn at once. Then the second month he can draw from his reserve—or use it to fight, or survive in the cold, or augment. Only he can't get at it by himself—he has to have a Gen to provide resistance. However, the Gen can be low-field, or even scared—and it still works."

"Do you think we all have it?" asked Carlana.

"I don't know. Jord seems to. It may be a new mutation, or there may have been Simes with the capacity all along—or every Sime may have it, but not use it. Maybe a trauma at changeover opens it. We just don't know enough yet. Every new piece of information brings up a hundred new questions."

"Such as why this reservoir of yours becomes an asset rather than a liability only when you have Gens willing to help you get at the selyn you have stored. Surely that is another indication that we're slowly finding out God's plan," said Abel.

"I think we're headed in the right direction," Rimon agreed. "I wish Jord had been here to zlin what I did to Jon, and I want to zlin Jord in healing mode again."

Abel frowned. "Where *is* Jord? He knew we'd be planning—"

Rimon said, "He's post. He doesn't want to sit around talking theories!"

"He's what?"

"Post-kill—or, in this case, post-transfer. If you're right, it's his first time. You'd better not expect his feet to touch the ground until sometime tomorrow."

Kadi looked up and said quietly, "Rimon—Willa's post, too."

For the first time, Rimon considered what that could mean. Jord and Willa were just as inexperienced as he and Kadi had been, and he recalled Kadi's concern that Willa's adolescent emotions were fixed on Jord.

Just then the door opened, and the truants entered. Both were smiling, both had the too-neat look of freshly tucked clothing and just-combed hair, and both were flushed with a fresh and innocent joy.

Jord took Willa's hand, and approached his parents. Willa looked up at him proudly, joyfully, as he said, "Father—Mother—I have good news. Willa has consented to become my wife."

Chapter 19

AN OLD FIGHT

Only Del shared Rimon and Kadi's concern over Jord's intention to marry Willa. Fort Freedom exploded in a rush of wedding plans, everyone as excited as if his own child were getting married. There was no use trying to talk to Willa—she was in paradise, certain that Jord was the husband Rimon and Kadi had promised her.

While the wedding plans went forward, Rimon and Jord tested everyone in Fort Freedom in turn, always a few days after a kill, hoping to find someone who could imitate the healing mode.

Their lack of success was disheartening.

The one thing that brightened Rimon's days was the security of having Kadi back for transfer. The next time, everyone left them alone with their son. That evening, with Zeth well-fed, warm, dry, and sound asleep, Rimon and Kadi prepared for transfer. He sighed. "At this moment I can't believe I've ever known sexual desire—and yet I know it will be there after transfer, and I won't be able to hold back. Kadi, what am I going to do when you're fertile again?"

"Let's not spoil this time by worrying about next time."

"Then let's worry about last time."

"Huh?"

"I didn't satisfy you. This time you take control. Don't stop until you're satisfied."

"But—"

"What do you think I'm going to do—burst?"

She giggled. Her nager bubbled with delight, but he could feel that she was relieved. How long he might have remained in anticipation, Rimon would never know—it was Kadi who could stand it no longer. She began to pour

254

selyn into him, deep into every nerve, a solid, sure torrent that coursed through his system—and on into that reservoir he could suddenly perceive etched in glowing force, yielding before the impact of Kadi's selyn until he began to feel he would indeed burst.

The warmth of Kadi's relaxation held him for a moment before his own pleasure took command of him, drawing him to physical consciousness of Kadi's body against his as she resumed control, making love to him hungrily, passionately.

On the wedding day, Rimon, Kadi, Willa, and Jon assembled early at the Veritt home. Jord was not there; Abel informed them that he was praying and meditating in the chapel.

"This will be an important day for all of us," said Abel. "Last month we found that Jord and Willa could have transfer; this month we'll prove that before the whole world. Sara Fenell, Dan Whelan, and the others have agreed to be here today. I pray that they will now return."

If not, neither community may survive, Rimon thought. He had had so much work in Fort Freedom's fields because they didn't have the labor force to raise and harvest their cash crops with twenty per cent of the population trying to work their land independently—but if Fort Freedom was having problems, the dissenters were even worse off. They had only one advantage: Dan Whelan had been Fort Freedom's blacksmith. Del, who would not go to Whelan over Carlana's objections, complained constantly about the sloppy blacksmithing done by the woman in town, always comparing her to the woman Syrus Farris had running his smithy.

Del and Carlana appeared about an hour before the ceremony, with their children freshly scrubbed and dressed in new clothes. Jana was a little angel in a yellow dress today, and Owen had a suit and cape like Del's. Everyone else was neat and clean, but none wore new clothes except the bride and groom. There were no luxuries this year.

As everyone was assembling before the chapel, the dissenters appeared. People made way for them, warily, silently. Dan Whelan led the group to the chapel door, where

Abel was standing. Sara Fenell hung back somewhat. Rimon understood her conflict. She would always remember that her son had died trying what Willa would do today. If only Abel could make her look to the future instead of the past. . . .

Abel greeted everyone warmly. "We're pleased that you've returned to share our joy in this day. Please come in, and send your children to the front of the chapel. We wish all the children to see what it can mean for Sime and Gen to be together."

Whelan stopped before Abel. "I said I'd come back and listen to you if you could prove to me that Simes could live without killing. I'm here to see that proof."

"Enter freely and be welcome," said Abel.

Families shooed their children into the front rows, hiding their own nervousness. It couldn't be that they feared Jord would kill Willa—anyone who had seen them together must be well over that fear. But the questions would come now, from children who didn't yet know of the kill, but who were old enough to have some idea of what they were witnessing.

Jord was waiting at the front of the chapel, as far from the tensions of the congregation as possible. He was edgy, like a normal Sime in need, but his smile when Willa approached was quite genuine, and he relaxed visibly as she stood beside him.

Abel took the lecture stand and briefly instructed the congregation that they must permit themselves to observe the transfer in duoconsciousness. Rimon felt the increased tension in Veritt's staunchest supporters and the blatant disapproval in the little group around Sara Fenell.

He remembered the first time they'd come into the chapel, how serene and healthy everyone had seemed compared to their own hardened and unkempt appearance. Now, despite their impeccable grooming, the people of Fort Freedom seemed gaunt with trial.

As Abel spoke, trying to convince them it was no sin to use their Sime senses in the presence of God, there was a stirring of excitement—even hope—among them. Today would see the beginning of the end of their guilt. Their increasing hope seemed to double the load Rimon carried.

Abel kept his remarks brief and to the point, not making the couple wait while he spun out philosophical theories. When he called Jord and Willa before him, he asked only for a short, silent prayer for the young couple embarking on a long life together.

The other Simes in the chapel were excited, focusing intently on what was about to happen. Sara Fenell had her arms crossed, hugging herself. Dan Whelan folded his hands in his lap, but the knuckles were white. The Lassiters were clutching each other's hands, tentacles retracted hard. Others knelt in prayer, eyes closed, but zlinning carefully.

Rimon, too, closed his eyes, letting himself be carried away with relief as Willa gave to Jord, her joy almost outshining his. When he looked up again, he saw Willa looking up into Jord's eyes with that same starry ecstasy she had shown after their first transfer. Around the room, disbelief fought with soaring hope. Many were crying. At the back of the chapel, where those in need had been seated, the door opened as some left hastily.

A murmur of spontaneous prayer rose from the assembly, as everyone shared that moment with Willa and Jord, poised at the edge of post-syndrome. Rimon relived that first moment of disbelief with Kadi, when she had given him transfer and they had both found themselves alive afterward—that indescribable sensation that at last everything was all right. He felt it from Kadi—she must be sharing the same memory. He put his arm around her, and reached with his other hand to touch Zeth, binding them together.

When the wave of emotion had ebbed, Abel broke his long silence to call Rimon and Kadi forward. They had the place of honor as witnesses while Abel performed the strange ceremony of vows that constituted the Fort Freedom pledge ceremony. Rimon had gathered that in Gen Territory his marriage to Kadi would not be recognized, because they had not pledged before witnesses—while Jord and Willa were now considered to be permanently married through the spoken words, and not through emotional commitment, living together, or having children.

Rimon's puzzlement was swept aside by the powerful

tonic of Willa's happiness. He and Kadi were caught up in the hope and joy of the people as they swirled out of the chapel singing out their strange, traditional songs, surrounding the bride and groom. Abel, in the midst of it all, was glowing almost as much as his son, happier than Rimon had ever seen him.

Out in front of the chapel, everyone crowded around Jord and Willa again, congratulating them, respectfully asking to zlin them. As the crowd began to disperse, Dan Whelan approached Abel. "I have seen," he said simply. "May God forgive me for doubting."

"God is merciful," replied Abel. "He will understand. Will you return to us now, Dan?"

Whelan's tentacles flicked nervously but were instantly restrained.

Veritt added, "Even though we believe you erred, we admire you for following the dictates of your conscience. Come back to us, Dan."

"Mr. Veritt, my son, Uel—knows. But he has never seen a kill. Today he saw—oh, surely he saw God's mercy in action!"

"He saw another witch in action!"

Kadi jumped, startled, and five Simes near her likewise started at the surge in her field. She settled immediately as she recognized Sara Fenell.

"No, Sara!" said Dan. "You saw it yourself—how could you think Willa a witch?"

"Will you all be taken in? Look at these women—demons in the bodies of Gens. Rimon Farris is a sorcerer sent to steal your souls. And he's succeeding. Look you how he has made his way into your midst, seducing your own son, Abel Veritt, with one of his succubi. Yonder stands Jon Forester—why is he not able to give selyn to someone? Not his own parents dare touch him, only Rimon Farris. And why is that?"

"Because Rimon's protecting me, that's why!" said Jon. "But you come on—I'll give you transfer right now. I'll show you Rimon's no sorcerer!"

On the wave of his anger, Jon might actually have been able to do it, Rimon thought. An overpowering emotion could wipe out fear, as Kadi had found at their first transfer. But it wouldn't sustain Jon. Abel on one side and Rimon on the other immediately pulled him back, as Sara Fenell said, "Shall I kill you to prove you are wrong, Jon? The Devil will not gain my soul so easily, although I see he has made progress toward obtaining yours."

She turned to the group of dissenters, who had formed a cluster between herself and Dan Whelan. "You see? This boy is being corrupted, the way Drust was corrupted. Can you not learn from my son's experience? How many of your children must die?"

Margid Veritt came up and put her arm around the distraught woman's shoulders. "Sara," she said softly, "you're upset. Please, come with me where you can rest—"

The other woman flung her off. "I'm not having a woman's hysteria! As a mother, Margid, think! Jord is your son!"

"Would you have me question what God has revealed to my husband?" asked Margid.

"There is nothing to understand except the bare facts. Rimon Farris has not yet bent Jon to his will; he has not yet gained the boy's soul. When he does, Jon will be like these women—a vessel for selyn, controlled by this sorcerer, and in turn used to control you and lead you to damnation."

By this time, Jord and Willa had moved close beside Abel. Now Jord said, "Mrs. Fenell, this is the second month I have not killed. Does that mean nothing to you? Rimon has taught Willa, who is teaching me—and while I learn, she can keep me free of the kill. Can you not envision a world in which Simes and Gens teach one another to live together in peace?"

"No! If God had meant that, Gens would not die when Simes took selyn!"

"But we don't," said Willa.

"You see, Jord Veritt? This demon has your soul in her grasp. There's no use talking to you. Is there no one here who can see how first the Gens are corrupted, and then used to corrupt the Simes?"

"Sara, please," said Abel, "won't you stay and pray with us? We'll listen to your objections, try to answer your questions."

"I listened to you, Abel Veritt, when you were on God's

true path. You taught me well, then. I shall pray for your return to the true way."

Once more Sara Fenell made her retreat from Fort Freedom—but this time far fewer people followed her. Rimon felt Kadi's astonishment, but he understood. Abel Veritt had placed his faith in Rimon, and though all it seemed to bring him was grief, his faith remained unshaken. *What do they want of me? Why won't he turn to Jord now? Why won't they all turn to Jord now? But maybe they will when they really understand what Jord and Willa are, maybe then they'll take some of the pressure off of me.*

The summer ended and the cold rains of fall began again. This time, though, Kadi was not so shut in. They had glass in the windows, and their new stove provided far more heat than the fireplace they had huddled around last winter. Zeth was a constant joy, a good baby who fussed only when there was something wrong, but whose curious black eyes soon followed everything that went on.

They missed Willa's help, and also the girl's sunny personality. Jon shifted from hope to fear to anxiety to pride each time Jord or Rimon drew from him in healing mode, and he would vow that next month he'd be ready to give transfer—but each month, as he grew high-field again, his anxiety grew with it until Rimon again ruled out the attempt.

They spent a good deal of time at Fort Freedom, but when they were home they never lacked company; if Jord and Willa were not there, it would be Del's whole family. Both Owen and Jana learned to ride quickly and loved going places on their ponies. Owen confided, "Jana's almost as much fun as a boy now, but I wish Zeth would grow up so we could play together."

"There are no boys Owen's age at Fort Freedom," Carlana explained, and Rimon remembered that the Fifes, who had a four-year-old son, had elected to stay with Sara Fenell in the half-empty row of houses along the creek. They had also heard that the Fife family had bought a female Gen from Slina and kept her for two months without killing her.

"Do you think they're trying to raise the girl to be like Willa?" Kadi asked Carlana.

"Yes, I think that's what they're doing. I wanted to do it myself, but Del said no."

"And you just let it go at that?"

"No, I—I talked with Mr. Veritt about Del. He said Del is right to make me take responsibility for my own decisions. And I think if I had insisted, Del would have given in. I don't know, Kadi. If anyone can tame a wild thing and make it love him, it's Del. But if he failed, he would hurt more than anyone else. So we'll wait. If others succeed, I will insist."

That was the state of all their friends, torn between hope and fear. And from time to time, especially during the last days before a transfer, Rimon would retreat to Billy's grave, carefully tending the plants and hedges there, the physical labor somehow easing his guilt.

Besides the emotional turmoil, there were simple problems of survival—for the first time, Rimon and Kadi were better off than their friends at Fort Freedom. With their manpower spread thin by the schism during the growing season, their cash crops had suffered. Now they were short of funds. Dan Whelan was working hard to repair all their equipment, but he was running short of metal.

The big argument wherever three men gathered in Fort Freedom was whether to do without the necessary metal or to break one of their most cherished principles and deal with one of the outlaw bands that raided Gen Territory for metal mined from the ruins of the Ancients. But Veritt would not yield on that point. He said there was blood on that metal—the blood of those Gens who mined it, those from whom it was stolen, and the blood of Simes who paid dearly for their raids into the heart of Gen Territory.

Nonetheless, the Year's Turning ceremony was a time of great celebration, as Abel detailed the progress from the year before. Two more children had established, and both had elected to stay with their families, giving their selyn to Rimon each month as Jon did. Even though both had the same problems Jon had, their presence was a ray of hope.

Willa seemed happy, easing Jord's growing tension without causing him to lash out at her. Zlinning Willa, Rimon found none of that tension in her that had bothered him for so long in Kadi. Kadi had had to learn not to hide her true feelings, something it simply never occurred to Willa to do. Nonetheless, around Jord and Willa, he felt a kind of precarious stasis, as if Jord would soon face something similar to what had happened to Rimon last winter, the day of Carlana's miscarriage. When he came through that, he'd be in control of himself.

Then one snowy day, as what looked like an all-day blizzard began to pile snow around their homestead, they had an unexpected visitor: Risko, the man who worked for Slina, and whom Rimon had healed the very first time he'd ever used his healing mode.

"Rimon, we got problems at the Pens," he explained.

"What's wrong?"

"Slina got in a prime Gen a few weeks ago—marked as Farris stock, he is, but I told her she shoulda asked you."

"You think she was cheated?"

"Worse than that. He's sick—and it's spreading through the Pens. We lost three already, and if we can't stop it, well—look at the snow comin' down. You may not need our stock, but everyone else does, and—"

"It's all right, Risko," said Rimon. "I'll come and do whatever I can. Kadi, Jon—you come along and—no, you might catch it. You go to Fort Freedom and tell Jord to come help me."

"Slina's already gone to ask Abel Veritt for help," said Risko. "We heard his son's a healer, like you."

"He'll help," said Rimon. "Everyone in Fort Freedom who can do anything will."

It was not only that they needed Gens to survive; it was that they knew full well that if the Simes in the little border town were shorted, they'd have no qualms about hunting across the border—and right across the border was the community where Fort Freedom sent their established children.

When Rimon reached Slina's, three wagons were just pulling away—Simes stocking up on Gens with an eye on the gathering storm. Inside, Rimon found both Abel and Jord in the office, Willa at Jord's side.

"Willa, it's a Gen illness," Rimon told her. "You mustn't stay here—see, I didn't even bring Kadi."

Jord shifted closer to his wife, his stance tense. "Willa stays with me. I say where she goes."

"Jord—" started Rimon.

But Slina interrupted. "Willa had this one couple years ago. Anyways, one like to it."

"You know what it is, then?" asked Rimon.

"Gotta be just a bad kind o' Reloc fever."

"Shen!" Reloc fever had been known to wipe out whole Pens.

Slina said, "If I can't do somethin' awful fast—"

"Now calm down, Slina," said Abel. "You've only had five cases, and we've got them isolated."

She glanced at him, but said to Rimon, "I picked up a bargain with a Farris brand—now, I ain't blamin' your dad, understand—I always did suspect it was a forgery, but it was a good buy. Big, healthy out-Territory male, and hung like a bull. Figured to expand my operation, breed the wild 'un to some of my best stock like them fancy outfits do."

Rimon nodded, his mind on the problem of Reloc fever loose where Kadi might encounter it—or Zeth. "It's not your fault, Slina. If his papers didn't indicate he'd been through Reloc, why would you suspect anything?"

"I did quarantine him. The day after I let him out—he falls down sick, and six days later I've got two pregnant females down with it, and two pre-Gens down a couple days later."

"Pregnant females?" asked Rimon.

"Yeah. May as well write 'em off as a complete loss." Slina was gloomier than Rimon had ever seen her, but he put it down to turnover.

"They're worth fighting for, Slina. Once in a while, you can beat even Reloc fever."

"Let's take a look at the victims," said Veritt.

Slina picked up her giant keys and led the way across the court yard to the small infirmary set apart from the Pens. As they walked, Rimon said, "What are you doing breeding Gens at this time of year?"

"You think I want them delivering at this time of year?

There's no late winter without some kind of illness in the Pens, so I don't want susceptible—unsellable—newborns around then."

Without thinking, Rimon quoted his father, "It's cheaper to lose a newborn than a good breeder. Besides, in the infant house you can isolate them from—"

"I can't afford no infant house, Rimon! I—"

Slina cut off, flicking a glance at Jord and Abel behind them, and Rimon became aware of the utter horror Jord was fighting down, the weary but sick feeling in Abel as they listened to the calm discussion between two Gendealers. Rimon shook his head ruefully as he held the outer door open while Slina fitted her keys into the massive lock on the inner door to the infirmary.

Inside, they found a small room with three beds. Two of the victims lay listlessly, staring at the ceiling. They were young boys, probably about to establish within the next few months. The third bed in the room was wrapped about with a strong though murky field.

"This must be the one," said Rimon. The Gen was a large full-grown man who slept fitfully, turning with a soft moan as Rimon approached. There was the briefest glimpse of the diagonal notch filed in his front tooth—the mark of prime Farris stock.

Rimon inspected the Gen, zlinned the nager, and shrugged. "He could have passed through Farris hands. He's well muscled, and even all but unconscious, he shows a nager with bite. This one is a troublemaker. Prime kill, yes, but no good at all for breeding stock."

How quickly it all comes back, he thought, shocked at himself. Secretly, he was glad Kadi wasn't here to listen—though she'd heard the like all her life.

Slina shook her head. "Anytime you want a job, Rimon—"

"Not me! I'm in the business of saving Gen lives now. But you're doing a great job running your own outfit, Slina. Really, you are."

With a sigh, she twitched the covers off the Gen to display the characteristic rash of Reloc fever. "He's been slow coming down with it," she said. "Just showed the rash this morning."

Just then, the man tossed restlessly, his movement wakening the characteristic headache of the fever. Rimon and Jord winced at the pain and went into healing mode together, while Abel stepped back behind them. Slina seemed unaffected. After all, she was accustomed to Gen pain.

The Gen's eyes came open, fever-bright and unfocused. "Where—who are you?" he asked in a raspy whisper.

Rimon had learned enough of the Gen language at Fort Freedom to answer. "I'm Rimon Farris. You're ill, but we know how to cure you."

The man's eyes slid past Rimon to the others and came into focus, memory returning. As weak as he was, he drew away from Rimon and said more clearly, "Get away from me!" The spirit was definitely there when he was awake. Prime kill—or prime transfer partner?

Rimon moved back a step, holding his hands out, tentacles sheathed, and then putting them firmly behind his back. He watched the Gen assessing that move, but Slina said, in Simelan, "Rimon! Don't let him think he can have his way—you know what'll happen!"

"Let me try this experiment," he said. "You can always take him—he's not going to get away from us!"

She stood back warily and let Rimon proceed. He waited until the weakened Gen could not hold up his head anymore, and said, "We're here to help you."

"For what! To get sold again? To get killed? You just try it, I'll—" He collapsed in a coughing fit.

Then Rimon said, "You ready to take some medicine now?"

"No—I'd rather die. Cheat this stinkin' place outa—" He began coughing again.

Abel said from the back of the group, "You don't really want to die. God doesn't expect us to give up—you have no idea why God sent you here at this time. Tell him, Rimon."

"God!" said the Gen. "What do you know of God!"

"We pray," said Abel, "just as we did when we were children. Our faith is always rewarded."

The Gen made the effort to raise his head and focus his eyes on Abel. "Church of the Purity? Here?"

"After our own fashion," said Abel, with a humility Rimon had seldom seen in the older man.

"Let me try," said Jord, moving forward with Willa. "Look at me," he commanded, taking Willa's hand and holding out her arm so the man could see clearly she was Gen. "There are some of us who don't kill, and others who are learning not to. You can be as safe here as Willa is—and Willa's my wife."

"Drugged!" scoffed the Gen.

"No," denied Jord calmly. In Simelan, he said to Willa, "Would you like to help this man get well?"

She nodded vigorously and said in Simelan, "Yes, Jord, what should we do?"

The Gen wiped beads of sweat from his forehead, his arm falling heavily back to the mattress. "God, what a dream! She's talkin' their lingo! Won't I ever wake up?"

Rimon said, "His fever's rising. We've got to get some fosebine into him. You do have some ready, Slina?"

"Sure—can't get them to drink it, though—not unless they've dehydrated from the fever. And I'm just not cruel enough to withhold the water that long."

"Get the fosebine and let me see what I can do." He turned back to the Gen as Slina left. "You *are* smart enough to take medicine even though it tastes bad?"

The Gen rolled his head on the mattress, a weak negative. Rimon was at a loss until Abel said, "Rimon, we've got to make him understand that we're trying to start a whole new way of life here."

Zlinning, Rimon could sense how Veritt was oddly attracted to the Gen. *He's probably having visions of training him!*

Veritt wasn't paying much attention to Rimon. He began talking to the Gen, urgently. "—and my own son no longer has to kill every month. Families aren't being broken when the children mature. Men and women can fall in love and marry—Sime and Gen together. Rimon and my son are both married to Gens—Rimon has a son by a Gen. Don't you see—you've work here, a place here, if you can survive this trial. Take the medicine—live—and join us."

Slina returned with a large bottle of pale gray liquid and a wooden drinking bowl. "For whatever good it'll do!"

Rimon took the bottle, examining the liquid. He could see right through it. "This isn't concentrated enough," he said. "Put in about four times as much powder to this amount of water."

"Rimon, it already tastes so foul they won't touch it!"

Rimon shoved a lock of hair off his forehead with one tentacle and poured some of the liquid into the bowl. "Come on, now—if you don't drink this down, Slina is likely to sell you to the next customer for immediate kill before you just die anyway."

"Rimon!" said Jord.

"What'd he say?" Slina asked Abel, who motioned her to silence.

Rimon offered the drinking bowl, his tentacles carefully retracted. "Show her you're intelligent, and she'll keep you alive long enough for us to get you out of here."

Warily, the Gen took the bowl and tasted the concoction with curled lip, and then drank it all down. He flung the bowl away at random and slid back onto the mattress, muttering something about hoping it was poison.

Rimon fielded the bowl in midair with two tentacles and flipped it into his hand. "There, Slina, see? Zlin that."

As the medicine took effect, the Gen relaxed, his aches and pains quieting, his fever leveling off. Rimon said, "Go prepare some of the stronger mixture, Slina, while we take a look at the two women."

Rimon and Jord with Willa beside him went to the next room, where two female Gens occupied the beds, one coughing spasmodically, the other watching and whimpering in fear. Again, Rimon realized just how unique Slina was among Penkeepers for not selling these two breeders when they first showed symptoms—certainly there were customers in town who'd relish a pregnant Gen. Intense disgust rose in Rimon, surprising him.

"What's wrong?" asked Jord, one tentacle around Willa's wrist.

"Nothing," answered Rimon, shaking off the mood and zlinning the two women. Immediately, he saw that the one coughing was about two and a half months pregnant. Her fever was skyrocketing.

Jord, too, was zlinning. "Rimon, Slina said the two females were infected after the males. But look at them—is Reloc fever always so fast?"

"I've dealt with it only once or twice before. Pregnancy weakens a Gen—any disease is serious then." Rimon found an empty basin on a side table and handed it to Willa. "Go fill this with water and get some rags. We're going to have to sponge down that fever."

The rest of the night, they nursed the five patients along, while Slina searched for new victims, and then returned to the infirmary with hot trin tea and a few biscuits.

Jord said, "I got the man to take concentrated fosebine by showing him how Willa would drink it if I told her to. Now she's fallen asleep!"

"Let her sleep," said Rimon. "She can't keep up with a Sime, you know."

Jord gave Rimon a wry grin. "You should have taught her that from the first!"

"Kadi hasn't learned it yet!"

In a moment of camaraderie, Jord said, "I rather doubt Henry ever will, either."

"Henry?"

"Steers. Henry Steers. I asked him his name. It was as if I'd given him his identity back—he said no one on this side of the border ever cared enough to ask even his name."

"You know why, Jord."

"Yes, of course," he replied. "It's only after you don't have to kill that you start to see your defenses. But did you notice that he isn't scared of any of us? I don't know if he assumes that no one would take a sick Gen, or if he's just naturally like Willa."

"More likely he's just emotionally wrung out. Slina's had him a while, and we don't know what he went through before that. If Fort Freedom does buy him, you'll probably end up sending him across the border. He's got a life out there somewhere."

"We'll get the money," said Abel. He turned to Slina. "We'll pay what you were asking—but it's going to take us a while. It's been a bad year, but things are getting better now."

"You've been good customers all these years, never making any trouble. But I can't let you have him on credit—

Rimon is right. He's a troublemaker and probably will get himself killed trying to escape. I'm doubling my security on this wing as soon as he's well enough to stand on his feet."

"Just don't sell him to anyone else," Abel said.

Rimon wondered if Abel was following Slina's thoughts as she nodded. "It's a deal, Veritt. I'll keep him for you until midsummer. But that's as long as I can guarantee you—then I may have to send him to auction to recoup some of my losses." She hadn't really wanted to sell Steers right away—she had other plans in mind.

All three males were out of danger before the next morning. The two females were another matter. Near midnight, Slina called Rimon in to support the field of one of them as she miscarried—not such a painful experience as Carlana's, since the pregnancy was so little advanced, but racking coughs added to the misery of her cramping, and she could not seem to get enough air. Rimon had to concentrate on bolstering her selyn production, alternating with Jord, who still could not hold very long in healing mode.

Willa was upset at the loss of another baby, although she was not frightened. When the worst was over, Rimon collapsed into a chair, letting Jord take over seeing that nothing went wrong after the fact. Willa asked Jord, "Why do so many babies die?"

"Not many, Willa. I know this is the second time you've seen it, but most women have their babies without even as much trouble as Kadi had."

"When can we have a baby?"

"Maybe next year."

"That's what you said last year. It's next year now. The Year's Turning is over."

"You know I don't want to wait, Willa, but we have to, for your sake."

It was obviously an old argument. Rimon lost track of their murmurings and drifted into a light doze.

He woke with the sound of a strangled wheeze dying in the air about him, a Gen field fading to nageric silence. He was on his feet with a start before he realized it was too late. One of the women had died. On the other bed, the one who had miscarried was having a coughing fit while Slina tried to coax her to drink some fosebine.

His knees suddenly weak, Rimon sank back into his chair. Jord and Slina hurried to his side, but he fended them off. "I'll be all right if I can just sit a few minutes." There was a weak, fluttery sensation somewhere inside him that he'd thought he'd never have to cope with again. "Jord, you'd better check out the other Gen."

"She drank some fosebine," said Slina. "She's asleep." She moved to look down at the dead girl. "Shidoni! A good, healthy breeder, and the kid, too—and the other one's kid. What am I gonna do?" Then she straightened. "Listen, I'm sorry—without your help, I'da lost the bunch of 'em. I owe you."

"All Fort Freedom asks is the right to buy Mr. Steers."

"You got that—my word on it." She turned to Rimon. "You look all dragged out. Come on—I got an empty bed in my office. You stretch out there for a while."

"I'll help you," said Willa. It was a simple, selfless impulse, typical of the girl's character. Jord was in no difficulty at the moment, and Willa had learned long ago how to ease Rimon's strain—but even as she moved from Jord's side toward Rimon's, her husband reached out in a sudden flare of blazing anger to thrust her away from Rimon.

"You leave my wife alone!" exclaimed Jord, reaching for Rimon.

"I didn't touch her!" Rimon gasped in astonishment that faded before the familiarity of Jord's reaction. "Abel—"

But the older man was impeded by Willa, who was trying to get back to Jord, as Jord reached for Rimon's throat. Rimon raised his arms to fend Jord off, only to find Jord's tentacles whipping about his forearms, laterals extended for contact. Jord's grip put pressure on Rimon's lateral extensor nodes, twining their laterals together. *What is he doing?*

Hideous familiarity told Rimon at once what Jord was in fact doing—what Rimon had done to Zeth, instinctively, on that far-off day of his First Kill. *No! NO!* Raw panic surged through Rimon, feeding Jord's attack. But Jord was jerking Rimon into lip contact at that very instant, and all Rimon could do was refuse—*refuse!* He felt the pain of Jord's denied draw, the shock of shen, and then Jord collapsed, unconscious, pulling Rimon down on top of him.

Chapter 20

FAILURE

Ignoring his own spinning head, Rimon scrambled to his knees, zlinning Jord. *I've killed him! He'll die of shock!* Willa dropped down beside Jord, grabbing for his arms.

"Jord, Jord! Wake up! Let me help you!" She looked up at Rimon in fury. "Why did you do that?!"

Jord was pre-turnover. Zlinning him, Rimon said, "I think he'll be all right, Willa. Just hold him and try to make him calm."

As Abel zlinned Jord, profound relief spread out from him. "Are you all right, Rimon?"

"Me? Sure. It's your son I nearly killed."

"Not this time," said Abel, with a flash of smugness.

Jord stirred. "Willa!" He hugged her close, then looked over her shoulder at Rimon to say, "God forgive me! I'm sorry, Rimon. I don't know what made me do that."

"Why did you hurt him?" demanded Willa. "Jord never hurt you."

"Willa," said Jord, tightly controlling agonized guilt, "I tried to kill Rimon!"

"You can't kill Rimon that way any more than you can kill me," she said.

Now there's a thought. There was so much they didn't know. "Jord," said Rimon, "I shouldn't have shenned you. I panicked. If you'd actually been in need, it could have killed you."

His head hurt suddenly—sympathetic reaction to Jord's pain, plus that great, looming burden that seemed to grow ever heavier on his shoulders. *I know I can kill a Sime in transfer. I know I never want to kill another Gen. But now I find out I can kill merely by defending my own life.*

I don't want that kind of power—power that can get out of control so easily.

Jord held out a hand to Rimon, tentacles neatly retracted. "I'd have deserved it if you'd killed me. I don't blame you, Rimon." His gaze strayed to Willa, then back to Rimon. "I should trust you, of all people—and Willa. In a sense, you gave her to me, like a father giving his daughter in marriage."

"That you don't trust him is a good sign," Abel said. "It's useless to try to make sense of your motives now. We just have to see that such a situation never occurs again. Willa, you must not approach any Sime except Jord, in any way, until he learns to deal with this, as Rimon did. Do you remember how jealous Rimon was of Kadi last year?"

"I remember."

"Well, Jord is going through the same thing, and you must be very understanding, and very careful, until he reaches the stage Rimon is in now."

"It feels like changeover all over again," said Jord. "I never know what to expect next. I've become something uncontrolled and dangerous."

"Jord," said Abel, "that's the right way to think of it—but as we now see changeover, not the hell I put you through. Look to the future. Look at Rimon. You're going to come through this unwilling, perhaps unable to kill. Then you'll teach others. My son, I'm relying on you to teach us all—to teach me."

As Rimon listened to Abel calming his son, a part of his bleak burden lifted. If Abel would just place his hope of salvation on Jord's shoulders, if Rimon could have responsibility only for Kadi and Zeth—that was enough. That much, he thought, he could handle.

Rimon felt good that early spring, with relief in sight from his burdens. He began to think that perhaps he could handle anything life decided to throw at him.

Willa was gone, but Jon continued to live with them for days at a time, helping with the chores and even taking care of Zeth as he grew more active. But Jon also spent a great deal of time in Fort Freedom, with his parents, with Jord and Willa, and talking to Abel Veritt.

Abel put Jon on a regimen of prayer and meditation to end on the first day of summer with Jon's first real transfer. With a target date now set, Abel hoped Jon would gain command of his nerves. Rimon wasn't too sure about that, but he conceded Abel knew more of Gen psychology than anyone raised in-Territory. And, with the date set, Jon did seem to settle down securely.

One difficulty refused to resolve itself. Fort Freedom was still struggling under the combination of the bad year, people's continuing guilt at the kill, and the financial burden of saving enough to purchase Henry Steers. Every time Rimon mentioned that to Abel, he would be put off sharply with one or another statement that added up to "Fort Freedom does not borrow money!"

Yet knowing what Slina was doing to Steers in her attempts to emulate the more elaborate breeding operations, Rimon felt more and more urgency to get the Gen out of there.

Jord Veritt spent a great deal of time at Slina's. The few times Rimon went with him, he observed a growing respect between the two men. Religion seemed to be as important to Steers as to Fort Freedom, and Rimon noticed a kind of nageric link between the two men when they were on that subject—even when they were arguing some point of theological disagreement. But then, each time Jord came back to the subject of Simes and Gens living together, the link would shatter under Steers' uncontrollable anxiety.

"How do I know you'd treat me any more as a person than that woman does?" Steers demanded one day. "Can't you convince her that I am not going to run away?"

"I don't think anything will convince Slina not to lock you in," said Rimon.

"That's not so bad," said Steers. "It's the drugs. I never know if I dare eat or drink—every few days I lose time to crazy dreams, and I know she put something in my food again. Afterward, I always feel I've been doing something, not just sleeping, but I can't remember it."

Rimon knew, but hesitated to tell Jord. Wild Gens would not cooperate for breeding, but there were combinations of drugs that could produce compliance without impairing virility. It was a dangerous practice. The hallucinations could lead the Gen to harm himself or his partner, but nothing could stop the newest fashion in Gen-breeding.

Jord was putting pressure on Abel to get Steers out of the Pens, privately explaining to Rimon, "My father has vowed not to die a killer. Steers has been sent to teach him, Rimon, I know it. I've got to see them work together."

Rimon could not ignore the vibrant hope in Jord, the carefully suppressed hope in Abel, the air of expectancy throughout Fort Freedom. *But what if they fail?* Yet he sensed that Jord was right; Steers no longer reacted hesitantly toward Jord, and he was losing his apprehension with Rimon, as well. If Slina entered, his nager shattered with resentment—but not fear.

"The most hopeful sign," said Rimon, "is that he reacts to us as individuals. But I'm afraid his first priority on getting out of here will be to go home. Mine would be."

"His wife was killed by the raiders that captured him. He doesn't know what happened to his twelve-year-old son—but he thinks he's probably on this side of the border. His only hope of finding him is staying here."

Rimon took a deep breath. "Jord—I don't know if you'll want to tell Steers this, but I do know the Trade. The boy's probably dead, especially if he was established, or did so since capture. I don't think it's fair to get Henry's hopes up—even if his son is alive, it would be a tremendous job to trace a single pre-Gen, even if I still had access to my father's information network. If he was still a child, the raiders would have sold him cheap, because nine out of ten Wild Gen children are dead within the month. Especially in winter."

Jord reached for Willa's hand. "I'll have to tell Henry. We can't give him false hopes. Still—we don't *know* his son is dead."

"He'd be better off, Jord," Rimon said softly.

"No," said Willa. "If he is alive, someday someone will take him from the Pens, the way you took me. When Simes don't kill anymore, they'll have to let all the Gens out. Then Henry and his son will find each other and be happy."

It was the longest speech Rimon had ever heard from Willa. Jord said, "I wish you spoke English, Willa. Henry would believe you—but he can't understand you."

"Then we must teach him to talk like us," said Willa.

That plan, however, was delayed by a new problem— the very outgrowth of Reloc fever both Slina and Rimon had feared all winter: pneumonia. As spring approached, the sparse snows melted and an early warm spell encouraged tender shoots of new grass while the daffodils poked up a month early in the yards of Fort Freedom. Inevitably, freezing rain and hail soon destroyed the premature signs of life. Another warm spell turned the rutted roads to slushy mud, but Rimon and Kadi managed to get through on horseback to Fort Freedom, where they were told that Abel, Jord, and Willa were at Slina's fighting a new illness.

Rimon left Kadi and Zeth at Fort Freedom and rode quickly back into town. Even light cases of Reloc fever were debilitating. Gens might recover completely, but for about six months after they were susceptible to anything that came along—and the recent thaw-and-freeze pattern was exactly what Rimon's father always called "pneumonia weather."

Slina's infirmary was full, and she had set up cots in several holding rooms. When Rimon came in, Risko was carrying out one blanket-wrapped form. "Third one today," he grunted.

Slina, busy with the fosebine, didn't look up when Rimon entered, but told him, "I'm out of healthy Gens. Everyone close enough to need to pick up his month's choice has been in the last two days. Everyone else will get sick ones—and the way they're dying, I may be out before I can get an emergency shipment."

"Out? Completely out?"

"Well, whaddya want me to do?" she snapped. Then, pushing back a lock of hair with one tentacle, she said, "Shen, Rimon, they're gonna raid, you know. And you know what'll happen this summer."

"The Gens will raid us," Rimon said heavily.

"Organized Gens!" spat Slina. "With their bloodyshen guns, killing right and left!"

"We've got to save enough Gens to get along until you get some more," said Rimon. "I'm here to help."

"Go spell Jord Veritt—he's about ready to drop. I never used to like the boy—the old man's a good sort, but Jord was a real lorsh. You done something to him, Rimon, or maybe Willa did—he's been going day and night for a week. Shidoni—who'd think I'd be beholden to them Fort Freedom characters?"

Rimon found Jord and Abel, both haggard and bleary-eyed, in one of the larger rooms. Willa, pale and exhausted, had fallen asleep in a chair. She was high-field, however, a support to Jord even though she was not consciously doing anything.

High-field? Rimon zlinned Jord. He was approaching need, and something in his pattern had changed. So Jord was almost in need, and Rimon past turnover—neither one of them in the best shape for this work. Rimon told Jord, "Willa's asleep. Take her with you, and get some sleep."

"Can't sleep now," Jord murmured.

"You can with Willa. Give yourself two hours." He took over support of the Gen Jord had been concentrating on, alert to the others, apparently the most critical cases.

Abel said, "Go ahead, Jord. Rest. Thank God Rimon is here now."

"How about you, Abel?" asked Rimon.

"I'm fine; I haven't been doing anything but physical work. It's healing mode that's so exhausting."

Rimon smiled. "Then I'd be glad if you stayed. When you're meditating—praying—your nager is almost as soothing as a Gen's."

The moment he could take his concentration off the worst patient, Rimon zlinned the other Gens. Two were slowly rallying. The three others were all critical. And one of them was Henry Steers. Rimon said to Abel, "Slina was keeping Steers isolated; he shouldn't be down with pneumonia."

"Isolated indeed!" replied Abel, his nager flaring more fury than Rimon had ever seen in the gentle old man. "Do you know what she was doing to him?"

Rimon sighed. "I knew, but I didn't know you did, and I was hoping he'd never find out."

"You knew?"

"Abel—I tried to talk her out of it. It's dangerous to try to breed the Wild males. But he was strong, and healthy after he got over the fever. She was just trying to recoup her losses."

"Rimon—I'm glad Jord isn't here right now. I find it hard to recognize you, and I've seen more of the world than my son has. I think I could understand if it were simply that Slina tried to use Henry—for breeding. It's *how* she used him! He would have refused, but still, she didn't ask, or tell him what she was doing—and don't say it's because she doesn't speak English, because we'd have translated for her."

"Would you have?" asked Rimon.

"If I couldn't have persuaded her to give up the attempt. He had a right to know—but she drugged him! You remember his telling of memory lapses? God forgive me, I had no idea there were such drugs—but you did, Rimon. How could you have hidden it from us?"

"What would you have done if I'd told you?"

Shaking his head, Veritt ran all his tentacles through his hair, looking very much like Rimon's father. But then he sheathed his tentacles self-consciously and met Rimon's gaze.

"If we'd known, we'd have gone to Mr. Erick. He's been very generous, but no one can give outright the huge price Slina has set. Yet I think Mr. Erick would have lent us the money—if you'd only spoken out! You concealed the truth, and because of that, Mr. Steers has lost his will to live."

"Oh, now, wait a minute, Abel! If you found out and told him, and that made him give up, don't blame me. I know you believe in telling the truth, but this time I can't see he's any better off knowing!"

"I didn't tell him," Abel protested. "He told us. The last time Slina drugged him—he remembered. Whatever she gave him—it turned him into an animal, unable to control his own desires; but that time he knew what he did, even though he couldn't stop himself. Afterward, he didn't want to talk to Jord or me. And in a few days he came down with pneumonia, and now all he'll say is that he'd rather die than be used as an animal, by Slina or by us."

"Abel, I'm sorry!" said Rimon. "I didn't think Slina'd ever get the dose right! It's tricky—"

"Oh, God help us, Rimon—how could you know that a human being was being used like that and keep silent?"

Abel's tone said clearly that Rimon, the first nonkilling Sime, had no right to be less than perfect. It was the same tone his father had often used to him.

"Abel," he said, suddenly angry, "this whole Pen uses human beings against their will, drugs them, buys and sells them for the kill. I don't see much difference between Mr. Steers and the nameless creatures grown in Pens. They're all people."

They're all people.

The words echoed in the room. The older man crumpled, head in his hands, defeated. Instantly, Rimon was on his knees before Veritt. "I'm sorry! I didn't mean it that way—Abel, listen to me; it's not your fault. Abel?"

Something crystallized in the old man. He raised his head, sheathed his tentacles tightly, and gazed up over Rimon's head. "I've vowed I'll not die a killer. One day, I will be able to look at the world as you do, Rimon—as my son does. I yearn for that day. I pray for it."

Rimon, kneeling at Abel's feet, realized something about himself. Veritt had made Rimon into an image to be worshiped. Rimon had resented that, yet the moment Veritt's image wavered, Rimon hastily rebuilt it. *They're all people, and I'm better than you are because I don't kill them.*

He turned from Abel, back to the patients. Something good might yet come of this night. Perhaps Abel would turn to Jord, now that Rimon had shown a flaw. Jord was maturing rapidly; he deserved his father's trust and faith, especially since he'd soon be through his "period of adjustment." If they could pull Steers through the pneumonia, surely things would straighten out, and they could get on with training another Gen.

Rimon set to work with Steers, barely noticing when Jord returned an hour later, a sleepy but determined Willa by his side. "I can't rest until Henry's out of danger. How is he?"

"About the same," Rimon replied. Jord zlinned the Gen in silence.

Abel helped Slina remove the two recovering Gens, then returned to aid in dosing the others with another round of fosebine. Steers muttered incoherently and tried to push them away.

"Henry!" said Jord, "you must take your medicine. We'll take you home with us as soon as you're well enough to be moved." The Gen opened feverish eyes, numb despair in his nager.

"Better off dead," he muttered, and tried weakly to turn away from Jord. He wheezed helplessly, and then his breathing became more labored as he fell into unconsciousness.

"Did Father tell you what Slina did to him?"

"I know," replied Rimon.

"I'm not here for her sake," said Jord. "It's to keep my friends alive, to help Henry—and to keep those foul creatures in town from raiding across the border. As for Slina—I hope she rots in hell!"

"Jord!" said Abel sharply. "Slina's not inherently evil. May God forgive me for thinking the poor creatures she raises were not people—and may He forgive Slina for thinking the same about Henry Steers."

"God may forgive her," said Jord, "but it will be a long time before I do."

A few hours later, Margid Veritt came and sent her husband home to rest. It was the first time Rimon had ever seen Abel defer to his wife. He was back at dawn, looking rested. By that time, Rimon was feeling a slight, nagging strain, and Jord was on the thin edge of exhaustion.

Willa said, "Jord, come on. You're in need. Let's go home and—"

"Not until Henry is out of danger."

"He's just the same," she protested. "He will sleep. Please, let me give you transfer, make you feel better."

"Willa, *I* will decide when we have transfer."

As Jord's parents eased out of the room, Rimon realized that the situation was not new. He hadn't been around Jord in need for several months; thus he hadn't seen this resentment in Jord, toward Willa. He recalled his own resentment of Kadi's control—but he had decided that was due to her attempts to hide her true feelings—his sense that she was lying nagerically. Willa was completely open—her concern was genuine and loving, and still Jord responded with resentment.

He decided to let Jord cool off, then try tactfully to send him home with Willa. Jord went to the foot of Steers' bed, staring at him, brooding. Willa tried again. "Look, he is sleeping. Sleep is good, Jord. He will be well soon."

"You don't know anything about it!" Jord snapped. "You don't know *anything!*" Then he pulled himself together, genuinely sorry. "Forgive me, Willa," he said with the tone of habit. "I shouldn't have said that."

"You are in need. Come home and have transfer—then you won't say things you shouldn't."

"Will you stop pestering me?! I said I'm staying here!"

Steers moaned, wheezed, and began to breathe stertorously. Rimon moved to where he could zlin him without Willa's field interfering. It was bad—his nager was fading. Apparently he had the strength of will to let himself die. Rimon moved in, one eye on Jord's reaction, and tried to support the Gen's field. Even unconscious, Steers resisted. Perhaps the best thing was to leave him in peace. Rimon zlinned Jord lightly, and knew that the Sime knew his friend was dying. Yet Jord was determined to stay with him until the end.

Rimon withdrew to check the other Gens. They had lost another one during the night, but the other two would survive. *Survive to be killed,* he thought with a shudder, the first time the thought had gotten through his carefully laid defenses. *I am getting tired.*

He was vaguely aware of murmuring between Jord and Willa. Suddenly a flare of anguished fury reached him, and he turned as Willa said, "But Jord—"

"Leave me alone!" he cried. "You don't understand anything about it! Just let me go pray for my friend in peace." And shaking Willa off, Jord ran out, leaving her staring after him.

Rimon hurried to her. Steers was dead. "What happened?"

"I don't know. The man died. So I told Jord we could

go have transfer now. I wanted to make him feel better—"

"Why didn't you go with him?" he asked, pulling her toward the door.

"He told me not to."

"But he's in need! Come on, Willa! We've got to catch him."

To pray, Jord had said. The chapel. Rimon took off after Jord at a run, Willa following. Foreboding weighed in the pit of Rimon's stomach. Jon would be in the chapel at this hour. Rimon speeded up, seeing Jord augmenting now, dashing for home and whatever solace he found in that chapel.

As they pounded toward the opera gates of Fort Freedom, Rimon zlinned a Gen nager crossing the square. He was still minutes behind Jord, Willa fallen so far behind he could hardly sense her. As Jord neared the gates, Rimon zlinned the Gen directly in Jord's path, but couldn't tell who it was.

My fault! Why did I let anyone keep their children here?

Zlinning Jord, Rimon saw that he was not interested in anything but escape. It would be all right. All right—

Jord was through the gate now—practically on top of the oncoming Gen. It wasn't that Jord failed to sense him—it was that he didn't care. He would have gone straight past, but for the sudden nageric screech of startlement as Jord almost ran the Gen down—and at that moment Rimon recognized Jon Forester.

The twinge of fear stopped Jord in his tracks.

Oh, Jon, hold it in this once—just this once! Rimon willed. Jord had taken Jon's field down three times—maybe he wouldn't fear. If he held steady for just a moment, Rimon could catch up and hold Jord until Willa got there.

For a moment he thought it was going to be all right. Jon's startlement dissolved into anger—*no augmenting inside the gates* was the rule in Fort Freedom, where people let their children play on the green, and it was strictly enforced now that there were Gens likely to be startled by exactly what had just happened.

Even as Rimon rounded the gates so that he could see what was happening, Jon turned on Jord, ready to snap at him, and *saw*—saw a Sime haggard with need, zlinning him. . . .

Thready fear pulsed through his field. Rimon shot forward, but Jord was reaching toward Jon already, sending the boy's fear flaring into a beacon that Rimon himself felt drawn to for a terrible moment.

Rimon launched himself at the pair in a desperate leap. In midair, he saw Jord grasp Jon, felt the fear, the pain, the insane pleasure of killbliss, and as he hit Jord in the chest, knocking him away from his prey, it was a dead body that fell from Jord's grip. Rimon rolled in a tangle of bodies, feeling Jord's frustration, not because the kill was interrupted, but because he had drawn all the life-force from Jon and still it was not enough.

Still in desperate need, Jord groped toward Rimon. With terror and guilt coursing through his nerves, Rimon didn't care this time—he couldn't shen Jord again, couldn't kill him when Jon, and Henry Steers, and God knew how many others had already died—killed by Rimon's own hand as surely as if he'd done it himself—because he had to try to live without killing Gens.

When Jord grasped him, lateral to lateral, he didn't resist. He didn't care. He was better off dead. Everyone would be better off if he were dead. As Jord made lip contact the pain began—aching, searing pain like the pain when he had driven selyn into Kadi, but worse—going on and on until blessed blackness blotted out his guilt, his pain, everything.

Chapter 21

SELF-DEFENSE

Rimon woke. He felt fine. He was in bed, and Kadi was in his arms, asleep, her head on his chest, the fragrance of her hair sweet in his nostrils. But it was not their bed.

Memory came back in a rush of impressions, all overlaid by overpowering need. Coming to in need and pain, being pulled from a tangle of bodies. Jon dead. Jord in shock. Hands moving him gently—Abel Veritt. Willa pounding up, breathless, taking in the scene and turning on Jord, hitting him on the face and shoulders while she made wordless cries of anger and frustration, Jord never lifting a hand to defend himself until Margid Veritt pulled Willa off him. And finally Kadi seeming to materialize out of nowhere, the anguish in her field disappearing at once when she saw Rimon was alive, dissolving into concern, her nager an instant, soothing support.

Through it all, the deep, aching, terrible need, the worst he had ever known. Somehow, the Veritts had gotten them all out of the street and into their house, where Abel had thrust Rimon and Kadi into—yes, that's where they were: Abel and Margid Veritt's bedroom. He'd never been in here before.

All Rimon had meant to do was shunt selyn from his reservoir into his own system, just enough to last the few days until his next transfer was due. Need impelling, raw nerves crying out for selyn, he faltered and suddenly Kadi took command, pouring life into him, completing the transfer on a wave of bliss that led them mindlessly to the inevitably physical conclusion.

But now he remembered. Henry Steers. Jord. Jon. All of Abel's hopes smashed at once.

Rimon gently extricated himself from Kadi's arms.

"Rimon?" she asked, sitting up to focus on him vaguely.

"Go back to sleep, Kadi. I've got to talk to Abel." He began sorting through the tangled heap of clothing.

Kadi got up to dress. "I couldn't sleep now. I'll go with you. Jord will be the biggest problem."

"Problem!" laughed Rimon bitterly. "Oh, Kadidid, how am I going to live with this?"

"It wasn't your fault, Rimon." It seemed she had been saying that to him all his life. No, she didn't understand. So far, she had survived her association with him, but sooner or later, she would become his victim, just like all the others.

Rimon's brief post-syndrome had evaporated. Jord was deep in the post-kill depression he had known in himself, in Del, in everyone he touched. Jord didn't look up when Rimon and Kadi entered, but Abel rose from his chair before the fire, and came to them anxiously. "Are you all right?"

Rimon brushed that aside. "Where's Willa?"

"We finally got her to sleep. Jord—"

Jord said dully, "My life should be forfeit to you, Rimon."

"You were driven beyond endurance," Rimon replied. "I never should have tried to teach others to be like me. I'm unnatural, abnormal—"

"No!" interrupted Abel. "It's not unnatural to refuse to kill."

"But I kill anyhow!" said Rimon. "Billy, Vee and Drust, now Jon—and look at my friends, eaten up by the same disease that devours me! Abel, I'm not what you think I am!" He pointed to the bedroom. "In there—I lost control just the way Jord did."

"No," said Abel. "You may have allowed Kadi to control you, but you would never have hurt her. I've seen it, zlinned you, Rimon—if you'd taken a frightened Gen, at the first pain you'd have gone to healing mode. You don't crave pain. *Think* about that! You say *you* are unnatural? How can the desire to feel pain be natural? No, Rimon, it was a test."

"A—test—I—failed!"

"No, a test Jon failed, and even Jord failed. But Rimon,

God does not put tests on us to make us give up. My son has to start over, to face the test again. Are you going to refuse to help him? Can you refuse to help?"

"Father," said Jord, a worn whisper. "I can't ask—"

Kadi went to sit beside Jord, saying, "You don't have to ask. We'll do anything we can for you."

Jord shrank from Kadi's presence. "I know what I am. You were right in the first place, Father—we are all cursed. Our strongest will is nothing before the compulsion of our nature. I had no malice toward Jon. He simply—came in the way! It could have been anyone. I no longer even distinguish between Sime and Gen—Father, instead of Rimon, it might have been you, Mother, anyone! Oh, God help me —I can't walk anywhere safely now. There is no place left for me."

How was it possible, Rimon wondered, for Jord to understand so well, while Abel with all his experience couldn't see it? *We are killers by nature. The Gens can refuse to die, but we cannot refuse to kill.*

Abel was saying, "Jord, there is one place for you: where Rimon stands—beyond the kill. Remember when Kadi was pregnant, and Rimon lived on Willa's selyn? That was before he passed through his crisis. Now he takes selyn routinely from any Gen who will offer it, and they feel no pain. You have done it, too. You know how."

"But I wouldn't dare anymore. I—"

"Don't say it," answered Abel. "Jord, my son—we have all erred. Accept that, and pray for forgiveness. But don't make one sin the excuse for others. Learn from your error —no one is safe until he has passed through the trail that Rimon passed through. Rimon, weeks ago I recognized that my son was approaching this crisis, and I was blinded by pride. I led you to presume we had found the key to safety for our Gen children here at Fort Freedom—but so long as there is any Sime in the community who has not passed through the test, we can't have them here. We must still be ready to give up our children when we must."

"Oh, Abel," said Kadi, her nager aching with Abel's pain. A thought cut through Rimon. What would it be like to give up Zeth after ten or fifteen years of watching him grow?

Zlinning him lightly, Abel said, "Rimon—if we help, perhaps you would be willing to take in any of our Gen children who elect to stay on this side of the border now?"

"Willa," said Jord, very painfully. "I hurt her—insulted her, and then left her. She may never forgive me, but if she does—what am I to do? I love her, and yet—oh, God, what if I kill her, too?"

"You can't," said Kadi. "That much I know. There is a test for Gens, too—and Jon failed it. If he had ever gotten beyond covering his fear with defiance, all that would have happened would have been a simple transfer. No one would have been hurt."

Jord got up and moved restlessly about the room, stopping at the fireplace to stare into the flames. "No," he said at last. "No, we can't blame it all on Jon. I should have been able to resist his fear."

"Not in that condition," said Abel.

"I agree," said Kadi. "Jord, does your God blame you for having human limits? We can go on trying to stay alive —or we can quit and die. I wasn't raised to be a quitter." She met Rimon's gaze and some of her fire flashed to him. "Neither were you, Rimon Farris."

Zeth. Rimon had gone on then; he could go on now. Killing was unnatural because it prevented people from staying alive. Life itself was the greatest value.

"All right, Abel. We'll take in your Gens—for a while. Until you can take them back."

"Father! No—send them across the border—"

"Jord, God will expect us to get up and go forward. But we must learn from what has happened. First, though, must come Jon's funeral."

Jord went dead white. "Father, I can't—"

"You will attend. Everyone will attend. Go ring the bell, Jord, and tell everyone to assemble in the chapel. I must go and tell the Foresters what I plan."

As if this whole thing were entirely his responsibility.

Within hours, a funeral cortege marched from Fort Freedom along the hill trail toward the border—where Jon was to be buried exactly on the border itself. The trail was frozen mud again, the digging of the grave difficult. Jord pitched into that work, as if the physical labor were a kind of expiation—or, perhaps, simply because it gave him something to do instead of standing to be stared at in horror.

The chill wind made Kadi shiver, and Rimon drew her close, warming her with his own body heat. Willa, still radiating a bewildered anger, remained near the Veritts until Kadi, seeing her start to shake despite her warm clothing, reached out and drew her to them, handing Zeth to her. Rimon didn't know why she did it, until the girl began to rock the baby, her attention at last on something besides her husband. Slowly the fury faded.

Occasionally, Rimon zlinned Gen Territory. This large a gathering of Simes was a perfect target for Gen guns should the border patrol happen along. Possibly the danger was a part of the penance; he didn't really understand Abel's methods. He sensed hostility toward Jord, but people quickly smothered it, as if waiting for permission to release their feelings.

When the Foresters stepped forward to place a wreath of evergreen branches on their son's casket, Abel spoke to them softly, and then took his place beside the grave.

"We have all faced death before," he said, "but it is never easy. Today we assemble to mourn the passing of Jon Forester. By now it is no secret to anyone here how Jon died: my son killed him."

At the bald statement, a shock ran through the listeners. Abel went on. "However, Jord was only the immediate instrument of Jon's death. We're all to blame, all guilty—and yet, most of all, we're guilty of demanding too much, too soon.

"Jon Forester had courage. Yes—the most difficult kind of courage; for although he failed, he overcame his failures to try again and again to learn transfer. Jon died a martyr to the cause of life. Because he knew Simes could and should live without killing, he remained among Simes when he could have gone across the border to his own safety. God cannot ask more of any man. Let us pray for the soul of Jon Forester, who is surely now in heaven."

As Abel prayed, Rimon noticed the Foresters and a number of other people crying—but in many, there was still a tight control. Jord, in particular, remained dry-eyed, pale, even his nager a kind of separate field, as if he could not touch or respond in any way.

After the prayers, Abel said, "Probably you wonder why we have come here to bury the body of Jon Forester, instead of interring it in the consecrated ground near the chapel. No consecrated ground is required; the body of a martyr consecrates the ground it is laid in. Jon is not the first martyr to the cause we have vowed to follow. We must all face the inevitable fact: he will not be the last."

Abel waited until the murmur of horror died down before he continued. "We are in a pitched battle with the forces of evil, and since the evil lies within ourselves, the casualties of that battle must come from among ourselves. Our goal must be to lose as few lives as we possibly can—and to be sure that *no life is wasted!*

"Jon Forester did not die in vain, unless you make it so. If you give up the hope of life without killing, Drust Fenell, Vee Lassiter, and Jon Forester all died in vain. If a second life is lost because we encourage Gens who have not learned not to fear, to walk freely among Simes who have not yet learned not to kill—then that life is wasted. Only if we learn that lesson is Jon's death not in vain.

"We must pray constantly that God will grant us to learn quickly." There were tears in the old man's voice. "I have asked myself, over and over, why God saw fit to place Jon in my son's path at just that moment. Why was Jord presented with the test when he was in no condition to pass it? I think it's a lesson for all of us: we *can* fail. I've failed—every time I've tried not to kill. So have many of you. We all had our hopes bound up in Henry Steers—we have all done without to contribute to the fund to buy his freedom. Was that, too, a vain effort? I think not. Henry Steers had a son, a boy who is somewhere in this Territory. Had he lived, his father would have sought for him—and now, we will do it for him. Rimon—"

"Abel, how can I—?"

"You know more than any of us. We must search. We must try. God always expects us to *try*." As far as Abel was concerned, it was settled. Rimon looked down at Zeth, and knew that he had been drawn into Abel's hopes and schemes again. But now, the general expiation assigned, Abel turned to the specific one.

"Jord, step forward."

As if hypnotized, Jord joined his father.

"My son, Rimon Farris was sent to teach the first lesson: that Simes do not have to kill. You have a second lesson to teach us: God does not condemn us for our failures. Will you teach us that lesson, Jord? Will you face the test again when God chooses to repeat it, and this time pass it?"

"If it is God's will," Jord replied.

"Do you repent of killing Jon Forester?"

"You know I do!" Jord choked out.

"Then will you do penance, in prayer and in works, to atone for your sin?" Jord's fierce control broke, and tears of healing grief rolled down his cheeks. He fell to his knees before his father. "Anything," he said. "Just tell me what to do."

Abel placed his hand on Jord's head. "You have taken Jon's selyn."

Oh no! thought Rimon. *Don't load that on him, too!*

But Jord only nodded, and Abel continued, "This month you will use that selyn in acts of penance for past mistakes, and of enduring hope for the future. First, you will fill in Jon's grave, obliterating any indication of the burial. This is not only that marauders may not desecrate the grave, but as a symbol that one day the border itself may be obliterated, when there will be no more divisions and no more martyrs."

"Yes, Father," Jord replied.

"And you'll spend the rest of this month preparing a monument for the chapel in Fort Freedom, that the names of those who've died for our cause shall never be forgotten. You will hew the granite alone, polish the stone, and carve into it the names of Drust Fenell, Vee Lassiter, and Jon Forester. All future generations who look upon that stone will be reminded that their lives rest upon the deaths of others, and will join in our pledge that those deaths will not be in vain."

As penance, the concept made little sense to Rimon—but as a mark of continuity, of a living dream, the idea moved him deeply. Around him, he felt the emotions change, anger and resentment at Jord disappearing. Jord, now sobbing in heartfelt cleansing grief, was returned to the community.

Willa stared at her husband, her frustrated resentment slowly fading. Finally, she handed Zeth back to Kadi, and went to kneel beside Jord, putting her arms around him. People began to withdraw. Rimon and Kadi went back to their home, leaving Jord and Willa to work out whatever they could to salvage their marriage.

Spring finally came to stay. This year Rimon waited to plow his fields until after the floods—but the floods didn't come. "Some farmer!" he told Kadi. "I should have guessed that less snow this past winter would mean less runoff in the spring."

But Rimon didn't allow the time to go to waste. Besides earning extra money working for Del and Fort Freedom, he consulted with Slina to determine the most likely location of Henry Steers' son—if he were still alive. They knew he hadn't been taken with his father to the Farris Genfarm. There were only two establishments that dealt in quantities of pre-Gen children. If he hadn't yet established —or possibly changed over—there was about a seventy-five per cent probability that he was at one of those Pens. Otherwise, he could be anywhere, in one of the scattered Pens like Slina's. In that case, a Pen-by-Pen search was the only way to find him, and there was no way to do that.

Twelve was still young; there was a good chance the boy would not establish for a year or more, so in early summer, when Rimon and Del took some horses to High Canyon, Rimon made a detour to check out the Villiers Genfarm. Only one of the Villiers pre-Gens was a boy of somewhere around twelve. Rimon managed to speak a few words with him in English, found that he was not Henry Steers, Jr., but learned that there had been a boy called Hank—and maybe it was Steers, but he didn't remember—in the same shipment he had been in at one point.

Except for the possible clue that Steers' son had survived to be sold, it was a dead end. Rimon found it grueling to have to leave the boy. However, he was lean and spare-framed, a typical pre-Sime build. If he changed over, he'd have to work off whatever price Villiers paid for him, but he'd be all right if he could face becoming Sime. The only way Rimon could walk away was to convince himself of that.

His own homestead was growing enough without adding more children, even if he could afford to buy the boy. Both the young Gens who had been living with their families in Fort Freedom decided to stay on this side of the border, even after Jon's death. Rimon feared it was Abel's speech at the funeral that had persuaded them. They were starry-eyed kids, caught up in Abel's dream and determined that they wouldn't "fail the test."

So they came to Rimon and Kadi, their families helping to build on to Rimon's house, providing supplies and labor, and also giving him the tax money for their children. The boys' skills were welcome. Sordal Kent was already a good farmer and Len Deevan had been apprenticed to the herb-alist. He took one stroll through their tunnel and asked Rimon, "Why aren't you growing mushrooms in here?"

"Mushrooms?" answered Rimon. They were a favorite food he'd missed lately. "I don't really know enough about cultivating mushrooms to attempt it. Neither does Kadi."

"Will you let me? I can get Mr. Lansing to help. Next year, you can take some to market when you go with Mr. Erick!"

Rimon authorized the plan, to be strictly supervised by Fort Freedom's master herbalist, and their first real industry was enthusiastically founded.

During all this, Rimon sensed a renewed unity among the folk of Fort Freedom. The month of Jord's penance had worked wonders. Jord labored hard, alone, Willa never far away. Zlinning them as she watched her husband, Rimon found that Jord was under control again. Abel's plan was working; this time, Jord was going to succeed.

The ceremony for the unveiling of the monument held a real surprise. Jord had added a fourth name that hadn't been there the previous evening. As the first rays of the rising sun struck the smooth granite surface, the name of Billy Kell leaped out at Rimon. Billy Kell. Drust Fenell. Vee Lassiter. Jon Forester.

Billy. Rimon forced himself to breathe evenly, not to give Kadi the slightest hint of his pain, as fresh as if it had happened yesterday. *Billy trusted me—they all trusted me. Who'll be next? Abel? Kadi?*

Beside him, Del was crying, Carlana observing serenely. And not a trace of surprise from Kadi. When the two women exchanged glances, Rimon knew that one of them had put Jord up to this. He didn't want to know which.

Yet, after the ceremony, Rimon noticed that Del seemed less tense than he had in months, and Rimon, despite refusing himself the luxury of tears, felt that some indefinable burden had been lifted. Thre was something to be said for Abel's methods after all.

Summer brought Gen Raiders. Slina seethed, for she had predicted the retaliations as she struggled to keep enough Gens in supply to provide for both the town and Fort Freedom. Although she hadn't run completely out before a shipment had come through, it was unclear whether she would have been able to provide for the whole town if some of the town Simes had not gone raiding across the border. She claimed she could have, though, loudly, to anyone who'd listen. But as the town had no mayor, council, or even any form of law officer, there was no one to whom she could make an official complaint.

The effects of the illness in Slina's Pens were widespread. Although Rimon's carefully shielded homestead survived, they lost half a field of wheat to the fire the Raiders set. One group of Gens defied the barrier of the mountains when what was usually a raging river slowed to a stream. They rampaged across Del's property, cutting his fences, carrying away some of the precious wire, and making off with twenty of his finest horses. Wryly, Del told everyone that he was glad their greed had sent them back across the border with their loot without attacking deeper in-Territory. But everyone knew he couldn't afford such a loss.

Rimon and Kadi were doing better financially—but they had to. This summer the two years would be up, and their homestead would no longer be a homestead, but their own land, free and clear—except for the property tax Rimon would have to start paying on it. Now Rimon took every job he could get.

Kadi would have been glad to work in the fields of Fort

Freedom with Rimon, but while the women of Fort Freedom worked hard in their own fields, none of them would ever hire out for pay. She and Rimon decided it might be best not even to mention it to Abel. Del, however, was constantly shorthanded.

So Kadi, who could handle horses just as well as Rimon, went to work for Del, leaving Zeth in Carlana's care most of the day. Rimon soon saw that Kadi had a knack for the work that he hadn't. The men from Fort Freedom who hired out to Del would escort Kadi and Zeth back and forth, and after a few raised eyebrows, it was accepted that Kadi was—as usual—different from the women they were used to, but not therefore bad.

Despite all his problems, Rimon felt a certain satisfaction when his homestead became his own property. He'd have to travel to the Territory Capital to obtain his deed: five days each way. It would be Summer Fair at the Capital —a time when all the largest merchants would display their wares. He promised Abel to look again for Steers' son, and if he wasn't there, to go on across the Territory to the Varnst Genfarm, their last hope of locating the boy. Abel, then, entrusted him with all the money that had been gathered to buy Steers—a fund Fort Freedom had kept intact in the constant hope that they'd somehow be able to locate Henry Steers, Jr.

Originally Del had planned to take a herd of horses along to the Summer Fair, but with the depletion through the raid as well as having to sell off stock to pay for extra hired hands, he didn't have enough to make the trip worth his while because he couldn't file the deed of ownership to his ranch until a month later. So Rimon and Kadi agreed to take five of Del's horses to sell for him.

Rimon had hoped the trip would be a chance to get away from his responsibilities—but here he was with horses and a large sum of money, and the burden of his thoughts and worries, which refused to be left behind. He wanted it to be a pleasure for Kadi, though; a treat after she had gone through so much and worked so hard. Neither of them could guess what to expect in the city from people who weren't used to seeing a Gen treated as a person, but

Rimon was determined to fight his way through any obstacle to show Kadi a good time.

Kadi reverted to the Krazy Kid he'd known before she'd established, as excited as any child on the way to a fair. Her cheerfulness was contagious. By the end of the first day, Rimon was feeling much more fancy-free than in years. The time passed swiftly, as Kadi marveled at each new scene—and Rimon recalled that until she'd established, she'd never been more than a day's ride from home.

They traveled across a plateau, into a land of small canyons with fantastic rock formations—but none of the roaring waterfalls Rimon had expected. They camped that night beside a drying waterhole, somber reminder of the advancing drought.

On the fourth day, they came into hilly green country. The horses wanted to crop the grass, and they had a hard time keeping them moving. Rimon told Kadi, "Tomorrow we get on the eyeway that cuts straight through the hills. We can stop early tonight, and still make the Capital easily tomorrow."

"It's been so nice, just the two of us together," Kadi replied. "I'm not looking forward to the crowds in the Capital."

"I'll take care of you," said Rimon, and Kadi turned to smile at him, her nager bright and serene.

"I'm not afraid, Rimon; you always take care of me." Then she said, "What do you suppose Zeth is doing now? I do hope he isn't tearing up Margid's clean house too badly."

"You know Abel and Margid love him like a grandson—" Just then, he zlinned a small group of Simes. "Kadi, travelers approaching: come over here beside me."

Even as he spoke, he realized that the Simes were not approaching; they were waiting just the other side of the ridge. Their fields were partly insulated—most Simes wouldn't have zlinned them at all. They were hiding—an ambush!

Reining in, he said, "I don't like it. They're not moving. It could be thieves lying in wait. Come on—let's turn the horses back."

But in order to do that, they had to ride to the front of the small herd. The horses were starting to spook with the tension—and maybe had smelled the waiting Simes. Rimon and Kadi uncoiled their whips, trying to drive the horses back. At their shouts and the crack of their whips, the Simes in ambush must realize that their prey had sensed them. Rimon hoped that with the element of surprise gone, they'd hesitate to attack. There were three—no, four of them. Would they attack two people? But they perceived only one person, he realized; one person and one Gen.

Both Rimon and Kadi were now between the horses and the ridge. The Simes' nager increased suddenly as they came over the top of the hill, riding full speed. Rimon turned to face them, and almost froze. Freeband Raiders!

Four scarecrow forms converged upon them. The horses raced away from them, but Kadi turned beside Rimon, fighting her mount and wielding her whip bravely, cracking it in front of the nose of the nearest Raider's horse. The horse reared, but the rider clung, and another came up on the other side of Kadi. She tried to swing her whip at him, but she couldn't match Sime speed and agility. In one motion, he pulled her off her horse onto his. She squirmed, kicked, and finally bit into the Sime's arm, at which he dropped her—but before he could reach down to grab her again, another rider—a woman?—yanked her out of his grasp.

Rimon tried to fight off the other two Raiders who, in full augmentation, were determined to separate him from Kadi. They expected him to give up on odds of four-to-one and simply let her go. Instead, he fought his way toward her, and managed to coil his whip around one of the Raiders and unseat him—but the man caught his whip and took it down with him, disarming Rimon as the other knocked him off his horse. They went down in a tangle, and in a moment there were two others on him, two holding him while the other beat him, and he heard Kadi screaming, "Stop! Don't hurt him! Rimon, Rimon!"

At least she's still alive, he thought as he lost consciousness.

They didn't let him stay blacked out. He was held by two of the Raiders, while one held Kadi where he could see her, and the other poured water over his head.

"What the bloodyshen hell is this?" demanded the Raider

to Rimon's left, her voice indicating she was indeed female. "You're more scared than that shendi-rippin' female!"

"Rimon, are you all right?" asked Kadi.

"Yeah," he lied hoarsely.

"Not for long," said the man who'd poured the water. He was tall, with a shock of tangled hair as red as Kadi's. Above his pale, skeletal features, it looked like a clown's wig.

There was nothing funny, though, about the menace in him as he turned to Kadi. She stared at him defiantly. When he came close enough, she made a deliberate attempt to knee him in the groin. He sidestepped and slapped her viciously. She responded with a flick of her field that made him stagger, and the Sime holding her winced and gasped in astonishment.

The female Raider cried, "A witch!"

"S'matter, Ina?" sneered the red-haired man. "You scared of a Gen?"

"You'd better be scared of me!" Kadi said defiantly. "You picked the wrong Gen to attack this time."

Don't goad them, Kadi, Rimon willed. He could see through her bravado, but was sure none of the Raiders could. Rimon brought augmented strength to bear against the two holding him, but they matched him bit by bit until they gave him a shake. "Stop that, or we'll kill the Gen and have done with it."

How can I get loose and rescue Kadi? I must—somehow! Think! he began to zlin as deeply as he could, seeking anything that would give him an opening. Their captors' fields were consumed with the frantic beat typical of the Freeband Raiders. Of the four, the one holding Kadi had the lowest field, but none of them were in need. Freeband Raiders never allowed themselves to reach real need, if they could help it.

Then he found it—in the woman holding him—her whole body was rotted away with her dissipated lifestyle, but the weakest point was her vascular system. She had a condition seen usually in the very old, and could die very suddenly of circulatory collapse or heart failure. But how could he use that information?

He drove himself down into hypoconsciousness as again

one of the Raiders, tentacles extended, delivered a ringing slap to Kadi's face. *This group isn't as imaginative as those others I saw—long ago.*

How can she be so calm? She expected him to do something—pull off some kind of miracle. *They all expect me to do miracles, and I'm nothing but an ordinary man!*

His despair registered with the Raiders. He felt them zlinning him, and then the woman said, "We can use this one! He's as good as a Gen. Torture her and feel him squirm!"

The red-haired man grinned malevolently, and slapped Kadi again. She broadcast the pain right back at them with all the power of her nager, making the flick of anger she had thrown at them earlier seem like a loving caress.

It knifed through Rimon, and for a moment everything went red as he felt his knees sag under him. He didn't quite lose consciousness, but his weight pulled the two stunned Raiders down with him. As he swam up to awareness again, he realized he'd lost the chance Kadi had given him to get loose. *If only I hadn't been zlinning!* By the time he had control of his paralyzed legs again, the two Raiders—coarsened by their lifestyle and not nearly as sensitive as Rimon—had recovered and were pulling him roughly to his feet.

"Shen and shid!" gasped the redhead, while the woman puffed mightily in Rimon's ear. "Bron, kill that Gen. She's no good for anything."

The man holding Kadi spun her into kill position, expecting fear, and got it: Rimon's. Rimon tugged and writhed, but he was helpless, his system in chaos, a huge, aching bruise spreading on his right outer lateral, his head beginning to throb. *I can't live without her! It'll kill me, too—it has to!*

Transfixed, Rimon felt the Raider reach peak killmode. He couldn't hold himself below duoconsciousness as Kadi's lips touched the Raider. There was a split instant of selyn flow—and a bolt of lightning searing through Rimon, blinding his Sime senses.

As his eyes adjusted, he saw Kadi's face twisted in disgust as the Raider, shenned, fell at her feet—nager flat—dead. Rimon was forced to duoconsciousness again. Free,

Kadi staggered for balance and then came toward Rimon. The red-haired Sime grabbed her. She looked up to the vicious face descending toward hers, and with a cold deliberation turned into his arms, her fingers digging savagely into the tender nerves.

The Rider screamed, stiffening and dying even as she held him. She dropped him in a heap and moved on toward Rimon as the woman to his left suddenly slacked her grip on him and fell—dead, he zlinned, of a cerebral hemorrhage brought on by stark terror—of a Gen.

The remaining Raider pushed Rimon toward Kadi with a mighty heave and leaped onto his horse, riding for his life.

Rimon fell to the dirt at Kadi's feet. She went down with him, clutching frantically at him. "Rimon! Rimon!"

Rimon pushed himself up. "I'm all right, Kadi—"

"Quickly," she said. "To the horses. We've got to get away."

He looked at the corpses blankly, then assured her, "They're all dead, Kadi—there's no—"

"Dead! No! I only meant to *stop* them—only—only I *killed!*"

And Rimon understood. Kadi wasn't using the word "kill" carelessly as a child might. She meant precisely that: kill by selyn movement.

"Kadi—that woman died of a brain hemorrhage—her lifestyle did it to her. And the others were trying to kill you. You had every right—"

"No—I—didn't—" Kadi said through clenched teeth, backing away from him, her anger rising again.

Rimon reached out, flooded with the strangest emotion. *I was supposed to protect her, and look what happened. What use can she possibly have for me after this?*

Fear—that was the emotion raging in him—fear.

Chapter 22

COMPARISONS

"Shenoni, Rimon, you of all people should understand!" But Kadi didn't reach for his outstretched hand. "I *killed*—just as viciously and reflexively as any killer Sime! I couldn't help it, Rimon!"

Rimon looked at the corpses about them. Slumped in grotesque positions, they were like the discarded Gen corpses Raiders left beside the road for others to take away. *Kadi—killed.*

He brought his eyes to focus on her, reading her nager. *A Gen who can turn our own weapon back on us. A Gen. A person.* If Gens were indeed people, then if there was any rhyme or reason to the universe, surely they could kill, too.

A great spreading warmth thawed his fears. "Of course, Kadi. It's only natural—you killed in self-defense. A Sime kills in self-defense against a Gen who refuses to give selyn."

A faint smile came over her face as she met his eyes, and Rimon could feel the shock receding. "Oh, Rimon, I love you, too."

She looked around, taking stock. The Raiders' horses had stopped some distance away, and their own mounts were scattered off in another direction. There was no sign of the herd. "Only God knows where those animals went. They're still half-wild," said Kadi.

Rimon tried to get up. Kadi was right. They had to run down the horses and move off a ways to make camp before tending their wounds. But dizziness washed over him, and the next thing he knew he was bent over, retching violently. He hadn't felt anything like this since he stopped killing.

"Rimon?" Kadi's voice came through the roaring in his

ears, her hands taking his arms as they always had after a kill. Her nager locked to his, firm and soothing.

"I'm all right, Kadi," he insisted, gathering himself to rise. That was the last thing he remembered for some hours. When he woke at twilight, there was a cheerful campfire burning near him. He was under a blanket. The horses were tethered to a line strung between two scrub bushes. And Kadi—

"I think you must have slept more than three hours!" she said when she saw he was awake.

She was calm, and Rimon felt the firm results of her ministrations. As he sat up slowly, his head stayed clear. "I guess I was in worse shape than I thought. I'm fine now —thanks to you."

She poured tea into a trail mug and brought it with a hard biscuit. "If this stays down, I'll believe you."

He took the mug, wanting to reject the biscuit, but decided not to fight her determination. There was no evidence of the Raiders' bodies. She couldn't have buried them. But he wasn't going to ask. "Kadi, you shouldn't have gone for the horses by yourself."

"Why not? I waited until you were sleeping naturally and then rode them down. No problem. Now drink."

He did, nibbling at the biscuit. Kadi ate with him, and that helped. He felt better by the moment. The bruise on his arm was visible now, and it still ached, but the worst of the shock was over. There was none of the blurring he had felt before he passed out.

Kadi asked, her field totally blank, "Should we take the bodies into the Capital and collect the bounty?"

"Kadi!" *Is this my wife?* And from somewhere a distant thought: *She did kill.*

She nodded. "I do stand out. If that Raider who ran away has spread the story and we come in with the bodies, we might get into trouble."

"Nobody would believe him!"

She shrugged. "I think we dare take the horses and saddles—anyone can see they've been used by Raiders— and we can say we found them."

"Kadi, what's wrong with you?"

"I'm trying to think rationally so I won't fall apart. We

can use the extra money—but I don't think it would be wise to let anyone examine those bodies, at least not with us there. I'm dangerous, Rimon. I don't even know how dangerous—but the important thing is not to let a city full of Simes at Summer Fair know that. I've gotten used to living free. I've forgotten how to act like a Gen, if I ever knew."

"You just act like my wife!" said Rimon, putting his arm around her. "All right, it's common sense not to attract the attention of the rabble at the Fair—but I never intended you to pretend to be my property, Kadi. We have to let people start to see Simes and Gens together."

She snuggled into his embrace and began to relax. As the fire danced against the sunset, she drifted slowly to sleep. Feeling her weariness, Rimon appreciated what she'd been through in the last hours—her first experience of the kind of uncontrollable reflex he had learned to take in stride. And then he had fainted dead away, leaving her to face it alone. *And she pulled it off—better than I could have. My wife. Kadidid.*

He bundled her up against the chill of evening, built up the fire, and checked their camp. He found the Raider corpses neatly stacked under a loose pile of rocks downwind of the camp. Then he settled down to mind the fire and rehearse his answers to the inevitable questions he would face in town. Would he be able to get them to register Kadi as a person, so she could inherit for Zeth if anything happened to him? Could he get all the Gens registered as people? Would anybody accept Kadi as his wife?

The Capital at Summer Fair was a madhouse in which Rimon and Kadi drew little attention simply because there was so much else to see, hear, and zlin. They were two weeks before the big Gen auction of the Fair, so it was still possible to find a room. The landlord didn't question Rimon's having a Gen with him, but Kadi shuddered at the cage in one corner of their room.

"They're in every hotel room," Rimon explained, "or else shackles are available. I'm sorry, Kadi—I forgot you've never stayed in a hotel before." In fact, until his eyes lighted on the cage, he'd forgotten they existed.

That afternoon, he went out to sell the horses. It was easy to find bidders on Del's fine animals, although Rimon had to haggle some, finally throwing in the Raiders' horses to bring the sum up to what he thought it should have been. Then he sold the saddles, one of which was almost new. What he got for them was extra money Kadi had more than earned—so he decided to use it to take her out to dinner, show her a time such as she'd never dreamed of before.

Dressed in the good clothes they had brought for tomorrow's business dealings, they sought out a small, excellent but reasonably priced restaurant that Rimon remembered from having been here with his father three years before. As they entered, he had a startling thought: *What if we run into him here?*

No, Rimon knew quite well that Syrus Farris would not bring his Gens in so early he had to pay extra stable and lodging fees. His advance men were probably here, lining up space and fodder, making appointments—Rimon had done that job for his father once. *But Kadi and I will be gone before Dad arrives.* Relieved, he put the worrisome thought out of his mind.

The headwaiter recognized him—or knew him as his father's son—for he came forward attentively and said, "Ah, N'vet Farris, good evening. I can have a table for you in a moment. Will you be meeting someone?"

Rimon was unused to that title of respect, normally reserved for people who wielded power. His father was N'vet Farris; he was just Rimon. "No, I'm not meeting anyone," he replied.

The man extended one handling tentacle, courteously indicating the heavy door to their right. "Then if you would like to place your Gen in the holding room . . ."

"She will eat with me," said Rimon.

The waiter registered shock, but then, perhaps at the thought that Farrises were eccentric but good tippers, bland concession. He led Rimon and Kadi to a table far at the back, almost under the stairs. No one in the room, however, could miss Kadi's presence.

Rimon felt her embarrassment as they crossed the room

—but at the table, she settled down to look around curiously. Remembering that she had never been in such a place before, he felt pleased to be able to bring her here.

As they examined the menu, Rimon pondered. What was it that made him so instantly recognizable as a Farris? His cousin, Lenara, had made many trips here with his father, before Rimon changed over and began working, too. Once the three of them had brought in the largest shipment of prime stock ever seen in the city and gone away—people averred—having cleaned out every bank in town. The next year, people had breathed exaggerated sighs of relief when only two Farrises had shown up, saying, "This town can stand up to two Farrises, but not three!" *Did people still remember that?* It had been over five years ago—just after Zeth died, Lenara died. He hadn't thought of Lenara in years. Now he wondered why she'd died. Vaguely, he remembered something about a man—had she been pregnant?

Farris women die in childbirth, too? But Kadi has survived giving me a son. Dad ought to know—someday—he has a grandson by a living woman.

"Why are you looking at me like that, Rimon? I don't know what half these things are. You'll have to order," Kadi said.

"Your order, N'vet Farris?" said the waiter, hovering.

Rimon pulled himself together, scanning the list of delicacies. A week from need, he wasn't very hungry, but Kadi was, and that would spur his appetite. Of course, there was nothing on the menu that Simes couldn't eat, but a good deal that was poisonous to Géns. Rimon selected foods he and Kadi could share, eliciting a supercilious reaction from the waiter. He surrendered the menu and relaxed, aware that he'd gotten through the ritual with as much ease as his father.

"Someday," he said to Kadi softly, "they'll have menus with Sime and Gen foods listed separately."

"Someday," said Kadi when their order arrived, "they'll learn to double the portions of Gens."

"You can have most of mine," said Rimon. "I just wanted to taste some of my favorites."

"Oh, Rimon! I should have thought—what a waste coming to such an expensive place when you can't enjoy it."

"I'm enjoying it, Kadi. I'm enjoying your enjoying it."

He meant that sincerely. The last time he'd been here, it had meant nothing to him. Now, everything leaped at him with fresh sparkle, as if he were seeing it for the first time. But he was also enjoying forcing others to accept him and Kadi as a couple, and feeling pleased it was so easy. Of course, no one knew their true relationship—*But it will come out. The name will identify me—no use ever trying to deny I'm a Farris.* His father would come into town soon. Would anyone mention Rimon's strange Gen to him?

They left the restaurant at twilight, as the nearby establishments were just opening for the evening's entertainment.

But the street of shut-up shops that they had traversed earlier was now brightly lit, doors open, shiltpron music wafting out to them on the odor of stale porstan. Barkers shouted the delights to be had inside some places.

"A kill like no kill you've had before!"

"Yer ma would never let you torture 'em? Come in here and try our techniques!"

"Wild Gens running the gauntlet! Biggest thrill in town!"

"Hey, friend!" A hand and tentacles wrapped around Rimon's upper arm. "You wanna sell that one? Wha'd you pay for 'er? I'll give you a nice profit."

"No thank you," Rimon said, trying to pull away.

"Come on, friend—I'll give you my choicest kill. That one shouldn't be wasted on a single kill—zlin that nager! Whip her a little, and send up the whole shenned town!"

Rimon turned on him, grasping the arm that had stopped him. "This lady is not for sale! She happens to be my wife!" The man fell back in astonishment, allowing Rimon to stride away, Kadi sheltered in the crook of his arm, their fields blending solidly for the onlookers. Behind them, horror and revulsion quickly gave way to disbelief. One faint voice raised in laughter triggered a rising tide of forced mirth. "A fair-clown out of costume!" yelled one, and as he and Kadi moved out of earshot, Rimon realized it wasn't going to be as easy as he thought.

At the very next place along the street the barker was shouting, "Wild Gens! Prime Farris stock! Come in for the kill, the thrill of a lifetime!"

Trapped in a nightmare, Rimon steered Kadi into the

next side street, not knowing where he was going except away from that street of perverse appetites. There was no lighting; he had to guide Kadi along, zlinning by her field, but they were out of the crowd. Finally he stopped to let Kadi catch her breath, drawing her to lean on him, taking strength from her presence.

"I'm sorry!" he said. "I didn't remember it that way! But it *was*—I used to think it was *fun* to come here! I used to be just like them!"

"No you weren't, Rimon," she reassured him. "You were never cruel. You never went into one of those places, did you?"

"No—never! Drunk on porstan and shiltpron, yes—but *that*—" he shuddered. *But was it because I didn't want to—or that I simply couldn't face the memory of killing Zeth in First Need?*

"You see? You were never like them. And now you're even more different."

He straightened. "And I'm glad! Kadi, I've been worried about what I've become—I thought it was unnatural. I wasn't sure it was right to try to teach others. But now I know. I couldn't go back to—*that*. Never again, Kadi—never again!"

The next morning, they made their way to the Territory Land Office. Though it was early in the morning, the crowds were already thick. Everybody who had business in the Capital waited until Summer Fair, making the trip an excuse for a vacation. The plaza in the center of the government complex was almost impassable, a cluster of people at the center creating an obstacle in the flow of traffic.

Clinging to Kadi's hand, Rimon was swept inevitably toward that center point—a nageric sore that gave him a headache even from a distance. Everyone seemed to want at least a glimpse of—oh no! Through the throbbing miasma of fields, Rimon finally discerned what it was they were all gloating over: a Sime criminal, caged, exposed to die of attrition. The man was in torment, and other Simes were gathered around, drinking in his pain.

"Serves 'im right."

"Oughta deal with all Raiders that way—that'd teach 'em to raid the Pens in a bad winter!"

"Zorg, let's bring the kids to see—learn respect for the law."

Rimon dragged Kadi away, hoping she didn't realize what was happening. They practically ran up the steps of the Land Office, to find a long line of deed claimants. An hour later, they were ushered into one of the cubicles, where a bored clerk asked, "Name?"

"Farris. Rimon Farris."

She looked up at that. "Oh—gettin' yer own place, eh? I'll get your file." She paused at the door. "That Gen's not drugged. It gonna behave?"

"I have no intention of causing a disturbance," said Kadi.

"You Farrises. Some new experiment?"

"You might call it that," Rimon replied.

The clerk soon returned with Rimon's file. "You picked an out-of-the-way spot, but I guess that's so you can expand, eh? Plannin' to compete with your dad?"

"No."

"You cleared any more land since this report?"

"No."

The clerk checked her papers against Rimon's. "Description of property all seems in order. Purpose of the homestead?"

"Farming," said Rimon.

The woman looked up sharply. "Just—farming?" She leafed through a sheaf of forms showing taxes paid on Kadi, Willa, Jon—but then just two Gens after Willa married Jord—the spring assessment had been made a few days before Jon's death had brought the other two Gens to live with Rimon, and another girl, Anni Suttin, had joined them since then. He would have a stiff Gen tax to pay in the office down the hall, but he had the funds ready, paid by their families.

"Seems in order. Now, how many people in your household?"

"Six," replied Rimon.

"Adults or children?"

"Five adults, one child."

"Names of all the adults?"

"Myself; my wife, Kadi Morcot Farris; Len Deevan; Sordal Kent; Anni Suttin."

"Hmmm? Three hired hands? You're doin' pretty well—at farming?"

"No, they're—more like boarders," said Rimon.

"Oh-ho. Income property!" The woman reached for another form. "That's different. What rent are you charging?"

"No rent." Rimon was in a fine tangle now.

The woman looked up. "It's not another of those communal things like that other place in your area—Fort Freedom? We figure that's some kind of tax dodge, but so far we haven't been able to prove they don't hold the property in common."

What would be the best thing to say? Rimon wanted his property in his own name and Kadi's, not held in common by everyone who lived there. "No; the land is mine. The kids staying with us work in return for room and board."

"Mmm. You got a good deal till they wake up and start demanding a salary. Property to be listed in the name of?"

"My name and my wife's."

"Then you have to bring your wife in to sign the papers."

"This is my wife." This was the crux. He had to try to have Kadi recognized as a person. If anything happened to him before Zeth changed over, his wife and son could lose everything.

The woman stared blankly for a moment. Then, as she realized he meant Kadi, intense anger spread through her field. "What stunt are you trying to pull? You claim this Gen is your wife?"

"Yes. I claim it, she claims it, and she has borne me a child. Under the law, that fulfills all the requirements."

"Under the law, you bred a Gen—no more." She scratched Kadi's name off the form and altered the section on Rimon's marital status. He felt Kadi tense at that, but she remained quiet.

When the tax assessor ran her pen down the column and scratched out the notice of a child in the household, Rimon felt Kadi fight off tears combined with the desire to attack. Willing her to remain calm was the only thing that allowed him to retain his own control.

The woman finally balled up the form, pitched it into the wastebasket, and took a new one. "Now let's start this right. I'm not reporting for you tax fraud this time, N'vet Farris, but we'll be watching you from now on—believe me." She hastily scratched in the basic information, through Rimon's name. "Now—how many other adult *Simes* in your household?"

"None," Rimon admitted.

"So. What it adds up to is four Gens and one pre-Gen—and you. A Genfarm."

"No! I do *not* sell Gens!"

She rested one tentacle significantly on the tax forms for Jon and Willa, as if challenging him to explain their absence. "That is not the definition, as any Farris knows. You have more than three Gens per Sime on this property —and you're breeding the Gens. You've admitted that. It adds up to Genfarm, and if you'd care to protest that to my supervisor, I'll inform him that you tried to defraud the Nivet Territory of tax revenue by claiming Gens as adult humans."

What could he do? He could be denied the deed, assessed fines—yet he couldn't help protesting. "For all the taxes we pay, we get no protection out along the border."

Intent on a column of figures, the woman muttered, "So move."

"We might have to. A lot of our friends have been talking about trying another Territory, where the taxes aren't so high."

"You want government Pens, guaranteed kills, you got to support the tax system. You don't like it, get out." She finished the column of figures with a flourish and passed the paper to Rimon.

Looking over his shoulder, Kadi gasped, "We can't afford that!"

"I won't pay it," Rimon said grimly. "You can just send your notice to our local dealer to cut off my Pen privileges."

The woman snorted. "When you grow your own? And live where you can slip across the border anytime you want to? You pay up here and now—or we confiscate your Gens, starting with this one."

Rimon could think of no further argument. He checked the figures; they were correct for a Genfarm, the highest assessment rate. After the way he'd fumbled the beginning of the interview, what could he do but pay? In order to come up with the entire fee, he had to use a part of Fort Freedom's money. *How will I ever pay it back? What will I do next year? Must I spend my whole life struggling just to stay alive?*

Numbly, Rimon finished his business in the building, and walked with Kadi out into the bright sunshine. She remained silently at his side, trying to support him despite her own cold despair. He steered her away from the grim display at the center of the plaza and headed up one of the radiating streets in the direction of the Pens, wondering what good it did to avoid the sight of an execution while heading toward the Pens full of condemned—and innocent—people.

Their last order of business before they could leave town was the search for Henry Steers' son. Rimon moved automatically through the streets, afraid to think.

"Rimon," Kadi said at last, "there is a solution, you know."

"Solution?"

"Suppose we invite Jord and Willa to build a house on our property. Then there will be two Simes and five Gens —we can even accept another Gen before the ration will be more than three-to-one again."

Some of the tightness in Rimon's chest melted. "Kadi, you're right! We won't get this year's money back, but we can plan against next year. I'm glad somebody in this family is thinking straight!" And he kissed her, right there on the street, oblivious to the stares of the passers-by.

When they came out into the midway, Rimon looked around for a directory. The search took them along a row of tawdry displays, cheap thrills aping the permanent parlors they had passed last night. Instead of barkers, there were performances before tents, exhausted Gens goaded through obstacle courses, poorly proportioned paintings depicting luridly, "100 Kill Positions—All Demonstrated Inside! Improve Your Personal Satisfaction With the Secrets of the Mysterious East!"

One display, however, brought Rimon up short. In a cage was a very large male Wild Gen, ragged, dirty, bearded. He stared morosely out at the passers-by, not knowing why he had been placed there, and too tired to care. But both

Rimon and Kadi stared incredulously at the freshly hand-lettered sign:

GIANT KILLER GEN

In smaller lettering, the gawking crowd was informed that the predatory Gen stalking the trails to the Summer Fair had been captured, and that for an exorbitant price they could buy one of the last few tickets left to see him killed the last day of the Fair.

"Is that the one?" someone asked. "Did you really kill five Freeband Raiders?"

"Nah—only three," said someone else. "Besides, how do we know this is the one? I heard it was a female."

"A *female* Gen? Killed three Simes?"

"Seven, I heard—sucked their blood right out!"

A little boy started to poke a stick at the Gen, when his mother pulled him back sharply. "Right you are, madame," said the manager of the display, seizing the opportunity to gather a crowd. "Keep the children back, and stay away from him yourself. We're not sure how many Simes he *has* killed—at least three, maybe eight or ten! He was captured last night in a life-or-death struggle. Step inside and see it re-enacted—Gen against Sime! Can you believe it? Is it real? You won't believe your senses until you zlin it for yourself—the most realistic representation ever of a Real Live Event! Step right this way—"

As the gullible ones filed into the tent, Rimon turned to Kadi and said, "I didn't know you'd grown a beard!"

"It's not funny!" she protested, but he saw that it was indeed as much funny as horrifying to her. So that Raider had been so frightened he had actually dared brave the Summer Fair crowds—rather than be out there alone with a Giant Killer Gen on the loose.

"Maybe what we ought to do to make up the tax money is put you on display for real. I could set up a tent, and—" She hit him in the shoulder, eliciting more curious stares, and still more as she dragged him away from the display.

They located the directory for Gen sales displays. Not all the spaces were filled in; the largest of all was empty, reserved, Rimon knew, for Farris stock. But they were in luck: the second largest was filled in with the name Varnst, Syrus Farris' largest and most successful competition.

Undoubtedly, they would have the best of their pre-Gen children here already—stock one traded before the wild bidding sessions of the last week of the Fair. If Varnst had Henry Steers, Jr., unestablished, chances were he'd be there —and Rimon could ask the keeper if they'd brought along all children of establishment age. If they had, Rimon would be saved a trip to the other side of the Territory.

He and Kadi were striding along a row between the tents when they came to another major crossway, where the crowd was pushed back on either side to let some wagons pass. As he looked to see the length of the line of passing wagons, Rimon froze. Despite the accumulation of trail dust, he saw these wagons were in good repair and recently painted in bold black and white: the Farris colors. Kadi's field registered shock, and she stepped closer to Rimon. He could see no way to get around the oncoming line. They'd just have to wait it out.

As they waited, Rimon's arm about Kadi's waist, he slowly became aware of something—someone—off to his left. Just behind the first row of spectators stood Syrus Farris, watching his men as they brought in the wagons. Farris would tolerate no rudeness to the public, no cruelty to the Gens; Rimon had seen his father do this before, riding ahead to make arrangements, then mingling with the crowd to see how the Simes he hired did their job when they thought themselves unobserved.

Syrus Farris might be observing his crew, but Rimon was observing Syrus Farris. How good his father looked! This was a bad year; Rimon and Kadi looked more prosperous than many people at the Fair because of Kadi's skill with a needle, but while their clothes might be skillfully made, Syrus Farris' were of the finest materials, and styled in a slightly different way that Rimon realized must have come into fashion since he'd left the center of civilization. The comfortable boots Rimon and Kadi wore had been excellently made by the shoemaker at Fort Freedom—but they were not of that exquisite imported leather that would hold a shine even through the dusty ride Farris had just negotiated, and come up gleaming with the flick of a cloth.

Afraid to zlin, Rimon watched his father, feeling for the first time slightly shabby, definitely not up to what his father would have expected. But then he also saw the sprinkle of white hairs through his father's thick black thatch—surely that had not been there two years ago? Or all those lines around his eyes? Come to think of it, why was Farris here early? He looked prosperous enough—but then he always took pains to look prosperous. The wagons passing by were loaded with unestablished children and older Gens—he was selling off breeding stock! Things were not going well on the Farris Genfarm, no matter what face Syrus Farris showed the world.

On one *of the Farris Genfarms,* came the disquieting thought. He would have to encounter his father with a freshly made deed to a Genfarm in his pocket. But perhaps he could avoid it. Did his father know he was here? Would he want to know?

Tentatively, Rimon dared to zlin his father. Even from a distance, over the fields of others, he could easily sense that distinctive nager. There had always been a barrier that kept him from reading his father; now it was gone. *No—my sensitivity has increased.* As he reached the core of Syrus Farris' being, he saw something else, something that stunned him, forced him to lean on Kadi's field. She looked up at him, and he muttered, "Kadi—he's like Jord and me: two selyn systems!"

"Then Zeth will—" she whispered.

"He'll have it, too! And be able to learn not to kill! Jord and Willa—Kadi, it does run in families!"

Rimon's eyes were still on Syrus Farris. The older man turned slightly toward where Rimon and Kadi stood, frowning. Rimon froze, waiting to see if his father would look at him; he was certain his father had zlinned him. But Farris did not turn. *He doesn't want to recognize me.*

The last wagon passed, and the crowd began to move. Rimon held Kadi right there, waiting. *I'll let Father make the decision. He can walk away, or he can turn and recognize us.*

Slowly, as if fighting a force he could not resist, Farris turned. Father and son faced one another over a distance of only a few paces. "Rimon," he said softly. Then, flatly, "I see you've kept that Gen."

"Kadi is my wife, Father," said Rimon. "I told you that."

Farris ignored that, openly zlinning his son. "You're well," he said, unable to keep surprise out of his voice. It was so long since Rimon had left behind the chronic shorting, the never-quite-healthy feeling, that he'd forgotten about it, until he'd seen that same tiresome strain in his father's field. "I'm pleased to see your health is good, at least."

"It's because I don't kill," said Rimon. "I didn't kill Kadi, as you see—and I've learned to draw from other Gens without killing."

Farris brushed that aside. "I heard you were homesteading at the border. Have you been successful?"

"I just got the deed to my land this morning."

His father nodded, holding back a faint surge of pride. "That is good. What will you do now?"

"Farm. We've had some success marketing trin, and now we're trying mushrooms. In a few years, you may find our produce on your table, Father."

"Perhaps," Farris said bleakly. "Did the drought hit badly in your area?" A safe topic, the weather.

"It's been difficult, but we can survive one bad year."

The twinge of irritation building in Farris suddenly broke free. "We! You and this Gen?"

"Yes," replied Rimon. "Kadi and I—and our son."

Farris stared at his son, going so pale Rimon feared he would faint. But he was back in control immediately. "You have a son, Rimon?"

"*Kadi* and I have a son."

"The Gen is alive," said Farris, as if that were enough proof that Rimon was lying. So Rimon had been right—Farris wives died in childbirth.

Kadi spoke softly, "You're welcome any time you wish to visit your grandson, N'vet Farris."

At being addressed by the term of respect between equals, Farris looked directly at Kadi for the first time. But he spoke to Rimon. "She still has you in her power."

"And Rimon has me in his. It's called love."

"Rimon," said Farris, "I must supervise the unloading of the stock. Will you join me?"

A courteous invitation between equals. Rimon could not refuse—and he didn't really want to. They walked down the lane to the large tent assigned to Farris. The crew had scrubbed and disinfected everything, and the flaps were up to air it out. The wagons pulled up one by one, unloading their cargo carefully, no cruelty allowed. That had always been important to his father. Farris Gens were treated kindly, never unnecessarily hurt, never left in discomfort. But nonetheless, his father was cruel. All the gentle treatment went only to assure the buyer a Gen who would be responsive to the pre-kill routines. *Prime Farris Stock. Human lives bought and sold.*

Rimon wanted to lash out—to demand that his father recognize Kadi as a person, all Gens as people—but as he watched Farris carefully inspecting, helping to lift one of the pre-Gen children down from a wagon, he was suddenly reminded so powerfully of Abel Veritt that it took his breath away. *He can't recognize Kadi as a person, any more than he dare think of the Gens he raises as more than animals. He doesn't have Abel's faith to sustain him. If he knew—he'd die!*

For the first time in his life, Rimon perceived his father as weaker than himself—there was a definite frailty at the edges of his nager that could only become worse with advancing years. *And what does he have to live for? His wife is dead, his son gone to a life he can't understand.* "Kadi," he said softly, "we should leave now." *Before we do any more damage.*

As Kadi stepped to his side, Syrus Farris turned back to them—and Rimon realized that he had perceived that strange state of their fields when Kadi was high-field and he was low.

"We're still here," he said with a chuckle, knowing others perceived it as if they disappeared nagerically. "But we must get on to our business."

Farris ignored that. "Let me zlin you without the Gen."

Obligingly, Kadi went over to watch the children being unloaded. Farris zlinned his son. "You're in need."

"Still a few days from it."

"But you're steady, calm—Rimon, I must admit that you're healthier than I've seen you since your changeover. If it's from living without killing, so be it. Come home, Rimon. I won't ask you to kill—you say you can draw from any Gen. You can have all the Gens you want. Come home, find a wife—"

"I *have* a wife."

Suddenly, from Kadi, he felt a shock, and she cried, "Rimon!"

Another wagon had drawn up; several Gens were being herded into the Pens—and one of them was Nerob.

"Kadi!" exclaimed Nerob, but she turned and ran to Rimon.

The Gen was the same mixture of defiance and cowardice Rimon remembered. He looked at them. "Rimon? Rimon!" The Gen began to beg, frantic as his line moved toward the holding cage. "Buy me, Rimon! We were always friends —don't let them sell me for a kill. I'll work for you— anything!"

As if he'd never tried to take Kadi away from me. Nevertheless, Rimon felt pity for Nerob. Kadi was silently pleading for mercy. He could send Nerob across the border and be rid of him. The money—shen! He'd get it somewhere. Nerob—Yahn—was a person. A person Rimon detested, but a person even so.

"All right, Yahn, I'll see what I can do," he said, marshaling his mind for a bidding duel with his father. "N'vet Farris, that old breeding male can't be worth much. Name a fair price, and perhaps we can do some business."

His father zlinned him, bringing his eyes to focus on him as well. There was astonishment and grudging approval in the older man's nager, and for a moment, Rimon thought he'd deal.

"I won't sell him to you," said Farris. "For your own good, Rimon, I won't sell Nerob at all. I'll put him back to breeding—if you'll sell me Kadi as a mate for him."

Such utter rage thrilled through Rimon's body that Syrus Farris took an involuntary step back, holding just as Kadi's field gripped and held Rimon, her hands clamped about his biceps to prevent him from going for his father's throat. Gone was every trace of sympathy he'd felt for him only moments ago.

Savagely, he said, "So this is how you choose which promises to keep! And I always wanted to be just like you!"

"Rimon!"

"If the Farris honor means anything to you, Father, then sell Yahn to me—for the sake of your promise to Keslic!"

"I can't do that, Rimon. I'd pay anything to get you to come home—live a normal—"

"Normal! I'll tell you how normal your life is. Mother died. Lenara died!" He paused as his father registered shock at the name. "All the Farris women die—but not Kadi. Kadi's given me a son, and I know from the way it happened he's going to be Sime like you and me. I've found the way Farrises can have children—without killing their women. We have to have them by Gens, Father. Take a good look at Kadi. Remember her. And remember that she has given me one child already. There will be others—and she won't die. You just think about that!"

And he turned and stalked out, Kadi close at his side.

Chapter 23

COMING HOME

It took the entire walk to the Varnst tents for Rimon to stop shaking. He had lost control again—control of his temper, this time. Even though he knew his father would never have sold him Nerob, the thought persisted: *I lost him his last chance to live.*

Kadi, too, was silent, her emotions in turmoil. Only when they reached their destination did she begin to give Rimon any support. Finally she said, "Your father was never like that."

"I think we're the ones who've changed. We're building a little corner of the Territory where people don't do things like that to other people. But I've been contaminated by just two days back in this environment—the way I lashed out at Father was meant to hurt him."

"You just told the truth."

"Maybe. I think so. But what good will it do him to know it? If he believes it, it can only hurt him. Kadi, let's check out the pre-Gens and get out of here."

They found their way to the small tent Varnst had set up to display children. "We got twelve for sale," one of the men told him, "from nine years on up. You buy a young one, you can get several years' work even if it changes over." He had sized Rimon up as a young man shopping for a servant. Amazing—someone who didn't place him as a Farris. Thinking of the way prices would rise if he were recognized, he kept quiet and looked over the children while the salesman was looking over Kadi.

"Now, that's some Gen! Want to sell her?"

"No, thanks," said Rimon. "There're only eleven children here."

The man turned, looked over the group of children in

318

red Varnst smocks, and said, "Trouble again! Hey, Treen, you were supposed to keep an eye on Trouble! He's escaped again."

"Shen!" said a young Sime woman at the end of the tent. "I only turned my back for a minute!" As she went out of the tent, zlinning, Rimon started to laugh.

"You've got one there who's already learned how to hide from Simes," he said.

"Hmmm?"

"He's under the platform."

The salesman zlinned, but obviously could not detect one child's nager separate and beneath the others'. "I don't think so, but I'll check—" He went to the back of the platform, looked under, and said, "Well I'll be shenned! How did you zlin him through the field of that crazy Gen?"

He hauled out a boy of about twelve, earning several ill-aimed blows and kicks in the process. He pulled the boy's hands behind his back and held him as the child regaled him with imaginative invective. But while the boy's Simelan was fluent, as far as it went, it was strongly accented.

While the salesman was distracted, Rimon whispered to Kadi, "Talk to him—I don't want them to know I speak English."

So Kadi asked, "Were you captured out-Territory?"

Hearing his own language, the boy stopped his struggles to study Kadi. "What do you care?"

"Tell me your name," she said. "Hurry, before they stop us from talking."

Perhaps it was the inclination to trust a Gen, or perhaps simply another chance to defy his captors, but the boy drew himself up proudly in spite of the hands and tentacles holding him. "My name is Henry Steers, Jr."

Rimon felt the thrill in Kadi's nager, but she did not betray her recognition of the name. Most Gendealers picked up a few words of the Gen language, and she wasn't going to risk being understood. "Henry, if you'll stop struggling, perhaps Rimon will buy you."

"He's got no right to buy me! I'm a freeborn man!"

"The only way you'll get out of here is if someone buys you—and you'll be best off with Rimon."

"Quiet that Gen of yours! She's exciting this one!"

"That's enough, Kadi," said Rimon, catching her eye. "We don't want a troublemaker."

She fell immediately into the game. "I'll win his confidence, Tuib. Look, he has good, strong shoulders. I can train him."

Rimon purposefully zlinned the boy. "No telling what he'll be—might be months of work in him if we can get him to do anything. If he turns Sime—well, he could work out his indenture—if he doesn't run away."

Spotting a chance to get rid of the troublesome child, the salesman said, "Oh, no, N'vet—he's spirited—he'll make a prime kill as a Gen, or a good worker as a Sime. It's just the carnival atmosphere made him play tricks today. Why, he didn't even try to escape, just hid. He'll probably become attached to you."

Rimon pretended reluctance long enough to purchase the boy for much less than the sum with which Fort Freedom had entrusted him. But he had purchased Trouble indeed. Twice on the way back to the hotel, the boy squirmed out of his grasp, and had to be plucked up bodily. When they finally reached their room, Rimon tossed him onto the bed and said, "Stay there while we pack, or I'll lock you in that cage!"

"You shendi-flayed, shidoni-be-shenned—Hey, you know English!"

"That's right," said Rimon, "and I also know who you are. In fact, I came here to find you—Hank."

"Who told you my nickname?"

"Your father told us," replied Rimon. "We've been looking for you ever since—since your father died."

"You killed him!"

"No. He died of pneumonia. He wasn't killed by a Sime."

Kadi sat on the bed next to Hank. "We'll take you to a place where Simes and Gens live together—the way Rimon and I do. See?" She held out her arms. "I'm Gen, but Rimon is Sime, and he's my husband. We have a little boy of our own."

Hank stared at Kadi's arms, then at her face. "You're crazy! How do you keep him from killing you?"

"Rimon doesn't kill. Ever."

The boy absorbed that slowly, then looked up at Rimon.

"I don't believe it," he said flatly. Nonetheless, Rimon could read a faint hope in the childish nager.

"Give us a chance to prove it, Hank," said Rimon. "I don't want you to ride for five days tied up and thrown across my saddle, but if that's what it takes to get you to Fort Freedom, I'll do it. If you'll promise not to try to escape, you can ride the horse we brought for you."

"You'd take my word?"

"Your father was an honest man. He wouldn't give his word unless he meant to keep it. I expect you to do the same."

For a long, quiet moment, Hank studied them. "You've got my word. I won't try to escape until after I see this Fort Freedom."

They discarded Hank's red smock, and dressed him in a spare set of Rimon's clothing, sleeves and pant legs rolled up. Clean, with hair combed, he emerged as a good-looking boy, with dark brown hair and wide blue-gray eyes like his father's.

When they finally had everything packed, and were looking around to see if they'd left anything, someone stopped at the door. Wondering who it could be, Rimon opened the door and found himself face to face with Erd Keslic, the father of Yahn, who had become Nerob. When Rimon invited him in, he glanced at Kadi and Hank and shook his head nervously. "I just—I've been looking for you all over, Rimon. It's—"

No—oh no, I can't go back and try to buy Nerob again!

But Keslic, radiating embarrassment, was saying, "When I got back today, N'vet Farris told me to put Nerob back—he isn't selling him. He said, bad year or no, he kept his promises. But then—the others told me what happened, and I—Thank you, Rimon." Having gotten the words out, he spun and hurried away. Rimon stared after him, a weight lifted from his soul.

Kadi put her arm around him. "Oh, Rimon, I'm so glad. You did the right thing—and so did your father!"

The ride home was uneventful. Hank tried to keep Kadi between himself and Rimon, but made no attempt to escape.

They reached Fort Freedom late in the afternoon, Rimon choosing to cross the creek below town and skirt Del's fence rather than take Hank through town. Let him see Fort Freedom first.

The crops were withering for lack of rain; nonetheless it was easy to see the care that had gone into the fields. Three houses by the creek were still lived in, but no one was in sight.

When they rode up to the stockade, though, the woman on guard called out in English, "You found him!"

"We found him," Rimon agreed.

"God be praised! Welcome, son—welcome to Fort Freedom!"

Hank stared at her, then looked at the neat, well-kept houses that made up the community. "It looks like home!"

People came out, sensed Hank's uneasiness, and hung back. When they reached the Veritt home, Abel came out, followed by Margid with Zeth. "Mama! Daddy! Come see. Puppy!" cried Zeth, tugging at Rimon.

"In a moment, Zeth," Rimon told him, picking him up with an agonized vow that there would never be the gulf between him and his son that he knew with his father.

Hank watched from his horse as Kadi embraced Abel and Margid, Jord and Willa converging from next door—another Sime/Gen couple. Then Abel went to Hank, looking up in awe. "Welcome to Fort Freedom, Henry. I'm Abel Veritt. I believe Mr. Farris has told you about our community?"

He held up his hands to help the boy off his horse, but Hank remained rigid until Abel stepped back. Then he slid down cautiously. "Mr. Farris said my father died here, and you were looking for me. I suppose to kill me, too."

"No, Hank!" Jord said urgently. "Your father and I were friends. If only he could have known you were alive and well—"

"Let's not crowd Henry today," Abel said, turning to the boy. "Will you accept our hospitality? I know it's difficult for you to believe we offer you a safe place to rest."

As Abel shook his head warningly, the people who had gathered left in silence. Only Abel, Margid, Rimon, Kadi, and Zeth accompanied Hank into the house.

Hank looked around, eyes wide. Rimon could easily guess that the things he'd always found alien in Fort Freedom spelled "home" to Hank. In the main room, Zeth squirmed down, and hurried to get something from a basket. "Daddy, look! Mama!"

Not very steady on his feet yet, Zeth overturned the basket and sat down hard on his bottom as he tried to lift out a puppy. Another pup tumbled out, and with a happy yapping ran straight at Hank's feet. He automatically picked it up, and got his face washed with a quick pink tongue.

Kadi, meanwhile, was asking, "What's going on here, Abel?"

"The Whelans' dog had pups, remember? Zeth couldn't decide between two of them, so we brought them both home for him to make up his mind. I told him he had to choose just one. As you see, he's made his choice," Abel explained, ignoring the fact that he hadn't consulted Zeth's parents about a puppy at all. Zeth was showing his puppy to Kadi now. As she petted the oversized head with loving strokes, Rimon decided not to object. The puppy would be Kadi's responsibility—but she'd missed having a dog since Wolf. He knelt down to be introduced to his son's new pet.

Hank stood cradling the other puppy as if it were the one real thing in an insane world. It didn't take Abel long to notice. "Would you like that puppy, Henry? The Whelans are looking for good homes for all of them."

"I don't have a home anymore," Hank said stolidly.

"We're offering you a home," replied Abel. "However, if you prefer, we'll escort you safely across the border."

"Why would you do that? I'm a Gen, and Simes kill Gens—the way you killed my mother and father."

Abel glanced at Rimon, who shrugged. No matter how many times they'd told him on the trail, Hank still resisted.

"We don't kill people like you," said Abel. "We're in the process of learning not to kill at all. Both Rimon Farris and my son Jord have learned to take selyn without killing the Gen."

"But you kill—don't you?"

"Yes. We won't lie to you. Not all of us have learned

yet. We ask you to wait until you know enough about us to decide if you want to stay—if you are Gen."

"No if about that," muttered Hank.

"I told you," said Rimon, "you haven't established selyn production. You're a child, not a Gen."

"How do I know that? You say Gens start producing this—selyn—in their teens. But if I were doing it, how would I *know?*"

"You'll know," said Kadi. "Somebody will tell you."

"Kill me, you mean."

"Not here," said Abel. He moved so that the boy had to turn to follow him with his eyes. "But you might go into changeover. There's only one chance in three you'll be Sime, but there's still that one chance, Henry, and even Rimon can't tell yet which way you'll go."

"No! My parents taught me to pray, and all through this, I've prayed every day. God will not desert me."

"You were taught," replied Abel, "as I was taught as a child. But I failed to learn the dangers of presumption, and found myself Sime, convinced I was cursed. It took me years to find that it was I who had deserted God, and to return to His service."

"You can't preach at me! You're a cursed Sime!"

Abel inspected his tentacled arms with an air of objectivity. "It would seem so. All of us here wakened one day to find ourselves Sime, unable to refrain from killing for selyn, though all our lives we'd been so sure it couldn't happen to us. Henry, you're welcome here; if you should be Sime, we'll pray for you, as for all our own, that you'll never have to kill. And if you're Gen, you may remain or leave with our blessing. Come now, you're tired. Accept our hospitality—at least to the extent of a meal and a bed."

"Supper will be ready soon," said Margid.

"In the meantime," said Abel, "would you like to visit your father's grave, and perhaps pray for him in our chapel?"

"You have a chapel? How can you—"

Abel smiled faintly. "Do you doubt that God can see and hear either side of the border with equal clarity?"

Hank regarded Abel over the puppy he still held. Then Kadi took it, putting it back in the basket. Hesitantly, Hank left with the older man. Rimon, Kadi, and Zeth joined Margid in the kitchen as she prepared a meal for Hank.

"I hope he'll stay," she said. "It's been so nice to have a child in the house—we're going to miss Zeth. Kadi, will you eat something?"

With Zeth falling asleep on her lap, Kadi said, "As long as you're making it, I'd like some."

"Rimon?" asked Margid. "No, forgive me—a cup of tea?"

And he remembered for the first time that day that he was in need. And tonight . . . a faint chill ran up his back. Tonight he and Kadi would have transfer. What was the matter with him? It would be like every other time—the most blissful experience he ever knew. Yet prying at the corner of his mind was that strange and terrible fact: *Kadi can kill.*

His thoughts were interrupted when Abel returned with Hank. The boy was grim-faced, but dry-eyed. He sat down beside Kadi at the table, lost in thought.

"Abel, you'll want Hank's papers," said Rimon, fishing them out and looking for his pen. Automatically, he spread his tentacles to search his pockets, and Hank started slightly. But then he just looked away without saying anything.

"I'm signing him over to you, Abel, and here's your change. I owe you some more—can the explanations wait till tomorrow?"

"Of course." Abel held the papers out to Hank. The boy stared at them, then up at Abel. "We don't believe in ownership of people," Abel explained. "But I wouldn't advise you to destroy them. We must abide by the laws of this Territory until one day we have the power to change them. If you change over, you become a free citizen of this Territory if you have no debts to indenture you. If you establish, a Sime must technically hold you as his property—or you're fair prey for any Sime."

"So you own me, either way," Hank said resentfully. "I don't understand Sime money, and I don't have any to give you."

"No. Fort Freedom had to pay to release you, but you

owe us nothing. You're free to seek your own way to salvation, Hank."

Cautiously, Hank took the very edge of the paper Abel held out, and plucked it away, as if afraid Abel would grab him.

"Go wash your hands and face before you eat, Henry," said Margid, as casually as if she spoke to her own son. Hank stared at her, almost said something, but went to wash up in silence.

At the table, when Margid came near him, Hank held himself carefully out of her way, so that she wouldn't touch him accidentally as she served his food. He seemed hesitant to eat at first, but as Kadi dug in, he followed suit. Then he looked up, surprised. "It's real food! Like we had at home!"

Everyone laughed, and some of the tension eased. "Margid is a wonderful cook," said Kadi. "You'll be happy here, Hank."

The boy put down his spoon to finger the papers Abel had given him. "I can't read these."

"You'll have to learn Simelan," said Abel. "Then you'll see they are exactly what we told you."

Hank said in heavily accented Simelan, "I've already learned to speak a lot of it. I knew I needed it to escape."

Rimon choked on his tea, both Kadi and Abel blushed, and Margid looked totally blank. This time it was not a deliberate use of foul language; but in all innocence, Hank used the verb for "learned" with connotations of sizing up a sexual partner, the word for "knew" that implied a Sime discerning a choice kill, and the word "needed" where the proper term was "required." Thus it came out the foulest of gutter language.

"I'm afraid," said Abel, "that you had best speak English, until we teach you proper Simelan in school."

"I'd have to go to school?"

"Of course. Didn't you go to school before—at home?"

"Sure, but . . . You sure do act like real people."

As Hank began to eat again, a young voice called from the front of the house, "Mr. Veritt? Mrs. Veritt?"

"We're in the kitchen, Uel," called Margid.

It was Uel Whelan, Dan Whelan's son. Like all the

children of Fort Freedom, he was meticulously polite before the Veritts, but curiosity was strong in his nager. He was twelve or thirteen, now, and, like Hank, showed no indication of becoming Sime or Gen. "Mr. and Mrs. Veritt. Mr. and Mrs. Farris. Hi, Zeth." Then he waited.

"Uel," said Margid, "this is Henry Steers, Jr. Uel Whelan is the son of our blacksmith, Henry."

"I wish everybody would call me Hank," the boy said. "My father was always Henry."

"Hi, Hank," said Uel. "You gonna stay with Mr. and Mrs. Veritt?"

"Maybe."

Snubbed, Uel turned to Kadi. "Did Zeth pick out which puppy he wants?"

"Yes," she said, "the one with the white patch over his eye."

"Well, I'll just take the other one home, then——"

"Uel," said Abel, "I think the other puppy has chosen Hank—if Hank wants him."

Hank stared at his plate, then looked up at Abel. "Can I really have him?"

"If you'll take care of him."

Uel, apparently sensing that Hank's rudeness had come from strain, tried again. "Want me to show you how to take care of him, Hank? I raised his mother from a pup."

"I know how to train a dog," said Hank, but the rudeness was gone from his voice. "This one looks like my dog, Bigfoot—his feet are too big for the rest of him, just like Biggie's were." He started to get up from the table.

"Hank," Margid said warningly.

The boy turned. "Uh, may I be excused?"

"Have you had enough to eat?"

"Yes, thank you. I think we ought to take the puppies outside, y'know?"

"Very well," said Abel. "Don't be too long, though. You should get to bed early tonight."

"Yes, sir," over his shoulder as he and Uel headed eagerly to play with the puppies.

As the door closed behind them, Rimon said, "I think he's decided to stay."

Abel nodded, smiling contentedly. "Yes. Margid, I think you've acquired another boy to raise."

It was very late by the time Rimon and Kadi had collected the other members of their household, packed up Zeth and the puppy, and gotten home. The pup, now separated from the last of its littermates, cried and cried when they tried to leave it in its basket. In order to ensure tranquillity, Kadi finally let Zeth take the puppy to bed with him. Rimon wondered if the other puppy were providing something warm for Hank to cling to, when he was afraid to let the people around him touch him.

Finally, Rimon and Kadi were alone. Rimon realized that any other month he would have chafed at the events that delayed satisfaction of his need. With Kadi at his side he was barely uncomfortable; nonetheless, it would have been more typical of him to carry Kadi off and leave Anni to put Zeth to bed.

At last he admitted it to himself: he was afraid. Since their last transfer, both he and Kadi had learned that Rimon was not the only one of them capable of killing in transfer. He had shied away from the disconcerting thought. No, he must face it. Kadi could kill him.

She faced it for me, he thought. Then: *She loves me.* But the nagging thought intruded. *What if she is afraid of hurting me? It doesn't matter what the fear is. If her fear makes me hurt her—*

He remembered the fear in Kadi's nager as she faced what she had done to the Freeband Raiders, as she said, "I'm dangerous!" Yes, dangerous was the word—but what could they do? A healing-mode transfer, in which Rimon could control even if Kadi felt fear? That would only put off facing the problem to next month, making it worse. No, they had to get through a normal transfer now, or risk upsetting their relationship—maybe forever.

As Kadi came to him, however, he discovered that there was no fear in her nager. Was she acting again? He zlinned her deeply, finding no trace of anxiety. What had happened?

"Rimon, you're disturbed. I don't blame you for being afraid I might hurt you, but I won't," said Kadi softly, her nager at an emotional level that kept real fright at bay. "I think I know what Simes must face when they can't keep from killing."

He reached out to put his arms around her, remembering all the time he had fought the kill reflexes—and lost.

"Not yet," she said, eluding his grasp smoothly. "It still gives me chills to remember it—that creature's touch. But I've made myself remember what I felt when it happened. I can almost convince myself that I felt my own nager, Rimon. I sometimes have to look at my arms to see I'm not turning Sime. Don't laugh at me—"

"I don't think I could, right now," answered Rimon, aware of the acute buildup of need as he tried to focus on her words.

"I have to say this. I know I won't hurt you because you don't feel to me like that Raider did. You don't trigger any reflex in me except love and pleasure. And if I ever did have to shen you, it wouldn't be like *that*."

Some flash of scientific curiosity broke through the pall of need, and Rimon had to ask, "Like what, particularly?"

She glanced up at him, gauging his humor. "It—felt a little like when Zeth was born and you had to get selyn to flow backwards through my system, to him. That's what I think I felt. And this unbearable—itch—I just couldn't stand it. You've never done anything like that to me, Rimon—and you never will. So you'll never make me shen you out like *that*."

But Rimon was momentarily lost in thought. Had Kadi made the Raider's system work backwards? Was that what had killed him? He didn't remember much of the incident except his terror and the paralyzing nageric clap that had ended it.

"Now, Rimon," said Kadi, quietly inserting herself into his grasp, fingers working their way tenderly up his tentacle sheaths until her palms closed gently around his arms. "Take your transfer; don't be afraid of me—not ever."

He whispered, "You control."

"Oh no, you've got to face it, or everything we've built will come crumbling down. You do it *to* me, and see how much I—still—enjoy—it."

Her nager had warmed about him, bringing need singing through his whole body. He wondered vaguely how he could do anything to her when she could turn him on and off like that. But at the same time, he found himself enjoying need itself, too caught up to appreciate the contradiction. Nature took charge, his awareness soaring into hyperconsciousness, enveloped by the purity of Kadi's distinctive nager, as her selyn became his own.

The drought persisted. Both Rimon's trin and the flax grown at Fort Freedom as a cash crop were nearly a total loss. The problem of taxes multiplied—even with their parents paying the head tax on the three young people in Rimon's household, he was hard put to pay just for Kadi. Next year's property tax loomed as a distant threat, although they talked with Jord again about moving out to their property to reduce their taxes. But Jord didn't want to move out of Fort Freedom, and he was becoming even edgier than when he had approached the crisis before. He was fighting with Willa again, and she didn't help by reminding him of what had happened the last time he had left her side when he was in need.

Early in the fall, Rimon and Abel were discussing financial plans with Del Erick, the only one of them who had come through with less than a devastating loss. Del said ruefully, "If you and I had taken adjoining land, Rimon, Carlana and I could move just across the property line and increase your ratio of Simes to Gens."

Abel shook his head. "I don't understand all the legalities, but we must do something to have Rimon's property reclassified."

"Wait a minute!" said Del. "Rimon, your father used to say it was worth the taxes on the Genfarm for the protection that part of the Territory got from the government."

"But the government gives us no protection," said Abel.

"Since our area now has a Genfarm, we just might be able to raise our own militia, or at least mostly our own people, paid for by the government. I, for one, would be willing to pay part of Rimon's tax bill if it means I won't have to put out a fortune to keep my fences from being stolen, and carried away on my own horses!"

"Pay somebody else's taxes—that sounds faintly illegal," said Abel dubiously. "After all, Rimon isn't really running

a Genfarm, and to dupe the government into thinking he
is . . ."

Rimon wondered what kind of government Abel had
grown up with. What was the government but a settled-in
band of Raiders? "Well, Abel, *I* didn't call it a Genfarm,
the tax office did; so by their own laws, they have to protect me."

"Besides," said Del, "if we have a Genfarm and get a
local patrol, we can kick some of the worst of the rabble
out of town—so they won't be raiding from here and bringing retaliations. Fort Freedom and the permanent residents
of town make a pretty fair population. Rimon's taxes plus
mine will show an influx from this end of the Territory. . . ."

"Del, what are you suggesting?" asked Abel.

"We can form a county!" said Rimon. "Fort Freedom
and our two places have enough people to outvote the
town—and then we can form a local government and make
our own laws!"

"Abel," said Del, "if we make the laws, we can declare
Gens to be people. Rimon's marriage would be recognized,
and Jord's—it will take years—but isn't it worth the effort?"

Abel looked at the two young men and smiled. "We had
to work hard to get the Territory government to accept
Fort Freedom. I'm willing to work just as hard to carve
out a part of the Territory where we can build our new
life."

Abel's personal plans for a new life, Rimon knew, rested
more each day on Hank Steers. Finally convinced that he
was not yet Gen, Hank had announced that he would remain in Fort Freedom—at least until he established or
changed over. He and Uel had become fast friends, spend-
ing most of their leisure time out with their dogs. There
was a friendly rivalry, as Hank tried to make his puppy
behave as well as the mother dog Uel had trained. Biggie,
as Hank named him, served another function, as well. Although Hank no longer shied away from Simes, his attitude
made it clear he'd rather not be touched—but he would
hug Biggie and tumble with him, and as the winter progressed and the dog grew, he'd lie by the fire in the evenings, studying, his head pillowed on Biggie's shaggy flank.

Rimon worried that Abel was too attached to the boy. The way Hank avoided anything warmer than courtesy with the Veritts suggested that if he established, he planned to go straight over the border. And what would happen to Abel's hopes if he changed over?

He decided to ask Abel. "What if Hank turns out Sime?"

"Do you mean, will I stop loving him, the way I did with Jord? Rimon, I've no intention of repeating the gravest mistake of my life. If Hank changes over, I'll have to help him accept that fact, and go on from there—as all the rest of us have done. It will be difficult for him, and—it will virtually force him to join our ranks. I'd prefer that he had a free choice in the matter, but if it's God's will— have you noticed some sign of changeover in him, Rimon?"

"The way he's shooting up and filling out, I think he'll establish before the winter's over. But I'm not infallible. Nobody can call it before it actually happens, you know."

Abel sighed. "Yes, we can only wait and pray."

Waiting and praying were the order of business at Fort Freedom that winter. The carefully tended kitchen gardens provided enough food for the tables, and there was wood to chop for fuel, but there was little beyond necessities. As the flax crop had been so poor, there was not even the steady whir of spinning wheels that ordinarily vibrated through the winter evenings—and in the spring, there wouldn't be cloth to sell.

There was some wool from a small herd of sheep, and Abel decided to add to the flock as soon as finances permitted. When Kadi saw Margid knitting, with hands only and just two needles, she said, "But that way is so hard and slow! Mama always used four or six needles."

Margid extended her tentacles and flexed them curiously around the needles. "Can you teach me, Kadi?"

"I wish I could! But Mama couldn't teach me until I got tentacles—and I didn't. Doesn't anybody here know how?" But none of Fort Freedom's women had had Sime mothers; they knew only the Gen method, which Kadi promptly set out to learn. She also asked Slina to teach Margid the Sime method—without consulting Margid first. Slina and Kadi just turned up one afternoon, and Rimon realized only then where Kadi had gone.

Margid was properly embarrassed, but Slina would brook no denial. "Shen—almost a year since you folks bailed me out, and what have you let me do for you?"

Put that way, the lessons could not be refused, and soon every woman in Fort Freedom was even busier making warm clothes for her family. Rimon recalled his own plans to run some sheep on the rocky ground he couldn't till—but so far he hadn't been able to afford any, so his two goats had the land to themselves.

It was another snowy winter, but no one complained—it would mean a good runoff in the spring, and water in the streams all year. However, aside from Fort Freedom's Year's Turning ceremony, there was another date that everyone hoped would be free of hazardous weather. Del Erick was throwing a birthday party for his children.

"A *what* party?" Rimon asked him.

"It's a Gen custom. Carlana told me about it. They don't have changeover parties, of course. They celebrate the day a child is born—I guess because Gens can't tell when they establish." It was actually Jana's third birthday, but since neither child had had a birthday party before, they decided to include Owen in it, too. "Maybe we'll make it an annual affair," said Del.

As the plans grew, they couldn't decide where to draw the line on the guest list. Soon no one in Fort Freedom could be excluded, so the party was moved to the Fort's chapel, cleared and set up with tables for food, games for the children, and plenty of room for parents to come and watch.

A few days before the big event, Rimon was at Abel's when Hank arrived home from school. "Brrr! It's cold out there!" he announced as he shucked his coat and headed for the fire. Biggie, loping in behind him, paused politely to shake the snow off his coat at the door before he proceeded to track wet pawprints across the clean floor.

"Hank," said Abel, "you've been told before about tracking in snow. There's a broom on the porch."

"Yes, sir," replied Hank. "But it's *cold!* I'll clean it up." He pulled off his boots and set them by the fire to dry, padding toward the kitchen with Biggie behind making more tracks.

Rimon didn't laugh out loud, but Abel looked over to him with an apologetic shrug. Hank returned, shivering, and began wiping up the melting snow. Slowly it dawned on Rimon that Hank shouldn't be shivering as he worked before the fire. Concerned, he zlinned the boy—and discerned the first faint trace of selyn production. Yes, he had seen that symptom before—in a Gen establishing in cold weather, there were sometimes chills as the body adjusted. "Hank," he said, "you look chilled through. Why don't you go have a cup of tea?"

"That sounds good. Would you like some?"

Both Abel and Rimon agreed, but the moment Hank was out of the room Abel asked, "Is something wrong?"

"Not at all. He's establishing, Abel."

"Thank God!" Abel closed his eyes, holding himself rigid, and Rimon knew the conflicting emotions his beliefs caused the older man. With a shudder, Abel said, "Thank you for not telling me in front of him, Rimon. He must make his own choice—not be influenced by my desires."

Hank returned with the tea, carefully proffering the cups so that neither Abel nor Rimon would have to touch him. Then he sat down before the fire and sipped gratefully at the hot tea. "I can't seem to get warm today!"

"Do you know why you're cold, Hank?" asked Rimon.

"Maybe I'm catching cold. Things smell funny. The tea sure tastes good though—guess I'm learning to like it."

"Hank," Abel said very softly, "you've begun to establish."

A wild stab of joy, fear and disbelief went through the boy. "Then—I'm a Gen!"

"Definitely," said Rimon. "Congratulations, Hank." It was what one said to a changeover victim. It was the first time Rimon had congratulated a Gen upon establishment.

"But—?" Hank stared from Rimon to Abel. "What should I do?"

As Abel regarded the boy, Rimon noted with relief the older man was pre-turnover and as stable as he ever was.

"Hank," said Abel, "you must decide what to do with your life. Pray for God's guidance."

"You don't think I should give thanks for not being Sime?"

"You might give thanks for reaching adulthood healthy and free."

Hank frowned. "You really will let me go, won't you? Even though you were hoping I could somehow teach you not to kill?"

"If it's what you want, Hank, I'll arrange a Farewell."

"I—I don't know! I've never been so confused in my life."

Rimon remembered Kadi's fear and depression, as she had contended with the effects of establishment. The other Gens had shown some signs, too—but none of them had faced such turmoil as either Kadi or Hank. "Don't try to decide at once," said Rimon. "You're undergoing changes that influence your emotions. For now, you're perfectly safe—your field is so low that most people won't even notice it for a day or two. Stay here until the birthday party. Then, I think you should come out to stay with me until you make up your mind."

"I like your place, but—if I stay, I want to live here in Fort Freedom," Hank said. "Willa does."

"Hank," said Abel, "let's not talk yet about your learning to give transfer as Willa does. First, decide if you want to stay on this side of the border at all. Remember, Willa learned from Rimon before she tried working with Jord."

The boy looked from Abel to Rimon and back again, his growing field a study in conflict. Then he turned to Biggie, put an arm around the dog, and leaned on him. The aching loneliness in that gesture pierced Rimon to the quick. There were tears in Abel's eyes, as he held back from reaching out. He'd give Hank up, let all his hopes go with him, rather than frighten him, let alone hurt him. *Does Hank know that? Surely he couldn't turn away like that if he knew—if he only knew.*

The birthday party was a huge success. The children played games while Del and Carlana and Rimon and Kadi saw to it that every child won some bauble from the collection the adults had pitched in to make.

Hank, suddenly elevated to adult status, didn't compete. Uel laughingly accused him of establishing just so he wouldn't have to be in the boys' obstacle race—which Uel won easily without Hank's competition. Rimon would have bet on Hank, who had gained strength as well as size this winter in the physical regimen of Fort Freedom's children—preparation for a hard pioneer life on the other side of the border. The hopes might have changed, but the training hadn't. However, Uel's teasing was tinged with envy; he'd grown up being told it was better to be Gen.

As everyone sat down to watch Owen and Jana cut the huge cake decorated with their names spelled out in small candies, Uel said to Hank, "It's not fair for you to establish before me. I'm older than you are."

"Only two months," Hank replied. "Maybe you'll establish soon. We could cross the border together."

Rimon glanced around to be sure Abel couldn't hear.

"Haven't I told you often enough? I really mean it, Hank. I'm going to stay here and learn to give transfer."

"You wait till everybody starts looking at you—and then *not* looking at you—that way! You could get killed."

"It's up to the Gen," said Uel. "Mrs. Farris has told you that the Gen keeps the Sime from killing. It's true, you know."

"Probably is," agreed Hank.

"Well, I'm going to learn. All the established kids are staying, Hank—if everyone leaves, how will our parents or our brothers and sisters learn not to kill? If your mom and dad had been Sime, wouldn't you want to be able to stop them from killing?"

"Len and Sordal and Anni—they haven't stopped anyone."

"Not yet. It's not easy—but look at Mrs. Farris and Willa Veritt. I figure if Willa can learn it, so can I. My mom and dad—they're not my mom and dad, you know."

"Huh?"

"My real father was my dad's brother. He and my mother were killed in a Gen raid when I was a baby—I don't remember them at all. But Mom and Dad took me in and raised me as their own son. Do you think I'd repay them by crossing the border when I establish? I saw Willa give transfer to Jord on their wedding day. *That's* what I want to do."

Rimon saw Hank look down the table to Abel and Margid. Perhaps he was realizing at last how much love they had to give a homeless boy who gave them nothing in return but hope.

They were seated at a distance because they had both passed turnover. Rimon had reduced the fields of the other three Gens, so they could mingle freely at the party, but Hank's field had climbed to a bright beacon, rivaling Willa's and even apparent against Kadi's nager. Thus the Simes of Fort Freedom had assumed their Farewell Ceremony configuration, with only those most recently satisfied coming anywhere near Hank.

Except for Rimon, of course. He was just below midfield, but had to think twice to recall where he was in his cycle. Recently, noticing that need didn't clamor at him even when Kadi wasn't nearby, he'd decided that the secret was security: he knew she'd be there, and so his fears were slowly receding. If only Jord would hurry up and reach this stage . . .

But Jord was on the ragged edge of need today, carefully avoiding Hank and the other Gens, but spoiling Willa's fun by refusing to stay with her as she helped the smallest children. Each time she'd get involved, Jord would wander off, and Willa would have to leave the children she loved to go after him.

Jord is paying for another of my bright ideas, thought Rimon. The month before, when Jord became edgy and started avoiding Willa, Rimon had suggested that they have their transfer a day early. The result was not a disaster, but Jord had come from the transfer high-field, yet with a sense of being shorted. So this month they were letting his full cycle run out.

Rimon knew he ought to send them home for transfer now, but he wondered if he could persuade Jord. Abel probably could, so Rimon got up and headed toward the low-field Simes at the end of the table. The children, having eaten their cake, were starting to move away from the tables, but Hank and Uel remained talking together, Hank's field a flare Rimon could keep pinpointed without trying.

He glanced over to the table where Kadi and Willa were cleaning up the smallest children before turning them loose to fingerprint the chapel. Jord stood back, watching impatiently, but at least he wasn't leaving Willa's sphere of influence. With grim humor, Rimon noted how Willa carefully kept herself between Jord and Kadi. Jord was not going to be allowed to slip up again, if Willa had anything to do with it.

Secure that Jord and Willa were safely placed, Rimon turned to Abel, leaning close so that his words wouldn't alarm anyone nearby. "Abel, can you help me get Jord and Willa to go home?"

"They shouldn't be here at all," said Abel, "but there was no way to keep Willa away from a party for the children."

"What's wrong?" Margid wanted to know.

"Nothing," Rimon replied. "We just think—"

"Rimon!" Margid interrupted him. "Jord!"

Rimon zlinned Jord headed out of the chapel. Well, at least he was going away from any Gen here. Before Rimon could move, Willa called, "Jord!" and started after her husband.

Jord stopped when Willa called his name. Then, to avoid her, he began weaving back through the scattered tables and chairs in the center of the chapel, moving with Sime agility that Willa couldn't match. She plowed through, shoving tables and chairs out of her way, and at the clatter both Uel and Hank rose, easing out of the path of the chase.

Rimon couldn't allow a disaster this time; he shot down an aisle of tables, vaulted over one, and came up behind Jord just as he approached the two boys. He zlinned curiosity more than fear from Hank—until Uel grabbed Hank's arm, saying, "Get behind me!"

A lot of good that will do! The thought had hardly formed in Rimon's mind when Uel's good intentions erupted in startlement from Hank, followed by real fear as Jord turned toward him.

Rimon lunged for Jord and spun him into Willa's arms as she panted up to them. From the opposite side, at the same instant, Abel came seemingly out of nowhere to grasp Hank by the shoulders and pull him back out of harm's way.

Willa grasped Jord's arms, and with a flick of her field threw him into helpless need—shocking every Sime in the chapel but immediately damping any effect as she attacked Jord with her own need to give, assuaging his pain, filling the bleak void in him, easing away all his tensions in one outpouring.

Rimon was so close, so involved, that the sudden strong surge in the fields made his head spin. He felt the effect on Abel, equally close, still tensed against Hank's momentary fear. Now Abel, nearly blacking out with the effects of the rapid nageric shift, sagged, leaning his whole weight on Hank.

The boy turned, gasped, "Abel!" and caught him before he could fall, then eased him onto the bench where he and Uel had been sitting, supporting him physically and nagerically.

"I'm all right!" insisted Abel although clearly he was not. "Jord?"

"I'm all right, Father—thanks to Willa again. God forgive me—I don't know why I want to run from her when I get like that. But—Hank?"

"You never touched me," the boy said. "What did you do to your father?"

Rimon, steady once more, said, "It was the selyn flow between Willa and Jord—Abel was too close."

Hank asked Abel, "Can I help?"

"You are helping, Hank. Thank God you weren't hurt."

"But you were—protecting me. I—I don't want you to be hurt—not because of me, or because of anything."

Abel turned to meet the young eyes. Rimon could almost hear the words the older man was holding back. *Then stay.*

All at once, Hank blurted out, "You want what Willa did for Jord just now—instead of killing. Now I know—I want to do that for you!"

Astonished, Abel raised his head sharply, paying for the move with a stab of pain, but Rimon saw that it was well worth it as he looked into Hank's eyes. "Y-you've decided to stay?"

The boy nodded. "You said God sent me. I believe it. He must want me to teach you—why else was my father sent here? I'm sorry I was rude to you—" He broke into the tears he'd been holding back all these months. "They killed my mother—I never saw my father again—and I was afraid—Now I'm home. Don't make me leave—don't take it all away. Not again." He ran out of breath, sobbing on Abel's shoulder as the older man held him, Rimon seeing the same helpless despair in the boy that he expected only in Sime refugees from out-Territory.

Finally Hank raised tear-drenched eyes once more to Abel's. "Next month I'll do it for you, Abel."

"No, son—not next month. But you will do it, I have confidence—we'll pray together. I've vowed not to die a killer, and every day I see some progress toward keeping that vow."

Uel Whelan came to kneel before Abel. "If Hank can't do it, I will, Mr. Veritt. Someone will. It has to happen."

The three Gens who lived with Rimon were scattered through the chapel, with their families. Eyes shifted to them, but they were silent, motionless—at the first opportunity, Rimon would have to remind people of the lesson of Jon's death—it was no use to pressure someone who wasn't ready. His attention, and everyone else's, was caught by the movement of the other children, gathering around Abel and Hank, slipping between the adults. So few children—the hope for the future. Even Zeth followed the crowd, stopping before Rimon, watching the solemn moment. Zlinning his son, Rimon found that the child understood something—small as he was. And he'd grow up with the repeated dedication to end the kill.

Kadi came up beside Rimon and picked Zeth up. Rimon put his arm around her, feeling a strange new lift—Jord had just passed a crisis.

Looking at Hank and Abel, surrounded by the children, Rimon began to feel that this was indeed what he was born to do—to found a way of life in which people didn't have to fear to love one another. And Zeth would grow up with it—he'd be Sime, Rimon was sure, but he'd never kill. Not once. To guarantee that, Rimon would give his life—anything—anything at all.

Chapter 24

FIRST CHANNEL

As the dreary late winter advanced, Jord and Willa got along much better, making Rimon hope that the birthday party had really been Jord's crisis. Both Rimon and Jord were kept busy with the usual assortment of late-winter illnesses, but there was no repetition of last year's epidemic in Slina's Pens.

At Abel's insistence, Hank Steers moved in with Rimon —temporarily, he reminded everyone daily. That meant two dogs in the household, too—and often Rimon thought Uel Whelan might as well be a member of the family for all the time he spent there. Kids and dogs everywhere— until the day Zeth decided to "walk the dogs" down the tunnel through Len Deevan's carefully tended mushrooms.

Then Rimon called a meeting, and, feeling rather like Abel Veritt, laid down the law. To his surprise, no one protested his rules. Nevertheless, he began thinking of expanding the house again, or even building a second house for everyone except Kadi, Zeth, and himself. Hank thought that was silly. "Everyone will be moving back to Fort Freedom, the way Willa did."

"You may, Hank—but I don't know about the other Gens."

It was becoming a problem now. Len had been with them for almost a year, and still he had a skittish fear of real transfer. The other two who had been there for months were also unable to prevent the emotion that could prove a kill-stimulus.

Hank, on the other hand, lost his nervousness after the first time Rimon drew from him. "Is that all?" he asked.

"That's it. You're low-field. You can go anywhere you

341

want to for the next few days—within reason. Don't go into town alone."

"Kadi does."

"Kadi," explained Rimon, "is an exception to every rule ever made. When you can do everything she can, you can use your own judgment about where you go."

"Oh, all right. But when can I give a real transfer?"

"Six months."

"Six months! That's forever!"

"Hank, Abel and I both agree that you're not to be rushed. You know about Jon Forester—we tried to push him too fast, and the result was tragedy."

"But Abel wants to stop killing! Rimon, I know I can do it!"

"If you can do it now, you can do it six months from now. How would Abel face himself if you tried before you were ready . . . and you made him kill you?"

Hank had no answer to that. Nonetheless, he kept pestering to have the date moved ahead. After his third transfer, Rimon felt he was ready, but Abel was adamant: they had set a date, and they would keep it. Rimon thought Abel's fear for the boy was unfounded. Hank had that same sense of confidence that Willa had.

He noticed, too, that each time he drew from Hank there seemed to be more selyn, just as with Willa; only Kadi's field outshone them. When Rimon began trying to measure the differences, with no set standard, certain facts about his own physiology began to fall into place. "I use more selyn than other Simes," he told Kadi. "I thought for a long time that it was just that some of what I took when I killed went into my reservoir, and that left me shorted for the month. But Kadi—not one of these kids can provide enough selyn for me, not even Hank—because there actually is a capacity difference!"

"It's my fault!" gasped Kadi. "After Zeth was born, that time you let me satisfy myself—you didn't burst—you stretched!" When Rimon laughed, she said, "All right, it sounds funny, but it isn't. I did something that increased your capacity for selyn, because ever since you have satisfied me. But Rimon—what will you do when we decide to have another baby?"

"Maybe someone will be up to your capacity by then. Kadi, people's capacities grow. I've become more sensitive since I . . . stretched, as you put it. So have you. There's a kind of growth that goes along with the things Jord and I can do—I've seen it in him, too, and you certainly had nothing to do with that. But Willa must have—they've both increased in capacity. I witnessed their first two transfers— and at the birthday party I zlinned a distinct increase in the selyn flow."

"Do you think when two people start having transfer they sort of—grow together? Adapt to each other?"

"I'm sure of that. But all the kids have increased their selyn production, even though they're not giving real transfers yet. I'm onto something, Kadi. The trouble is, I haven't figured out exactly what it is."

One thing disturbing Rimon was that he and Jord received all the extra selyn from the Gens in Rimon's care. They could use it for extra work—but it seemed grossly unfair that two Simes should be using extra selyn while others still had to kill to live.

If only there were a way to transfer the selyn to other Simes. Each time his mind circled back to that thought, however, Rimon shuddered. There was a way, all right; he had experienced it twice, and was now certain it was what had killed his cousin Zeth. No, the Sime system wasn't meant to work backwards. The only way was to train Gens —and it looked as if there would soon be another success in Hank.

Meanwhile, Rimon used up some of his extra selyn in Fort Freedom's fields. They could no longer pay him, but he had a debt to work off, and when that was done, he helped out whenever he could. At foaling time, Kadi went back to work for Del; that spring her tax was paid entirely with money she earned herself.

Rimon and Del braved the threat of a late snow to get to the first market of the year, selling horses and mushrooms and the few items Fort Freedom had salvaged. Prices were down; no one had much money after last year except the government, which collected taxes no matter what. They sold a herd of horses to the border guard at a nice profit, and at the same time, filed the first petition to have their section of the Territory declared a county.

Spring planting went well, the crops soon sending up bright shoots in neat rows. There was renewed hope of healing the rift in Fort Freedom. Dan Whelan organized all those dissenters who'd returned, and offered to help Sara Fenell and the other two families still living along the creek with plowing and planting. When the help was accepted, they didn't push further—but Abel was laying plans, Rimon knew, to try again to bring them home when he could say he himself didn't kill anymore.

With that hope, Abel was glowing with good spirits. Hank bent Rimon's rules practically backwards, "living" with Rimon only in the sense that he slept there most nights. As Abel and Hank were deliberately getting into phase, though, Abel did send the boy home when he was in need. Uel Whelan often turned up on those days, and the two boys would go off together, much to the distress of Zeth, who always wanted to tag along.

One morning when Hank had been out with Rimon for two days, the boy was growing restless. "Come on, Rimon —if you won't let me try transfer this month, take my field down so I can go over to Fort Freedom."

"Next month, Hank, and that's why it's important that I not take your field down until this evening. That's when Abel has scheduled his kill."

"But it wouldn't hurt for me to be *ahead* of him."

"No, but he doesn't want you to see him today—especially not this evening. You can understand that."

"Yeah, I guess so. Maybe Uel can come out today."

But Uel didn't show up, and Abel did, just at midmorning. "Rimon, Uel Whelan's gone into changeover, and he's having a bad time of it. Jord says he thinks the problem may be a dual system, like yours."

"I'm coming," Rimon said at once. "Kadi!"

"I'll get the horses," said Hank, and was off before anyone thought to stop him. He had saddled three horses by the time Rimon and Kadi were ready, and Rimon decided not to protest. Hank was Uel's best friend, and his presence these days was almost as soothing as Kadi's.

When they reached the Whelan home, Rimon soon discovered that the problem was not physical complications at all, but Uel's lack of cooperation. He was in the final stages, tentacles well developed in their sheaths, but he lay still, pale and grim, turning his face away from Jord.

"Zlin him, Rimon," Jord said when they entered. "It's completely evident now—two selyn systems."

Rimon zlinned the boy, looking around at his parents, Jord, and Willa—what had they been saying to him to put him in this state? Rimon sat down on the edge of the bed and said, "Congratulations, Uel. It's almost over now."

"I won't kill! I'll die first!"

Jord said, "Uel, you want to save lives. Then listen to us. You can learn to heal the way Rimon and I do. That's the gift God has given you—to heal the sick and injured."

"What kind of God wants me to save some people by killing others?"

"Uel!" Abel said sharply, his need sapping his patience.

Rimon said, "He's not responsible for what he's saying, Abel. Jord's right about the dual system. Zlin his selyn consumption. If we can't get him to cooperate in breakout, he might succeed in killing himself."

"Let me try," said Hank. When he approached the bed, Uel turned toward him, drawn by Hank's field. "Come on, Uel—you know the exercises. Remember how silly I looked when I first tried them?" He held out his hands, clenching his fists, snapping his fingers open. "I can do them now, though. See?"

"You never required them," Uel muttered resentfully.

"Sure I did—I require them right now, and I've got to teach them to my kids, haven't I? Come on, Uel, do it with me. You can do it."

Rimon watched Hank concentrate, felt him actually trying to project the muscular contractions to Uel, who by this time was fighting involuntary spasms. Unconsciously, the other Simes in the room were imitating Hank's actions. Kadi had been teaching Hank her techniques; obviously, he was an apt pupil.

"Good!" said Hank when Uel moved his hands. "Again now."

But then the fluid swelled the membranes at Uel's wrists, the tentacles threatening to break through at any moment. Rimon turned to Jord. "Where's the Gen?"

"I'll get her," Jord replied.

"No—oh—oh!" With an agonized howl, Uel convulsed and the tentacles tore free. Rimon wrapped an arm around Hank's waist, intending to snatch him out of Uel's reach, but Uel twisted away to face the wall, curled up with his arms hidden, just the way Rimon himself had rejected all attempts to make him kill after Zeth. But Uel was in First Need. He should be unable to do anything but attack the nearest source of selyn.

Kadi said, "Rimon, can I help him the way I used to help you?"

"I'll do it," said Hank.

"You don't know what to do," said Kadi.

"I'll give him transfer. Why should he have to kill, when I'm here?"

Rimon felt the shock surge through Abel, exacerbated by his need. Yet in moments the older man had gained control of himself. "Rimon—can he do it? If Uel should never have to kill . . ."

"It's First Need, Abel. And Hank has never given transfer at all." *Give Abel a way out.*

Hank protested, "If I can't save my best friend's life, what good am I?" He pulled the smaller boy over onto his back.

Rimon started to reach out for Hank again, but Abel put a hand on his shoulder. "Let him try. Think of it, Rimon —the first of our Sime children never to kill at all—with your abilities—with Jord's."

Uel remained curled into a tight ball. "Won't kill," he murmured as Hank tried to pry his fingers from their painful clamping over his own arms. His tentacles were tightly retracted, even the laterals.

"Use your field," said Kadi. "You can't fight Sime strength with Gen muscle."

Hank concentrated, willing Uel to relax, coaxing softly, "Hey—come on—just let me help—come on now. . . ."

Painfully, Uel focused his eyes. "Hank? Hank—I can't—

do anything for my parents now. You—take care of them —please."

At that, Mrs. Whelan began to cry against her husband's shoulder. Rimon realized that if there was any chance of this transfer working, he had to get them out of the room —and Abel, too.

Hank was close to tears. "Don't be dumb, Uel," he said gruffly. "You'll take care of them yourself."

Uel gave a grim smile. "Don't put on any act with me, Hank. I'm dying."

"You wouldn't let me quit—you wouldn't hear me talking about going across the border. Well, now you're quitting, only I'm not going to listen. I'm going to give you transfer."

Uel's resistance began to crumble. "I can't kill you!"

"You're not going to because I'm not going to let you."

At that moment, Jord came in with the Gen for Uel. The fields in the room shifted painfully at that reminder, and Rimon said, "Jord, clear the room. Kadi, stay here. Everybody else out."

"But—" Abel began.

"Especially you, Abel. Don't put yourself through this— you could distract them at a critical moment."

"We'll go outside and pray," Abel said firmly, and led the exodus. Rimon zlinned the party through the closed door. He hoped Jord would have the sense to have that Gen ready for Abel. If this transfer worked—or worse, if it didn't—the repercussions would reach Abel strongly, as deep into need and as bound up in Hank as he was.

Rimon narrowed his concentration to the two boys as Kadi came up and put her hands on his shoulders. Within the insulated room they created an area of calm. Rimon was in healing mode; Kadi was a supportive presence. Hank was tense, but there was no fear in his nager. Uel's need was increasing more rapidly now, so that despite his efforts, his laterals began to lick out of their sheaths.

"Hank, if I kill you—"

"If I die, you take care of Biggie for me, all right?"

". . . all right."

He took Uel's arms in transfer position, his friend's tentacles automatically wrapping about him, the laterals seeking his flesh. But that didn't frighten Hank—he'd been through it many times with Rimon.

Rimon went completely hyperconscious as Hank bent to press his lips to Uel's. He'd known it before, with Kadi, had seen it with Willa and Jord, but Hank's incredulous surprise and delight when the flow brought exquisite pleasure was as exciting as if it were the first time for Rimon, too. And it was different—release from need without the savage wrenching of pleasure out of the brink of agony. *Innocence. Uel has never killed—now he never will.*

Kadi was clutching at Rimon's shoulders. Did she perceive somehow that Rimon had just seen a vision of untainted bliss, that he—and she—would never know? *But Zeth will!*

Then Hank and Uel were untangling themselves, staring at each other, too young to bear the embarrassment of solemnity. They both broke into giggles. "We did it!" Hank cried.

"Mom! Dad! We did it!" Uel shouted, jumping up, oblivious to the post transients in his body. His secondary system had been involved in the transfer, and Rimon zlinned the wave of dizziness that drove the boy to his knees. Rimon caught him up onto the bed again.

"Easy." Rimon couldn't help chuckling. "Give yourself time to get used to being Sime."

Uel stared at him, and broke into laughter again. "I am! I'm Sime and it doesn't matter! It really doesn't matter!"

By this time, Hank had opened the door. Dan Whelan and his wife were already there, followed by Willa, then Jord. The Whelans embraced their son and Hank, both crying unashamedly. Then Dan said, "God has blessed us after all our doubts. Mr. Farris, can you ever forgive me for my accusations?"

"That was all forgotten long ago," said Rimon. "Anyway, it's Hank and Uel's celebration today." Where was Abel? He was about to ask Jord, when Abel entered, pale—and high-field. So he'd had to take the Gen. Rimon had expected that, and now he recalled that sometime immediately after Hank and Uel had achieved their transfer, he'd felt a faint sensation. Yet it had hardly attracted his attention. The room was not very well insulated, and Abel's emotions upon being forced to kill at the same moment that Hank was giving his first transfer should have flared through the whole town.

But Abel's inner strength, bolstered by the physical relief from need, carried him through in his usual fashion. "Hank, you were truly sent to us; and Uel, God has blessed you in a way no Sime has known before. Rimon, Jord—all the rest of us as we learn not to kill—we will always have to live with the fact that we have killed. You're the first of your kind, as Rimon Farris is the first of his. May God guide you to use His blessings wisely."

Hank was staring at Abel. By now he had no trouble recognizing need—nor satisfaction. "Abel!" he whispered. "Oh, Abel, I'm sorry! I could have—"

"You could not do both, Hank, and what you did for Uel is far more important than what you may one day do for me."

"Next month. As we planned—"

At the stab of fear/resentment/jealousy from Uel, Rimon put a hand on Hank's arm. "Not next month. Uel needs you until he learns for himself not to kill. But in the meantime, no one's going to give up the attempt to stop everyone from killing." *But especially Abel. How can I let him go through this again? I've got to find a way—and soon.*

To that end, he sought more information, for he sensed that somehow, some way, he'd find some bit of knowledge that would make everything else fall into place. And then he'd know how to stop any Sime from killing. So he consulted Jord about Abel's kill on Uel's changeover day.

"Rimon! I wouldn't zlin my father's kill!"

"I know you wouldn't deliberately, but how could you help it that day? You must have had to force that Gen on him."

"Well—I did shove them into the storeroom together, but then I put Willa between me and them, and tried to stay completely hypoconscious until it was over."

Rimon fought down an irrational anger at the loss of

information. He knew how sensitive the people of Fort Freedom were about their privacy—especially about the kill. Nonetheless, he screwed up his courage and approached Abel with the request to witness his next kill.

Abel fought down a series of emotions, and finally managed to ask, "Why, Rimon?"

"I wish I could tell you exactly what I'm looking for, but I don't know. I think I'll know it when I zlin it. There was something about your kill at the Whelans'—something that could be the key to stopping you from killing. But I wasn't focused on you, and I don't know what it is."

"Something to stop me from killing?"

"I can't promise. It's just a hunch, Abel."

"I understand." But he didn't say yes. He shuddered. "When I was a Freeband Raider, we used to zlin each other's kills. While I know God forgives everything if one is truly repentant, I sometimes wonder if, after all my sins, I'm asking too much."

"No!" Rimon recalled his own vision of what transfer was like if one had never killed—a knowledge he could have only vicariously. That was enough frustration for anyone to live with. "Abel, I'm going to find the way. What we're doing is too slow; only one Sime separated from the kill for each Gen we train—and a majority of Gens who simply can't learn not to fear transfer. We've got to have every scrap of information!"

So, hesitantly, Abel agreed. "When the times comes, you may have to remind me of my promise."

They were interrupted just then by Jord and Willa, hand in hand and bursting with good news. Willa could not wait to break it easily. "I'm going to have a baby!"

"Willa!" exclaimed Abel. "Jord! Oh, that's wonderful—have you told your mother yet?"

"Congratulations," said Rimon, trying to hide the conflict in his emotions. On the one hand, the news that at last there would be another child in Fort Freedom assuaged a part of his guilt. Still, he was not sure that Jord should have allowed it yet; he seemed stable enough these days, yet Rimon sensed that he didn't have that deep inner security Rimon himself felt.

As Margid and Kadi, who had already been told the news, came in from the kitchen with tea, Abel heaved a happy sigh. "A grandchild. We are blessed indeed."

When the day came for Rimon to observe his kill, Abel was more nervous than Rimon had ever seen him. It was Rimon who almost backed out, though, when he saw the Gen waiting in the killroom, drugged, uncomprehending. He'd been thinking in terms of selyn flows, field gradients, experiments—but there before him was a person, about to die. He felt the same reaction from Abel. *Every month he goes through this!*

It was far worse than Rimon remembered. Even that terrible time—his last kill—when the boy had spoken to him . . . even then he'd more than half believed that Gens were not people. But that was three years ago, before Kadi —Willa—Hank . . .

The girl looked up at them with dull brown eyes, expecting nothing, her field high but lusterless. Like an animal, but not an animal. A human being. Somehow he had to make himself zlin one more kill. For Abel. For Zeth. *I can't let all those deaths be in vain.*

Steeling himself, he went hyperconscious, seeing the Gen's bright field, Abel a shadow of need, a void aching to be filled. Abel allowed his need to rise in full force and stepped forward. Even now, he was gentle as he drew the girl to her feet, not frightening or hurting her. Like all Slina's Gens, she showed no reluctance to be handled, waiting dumbly for whatever Abel might do.

There was a horrifying familiarity to the scenario. Abel took the Gen in kill position, the draw began without fear, painlessly—but as the draw increased there was resistance —pain—fear—the fear fed need, increasing the draw voraciously, a feed back of pain/pleasure—killbliss.

Abel dropped to hypoconsciousness on a wave of guilt as vicious as the killbliss had been, turning his post-kill reaction to depression. He let the limp body pull him to his knees, then disentangled himself, closing the Gen's staring eyes and composing her limbs before wrapping the body in a cloth laid by for the purpose.

Rimon didn't interrupt the ritual. Finally Abel rose to face him, raw pain in his voice as he asked, "Did you learn anything?"

"Yes," Rimon replied. "Abel—you drew so little!"

"I drained her."

"No! That's just it: it wasn't your draw that killed her—it was her reaction. Come on—I've got to tell Kadi."

"You go," said Abel. "I must pray first. Each time . . . I pray it may be the last time."

"Abel—I must talk with Kadi first. But I have an idea."

The problem was that the idea terrified Rimon, and he couldn't understand why. He felt an overwhelming relief when he was back with Kadi in the main room.

"What happened? Where's Abel?" she asked anxiously.

"Praying. Kadi, I can't believe it. Abel uses so little selyn, I don't know how he can live on it! More selyn is wasted—dissipated—than he actually draws."

"Rimon—what—"

"You could give Abel transfer and never know you'd done it."

"But—"

"I'd never miss that amount, Kadi!"

"Rimon—I don't know if I can stand to give transfer to anyone but you. What I did to that Raider—"

Rimon forced himself not to grasp at the excuse. He hated the nagging jealousy that sought to keep him from what he knew was right. It had to be right! Why else did Gens produce more selyn than most Simes needed? Why did they grow constantly in capacity? If selyn were not wasted in the kill, there'd be plenty to go around, even if some Gens never learned to give real transfer.

"Kadi—Abel's not a Raider. You won't want to hurt him—there won't be anything unnatural, like running your system backwards, or his. The worst that can happen is that he'll draw more than I expect—and for one month, if necessary, I can draw from the kids and balance my fields."

"I—I don't like it, Rimon. I don't know why I feel it's wrong."

"Try it—just once."

"Try what?" asked Abel from the doorway.

When Rimon told him, he shook his head. "No. Absolutely not. I cannot interfere between you and your wife." But the surge of desire in his nager belied his words, even as heartfelt relief emanated from Kadi.

Putting his arm around her, Rimon told Abel, "That's just it—you wouldn't interfere. As little selyn as you need, I wouldn't notice any difference at my own transfer. And Kadi has that ability to produce—on demand, it seems. All Gens may have it. Every Gen I've worked with has increased production.

"And the waste! I haven't witnessed a kill by an ordinary Sime since Vee Lassiter's changeover, and that time I either didn't know what to look for, or wasn't sensitive enough to see the difference. More than half the selyn in that Gen today was lost, not consumed. Abel, you don't have problems with shorting, do you?"

"Almost never. Jord always had. Apparently, I'm just an —'ordinary Sime,' " he finished painfully.

Rimon winced. "I'm sorry. I didn't mean to imply that we're better, just different. If anything, needing extra selyn is a detriment, except that we may pay back by healing. I think the dual system is hereditary—my father has it, and I had cousins with shorting problems. Dan Whelan doesn't have it, but he recalls that Uel's mother did."

"Yes," said Abel. "She faced a terrible moral dilemma during her pregnancy, taking many extra kills in order to produce a new life. If only she could know—but she must. If God is just, she knows her child has found a new way of life."

"Then the only exception is Jord. Neither your nor Margid seems to have an extra selyn reservoir."

"Margid is not Jord's mother, although he never knew the woman who gave birth to him. Her death may have been due to this very condition, for she died of attrition in childbirth."

"I'm sorry," murmured Kadi.

"It was long ago," Abel replied. "But what you're saying is, I may be physically incapable of learning not to kill."

"We don't know that!" Rimon said fiercely.

Kadi clung to him, seeking strength as she said, "It's important that we try, Abel. Now that Willa's pregnant, Jord is going to require help soon. Remember what Rimon went through? We may learn something that will help Jord and Willa—and your grandchild."

With great, wrenching pain, Abel said, "Yes, of course. I can't refuse to try."

Abel was not the only one to relinquish his privacy that day. Hank and Uel had agreed to have their second transfer in the chapel, as Jord and Willa had done, before the whole of Fort Freedom. It was another bit of progress, a boost to everyone's morale—especially as Uel represented a future in which no Sime would ever have to kill.

Rimon had worried that there might be a tendency among the people of Fort Freedom to consider Hank and Uel saints, on some untouchable moral plane. The boys, however, saw to it that any such image was immediately shattered, by acting like what they were: two adolescents testing their newfound abilities. When no one managed to snag them for chores or lessons, they ranged as far from authority as they could get, each trying to outdo the other in a happy contest of Sime versus Gen. Uel, unhampered by conscious or unconscious guilt, had no aversion to augmenting, or to using his tentacles. Rimon watched him explore the world anew with Sime senses, envying his untrammeled delight. *It will be that way for Zeth one day.*

Hank, freer with Uel than with any adult, used his friend to try what he could do as a Gen—discovering such useful abilities as how to tickle someone from ten paces away. Uel soon found that although he could overpower Hank physically, whenever he came close enough to do so he was in range of Hank's nageric tricks. Rimon let them alone, figuring that the lessons they learned were good for both of them.

They capped their adventures by sneaking off into town one evening, where both had previously been forbidden to go. No one ever found out exactly what they did there, but the next day was Uel's turnover, complicated by a headache for which he got no help from Hank because he had one too.

Both boys settled down after that—apparently having proved something to themselves—and the lessons went apace. Like Jord, Uel was able to imitate healing mode the first time he zlinned it. After a few successful experiments, and before Uel hit turnover and the risk of instability, Rimon had him try drawing in healing mode from Anni Suttin, the most stable of the Gens staying with him. The result was a successful lesson and a tremendous vitalization of Uel's secondary system.

As Uel approached need, his high spirits dampened somewhat, but even the last few days he continued surprisingly steady, and Hank could still coax a smile out of him even on their transfer day. Both boys were subdued, though, when Rimon went to seek them after he left Abel. They were in the chapel together, praying, in that solemn mood of adolescents facing a public responsibility.

"It's over an hour, yet," said Rimon. "Do you want to stay here, or come have some tea?"

Hank looked to Uel, properly respecting his friend's mood.

"I'd rather stay here," said Uel. "I really don't want to talk to anybody—till afterward."

"I'll take care of him," said Hank, back in the protective mood of last month. Rimon zlinned him carefully. He was like Kadi and Willa. There was something wonderfully reassuring about these particular Gens—imagine living in a world full of them.

Rimon returned to Abel's house, just in time to see Dan Whelan leaving. "Uel and Hank are already in the chapel."

"I know," said Dan. "I don't blame them for not wanting to be on public display. I've just been telling Abel—I've managed to talk Sara Fenell into coming to see."

And to walk out again? Rimon wondered. The boys' relationship was only a month old, and both had been raised in a heavily religious atmosphere. If Sara made her charges of demonic possession and witchcraft again, what would that do to two impressionable boys? He could only hope their experiences together would outweigh anything anyone might say to them.

Rimon and Kadi sat on either side of Hank and Uel at

the front of the chapel, giving them what protection they could from the emotions of the people entering. Uel's parents came up front, with the Veritts—and with them was Sara Fenell. He felt the start of surprise from Uel; Hank, of course, knew of her only secondhand.

Rimon's gaze drifted to the monument to the martyrs. But there would be no martyrs today; joy filled the chapel. The wave of hopeful anticipation reached Uel; he reached for Hank's hand, and wrapped his tentacles about their two hands united. A soft gasp from the congregation reminded Rimon of the time Abel had deliberately displayed his tentacles in the chapel—and Sara Fenell had led away so many of his followers.

When everyone was seated, Abel rose. "You all know why we're here. God has blessed us time and again—the most recent miracle just one month ago. We give thanks that one of our own children, Uel Whelan, has been doubly blessed. Like Rimon Farris, like my son Jord, he has healing powers. But, unlike them, Uel will never have to learn not to kill—for God sent Henry Steers, Jr.—Hank—to us, to befriend Uel, and to give him transfer at his changeover itself. Anyone," he looked toward Sara Fenell, "must recognize God's plan in action in our community. Tonight we gather to witness the miracle. Once more, I urge you to use your Sime senses to witness. Witness truly, in Uel, that there is no curse in being Sime. The curse is in killing. Behold—before you is a Sime who has never killed."

"And I never will," Uel said solemnly.

As the boys stood and assumed transfer position, Rimon felt everyone going hyperconscious. He didn't want to—he'd had one glimpse of what was denied him—but he couldn't resist. Again, that unadulterated bliss, that painless, joyous giving. Again the embarrassment of the boys afterward, unable to face it as a solemn occasion—unable, Rimon realized with a shock, to perceive the meaning of their innocence because they'd never known corruption.

But in the audience, everyone understood. The chapel bore the aura of killbliss—the ambience of joy and sorrow, too mixed to conceive of one without the other. Even Kadi was crying, and Rimon realized his own face was wet.

Hank and Uel looked about them, at a loss to comprehend the tears. Last month, Rimon recalled, they had laughed. Abel, smiling through his own tears, told them, "Thank God you don't understand—may it be God's will that in another generation there will be no Sime capable of understanding how we feel tonight."

And then Sara Fenell came forward to kneel at Abel's feet. "God forgive me," she sobbed, "what I thought was a demon was the reflection of my own sinful nature. These blessed children—surely they're God's angels sent to give us a glimpse of paradise. And surely God is all-merciful, for despite my sins, my denials, my pride, He has allowed me to bear witness to this miracle." She collapsed in tears. Dan Whelan helped her back to her seat as Abel calmed everyone.

Rimon had a sudden moment of terror that Abel was about to announce the plan for his own transfer next month; but no, he merely led the prayer of thanksgiving and dismissed the congregation. *Why am I so afraid of it?* Rimon wondered. *If I only knew what I was afraid of, I'd either have a concrete problem to solve, or I'd get rid of my fear by understanding it.* Watching the three Gens in his care struggling with their own fears, though, he doubted whether understanding could help. They certainly knew what they were afraid of, but that didn't end their fears.

Kadi was no help. Her fear was that she'd hurt Abel. Rimon didn't understand how she could think that, unless it was the same guilt that had kept her silent about her encounter with the Freeband Raiders. "I think you should tell Abel," he told her.

"That I killed?"

"He has the right to know what you can do, Kadi."

Abel was astonished. "You killed three Freeband Raiders?"

"Only one of them intentionally," she replied. "That doesn't disturb me, Abel—that to save my own life and protect Rimon, I used my hands as weapons. The terrifying thing is that I—I killed in transfer."

"But the man was trying to kill you. I don't believe God

expects us to allow ourselves to be brutally murdered. In such a case, the kill becomes a weapon."

"An uncontrolled weapon is very dangerous," said Kadi.

"Ah—I see. Because I was once a Freeband Raider, you fear you'll react toward me in the same way."

"Abel, no!" gasped Kadi. Then, "Yes, that's what I'm afraid of, but not because you were a Raider years ago, before I was even born! You're nothing like those— creatures."

"Perhaps," he said. "And perhaps, on the other hand, so long as one kills, there is no difference." He studied Rimon thoughtfully. "I wonder what the true test is?"

After that, Abel made no further protest against the experiment. "It's in God's hands," he told Rimon.

Rimon deliberately thrust his own doubts aside. Abel was rising to a challenge he expected to win—and Rimon wanted it for him. If he could not overcome his selfishness just one time, for the most selfless man he'd ever known, then he deserved any punishment Abel's God could mete out.

They told no one of their intentions. Rimon had meant to have Jord there to observe, but Abel's son had fallen back into those eccentric mood swings that had preceded both his last kill and the scene at the birthday party. "I thought Jord's crisis was past," Rimon told Abel. "When he was prevented from attacking Hank and he accepted Willa's transfer, I thought that was the end of it. He seemed so much better afterward."

"It was Willa's decision," Abel said, "not Jord's. Apparently the final crisis was only forestalled. I'm praying daily with my son, Rimon. The next time, he'll be prepared. I have faith that he'll not fail again."

In the meantime, though, poor Willa had to bear the brunt of Jord's instability. Still in the early months of pregnancy, she was able to give him transfer, but bewildered to find herself unable to control him as she was used to. From gleeful happiness at having a baby at last, she was plunged into the terrible anxiety of trying to deal with forces she could not understand.

I know how she feels, thought Rimon, as the day approached when he'd promised Abel Kadi's transfer. Abel's hope carried throughout Fort Freedom—even though no one outside their small circle knew the plan, spirits were high.

Everything was going well. The crops were growing lustily, as if to make up for last year. The Wild Gens, undoubtedly busy tending their own fields, remained on their own side of the border. The petition for recognition as a county was accepted and work began on the necessary census.

And no children changed over.

There were three to whom it could happen at any moment, and five younger but still within the possible range— but it seemed to Rimon as if nature were holding off until he found out if the experiment would work, if one Gen could provide transfer for more than one Sime.

The day of the experiment, Rimon wanted Jord and Uel, both too sensitive to miss a transfer experiment a few houses away, well out of Fort Freedom. Thus he enlisted the aid of Del Erick, who, without asking what was going on, agreed to keep both Jord and Uel occupied. Uel's need was still in phase with Abel's; otherwise, Rimon would have had the boy there to observe—he was already incredibly steady, learning voraciously. Del quickly found the answer in Dan Whelan's plan to tear down the row of dissenters' houses along the creek and salvage the building materials for Fort Freedom. In the next town meeting, he managed to volunteer Jord and Uel, along with several other people as well as himself. Rimon watched his friend's maneuverings with concealed delight—people might not remember how they got involved in the scheme, but would be certain that Rimon had nothing to do with it.

Willa naturally went with Jord, and Hank with Uel. The final step was to send Margid Veritt, with Zeth "helping," out with lunch for the workers. Del would enlist her aid at the scene, and keep her there until the all-clear was given. By this time, Del was flaring curiosity, but he told Rimon, "Unless whatever you're plotting works, I don't want to know about it." But there was a painful tremor of hope in his nager, which renewed Rimon's determination.

And then, at the crucial moment, Rimon discovered that Abel had not collected a Gen from Slina's pens. "I don't intend to need one," he explained.

"Abel!" exclaimed Kadi. "Are you *trying* to frighten me? If we fail, you'll be in no condition to make a trip into town. I won't do it if there's no Gen for you to fall back on." She was clutching Rimon's hands, as if drawing strength.

Thinking perhaps it would be good to leave Kadi and Abel alone together for a while, Rimon said, "I'll go to Slina's and claim one for you."

"No," Abel replied. "It's my responsibility; I'll make my claim—for the last time."

Abel's certainty brought the weight of responsibility back onto Rimon's shoulders. Abel's dream had become his own dream—and yet he was not prepared for the test Abel was forcing on him, for he knew what Abel meant by "for the last time." Either Rimon would make the experiment work —or Abel would die.

He realized that Kadi had known that all along. His field affected hers as hers did his; he had to free her to serve Abel's need—Abel's life depended on it now.

When Abel returned with the Gen, he said, "I'll put him in the insulated room for now."

. No, Abel would not call it a killroom. "Perhaps—" began Rimon, thinking the Gen should remain within easy reach. Something impinged on his consciousness. "What the—"

Jord Veritt, a cloud of anger and need, stormed up the porch steps and in through the front door. Rimon had not seen him for two days—had not realized that he must have been shorted this month because of Willa's pregnancy, and was approaching need two or three days early.

"Father, will you stop Willa and Mother from ganging up on me? Nag, nag, trying to run my life, never satisfied—"

"Jord!" Abel's voice cut across Jord's tirade. "You will not speak that way of either your mother or your wife."

Rimon felt Kadi automatically try to resonate calm, but Jord was too used to fighting off Willa's efforts to be affected. Abel asked, "Where is Willa?"

"Oh, back there stuffing herself, with the rest of the Gens. I suppose she'll follow me soon enough—I can't get rid of her."

But at Gen speed, it would take Willa some time to get here, and she was pregnant. . . .

"She can still give you transfer this month," said Abel. "Come, I'll take you to her."

Rimon marveled at Abel's strength—at this critical moment, he would try to solve his son's problems before his own.

"I don't want Willa!" said Jord. "All the damned women trying to control me, and she's the worst. She thinks she owns me!"

To find the strength to contend with his son, Abel was leaning on the nager of the Gen he led, becoming fixed on him. He was deeper into need than Jord, by several crucial hours. "Willa loves you. Everything she does is intended to help you."

"Help me—help me. You sound as stupid as she does. I don't want Willa helping me—I don't want her to touch me!"

"Then what do you want, Jord? Do you want to kill again? Right now there's no one who can keep you from killing except Willa. Go back to her, Jord."

"You have no right to order me around!" said Jord, pacing. "You, with your kill waiting—how can you tell me what I ought to do, when you can't do it yourself!"

Rimon was surprised at Abel's answer. "I have no choice! You have. Do you want to choose, Jord? Here's a choice for you: go back to Willa, or stay here and kill!" He shoved the Gen forward as Kadi gasped in horror. But Rimon saw that Abel actually expected Jord to walk away from that high-field Gen, his father's Gen, as Rimon would have done.

And incredibly, Jord was hesitating. Rimon suddenly saw what Abel saw: it was Jord's test. A true test, when Jord was under no strain but need, and that not even at its greatest force. *He's going to make it!* Rimon was swept up in Abel's certainty as Jord remained frozen, his eyes fixed on the Gen that Abel had thrust before him. Seeing him, not zlinning him—yes, he was resisting the temptation—and then he broke!

In a flash of augmentation, Jord grasped the Gen and had him in kill position before Abel could recover from his astonishment—and then Abel was on Jord, mad with the full fury of a Sime whose kill has been stolen. Rimon leaped to pull Abel off Jord as he lunged at his son's neck, grasping him in a stranglehold that Rimon could not break, his hands and tentacles slipping over Abel's as Jord fought to breathe and Rimon expected at any moment to hear the crunch of his neck breaking.

But now Kadi came in from behind Jord, reaching for Abel's arms, projecting the sweet promise that he would not be denied, all the strength of her field enveloping them.

Abel's need overcame his rage as he was touched by a Gen. He dropped Jord, who collapsed into Rimon's arms as Abel's fingers and tentacles whipped over Kadi's flesh, pulling her toward him, not knowing her as anything but the life that had been denied him. As Rimon held tight rein on his frozen emotions, not daring to breathe lest he explode into insane jealousy again, she pressed her lips to Abel's and let the selyn flow—a maddeningly tiny trickle, an itch, a torture that ran like fiery ants through Rimon's nerves, too—unbearable—he wanted to scream as she had to scream, to break contact—

The shock of Abel's shen ricocheted through Kadi to Rimon as her knees gave way. Abel fainted from the shock and crumpled with her. She struggled up, terror and guilt shattering her nager. "Rimon! I've killed Abel!"

"No!" No, there was life yet. "He's alive, Kadi. Let me—"

He scrambled over to where Abel lay, dying because Rimon had assured him, assured Kadi, that the experiment would work. *My fault, my fault. Must I kill everyone I love? Think!*

Abel was deep in shock, as well as in need. But the Gen was dead. Never mind—help Abel. He went into healing mode, zlinning the bleak emptiness of need, the dark void threatening to swallow him. In healing mode, Rimon could project himself to Abel as a Gen, a promise of life to support his failing strength until they could get another

Gen for him. *Don't die, Abel! You've always had more strength than the rest of us.*

But that strength was moral courage, not physical stamina. Now, in deep rapport with him, Rimon could sense the inroads two years of bad kills had made on his system. *And that's my fault, too.*

If I can bring him out of this, I'll take Kadi and Zeth and go where no one will expect me to perform miracles, where I won't kill anyone else.

The strength of that decision eased his guilt enough to let him work, reaching into the depths of Abel's need with the promise of life, drawing him back toward warmth and hope.

Finally, he felt a stirring of response. Awakening in need, Abel was hyperconscious, reaching automatically to the source of life before him, grasping Rimon's arms, pulling him into transfer position. Rimon did not resist, remaining in healing mode, projecting himself as a soothing Gen field to help Abel orient himself. *Take as long as you want. Rest with me, Abel, until you have the strength to let go. You're safe.*

But Abel could not do it. The shocks his system had just taken had weakened him so that if he were to survive, he had to have selyn now, and there was no one to give it except Rimon.

Braced for pain, ready to force himself to allow Abel to fulfill his need if it killed him, he remained in healing mode to be Gen for Abel—to entice the draw that would heal the older Sime—after all, he didn't require much selyn. The flow began, that momentary pleasant sensation, to be followed by—

Abel's draw increased, speeding, but not hurting. Compared to Rimon's draw, or Jord's, it was slow—yet he sought something more than selyn. As they approached termination, with Abel still frantically unsatisfied, Rimon realized what was missing—the killbliss—the satisfaction that was equally pleasure and pain. As he thought of it, recalled it, the memory seemed to flow from him to Abel, satisfying the deepest need and at the same time whipping back into guilt—Abel's standard reaction to a kill.

But there should be no guilt. With a flick of his field like the fresh laughter of Hank and Uel, Rimon wiped out that emotion and drew Abel to hypoconsciousness. He broke contact, saying, "Abel! Come on! You're all right! Everything is all right!"

Abel opened his eyes, stared at Rimon, then down at his hands, still clasping Rimon's arms as if he feared to let go. "You—! Rimon—that was you? I didn't kill?"

"You didn't kill."

"A miracle! Another miracle—God be praised!" He burst into tears. "You have let me keep my vow!"

Kadi was kneeling by Jord, who was groggily awake now. Wide-eyed, she asked, "Rimon—what did you do?"

"I—" He paused to swallow as the enormity struck him. "I gave transfer to Abel."

"But how?"

They were interrupted as the door was flung open and Willa ran in, breathless. "Jord!" she cried, falling to her knees beside him.

"Don't touch me!" he said. "I don't deserve you, Willa— I've killed again."

By this time other people were entering—Uel, Hank, Zeth, Margid. Others were outside on the porch—everything had happened right here in the unshielded main room. Curious Simes were converging from every direction.

Margid, finding her husband in tears, asked in a panic, "Abel! What's happened?"

"When I least deserved it," he whispered, "when through my pride I had just provoked our son into killing—" Margid started, looking over to Jord and Willa in horror. Abel clutched her. "Margid! Jord killed—but I did not!"

"What?" Her attention focused on her husband, taking in the fact that he was high-field.

"I have sinned—pride, presumption, impatience. I goaded Jord into killing, and then would have murdered him in my despair—and at that moment God chose to show His infinite mercy. Rimon—"

All eyes fixed on him. Rimon said, "Abel, it's not a miracle. It's just—a logical extrapolation of all the other things I've done. I just couldn't see it!"

Just then Del Erick entered, grimly pushing his way through the crowd, trailed by Carlana. "Rimon—can I help?"

At Del's anxiety, Rimon realized that no one knew what had happened. It was a frightening scene; the dead Gen, Abel on the floor with Margid worriedly examining him, Abel's elation overshadowed by Jord's self-loathing as he tried to get to his feet, hampered by Willa. But Del had come to help—always he came back, no matter how it hurt him.

"Del, it's all right!" Rimon told him. "We've found the answer!"

"The . . . answer?"

"I should have known all along," Rimon said. "It's what my selyn reservoir is for—to give to others!"

Margid's head snapped up. "You—gave transfer to Abel?"

"Yes! And it didn't hurt!" Oh no, it didn't hurt—in fact, he was slowly becoming aware that he felt better than he had in months. He wasn't meant to store that overbalance of selyn in his system—it was there to be given!

As the slow surge of understanding in the other Simes bloomed into awe of Rimon, Jord's nager showed his desperate desire to escape. He tugged away from Willa as if to go out toward the kitchen, but Abel stopped him with a word. "Jord—my son, forgive me."

"Forgive you? Father, I'm the one who killed today, and I don't know why! I should have returned to Willa, but I couldn't—I couldn't!"

"God's ways are not always simple," said Abel, picking himself up off the floor to face his son. "Your failure provoked Rimon into his discovery. But now we know, Jord. There will be no more killing in Fort Freedom."

"And how will you stop me next time?" Jord asked bitterly.

"Rimon can stop you, as he stopped me—as you will stop others, Jord. God has blessed you with the same abilities Rimon has. Be thankful for the blessings God has granted to this community. Yes, be thankful even for your weakness, and mine, which forced Rimon Farris to discover the extent of his powers."

"Can you do it again, Rimon?" Kadi asked. "Do you know what you did?"

"Yes!" he said in elation, plucking Zeth up and holding him close. "It's healing mode, Kadi—the very first thing I learned after you freed me from killing. In healing mode, I can draw from Gens who are afraid without hurting them —and in healing mode, I can give that selyn to other Simes, and not be killed!"

"Then I can learn it, too!" said Uel Whelan. He turned to hug his father, then his mother. "I said I'd do it! I said I'd teach you not to kill. Now I can—in spite of being Sime —because I'm Sime—I can do it!"

Abel said, "Yes, Uel, you can do it. Jord can do it. And Rimon—Rimon Farris, you are a channel of God's grace from heaven."

"A channel of life!" said Del. He put his arm around Carlana and looked down at Owen and Jana, who had followed their parents in. When he looked back at Rimon, the pain was gone from his face, the wound of Billy's death healed at last. "I could never have brought myself to touch Hank or any of the Gens you're working with. Not after Billy. But if you can channel selyn to me, to all of us—then there's a future worth living for!"

"Pa—can I be a channel, too?" asked Owen.

"Me, too! Me, too!" chimed in Jana.

Del knelt to hug them both. "Maybe you will," he said, "but it doesn't matter. All that matters is that, Sime or Gen, you won't kill—and you won't be killed!"

"Our prayers have been answered," Abel agreed. "Come, let us go to the chapel. Someone ring the bell. We must tell everyone of this miracle, and give thanks to God, Who has forgiven all our sins, all our doubts. We must dedicate ourselves to the new way of life Rimon Farris has brought to us."

For the first time, Rimon was not even faintly embarrassed at the faith Abel placed in him. *I can do it! Now I know I can do it! I'm in control of my own life at last—and I can teach others.*

Kadi at his side, Zeth in his arms, he listened with equanimity to the vow that had so frightened him the first time Abel had made it contingent upon him. He would see that Abel's faith was not misplaced—teach the young people, like Uel, and Zeth one day, so that no Sime would ever be forsworn if he vowed as Abel Veritt did, "As God is my witness, I shall not die a killer!"